The Best
AMERICAN
SHORT
STORIES
2017

GUEST EDITORS OF
THE BEST AMERICAN SHORT STORIES

1978 TED SOLOTAROFF
1979 JOYCE CAROL OATES
1980 STANLEY ELKIN
1981 HORTENSE CALISHER
1982 JOHN GARDNER
1983 ANNE TYLER
1984 JOHN UPDIKE
1985 GAIL GODWIN
1986 RAYMOND CARVER
1987 ANN BEATTIE
1988 MARK HELPRIN
1989 MARGARET ATWOOD
1990 RICHARD FORD
1991 ALICE ADAMS
1992 ROBERT STONE
1993 LOUISE ERDRICH
1994 TOBIAS WOLFF
1995 JANE SMILEY
1996 JOHN EDGAR WIDEMAN
1997 E. ANNIE PROULX
1998 GARRISON KEILLOR
1999 AMY TAN
2000 E. L. DOCTOROW
2001 BARBARA KINGSOLVER
2002 SUE MILLER
2003 WALTER MOSLEY
2004 LORRIE MOORE
2005 MICHAEL CHABON
2006 ANN PATCHETT
2007 STEPHEN KING
2008 SALMAN RUSHDIE
2009 ALICE SEBOLD
2010 RICHARD RUSSO
2011 GERALDINE BROOKS
2012 TOM PERROTTA
2013 ELIZABETH STROUT
2014 JENNIFER EGAN
2015 T. C. BOYLE
2016 JUNOT DÍAZ
2017 MEG WOLITZER

The Best AMERICAN SHORT STORIES® 2017

Selected from
U.S. and Canadian Magazines
by MEG WOLITZER
with HEIDI PITLOR

With an Introduction by Meg Wolitzer

MARINER BOOKS
HOUGHTON MIFFLIN HARCOURT
BOSTON • NEW YORK 2017

hmhco.com

ISSN 0067-6233 (print)
ISSN 2573-4784 (ebook)
ISBN 978-0-544-58276-7
ISBN 978-0-544-58290-3 (pbk.)
ISBN 978-1-328-76673-1 (ebook)

Printed in the United States of America
DOC 10 9 8 7 6 5 4 3 2 1

In Memory of Carla Gray
1965–2017

Around us the meantime is already overflowing.
Wherever I turn its own almost-invisibility
Streams and sparkles over everything.
—Galway Kinnell

Contents

Foreword

EACH VOLUME OF *The Best American Short Stories* is a literary time capsule, a gathering of characters, settings, styles, voices, and conflicts more or less specific to their moment in history. *The Best American Short Stories 2017* features some of the last stories written and published before November 8, 2016, and what must have been one of the most acrimonious and wearying presidential elections for Americans.

I have a theory that it's more difficult to hide ourselves when writing fiction than nonfiction, even certain memoirs. So much is revealed in the poses that we choose to strike, the silences we allow, and the conflicts we dramatize. And if fiction tends to be more successful without forceful agendas, the genre does tend to offer at least a window onto an author's aesthetics and emotionality, and often their values.

The stories in this volume—bold, intimate, enlightening, entertaining—reflect a country profoundly divided. In Mary Gordon's "Ugly," a New York City woman temporarily moves to the Midwest and reckons with her own calcified urban superiority. The faithful chafe against the faithless in Kevin Canty's "God's Work." The young Asian woman in Sonya Larson's "Gabe Dove" grapples with internalized racism when dating an Asian man for the first time. The public and the private spheres go head-to-head in Fiona Maazel's "Let's Go to the Videotape." The wealthy grate against the support staff in Kyle McCarthy's "Ancient Rome." Misogyny brews beneath the surface of Eric Puchner's "Last Day on Earth." Acrimony between the genders appears often in these pages. After meeting a celebrity at a party, the narrator of Jess Walter's "Famous Actor" says, "I disliked him from the moment I decided to sleep with him." Amy Hempel explores the devastating echoes of a failed marriage in "The Chicane." The fractured condition of our country is most overtly referenced in Curtis Sittenfeld's story, in which a professor of gender and women's studies and a Trump-supporting shuttle driver have an awkward and ill-fated one-night stand: "Again when they look at each other, she is close to puncturing the theatrics of her own anger . . . but she hasn't yet selected the words that she'll use to cause the puncture."

Guest editor Meg Wolitzer and I spoke soon after the election, and we admitted to feeling daunted by the task before us. How did one even read short stories now? How could one read anything but the rapid-fire revelations that came in November, December, and January (and as of now, continue to come) about everything from fake news to the Russian involvement in our electoral process to the spike in hate crimes? And how was it possible to stay informed without becoming inundated and overwhelmed? After 9/11, series editor Katrina Kenison wrote, "All of [these stories] had been written well before September 11, and yet often I found it hard to believe that this could be the case; the truths they spoke seemed so timely, so necessary now." Back in 1942, series editor Martha Foley wrote, "In its short stories, America can hear something being said that can be heard even above the crashing of bombs and the march of Panzer divisions. That is the fact that America is aware of human values as never before, posed as they are against a Nazi conception of a world dead to such values." The difference now is the widespread availability of news—fake and real—due to the primacy of the Internet. I have friends and family who read no news and others who read just some. I must say that at the moment, I am working through a rampant news addiction. If you share this affliction, you know that it's no good, that it stimulates anxiety and robs you of the ability to be mindful in your day-to-day life. The antidote to depletion is, of course, nourishment. This year, the best stories provide necessary sustenance.

Ms. Wolitzer and I went back and forth about these stories numerous times. The job felt different this year. In a time when truth has become a pawn in a dangerous game of partisanship and influence, honest and emotionally true writing felt especially important. We strove for a mix of content and style, a collection of stories that gave voice to something urgent and meaningful.

The Best American Short Stories 2017 celebrates all that is our country: crowded and lonely, funny and sad, fame-obsessed and fame-wary. Here are immigrants, a cabdriver, a person with a boyfriend and a girlfriend, a bartender, a racecar driver, sex workers, a human resources manager, a Ukrainian packaging specialist, a bridesmaid, a Cuban writer. Here are trapped naval officers, a contestant on *America's Funniest Home Videos*, a gay man desperate to be a father.

I love these stories. I feel irrationally proud and protective of these characters, these Americans in their fragility and grace, their division and desire, all of them unaware of what is to come. I am eager to read next year's stories and to meet their characters, and to encounter their strength and resilience and wisdom.

The stories chosen for this anthology were originally published between January 2016 and January 2017. The qualifications for selection are (1) original publication in nationally distributed American or Canadian periodicals; (2) publication in English by writers who have made the United States their home; (3) original publication as short stories (excerpts of novels are not considered). A list of magazines consulted for this volume appears at the back of the book. Editors who wish their short fiction to be considered for next year's edition should send their publications or hard copies of online publications to Heidi Pitlor, c/o The Best American Short Stories, 125 High St., Boston, MA 02110.

HEIDI PITLOR

Introduction

IT STARTS, SOMETIMES, with an ending. The portal leading to
a lifetime of slavish short story love can come in the final passage
of a piece of fiction, which might contain some kind of full-body
startle or revelatory shock. Teachers know this—after all, students
return year after year, too big for the classroom and bringing tales
of How I've Grown as a Reader, Thanks to You—and so when
we're young and our brains are still forming and cooling, we may
be given an Amway hard-sell of de Maupassant and O. Henry by a
well-meaning teacher.

Or at least that used to happen. Do teachers still teach those
stories, or is everything different now? Friends with school-age kids
tell me they lament the fact that the Common Core has moved
the curriculum away from the supposedly soft shoals of fiction and
instead into the harder and more overtly preparatory realm of
nonfiction, a place where facts line up like sharp stones, and truth
rules. (Unless, of course, you're a fiction writer, in which case you
might feel that nonfiction practitioners have no corner on truth,
and you are willing to go toe to toe on this particular point.)

Maybe in assigning surprise-ending stories again and again, our
teachers did us the favor of digging new neural pathways in our
brains, and somehow actually created in us an unconscious, communal thirst for a big finish. I am certain that my earliest dips
into reading short fiction included the *de rigueur* electric jolt that
closed the thing; and so, after a while, armed with my new-smell-
ing reader, which was published by a company such as Ginn (I
am drawing that name up from my brainpan, though I haven't

thought of it in several decades), and called, perhaps, *Paths of Imagination*, Third Edition (okay, I made that one up, but maybe it exists), I came to deliberately trawl for the big moment at the end of a story, and to expect that it would definitely be there. My classmates and I were positive that such an ending was inevitably waiting for us, and we were monomaniacal about finding it, as if we were nonviolent little versions of the killers in Truman Capote's *In Cold Blood*, who were convinced that the Clutter family *definitely* had a safe in their Kansas home. A big ending began to seem to me like a requirement—the single element that could somehow make any story memorable. I had a jones for it; I wanted it every time. To me it was distinctive, necessary, a singular taste to be craved and hunted down: a literary kind of *umami*.

But of course if everything is surprising, then nothing is. Because we had all been raised on the power of surprise, the short stories that my class wrote for the creative writing unit, which has by now maybe been expunged from the curriculum like asbestos from an old school building, sometimes attempted a cheap and lazy mimicry of the kinds of fiction we'd already read. I recall more than one kid standing up and reading his or her own short story aloud; it was invariably full of action and suspense and a touch of Borges-like surrealism, and finally there came the last line, the kicker: "Then I woke up, and it was all a dream!"

Oh ho, a dream, you say? Teachers were tolerant of dreams, but we other students could be sour, exacting critics. Those clever endings taught us not only what to want and expect, but also what not to want: an unearned surprise for a surprise's sake.

While "The Gift of the Magi" is perhaps the standard-bearer of surprise-ending fiction, not to mention the winner of the M. Night Shyamalan Prize for Unexpected Closure, it was a somewhat lesser-known O. Henry story, "The Last Leaf," that first obsessed me. The plot concerns two girls who are roommates in Greenwich Village. It's wintertime, and one of them becomes gravely ill with what's referred to as "Mr. Pneumonia." Day after day, as she gets no better, she becomes preoccupied with the vine growing on a wall across the way, visible from her window. As the weather grows worse, she insists to her roommate that her fate is coupled with that of the leaves on the vine. When the last leaf falls, she knows she will die.

One night a tremendous storm hits, and by morning there's no way that the last leaf could have hung on. Raise the shade! the ill girl demands of her roommate, who is terrified to do so, knowing that the vision of the naked vine will cause her friend to lose the will to live. But when the shade is raised, a single leaf still clings to that vine, and the ill girl finally feels encouraged. Soon, her fever breaks and she begins to get better. But what she doesn't know is that the old artist who lives across the way, and who knew of the girl's obsession, went out at night in the snowstorm to paint the leaf on the wall, and in doing so, he himself got sick (also with pneumonia), and died.

Oh god, I loved this story, with its focus on magical thinking and death. To me, the notion that death was under our personal jurisdiction was a big draw—this idea that if only you had the *right attitude,* you could control death as if it were a thermostat in a hotel room. The story is really a sentimental sketch, and here is a bit of dialogue, spoken by the artist when he hears of the ill girl's conviction: "Vass! . . . Is dere people in de world mit der foolishness to die because leafs dey drop off from a confounded vine? I haf not heard of such a thing."

If you stay with "The Last Leaf" all the way through, you wind up at the ending, which you just know William Sydney Porter had worked out before or at least at the same time that he came up with the rest of it. For without the ending, the story rests on shaky legs, and the whole thing could easily blow away like an eponymous leaf in even the lightest of storms.

Later on in my reading life, though I had been fed on thriller endings, I started to want more than that when I read. But the idea of the "surprise" wasn't abandoned entirely; instead, it was given a shine and polish and a more mature translation. It's possible to see that a whole story—not just the ending—might itself take on what had been considered the function of an ending. I once heard someone paraphrase a writer (Donald Justice, she thinks, but I can't seem to find the quote), who said that in all good stories, someone needs to turn a corner, or a hair. No longer on the lookout for the socko shift, the reader surrenders, and it's then that surprises can flourish. By which I mean that you might not necessarily gasp; but without a doubt you will find yourself in a place you didn't know about before. A place where you didn't expect to be.

We live in a moment when change is continually demanded and fetishized. "Advice, How-To and Miscellaneous" is its own category among the *New York Times* bestseller lists, the first two entries suggesting a hunger for finding a way to be different from the way you are right now, while the third, "Miscellaneous," suggesting . . . I'm not sure what. I once asked a therapist friend if any of her patients ever actually "changed." I said to her, essentially, "Come on, you can tell me, I won't tell anyone," thinking that maybe she would lean over and confide in me that no, no one ever really changed. That "change" was a grail too far. Maybe *modification* was a better word. Maybe *subtle shift* nailed it more accurately. Maybe *learning experience* was the closest way to describe what actually transpired in therapy. But instead she was mildly offended by this question, and she said to me, "Of course they do."

So okay, maybe they do, in therapy and in life. In short stories, I don't think characters or their situation or their surroundings *change* as frequently as they *turn*.

The stories in this year's edition of *Best American Short Stories* live, and breathe, and again and again in them there is some kind of turn. After I came up with my final list and discussed it with the series editor, Heidi Pitlor, I thought about what it meant that these were the particular stories I had chosen. I considered what I was trying to say, in choosing them. Why they spoke to me as they had. I remembered once reading a book about someone with autism who had a tremendous facility for numbers. Patterns would jump out at her from a page filled with numbers. She was unable to describe how or why she saw them, but she did.

I, too, can't say exactly what made these stories "jump out" at me either, except to note that among the large number of superb entries I had the pleasure to read—and the quality of the stories given to me was consistently high—the ones I chose all feel like surprises in one way or another, and the surprises seem *right*. I think it's true that stories that are surprising in an overarching way are also often surprising on a granular, language level. The macro-surprise and the micro-surprise work together to form something that is original and exciting and exists outside the world of the ordinary.

That's true of Leopoldine Core's "Hog for Sorrow," included this year, in which a man who has hired a prostitute is described as "a little desperate. Like someone on *Judge Judy*, fighting for old furniture." I laughed when I read that, and part of me wanted to be an English teacher at that moment, so I could write in the margin, "How true!" (Not that Leopoldine Core, with her spare, lucid prose about desperation and love, needs an English teacher at this point.) T. C. Boyle, whom I have read and admired for years, offers in the first sentence of "Are We Not Men?" a jarring and almost physical surprise-pull into a world that is his own: "The dog was the color of a maraschino cherry, and what it had in its jaws I couldn't quite make out at first, not until it parked itself under the hydrangeas and began throttling the thing." Chad Anderson uses the second person in a strong and sure way in "Maidencane," and if the voice makes for clear, rhythmic reading, time suddenly intrudes: "Two decades drop away. The past and the present spring together like a clap." Sonya Larson's first-person narrative is vivid with wit; humor works organically in this examination of race, coupledom, compatibility: "I met Gabe Dove when I was sad and attracting men who liked me sad." Noy Holland's short story "Tally," weighing in at a far lower word count than anything else in this volume, is bold as well as economical: "The man, the men—the sober man, the dead man—had a sister, inscrutable as a turtle." Jai Chakrabarti's "A Small Sacrifice for an Enormous Happiness" gives us a drama about the delicate interlace of the exigencies of desire and family: "Nikhil convinced himself that Sharma had opened his heart to the idea of fathering, but the exuberance of this conclusion led to certain practical questions." A very different fatherhood milieu exists in Fiona Maazel's "Let's Go to the Videotape," in which supposedly private experiences are fiercely plumbed: "Who doesn't film his kid experiencing a threshold moment?" Maazel asks. Jim Shepard's "Telemachus" situates its characters in the close quarters of a short story and the equally close quarters of a British submarine during World War II, where, during a storm, "we alternated at the watch, poking our faces and flooded binoculars into the wind's teeth . . ." Eric Puchner writes of adolescence and the residue of a boy's parents' broken marriage. The boy observes his father's girlfriend, who had "done up her shirt wrong, and I could see her belly button, deep as a bullet wound, peeking between buttons."

Each story is a discrete surprise, the whole of them a collage of distinctness and distinction. This is true, too, of the stories honored in the back of the book, including ones by (to name just a handful of authors) Smith Henderson, Shruti Swamy, Lydia Conklin, Rebecca Makkai, Wells Tower, Caitlin Horrocks, Lee Conell, Manuel Muñoz, Corinna Vallianatos, Michelle Herman, John Fulton, Sarah Shun-lien Bynum, Helen Schulman, Jennifer Haigh,

Joan Frank, Bret Anthony Johnston, and David Bergen. It goes without saying that choosing twenty for a collection such as this one is always going to be difficult, and is a kind of skill that you figure out how to do on the job. This year, though, it was perhaps difficult in a different way; and here is the moment in this essay in which I want to talk about a very different kind of surprise, in order to give some context for how I approached the reading of these stories. As it happened, I was sent the first batch of them right before the 2016 presidential election. Like everyone I knew, I felt hope and excitement mixed up with unrelenting ambient worry and dread. I would watch the news at night and then shut it off after a while and return to the task of reading for *Best American Short Stories*.

Then, after the longest vamp ever, November 8 arrived, bringing with it its own surprise ending, and one that seemed, to so many people, wrong on a few different levels. Wrong, by my view, as in outrageous, wrong as in puzzling, wrong as in unearned. As of this writing, all those feelings remain in place. Here's a difference between life and art: the first might or might not contain a surprise or turn that feels wrong, while the second should contain one that feels somehow right, even if in being "right" it reveals injustice or tragedy or the unexplainable. And after the surprise has been revealed, it might well have an afterlife—which, if it's a wrong life-surprise we're talking about, can feel deadening, and create the sensation of time standing still. People want to know: Will it always be this way? Will the molasses of time ever thin out and flow? Will we ever have reason to feel hopeful?

At some point during election night, when I was the only one still awake in my household, I felt I really shouldn't sleep. It was as if I had to keep vigil. I was waiting for the results to become official; waiting to find out what was what, for sure, and then start to face it in a way that would no longer be theoretical. Waiting for the last leaf to drop off the vine. Pacing around the apartment, I wandered up to the big pile of short stories I'd been sent. At 2 a.m. I found myself trying to read them, but it was tough. Almost immediately I put them aside, realizing that this was not the time for this. But when would that time be? Each one had been written with care and command; and I wondered how reading fiction after this election was going to remain an imperative act; and I wondered what, too, would happen to its sister act, writing fiction.

To say, merely, "We need art now more than ever before," in answer to the questions that surround us, is sort of an unsatisfying response, and a little sanctimonious, and maybe not entirely true. Okay, we do need art more than ever before, but we still want it to perform the same magic that it once performed, when in fact we are living in a different moment. What is art going to give us now? Will the leaf clinging to the vine be proven to be not art but purely artifice, a false comfort that can't actually save anyone's life and in fact is pretty much good for nothing?

As the stories piled up in drifts around me in the weeks after the election, I found some answers, because among the stories, when I dug in fully, were stellar moments of profound change and beauty and weirdness and singularity. And while the election had made me feel that there was nothing on earth powerful enough to drown out this particular bad surprise, that turned out not to be true. Life kept getting lived, though with different emotions attached now. I returned to the well of stories again and again, finding myself drawn there not for distraction, not for, "Take me away from 2016," but for many reasons, none of them easy to describe. If you know exactly what you are going to get from the experience of reading a story, you probably wouldn't go looking for it; you need, in order to be an open reader of fiction, to be willing. To cast a vote for what you love and then wait for the outcome. You need to have faith in the reading experience of the past to allow you to read now, in the present, and to keep reading into the future, regardless of what dark shape it takes. And once you start reading, you may well find that you are launched out of despair. The launching isn't necessarily from a cannon; it might be from a slower kind of transport. Slow and deliberate, with the particular tang and feel of the writer whose work in particular launched you.

Joseph Conrad wrote about how art, when it succeeds, can offer "that glimpse of truth for which you have forgotten to ask." This year was a strange year to be reading so much fiction in the midst of what I think of as a bad surprise. But the glimpse of truth, as ever, is on display if you make the effort to look for it. So I raised the shade.

MEG WOLITZER

The Best
AMERICAN
SHORT
STORIES
2017

CHAD B. ANDERSON

Maidencane

FROM *Nimrod*

NOWADAYS, THE MEMORY starts like this: there's a rush in the red dirt, and you and your brother snatch up the tackle box and run from the girl. She flings her fishing pole at you and yells that her daddy will just buy her another tackle box. And another, and another. The girl's echoes follow you along the riverbank.

The river is green and appears desolate—no motorboats, no fishermen, no teenagers cannonballing, no herons stretching, no feral cats pawing the muck for crayfish, frogs, or mice—which only sharpens the sounds: the orchestra of insects, the whistles of birds, the girl's fading echoes, your steady breath. Your and your brother's white T-shirts are smeared with mud, and he has a cassette tape in the back pocket of his jean shorts. You wish you could remember the songs he liked. There's only this Saturday left, and you two are only a day from losing one another.

You remember the red riverbank and the sagging dock jutting into the water and how later that afternoon a dirty fishing hook snagged your thumb, and you imagine how the girl would've laughed because you stole it from her and the snag was deep and bloody.

You remember that you both caught a fish and brought them home. Your mother spread newspaper over the kitchen table and began to clean the fish while your father sat outside on the porch, chopping potatoes. You and your brother sat next to your mother at the table, but every few minutes he jumped from his chair to rewind a cassette tape to the start of the song he liked most. He had borrowed the tape from a school friend. You didn't really under-

stand the song, but you admired so much how easily your brother
had learned it, how he mouthed it aggressively, as if he could will
the people around him, the whole house, to match the song's exuberance.

Your mother chopped off the heads of both fish and then
started to cut one open along its belly but suddenly stopped and
just stared at the mess she'd made soaking into the newspaper. Your
daddy came in from the porch with a plastic bowl filled with the
chunks of potatoes and stared at her. She asked him to help her,
and he said he didn't know how to clean fish. Your mother started
to cry, and your father just stood there, hunched over, as if he
might fall over any minute, and only now do you get that they felt
guilty because this was your last supper together and they couldn't
even get this right. The song playing on the stereo descended into
a garbled moan as the cassette player began to eat the tape, and
your brother sprung from his seat, but your father was quicker. He
yanked out the cassette, its tape snapping and trailing from it like
spilled entrails, and he flung the cassette onto the table where it
slid into the fish heads. All fell quiet, even your mother. To break
the silence, you lifted your snagged thumb for them both to see.
It had started to sting sharply, and your flesh was red and angry.

Your parents bickered about what to do with you, complaining
because they feared you'd get tetanus and they couldn't really afford the shot. That's not who you were back then, a person who
could afford tetanus shots willy-nilly. In the end you piled into your
father's truck and they all took you to get the shot. It was only later,
back at home, while your daddy wrapped up the mess of a fish and
took it away, that your mother explained to you and your brother
what was happening as she uselessly rewound the tape back into
the cassette with a pencil. She and your brother were taking a long
trip, but you were staying with your daddy. After, your mother disappeared to her bedroom and your daddy to the front porch while
your brother microwaved canned pasta for you both to eat for dinner. That night, you and your brother made plans to run away, but
your father stayed awake all night, watching loud war movies on
the television, only falling into his usual snore at 7 a.m. when your
mother awoke, as if they anticipated your plans and coordinated
a watch schedule. A few hours later, your brother and mother
boarded a westbound Greyhound bus, leaving Florida for good.

The details of those twenty-four hours stick with you like bread caked to the roof of your mouth, like fat in your arteries, like dirt under your fingernails. You are the trees that day, deep green and drooping with humidity. You are your brother's sneakers in the red dirt and the rubber band he used to tie his dreadlocks back. You are the girl on the dock and the snagged hook in your finger. You are the pencil your mother used to wind up the cassette. And you are the scar your daddy got the next day from slamming the metal screen door on his ankle after they left. The ankle of a man who only knew how to love one person at a time. Your mother chose you for him and took herself and your brother out of the equation to make it easier.

All of this and what you'll think about most is the girl on the dock, from the scab on her elbow to the purple galoshes that her sister passed down to her.

Of course, that is the past. You don't know your brother anymore, and the girl on the dock is dead. You live in Baltimore now. You've got two dogs and a sleeve of tattoos on your left arm. You're contemplating one on your right. Your boyfriend wishes you wouldn't do it, but your girlfriend is encouraging. The girlfriend knows about the boyfriend, but he doesn't know about her.

Your brother lives in Wisconsin. From time to time, you call the number your mother sent you, but the phone just rings and rings, and there is no voicemail. If he calls you, you don't know—he's never left a message. You're one of those people who doesn't own a cell phone—just a landline—which your boyfriend finds endearing and your girlfriend is on the fence about. Your boss has threatened to fire you if you don't get a cell phone, but you always show up when you say you will, and if he calls any one of the bars or restaurants that he owns and you manage, he'll find you there or you'll return his call in fifteen. You spend your day with the type of people your mother would hate: people who chose the service industry willingly, not out of necessity. Since you are a manager you feel it isn't quite the same, and you haven't disappointed her. You wear a wooden rosary she once sent you around your right wrist. The small cross clicks against tumblers of whiskey and glass bowls filled with fresh herbs as you craft drinks. Sometimes restaurants that do not belong to your boss invite you to create their new seasonal cocktail menus and you say sure, but you keep it under the table. You don't have a do-not-compete clause, but still.

Your father once said that black people in red cars only attract bad attention, and you should never buy one. You never bought a car at all, sticking to a motorcycle. Once a year you have to remind yourself that your father is still alive, and you call him. The conversations are pleasant and last a few hours—you cover politics and recipes and your boyfriend and your girlfriend, about which he casts no judgment—but there is no need at the end of these talks to pretend that you'll speak any sooner than a year or so from that moment, give or take a month. All the plates in your house are from your father's mother. He gave them to you wrapped in newspaper, and they are pale green and very sturdy.

Your mother sends you a long letter once or twice a year, usually nonsensical but beautiful, drifting between English and Spanish, including long descriptions of your birth, or the glacier she saw on a recent trip to Alaska, or the invasive species of grass in her garden, or the brief affair she had with her distant cousin when she was seventeen. Her handwriting is always exquisite. Her ink is always blue. Once it was red, and she apologized for it. You've framed some of her letters, creating in your living room a gallery wall of smooth, intricate streams tracing across white or yellow stationery. Like maps with no cities, just rivers. Her address is in New Orleans, but you do not think about her when you visit that city, which is at least twice a year because your girlfriend and boyfriend both have best friends who live there, coincidentally. When you write her back, it's always brief, and you include a blurry snapshot of your face.

You are svelte and well shorn. You can be bright and kind but it took a long time for you to realize that those traits wouldn't make anyone actually like you more or less. Of all the bars you manage, you like the one by the harbor the best, despite all the tourists it attracts. You work the late shifts, and when it's closed and the crew is mostly gone, you stare at the water. It is here where your mind becomes its most acrobatic, its most macabre and fantastical. You imagine the bodies of the dead in the bottom muck; you imagine sunken boats and cars and guns rusting, breaking down; you imagine sick, rugged, bruised fish, no-nonsense and one-eyed. You imagine walking among the fish, joining them, just stepping off the edge and plunging into the water, and the fish swarming you, using the hooks of failed fishermen to snag your skin and drag you down to live in the metallic postapocalyptic landscape they've created among the skeletons of people and machinery. They will eat you, bit by bit, and it won't hurt at all, and you'll be just a few little pieces, feather-light and scattered across the waters of the harbor and the Patapsco and the Chesapeake and the Atlantic. And one day, you'll rise, evaporate into a cloud, and rain down on anyone who ever said they loved you, cling to their hair and drip into their ears, explore the thickets and tunnels of their minds for every thought they've ever had of you. You think about this all the time, enough that you'd alarm people if they knew it. You like alarming people because it's so unlike you.

At the harbor, over the groan of water taxis and the soft night traffic of Baltimore, you also think of the girl on the dock, more than a dozen years ago and hundreds of miles down the coast in northern Florida. Some nights you think: Rush me back to the red riverbank and let me tell the girl on the dock that she can't let us steal her tackle box. Let her know that if she lets us take it, she'll let anyone take anything from her.

You don't know this, but that's what happened two decades later when she is just-turned thirty, living in a house in coastal South Carolina with a yoga instructor, a chemistry teacher, and a hairdresser. She will let them take her food, her money, her car, her dog, her clothes. After a year of it, she will finally confront them, and they will all admit, yes, they ate her asparagus, and yes, while she was in class at the culinary school, they borrowed her car to go to the beach and didn't invite her. And yes, they took her Labradoodle with them. It was a bright March day and lovely. Her roommates tell her they left the beach when the storm clouds rumbled in off the water and the cold front hit the shore. This conversation shames her because it means they aren't even frightened enough to lie to her, and she runs outside into the hail and slips on the slick wooden porch and bangs her head against the edge of the step. It wouldn't have been a fatal blow if it had struck just a little lower or just a little higher, or to the right or to the left. It was just perfect.

She rests in a grave overlooking the river near her family's home. The dock is rotted and buried at the bottom of the river. Even the red dirt is covered by maidencane and trees of heaven, as the girl's parents lost interest in going to the river and neglected the dock once their children grew and left them. Now they simply prefer to look at the water from the comfort of their balcony. The girl's sister, who gave her the purple galoshes, grew up to sit in large rooms with large windows and contemplate the skyline and say, this is what the city is now and this is the way it should be, and then parks and hospitals and schools and roads are built, and she nods and checks a list and frowns and bites her nails and says, "More." She married a man from New Jersey with the same last name as you. All of this you don't know.

On any given day, you think more about that girl on that rickety dock than about your own family, who seem more like characters in a favorite book you lent out but never got back than people you're supposed to know. Sometimes you think of her as your sister even though she was pale and red-haired and the furthest thing from you. You only talk to your boyfriend about her, about the day your family halved like an orange. You tell him everything you remember—the old dock, your brother's cassette tape, the hook in your thumb—because he is the most patient person you know. You tell him, in so many clumsy words, that in your child's mind, losing your brother and your mother was a punishment for having stolen the girl's tackle box. The child-you believed this and locked it inside your brain, and your adult mind grew up around that idea like a tree that grows next to a barbed wire fence, its trunk expanding year by year, ring by ring, burying the barbed wire deeper in its bark. It's a silly notion, you say, and your boyfriend says people have believed sillier things. Sometimes you think that you'd like to go see the dock. Maybe figure out how to track down the girl, apologize for snatching that tackle box from her. Because even if she did just get another tackle box and everything turned out fine for her, it was still one thing she could never get back, a cherished thing, a piece of time and a piece of her that was just gone.

Your boyfriend is supportive, but then you talk yourself out of it, because is the dock still there? Who is there? Your father moved on, remaining in Florida but going farther south where he married another Cuban woman who is not your mother. And you don't remember the name of the girl on the dock and you're not in touch with anyone from those days who might know her. And if you could remember how to get to her house and climb those blue-painted steps and cross beneath the hanging ferns to her family's front door, which you've never seen but only imagined, what would you say? What would you find? Once or twice, you've dreamed about that front door: you're standing in front of it, mosquitoes buzzing around your neck, the air smelling of rain and smoke, and you tremble as that door eases open to furniture and stair bannisters and light fixtures all coated thick with dust. A shadow plods towards you, but before it reaches the door, you wake up.

Your boyfriend nods and kisses your hand. You shake your head, signaling the end of this conversation, and ask him what he's doing for the day. He says he's going to wash his car. He washes his car a lot, and if he's not doing that, he's reading, and if he's not reading, he's planning lessons. He teaches middle school history. You admire the way he refuses to talk shit about his students, even the ones that deserve it. He is tall and plays soccer with his brother and cousins on weekends because they are all very close and remained in Baltimore.

While your boyfriend washes his car, you call your girlfriend and then take the dogs for a run in Druid Hill Park. Since you're not in a hurry, you let them splash in the lake. Soon your girlfriend arrives on her bicycle, and you sit, knees touching, while you get her opinion on your new cocktail ideas for a few bars around the city. Your girlfriend lives in an apartment that is beach-themed because she grew up in Iowa and always dreamed of the sea, and her salt and pepper shakers are mermaids she named Daphne and Adelaide. She writes computer software and runs social media campaigns, and she is quick to tell people that they are two very different skill sets. She fixed your boyfriend's laptop once, and you told him it was a coworker who's good with computers.

She tells you now that she's just learned that her parents, after seven years of being divorced, are getting remarried in a few months, and the rest of her family seems happy about it, but for her it seems like they all must suddenly dig up the skeletons and the garbage they'd only just finished burying. You scratch her back and say you get it, and you do, because how disorienting, how messy, how exhausting it can be to drag from the depths what should remain settled at the bottom. You offer to go with her to the wedding, and she says she'll think about it, but maybe, probably, yes.

The dogs finish their play and shake the water from their necks, and you imagine drops flung from a taut line, and you wonder where the girl on the dock is now and if she ever got more hooks and lures and how many fish she caught. You and your girlfriend stand and brush the grass off, and she asks if you've thought any more about a new tattoo. You say you don't know, but you'd like to take her fishing sometime. She lowers her sunglasses over her eyes, straddles her bike, and shrugs, but you know this idea pleases her.

The girl from the dock did get more hooks and caught plenty of fish. Some she froze for later, and her roommates stole them. Others she prepared immediately, gutting and stuffing them with fresh rosemary, lemon, and onions, never thinking of you.

It's your birthday, and you've arranged to spend the day with your boyfriend and the night with your girlfriend. He is making mimosas for you both when your brother calls and by chance you finally answer.

Two decades drop away. The past and the present spring together like a clap. Your brother's voice is clear and high, so unlike you imagined it would be. It's like a long, airy, nervous laugh. He wishes you a happy birthday and says he's tried to reach you before but never felt right just leaving a message out of the blue. You say you understand. You ask him who he is now. He's a music teacher, he says. You tell him that your boyfriend is a teacher, too. This prompts your boyfriend to step from the kitchen with his ceramic mug of mimosa and sit across the room from you on the couch, smiling encouragingly. He wears boxers and one of your sweatshirts.

You and your brother talk about your parents and all the things you don't know, and you give him your father's phone number, and he offers your mother's information but you say you have it. You ask him what he remembers about that day, that last day. He says, "You first," which is something he always did when you were young and he wanted to see you try something before he dared to. So you tell him about your mother crying over the poor, mutilated fish and your dad throwing the broken cassette and your infected thumb and the SpaghettiOs and your mother slowly explaining the plan.

"Well, that's kind of how it happened," he says. He tells you that, yes, you'd each caught a fish and brought them home, but it was you two who cleaned them on the kitchen table. No newspaper or towels down. Neither of you had ever cleaned fish before, but that didn't stop you. The two of you did a terrible job, hacked them up, covered the table in guts. He laughs. "Then Daddy and

Mama came home from wherever they'd been, fighting and making their plans, and it was Mama that pulled the tape from the stereo and she threw it into the mess on the table. Daddy blamed me, mostly. He was like, 'You butchered a perfectly good fish,' and then pointed at you and said, 'And you butchered a perfectly good thumb.' We all got in the truck and took you to the doctor to get a shot, and after that they bought us McDonald's, and Mama told us what was what while she cleaned the table with the windows wide open to let out the stink of fish. Daddy sat in the corner, like he was pouting. I don't remember us trying to run away, but it would make sense. Maybe we should've."

He laughs, and so do you. You're a little disappointed that his memory isn't the mirror image of yours, but that's how memory works, you realize, and you're just glad the basics are right, and you can share this with him, and you feel close to him suddenly. You throw a grin at your boyfriend, and he winks supportively. There's a comfortable silence, you think, between you and your brother, and then in a rush you ask him if he remembers the girl in the purple galoshes on the dock. You stole her tackle box, and it was covered in mud that got all over you both. He laughs and says no, he doesn't remember much more about those days at all, mostly just the sun, the constant sun. You tell him in the most sardonic voice you can manage that you used to think that your parents' split and your separation from him were karma for stealing her tackle box. You explain this to your brother, and he just says, "Our parents were two weeds strangling each other out."

You describe the girl more, almost breathlessly: how she lived down the river from you, in a big blue house, and she was in your class, actually, and on the last day before summer break, she drew an octopus and you told her you liked it, and she said thanks and asked if you wanted to come fish with her, and you said yes, but he—your brother—said no, let's just take her stuff and go somewhere else to fish and bring home a catch for Mama and Daddy so maybe they'd be less angry about everything. You never saw the girl after that. When school started again in the fall, someone told you her parents sent her to a private school or something.

He still doesn't remember, and you ask him, "Where did we get the fishing gear, then?"

"Who knows," he says. "We were always scavenging junk from one place or another."

You persist, saying it was the girl.

"It was a long time ago," he says, and you imagine him rolling his eyes or flicking his hand dismissively, the way your father did when you were growing up. You feel embarrassed, as if you've foolishly believed something for a long time and suddenly your brother has revealed to you what maybe, just maybe, everyone else has known all along: the girl on the dock does not exist and your brother never thought much of you and you are more broken than you ever understood.

"Never mind," you tell your brother. Across the room, your boyfriend looks at you with such pity, as if, he, too, has always known during all of your stories and memories and confessions that you were misguided, silly, a fool. That look of pity, which you've never seen on his face before, at least not for you, feels brutal, like a betrayal, like a hook snagged in flesh. You want to hurt him.

"Sorry," your brother says. "If that's how you remember it, I'm sure that's how it was."

"Never mind," you say again. You feel now that there is nothing left to talk about. You think that most likely you'll never talk to him again until one of your parents dies.

He asks if you would like to Skype sometime. You say you don't know much about it—you're a bit of a technophobe—but your girlfriend could probably help you out. Your brother is puzzled now, and your boyfriend slurps from his mug with a violent smirk and pats one of the dogs come to sniff his bare feet. You repeat yourself, and your brother asks you to explain it—having a boyfriend and a girlfriend both—and you say that it's a tale for another time, a cliffhanger, so he'll have to call again to hear the rest of the story. You hang up the phone and say your boyfriend's name. He continues to pat the dog, and when you say his name again, he speaks with the same calm, flat voice he uses when disciplining a student. He has an idea for a tattoo for your right arm, if you still insist on getting one: a cassette with the tape unraveled and a fish tangled in it, gasping for breath.

T. C. BOYLE

Are We Not Men?

FROM *The New Yorker*

THE DOG WAS the color of a maraschino cherry, and what it had in its jaws I couldn't quite make out at first, not until it parked itself under the hydrangeas and began throttling the thing. This little episode would have played itself out without my even noticing, except that I'd gone to the stove to put the kettle on for a cup of tea and happened to glance out the window at the front lawn. The lawn, a lush blue-green that managed to hint at both the turquoise of the sea and the viridian of a Kentucky meadow, was something I took special pride in, and any wandering dog, no matter its chromatics, was an irritation to me. The seed had been pricey—a blend of Chewings fescue, Bahia, and zoysia incorporating a gene from a species of algae that allowed it to glow under the porch light at night—and, while it was both disease- and drought-resistant, it didn't take well to foot traffic, especially four-footed traffic.

I stepped out onto the porch and clapped my hands, thinking to shoo the dog away, but it didn't move. Actually, it did, but only to flex its shoulders and tighten its jaws around its prey, which I now saw was my neighbor Allison's pet micropig. The pig itself—doe-eyed and no bigger than a Pekinese—didn't seem to be struggling, or not any longer, and even as I came down off the porch looking for something I could brandish at the dog I felt my heart thundering. Allison was one of those pet owners who anthropomorphize their animals, and that pig was the center of her unmarried and unboyfriended life. She would be shattered, absolutely, and who was going to break the news to her? I felt a surge of anger. How had the stupid thing got out of the house anyway, and, for that matter, whose dog was this? I didn't own a garden rake, and there were no sticks on the lawn (the street trees were an edited variety that didn't drop anything, no twigs, seeds, or leaves, no matter the season), so I stormed across the grass empty-handed, shouting the first thing that came to mind, which was "Bad! Bad dog!"

I wasn't thinking. And the effect wasn't what I would have hoped for even if I had been: the dog dropped the pig, all right, which was clearly beyond revivification at this point, but in the same motion it lurched up and clamped its jaws on my left forearm, growling continuously, as if my forearm were a stick it had fetched in a friendly game between us. Curiously, there was no pain—and no blood, either—just a firm insistent pressure, the saliva hot and wet on my skin as I pulled in one direction and the dog, all the while regarding me out of a pair of dull, uniform eyes, pulled in the other. "Let go!" I demanded, but the dog didn't let go. I tugged. The dog tugged back.

There was no one on the street, no one in the next yard over, no one in the house behind me to come to my aid. I was dressed in the T-shirt, shorts, and slippers I'd pulled on not ten minutes earlier, when I'd got out of bed, and here I was caught up in this maddening interspecies pas de deux at eight in the morning, already exhausted. The dog, this cherry-red hairless freak with the armored skull and bulging musculature of a pit bull, showed no sign of giving in: it had got my arm and it meant to keep it. After a minute of this, I went down on one knee to ease the tension in my back, a gesture that seemed only to excite the animal all the more, its nails tearing up divots as it fought for purchase, trying, it occurred to me now, to bring me down to its level. Before I knew what I was doing, I balled up my free hand and punched the thing in the head three times in quick succession.

The effect was instantaneous: the dog dropped my arm and let out a yelp, backing off to hover at the edge of the lawn and eye me warily, as if now, all at once, the rules of the game had changed. In the next moment, just as I realized that I was, in fact, bleeding, a voice cried out behind me, "Hey, I saw that!"

A girl was striding across the lawn toward me, a preternaturally tall girl whom I at first took to be a teenager but who was actually a child of eleven or twelve. She marched directly up to me, glaring, and said, "You hit my dog."

I was in no mood. "I'm bleeding," I said, holding out my arm in evidence. "You see this? Your dog bit me. You ought to keep him chained up."

"That's not true—Ruby would never bite anybody. She was just . . . playing, is all."

I wasn't about to debate her. This was my property, my arm, and that lump of flesh lying there bleeding into the grass was Allison's dead pet. I pointed to it.

"Oh," she said, her voice dropping. "I'm so sorry, I didn't . . . Is it yours?"

"My neighbor's." I gestured to the house just visible over the hedge. "She's going to be devastated. This pig"—I wanted to call it by name, personalize it, but couldn't for the life of me summon up its name—"is all she has. And it wasn't cheap, either." I glanced at the dog, its pinkish gaze and incarnadine flanks. "As I'm sure you can appreciate."

The girl, who stood three or four inches taller than me and whose own eyes were an almost iridescent shade of violet that didn't exist in nature, or at least hadn't until recently, gave me an unflinching look. "Maybe she doesn't have to know."

"What do you mean she doesn't have to know? The thing's dead —look at it."

"Maybe it was run over by a car."

"You want me to lie to her?"

The girl shrugged. "I already said I'm sorry. Ruby got out the front gate when my mother went to work, and I came right after her. You saw me—"

"What about this?" I demanded, holding up my arm, which wasn't so much punctured as abraded, since most of the new breeds had had their canines and carnassials genetically modified to prevent any real damage in situations like this. "It has its shots, right?"

"She's a *Cherry Pit*," the girl said, giving me a look of disgust. "Germline immunity comes with the package. I mean, everybody knows that."

It was a Tuesday and I was working from home, as I did every Tuesday and Thursday. I worked in IT, like practically everybody else on the planet, and I found I actually got more done at home than when I went into the office. My coworkers were a trial, what with their moods, opinions, facial tics, and all the rest. Not that I didn't

like them—it was just that they always seemed to manage to get
in the way at crunch time. Or maybe I didn't like them—maybe
that was it. At any rate, after the little contretemps with the girl
and her dog, I went back in the house, smeared an antibiotic ointment on my forearm, took my tea and a handful of protein wafers
to my desk, and sat down at the computer. If I gave the dead pig
a thought, it was only in relation to Allison, who'd want to see the
corpse, I supposed, which brought up the question of what to do
with it—let it lie where it was or stuff it in a trash bag and refrig-
erate it till she got home from the office? I thought of calling my
wife—Connie was regional manager of Bank U.S.A., by necessity a
master of interpersonal relations, and she would know what to do
—but in the end I did nothing.

It was past three by the time I thought to take a lunch break,
and, because it was such a fine day, I took my sandwich and a glass
of iced tea out onto the front porch. By this juncture, I'd forgotten all about the pig, the dog, and the grief that was brewing for
Allison, but as soon as I stepped out the door it all came back
to me: the trees were alive with crowparrots variously screeching,
cawing, and chattering among themselves, and they were there
for a very specific reason. (I don't know if you have crowparrots
in your neighborhood yet, but, believe me, they're coming. They
were the inspiration of one of the molecular embryologists at the
university here, who thought that inserting genes from the common crow into the invasive parrot population would put an end to
the parrots' raids on our orchards and vineyards, by giving them
a taste for garbage and carrion instead of fruit on the vine. The
only problem was the noise factor—something in the mix seemed
to have redoubled not only the volume but the fury of the birds'
calls, so that you needed earplugs if you wanted to enjoy pretty
much any outdoor activity.)

Which was the case now. The birds were everywhere, cursing
fluidly (*"Bad bird! Fuck, fuck, fuck!"*) and flapping their spangled
wings in one another's faces. Alarmed, I came down off the porch
and for the second time that day scrambled across the lawn to the
flower bed, where a scrum of birds had settled on the remains of
Allison's pet. I flailed my arms, and they lifted off reluctantly into
the sky, screeching, *"Turd-bird!"* and the fractured call that awak-
ened me practically every morning: *"Cock-k-k-k-sucker!"* As for the

pig (which I should have dragged into the garage, I realized that now), its eyes were gone and its faintly bluish hide was striped with bright-red gashes. Truthfully? I didn't want to touch the thing. It was filthy. The birds were filthy. Who knew what zoonoses they were carrying? So I was just standing there, in a quandary, when Allison's car pulled into the driveway next door.

Allison was in her early thirties, with a top-heavy figure and a barely tamed kink of ginger hair she kept wrapped up in various scarves, which gave her an exotic look, as if she were displaced here in the suburbs. She was sad-faced and sweet, the victim of one catastrophic relationship after another, and I couldn't help feeling protective toward her, a single woman alone in the big house her mother had left her when she died. So when she came across the lawn, already tearing up, I felt I'd somehow let her down and, before I could think, I stripped off my shirt and draped it over the corpse.

"Is that her?" she asked, looking down at the hastily covered bundle at my feet. "No," she said, "don't tell me," and then her eyes jumped to mine and she was repeating my name, "Roy, Roy, Roy," as if wringing it in her throat. *"Fuck you!"* the crowparrots cried from the trees. *"Fuck, fuck, fuck!"* In the next moment Allison flung herself into my arms, clutching me to her so desperately I could hardly breathe.

"I don't want to see," she said in a small voice, each syllable a hot puff of breath on the bare skin of my chest. I could smell her hair, the shampoo she used, the taint of sweat under her arms. "The poor thing," she murmured, and lifted her face so I could see the tears blurring her eyes. "I loved her, Roy. I really *loved* her."

This called up a scene from the past, a dinner party at Allison's —Connie and me, another couple, and Allison and her last inamorato, a big-headed boor who worked for Animal Control, incinerating strays and transgenic misfits. Allison had kept the pig in her lap throughout the meal, feeding it from her plate, and afterward, while we sat around the living room cradling brandies and Bénédictine, she propped the thing up at the piano, where it picked out "Twinkle, Twinkle, Little Star" with its modified hooves.

"It was a dog, right? That's what"—and here she had to break off a moment to gather herself. "That's what Terry Wolfson said when she called me at work—"

I was going to offer up some platitude about how the animal hadn't suffered, though for all I knew the dog had gummed it relentlessly, the way it had gummed my arm, when a voice called "Hello?" from the street behind us and we broke awkwardly apart. Coming up the walk was the tall girl, tottering on a pair of platform heels, and she had the dog with her, this time on a leash. I felt a stab of annoyance—hadn't she caused enough trouble already?—and embarrassment, too. It wasn't like me to go shirtless in public—or to be caught in a full-body embrace with my unmarried next-door neighbor, either, for that matter.

If the girl could read my face, she gave no indication of it. She came right up to us, the dog trotting along docilely at her side. Her violet gaze swept from me to the lump on the ground beneath the bloodied T-shirt and finally to Allison. *"Je suis désolée, madame,"* she said. *"Pardonnez-moi. Mon chien ne savait pas ce qu'il faisait—il est un bon chien, vraiment."*

This girl, this child, loomed over us, her features animated. She was wearing eyeliner, lipstick, and blush, as if she were ten years older and on her way to a nightclub, and her hair—blond, with a natural curl—spread like a tent over her shoulders and dangled all the way down to the small of her back. "What are you saying?" I demanded. "And why are you speaking French?"

"Because I can. My IQ is 162 and I can run the hundred meters in 9.58 seconds."

"Wonderful," I said, exchanging a look with Allison. "Terrific. Really. But what are you doing here, what do you want?"

"Your mother!" the birds cried. *"Up yours!"*

The girl shifted from one foot to the other, suddenly looking awkward, like the child she was. "I just wanted to please, *please* beg you not to report Ruby to Animal Control, because my father says they'll come and put her down. She's a good dog, she really is, and she never did anything like this before. It was just a—"

"Freak occurrence?" I said.

"Right," she said. "An anomaly. An accident."

Allison's jaw tightened. The dog looked tranquilly up at us out of its pink eyes, as if none of this were its concern. A bugless breeze rustled the trees along the street. "And what am I supposed to say?" Allison put in. "How am I supposed to feel? What do you want, forgiveness?" She gave the girl a fierce look. "You love your dog?"

The girl nodded.

"Well, I love—*loved*—Shushawna, too." She choked up. "More than anything in the world."

We all took a minute to gaze down on the carcass, and then the girl lifted her eyes. "My father says we'll pay all damages. Here," she said, digging into her purse and producing a pair of business cards, one of which she handed to me and the other to Allison. "Any medical treatment you may need, we'll take care of, one hundred per cent," she assured me, eyeing my arm doubtfully before turning to Allison. "And replace your pet, too, if you want, *madame*. It was a micropig, right, from Recombicorp?"

It was a painful moment. I could feel for Allison and for the girl, too, though Connie and I didn't have any pets, not even one of the new hypoallergenic breeds. There was a larger sadness at play here, the sadness of attachment and loss and the way the world wreaks its changes whether we're ready for them or not. We would have got through the moment, I think, coming to some sort of understanding—Allison wasn't vindictive, and I wasn't about to raise a fuss—but that same breeze swept across the lawn to flip back the edge of the T-shirt and expose the eyeless head of the pig, and that was all it took. Allison let out a gasp, and the dog —that crimson freak—jerked the leash out of the girl's hand and went right for it.

When Connie came home, I was in the kitchen mixing a drink. The front door slammed. (Connie was always in a hurry, no wasted motion, and though I'd asked her a hundred times not to slam the door she was constitutionally incapable of taking the extra two seconds to ease it shut.) An instant later, her briefcase slapped down on the hallway table with the force of a thunderclap, her heels drilled the parquet floor—*tat-tat-tat-tat*—and then she was there in the kitchen, saying, "Make me one, too, would you, honey? Or no: wine. Do we have any wine?"

I didn't ask her how her day had gone—all her days were the same, pedal to the metal, one *situation* after another, all of which she dealt with like a five-star general driving the enemy into the sea. I didn't give her a hug or blow her a kiss, either. We weren't that sort of couple—to her mind (and mine, too, to be honest), it would have been just more wasted motion. Wordlessly, I poured her a glass of the Sancerre she liked and handed it to her.

"Allison's pet pig was killed today," I said. "Right out on our front lawn. By one of those transgenic pit bulls, one of the crimson ones they're always pushing on TV?"

Her eyebrows lifted. She swirled the wine in her glass, took a sip.

"And I got bit," I added, holding up my arm, where a deep-purplish bruise had wrapped itself around the skin just below the elbow.

What she said next didn't follow, but then we often talked in non sequiturs, she conducting a kind of call-and-response conversation in her head and I in mine, the responses never quite matching up. She didn't comment on my injury or the dog or Allison or the turmoil I'd gone through. She just set her glass down on the counter, patted her lips where the wine had moistened them, and said, "I want a baby."

I suppose I should back up here a moment to give you an idea of where this was coming from. We'd been married twelve years now, and we'd agreed that at some point we'd like to start a family, but we kept putting it off for one reason or another—our careers, finances, fear of the way a child would impact our lifestyle, the usual kind of thing. But with a twist. What sort of child—that was the question. Previous generations had only to fret over whether the expectant mother would bear a boy or a girl or if the child would inherit Aunt Bethany's nose or Uncle Yuri's unibrow, but that wasn't the case anymore, not since CRISPR gene-editing technology had hit the ground running twenty years back. Now not only could you choose the sex of the child at conception; you could choose its other features, too, as if having a child were like going to the car dealership and picking which options to add onto the basic model. The sole function of sex these days was recreational; babies were conceived in the laboratory. That was the way it was and that was the way it would be, until, as a species, we evolved into something else. The result was a nation—a world—of children like the tall girl with the bright-red dog.

To my way of thinking, this was intrusive and unnatural, but to Connie's it was a no-brainer. "Are you out of your mind?" she'd say. "You really want your kid—*our* kid—to be the bonehead of the class? Or what, take career training, cosmetology, *auto mechanics,* for Christ's sake?"

Now, tipping back her glass and downing the wine in a single belligerent gulp, she announced, "I'm thirty-eight years old and I'm putting my foot down. I've made an appointment at GenLab for ten a.m. Thursday. Either you come with me"—she was glaring at me now—"or I swear I'm going to go out and get a sperm donor."

Nobody likes an ultimatum. Especially when you're talking about a major life-changing event, the kind of thing *both* people involved have to enter into in absolute harmony. It didn't go well. She thought she could bully me as if I were one of her underlings at work; I thought she couldn't. She thought she'd had the final word on the subject; I thought different. I said some things I wound up regretting later, snatched up my drink, and slammed through the kitchen door and out into the backyard, where for once no birds were cursing from the trees and even the bees seemed muted as they went about their business. If it weren't for that silence, I never would have heard the soft heartsick keening of Allison working through the stations of her grief. The sound was low and intermittent, a stunted release of air followed by a sodden gargling that might have been the wheeze and rattle of the sprinklers starting up, and it took me a minute to realize what it was. In the instant, I forgot all about what had just transpired in my own kitchen and thought of Allison, struck all over again by the intensity of her emotion.

We'd managed to get the dog off the carcass, all three of us shouting at once while the girl grabbed for the leash and I delivered two or three sharp kicks to the animal's hindquarters, but Allison's dead pig was none the better for it. The girl, red-faced and embarrassed despite her IQ and whatever other attributes she might have possessed, slouched across the lawn and down the street, the dog mincing beside her, while I offered to do the only sensible thing and bury what was left of the remains. I dug a hole out back of Allison's potting shed, Allison read a passage I vaguely remembered from school ("The stars are not wanted now: put out every one; / Pack up the moon and dismantle the sun"), I held her in my arms for the second time that day, then filled the hole and went home to make my drink and have Connie slam the front door and lay her demands on me.

Now, as if I were being tugged on invisible wires, I moved toward the low hedge that separated our properties and stepped across it. Allison was hunched over the picnic table on her patio. She was still dressed in the taupe blouse and black skirt she'd worn to work, and she had her head down, her scarf bunched under one cheek, and that got to me in a way I can't explain, so that before I knew what I was doing I'd fallen down a long dark tunnel and found myself consoling her in a way that seemed—how can I put this?—so very *natural* at the time.

It was dark when I got home. Connie was sitting on the couch in the living room, watching TV with the sound muted. "Hi," I said, feeling sheepish, feeling guilty (I'd never strayed before and didn't know why I'd done it now, except that I'd been so furious with my wife and so strangely moved by Allison in her grief, though I know that's no excuse), but trying, like all amateurs, to act as if nothing were out of the ordinary. Connie looked up. I couldn't read her face, but I thought, at least by the flickering light of the TV, that she looked softer, contrite even, as if she'd reconsidered her position, or at least the way she'd laid it on me.

"I'm sorry," I said, "but I was upset, okay? I just went for a walk. To clear my head."

She had nothing to say to this.

"You eat yet?" I asked, to change the subject.

She shook her head.

"Me, either," I said, feeling the weight lift, as if ritual could get us through this. "You want to go out?"

"No, I don't want to go out," she said. "I want a baby."

And what did I say, from the shallow grave of my guilt, which was no deeper than the layer of earth I'd flung over the shrunken and lacerated corpse of Allison's pet? I said, "Okay, we'll talk about it."

"Talk about it? The appointment is Thursday, ten a.m. That's non-negotiable."

She was right—it was time to start a family—and she was right, too, about cosmetology and auto mechanics. What responsible parent wouldn't want the best for his child, whether that meant a stable home, top-flight nutrition, and the best private-school education money could buy, or tweaking the chromosomes in a test tube in a lab somewhere? Understand me: I was under duress. I could smell Allison on me still. I could smell my own fear. I didn't want to lose my wife—I loved her. I was used to her. She was the only woman I'd known these past twelve years and more, my *familiar*. And there she was, poised on the edge of the couch, watching me, her will like some miasma seeping in under the door and through the cracks around the windows until the room was choked with it. "Okay," I said.

Which is not to say that I gave in without a fight. The next day —Wednesday—I had to go into the office and endure the usual banalities of my coworkers till I wanted to beat the walls of my cubicle in frustration, but on the way home I stopped at a pet store and picked up an eight-week-old dogcat. (People still aren't quite sure what to call the young, even now, fifteen years after they were first created. Kitpups? Pupkits? The sign in the window read simply BABY DOGCATS ON SPECIAL.) I chose a squirming little furball with a doggish face and tabby stripes and brought it home as a surprise for Connie, hoping it would distract her long enough for her to reevaluate the decision she was committing us to.

I tucked the thing inside my shirt for the drive home, since the minute the girl behind the counter put it in its cardboard carrier it began alternately mewing and yipping in a tragic way, and it nestled there against my chest, warm and content, until I'd parked the car and gone up the steps and into the house. Connie was already home, moving briskly about the kitchen. There were flowers on the table next to an ice bucket with the neck of a bottle of Veuve Clicquot protruding from it, and the room was redolent of the scent of my favorite meal—pipérade, Basque style, topped with poached eggs—and I realized that she must have made a special stop at Maison Claude on her way home. This was a celebration and no two ways about it. In the morning, we would procreate—or take our first steps in that direction, which on my part would involve producing a sperm sample under duress (unlike, I couldn't help thinking, the way it had been with Allison).

We didn't hug. We didn't kiss. I just said "Hey," and she said "Hey" back. "Smells great," I said, trying to gauge her expression as we both hovered over the table.

"Perfect timing," she said, leaning in to adjust the napkin beside her plate, though it was already precisely aligned. "I got there the minute they took it out of the oven. Claude himself brought it out to me—along with a fresh loaf of that crusty sourdough you like. Just baked this morning."

I was grinning at her. "Great," I said. "Really great."

Into the silence that followed—neither of us was ready yet to address the issue hanging over us—I said, "I've got a surprise for you."

"How sweet. What is it?"

With a magician's flourish, I whipped the new pet from the folds of my shirt and held it out triumphantly for her. Unfortunately, I startled the thing in the process, and it reacted by digging its claws into my wrist, letting out a string of rapid-fire barks, and dropping a glistening turd on the tiles of the kitchen floor. "For you," I said.

Her face fell. "You've got to be kidding me. You really think I'm that easy to buy off?" She made no effort to take the thing from me —in fact, she clenched her hands behind her. "Take it back where you got it."

The pupkit had softened now, retracting its claws and settling into the crook of my arm as if it recognized me, as if in the process of selecting it and secreting it in my shirt I'd imparted something essential to it—love, that is—and it was content to exist in this new world on a new basis altogether. "It's purring," I said.

"What do you want me to say—hallelujah? The thing's a freak, you're always saying so yourself every time one of those stupid commercials comes on—"

"No more a freak than that girl with the dog," I said.

"What girl? What are you talking about?"

"The one with the dog that bit me. She must have been six-four. She had an IQ of 162. And still she let her dog out, and still it bit me."

"What are you saying? You're not trying to back out on me, are you? We had a *deal*, Roy, and you know how I feel about people who renege on a deal—"

"Okay, okay, calm down. All I'm saying is maybe we ought to have a kind of trial or something before we—I mean, we've never even had a pet."

"A pet is not a child, Roy."

"No," I said, "that's not what I meant. It was just, I'm just—" The crowparrots started up then with one of their raucous dinnertime chants, squawking so piercingly you could hear them even with the windows shut—"*Big Mac, Big Mac,*" they called. "*Fries!*"—and I lost my train of thought.

"Are we going to eat?" Connie said in a fragile voice, tearing up.

"Because I went out of my way. Because I wanted this night to be special, okay?"

So now we did hug, though the pupkit got between us, and, coward that I am, I told her everything was going to be all right. Later, after she'd gone to bed, I took the pupkit in my arms, went next door, and rang the bell. Allison answered in her nightgown, a smile creeping across her lips. "Here," I said, handing her the animal. "I got this for you."

Fast-forward seven and a half months. I am living in a house with a pregnant woman next door to a house in which there is another pregnant woman. Connie seems to find this amusing, never suspecting the truth of the matter. We'll glance up from the porch and see Allison emerging heavily from her car with an armload of groceries, and Connie will say things like "I hope she doesn't have to pee every five minutes the way I do" and "She won't say who the father is—I just hope it's not that a-hole from Animal Control, what was his name?"

This is problematic on a number of levels. I play dumb, of course—what else can I do? "Maybe she went to GenLab," I say.

"Her? You're kidding me, right? I mean, look at that string of jerks she keeps dating. If you want to know the truth, she's lower-class, Roy, and I'm sorry to have to say it—"

I'm not about to argue the point. The fact is I tried everything I could to talk Allison out of going through with this—finally, to my shame, falling back on the same argument about the whole *Übermensch-Untermensch* dynamic that Connie used on me—but Allison merely gave me a bitter smile and said, "I trust your genes, Roy. You don't have to be involved. I just want to do this, that's all. For myself. And for nature. You believe in nature, don't you?"

You don't have to be involved. But I *was* involved, though we'd had sex only the one time (or two, actually, counting the night I brought her the pupkit), and if she had a boy and he looked like me and grew up right next door playing with our daughter, how involved would that be?

So there comes a day, sometime during that eighth month, a Tuesday, when I'm working at home and Connie's at the office, and I'm so focused on the problem at hand that I keep putting off my bathroom break until the morning's nearly gone. That's

the way it always is when I'm deeply engaged with a problem, a
kind of mind-body separation, but finally the body's needs prevail
and I push myself up from my desk to go down the hall to the
bathroom. I'm standing there, in mid-flow, when I become aware
of the sound of a dog barking on the front lawn and I shift my
torso ever so slightly so that I can glance out the window and see
what the ruckus is all about. It's the red dog, the Cherry Pit that
set all this in motion, and it's tearing around on my hybrid lawn,
chasing something. My first reaction is anger—anger at the tall
girl and her fixer father and all the other idiots of the world—but
by the time I get down the stairs and out the front door the anger
dissipates, because I see that the dog isn't there to kill anything
but to play, and that what it's chasing is being chased willingly:
Allison's dogcat, now a rangy adolescent and perhaps a third the
size of the dog.

For all my fretting over the lawn, I have to say that in that moment, with the light making a cathedral of the street trees and
the neighborhood suspended in the grip of a lazy, warm autumn
afternoon, I find something wonderfully liberating in the play of
those two animals, the dogcat especially. Allison named him Tiger
because of his coloration—dark feral stripes against a kind of Po-
meranian orange—and he lives up to his name, absolutely fearless
and with an athleticism and elasticity that combines the best of
both species that went into making him. He runs rings around the
pit bull, actually, feinting one way, dodging the next, racing up the
trunk of a tree and out onto a branch before leaping to the next
tree and springing back down to charge, doglike, across the yard.
"Go, Tiger!" I call out. "Good boy. Go get him!"

That's when I become aware of Allison, in a pair of maternity
shorts and an enormous top, crossing from her front lawn to ours.
She's put on a lot of weight (but not as much as Connie, because
we opted for a big baby, in the eleven-pound range, wanting it—
her—to have that advantage right from the start). I haven't spoken
with Allison much these past months, but I still have feelings for
her, of course—beyond resentment, that is. So I lift a hand and
wave and she waves back and I watch her come barefoot through
the glowing grass while the animals frolic around her.

I'm down off the porch now, and I can't help but smile at the
sight of her. She comes up to me, moving with a kind of clumsy
grace, if that makes any sense, and I want to take her in my arms

but can't really do that, not under these conditions, so I take both
her hands and peck a neighborly kiss to her cheek. For a minute,
neither of us says anything, then, shading her eyes with the flat of
one hand to better see the animals at play, she says, "Pretty cute,
huh?"

I nod.

"You see how Tiger's grown?"

"Yes, of course, I've been watching him all along . . . Is that as
big as he's going to get?"

The sun catches her eyes, which are a shade of plain everyday
brown. "Nobody's sure, but the vet thinks he won't get much bigger. Maybe a pound or two."

"And you?" I venture. "How are you feeling?"

"Never better. You're going to be seeing more of me—don't
look scared, that's not what I mean, just I'm taking my maternity
leave, though I'm not due for, like, six weeks." Both her hands,
pretty hands, shapely, come to rest on the bulge beneath her oversized blouse. "They're really being nice about it at work."

Connie's not planning on taking off till the minute her water
breaks, because that's the way Connie is, and I want to tell Allison
that by way of contrast, just to say something, but I notice that she's
looking over my shoulder and I turn my head to see the tall girl
coming up the walk, leash in hand. "Sorry," the girl calls out. "She
got loose again. Sorry, sorry."

I don't know what it is, but I'm feeling generous, expansive. "No
problem," I call out. "She's just having a little fun."

That's when Connie's car slashes into the driveway, going too
fast, and all I can think is she's going to hit one of the animals,
but she brakes at the last minute and they flow like water around
the tires to chase back across the lawn again. It's hard to gauge the
look on my wife's face as she swings open the car door, pushes herself laboriously from behind the wheel, then starts up the walk as
if she hasn't seen us. Just as she reaches the front steps, she swivels
around. I can see she's considering whether it's worth the effort to
come and greet our neighbor and get a closer look at the tall girl
who hovers behind us like the avatar she is, but she decides against
it. She just stops a moment, staring, and though she's thirty feet
away I can see a kind of recognition settle into her features, and
it has to do with the way Allison is standing there beside me, as if
for a portrait or an illustration in a book on family planning, the

XY chromosomes and the XX. It's just a moment, and I can't say for certain, but her face goes rigid and she turns her back on us, mounts the steps, and slams the door behind her.

When the CRISPR technology first came to light, governments and scientists everywhere assured the public that it would be employed only selectively, to fight disease and to rectify congenital deformities, editing out the mutated BRCA1 gene that predisposes women to breast cancer, for instance, or eliminating the ability of the *Anopheles* mosquito to carry the parasite that transmits malaria. Who could argue with that? Genome-editing kits ("Knock Out Any Gene!") were sold to home hobbyists, who could create their own anomalous forms of yeast and bacteria in their kitchens, and it was revolutionary—and, beyond that, fun. Fun to tinker. Fun to create. The pet and meat industries gave us rainbow-colored aquarium fish, seahorses that incorporated gold dust in their cells, rabbits that glowed green under a black light, the beefed-up supercow, the micropig, the dogcat, and all the rest. The Chinese were the first to renounce any sort of regulatory control and upgrade the human genome, and, as if they weren't brilliant enough already, they became still more brilliant as the first edited children began to appear, and of course we had to keep up . . .

In a room at GenLab, Connie and I were presented with an exhaustive menu of just how our chromosomes could be made to match up. We chose to have a daughter. We selected emerald eyes for her—not iridescent, not freakishly bright, but enhanced for color so that she could grow up wearing mint, olive, kelly green, and let her eyes talk for her. We chose height, too, as just about everybody does. And musical ability—we both love music. Intellect, of course. And finer features, like a subtly cleft chin and breasts that were not too big but not as small as Connie's, either. It was a menu, and we placed an order.

The tall girl is right beside us now, smiling like the heroine of a Norse saga, her eyes sweeping over us like searchlights. She looks to Allison, takes in her condition. "Boy or girl?" she asks.

The softest smile plays over Allison's lips. She ducks her head, shrugs.

The girl—the genius—looks confused for a moment. "But, but," she stammers, "how can that be? You don't mean you—?"

But before Allison can answer, a crowparrot sweeps out of the nearest tree, winging low to screech *"Fuck you!"* in our faces, and the smallest miracle occurs. Tiger, as casual in his own skin as anything there is or ever was, erupts from the ground in a rocketing whirl of fur to catch the thing in his jaws. As quick as that, it's over, and the feathers, the prettiest feathers you'll ever see, lift and dance and float away on the breeze.

KEVIN CANTY

God's Work

FROM *The New Yorker*

SANDER LOVES HIS MOTHER. He walks a few steps after her, wearing a new black suit that has room for him to grow into, carrying a big black valise of pamphlets. When his mother goes to the front door, rings the bell, waits for an answer, Sander stands behind her, looking over her shoulder, with an expression on his face that he means to be pleasant.

It's the second day of his summer vacation, but it still feels like spring. Lilacs bloom in every yard; irises wag their pink and purple tongues at him.

His mother is plain. She wears a gray sweater, despite the sun, and a black skirt that reaches nearly to her ankles. No lipstick, short, practical hair. Her name is Anna. She makes up for her plainness with a big galvanic smile. People are on her side right away, though they rarely open the screen door and almost never take a pamphlet. Nobody new ever comes to Fellowship. Anna doesn't take this as permission to stop trying. She thinks the men and women and children in these sleeping houses will lose the chance to live life as God intended unless they take the message she brings them in the pamphlet. Sander thinks she is lovely and brave and admirable. Every day, she tries to save strangers. Selfless. Sander loves his mother.

Today! is the name of the pamphlet.

Sander has just finished his sophomore year. At the first breath of spring, the girls all started to dress like prostitutes. With his own eyes he has seen a pretty junior bicycling in a tank top with one pale breast riding free. In his dreams he sees the delicate tuft of blond pubic hair he witnessed poking out of a pair of low-slung jeans in study hall. This is what Sander thinks about as he walks behind his mother, feeling the hot sun wherever it touches the black fabric of his suit. That and the bad haircut he got yesterday.

The haircut! He feels tears start again at the thought of it. Some friend of his mother's, in her kitchen. When she brought out the mirror: death. As if every single thing in his life were there to disqualify him.

A nice enough street, anyway. Lots of students from the college. It's a Tuesday afternoon, so nobody much answers the door. Those who do are mostly wearing flannel pajama bottoms and flip-flops. Some of the men don't even have on shirts. His mother rings the bell, and a college girl comes to the screen door, and if she came outside Sander could tell if she was wearing a bra under her thin little shirt. But she says no, thanks, not interested, thanks, and closes the inner door on them, though it was open before.

Another soul misses out on eternal life in an earthly Paradise.

Why can't he be like his mother? Why can't he just be good?

Immense transparency of light, the sky a luminous blue. He takes a deep breath and lets God's grace fill him. All this great gift, this flowering world. It is not Sander's place to question why a God so generous can also be so exacting. Why do they have to work so hard to come to Him? Sin is everywhere, the path to goodness narrow and sometimes hard to find. But this is nothing next to His generosity.

"Another block or Taco Bell?" his mother asks.

"I don't know," Sander says. "I don't care."

"Are you hungry or are you not?" He is hungry. He is always hungry. But he doesn't want to go there in his new suit and with his haircut, and he doesn't want to go with his mother. He says, "I'll pass, I guess."

"Well, I'm starving," his mother says.

They load the valise into the back of the blue Aerostar and drive to Broadway, where Sander watches as his mother consumes a Gordita Supreme and an order of tortilla chips. She eats slowly and carefully, and she reads from a small black Bible as she does. Next to them, a tableful of senior girls laugh and scream like girls at a swimming pool: Elin Peterson, Morgan McKay, Nora Austin. Anna doesn't seem to notice, but Sander is worried for her. Something dangerous in that screamy life.

After lunch he is twice as hungry and feels like an idiot. They go back to the same neighborhood and begin to canvass. Two houses into it, a screen door is open, and a man in an undershirt, his hair pulled back in a graying ponytail, answers.

"I'm here to invite you to a special event," Sander's mother says.

"All right," the man says.

"I have some good news about God's love," she says, holding a pamphlet out toward the door.

"Come on in," the man with the ponytail says. This is not quite a surprise—every day or two they are invited in somewhere. Usually it's a drunk person or someone lonely and old. This man just looks angry.

"You want some coffee?" he asks. "I've got hot coffee. I've got plenty."

"No, thank you," Sander's mom says.

"Is that against your religion?" the man says. "You don't look like Mormons."

"We are not of that faith."

"Well, do you want some coffee?"

"I'd love some," Sander's mother says, and settles with a small ladylike sigh onto the sofa and takes the valise. Sander doesn't know about this. Maybe the man is not drunk, but there is certainly something wrong with him.

"So am I going to Hell?" the man asks, setting a steaming mug of coffee in front of Anna.

"By my lights, you are not," she says. "No hellfire and no eternal damnation."

"What, then?"

"Nothing."

"Just nothing?"

"A blank eternity."

"That doesn't sound so bad."

"Consider the alternative," Sander's mom says. "An eternity of bliss in the company of God Himself."

"You want to get high?" the man asks Sander's mom.

"Why, no, thank you."

That eagle stare he gives her, ignorant and proud. Why do the heathen rage? This happens, not too often, every couple of weeks and then not at all for a month or two, the sinful man who is proud of his sin. Sander is a sinful boy—he knows this about himself. But he has the grace to be ashamed of it.

"Oblivion," the man says, lighting a little brass pipe, smoking, pointing it toward Anna, who shakes her head no. Then toward Sander.

"I'd ask you not to do that," Anna says.

"Why not? If it doesn't matter, it doesn't matter."

"Your soul is at stake."

"If it's just nothing," the man says, and takes another hit off the brass pipe. Sander has seen it done, in the smokers' pit behind his school, though it's odd to see a grown man puffing on a tiny pipe.

"If it's just oblivion," he says, exhaling the words through thin smoke, "then I don't care. I like oblivion. I seek after it."

"Think of what hangs in the balance."

"Or not," he says. "Clara!"

"What?" a petulant voice answers from the kitchen.

A needle of fear. Sander knows that voice, that name.

"Come on out here."

"Why?"

"Come on out here is all."

It is exactly the person he was afraid it was, Clara Martinson, she of the ripped T-shirt, raccoon eyes, pierced anything, the next grade up from his, this girl who looks and dresses the way every teen girl would if there was nobody to tell her she couldn't. Which there isn't. Please, dear God, make me disappear, Sander thinks. Send me to the solar surface and vaporize me.

"What do you want?" she says. Then she notices Sander in his black suit and haircut. Okay: there is something in each of us, in every sinner (and Sander knows that we are all sinners), that wants to climb toward the light, and for a moment, in Clara's eyes, Sander sees the longing for grace.

Then, just as quickly, the window shuts. She says, "Oh, for fuck's sake, Dad."

"Come have a hit with your old man," he says. "Just a little toke."

"I'm sorry," Clara says to Anna. "He gets like this. You should go."

"This is a value, too," Clara's dad says. "This is a family."

Anna presses a pamphlet into Clara's hand, into her father's as well, as she rises to her feet. "Please come to the meeting," she says. "We have good news for you."

One more glance from steely Clara is all it takes to set Sander off into a fury of blushing. She trails them to the door while her father sits fuming on the couch. As Anna leaves, Sander turns to Clara.

"I'm sorry," he says. "She's just . . ."

"Don't apologize for her," Clara says.

"Then me," he says.

"No." Clara shoves him out, blinking, into the bright miracle of the day. The door closes firmly behind them. Sander sits on the curb, his big black valise between his feet, and wishes he could cry. He can't—he doesn't know why. Doesn't remember the last time.

When he looks up, his mother is beaming. She says, "That was really something, wasn't it? You never know what's going to happen."

"But the two of them . . ."

"We plant our seeds on stony soil," she says. "It is not up to us which grow and which do not. Are you hungry yet?"

"No," Sander says, although he is starving.

Clara turns up at Fellowship on Wednesday.

She seeks out Sander and says, "There's no Hell. There's really no Hell?"

"No."

"Then I'll stick around and listen."

She melts off toward the back of the hall before the meeting starts. It's a basement—knotty-pine paneling and framed pictures of the ex-presidents of the Elks on the walls. Sander is out of the suit, but the haircut remains. And he dresses as if his mother dressed him, which she does: chinos, plaid shirt. What had Clara been wearing? He can't remember—only her face, which was mostly clean of makeup and had a look of inquiry. He wants to turn around and look at her. But he must keep his mind on God's path. Then they stand and sing, all of them at once, "What God Has Yoked Together."

They are in the same room and singing together. They are one soul, one breath, at least in this tiny moment. That's what Sander feels.

After Fellowship, the hens and chicks of the congregation spirit

Clara away, and he doesn't see her again. He will never see her again. The skirts alone, down to the ankle, will drive her away, and the plain faces, the blouses buttoned to the neck. Clara will never have the vision to see through the shell, the earthly costume, to the joy that waits for her. Words, words, words, Sander thinks. She is a girl who might talk to him. These women will spoil it for him, these women he has lived among all his life. Just now, he hates them for it.

But she comes to Fellowship again on Saturday, and afterward, before the hens and chicks take her away, she asks Sander if they can go for a walk on Sunday. No, he tells her, but Monday might be all right.

"And what are your intentions?" his mother asks.

"I don't have any," Sander says.

Anna laughs out loud. They're in the kitchen, Sunday afternoon, summer rain beating against the windows. Sander still in his Sunday suit, though he's taken his tie off.

"That's impossible," his mother says. "Everybody has intentions, good or bad or all mixed up. What we want. It's what sets people in motion. But you," she says, and leans closer. "I don't want you to lose your way. She's a very pretty girl."

Not really, Sander thinks. Compared with the chicks, maybe. But there are some real knockouts at school. Clara's got the edge, maybe, the interest—she's got a snake tattoo that curls out from under her shirt, a little ways up her neck, emerald and garnet—but there are definitely prettier girls.

"She doesn't know what she's doing," his mother says. "You've seen how she dresses. She has no compass."

"We're just going for a walk," Sander says.

"Do you wish me to come along?"

Oh, no, Sander thinks. A hot ball of disappointment rises in his throat. He forces himself to speak: "I'd rather you didn't."

"Then think of what you are asking."

"I'll pray on it," Sander says, and his mother radiates approval, and at that exact moment he splits into two people, the one he has always been and some itchy, wayward newborn.

The old Sander will do as his mother asks, will pray and puzzle, working toward the light and out of the morass of sin. The old Sander thrills at his mother's smile, at her approval. Old Sander, full of grace.

The newborn Sander schemes. That night, in his bed, as he is supposed to be searching his conscience, he thinks instead of the snake tattoo. He thinks about what exactly he might say to his mother to keep her from chaperoning, without thinking whether this might be lies or truth. His dreams are full of open windows, speeding cars. The ex-presidents of the Elks laugh down at him.

At four o'clock Monday, after Sander and his mother have returned from a short, hot day, Clara shows up on her bicycle. The sun is shining and the sky is an empty, mindless blue. She parks her bike alongside the house. Sander is surprised: Clara's wearing a skirt down to her ankles, a turtleneck that hides her snake, even a beret on her head. Plain-faced. He barely recognizes her.

True, she's wearing combat boots, but Sander's mother approves. She says, "Very becoming."

Clara knocks politely. His mother invites her into the parlor and offers her tea, which Clara accepts. Sander hangs around the edge of the room like a curtain, a piece of furniture, while they talk about nothing: the weather, the summer, the beautiful yellow irises that Anna planted by the ditch in front of the house, now in full stalky bloom.

Clara has tits under her clothes, little ones, as far as he can tell, or maybe medium. And she has a pussy, too, a hairy one, or maybe a smooth, pretty one—he'll never know. Last year, when he was fifteen, he let this thought torment him until he was undressing every counter girl and lady cop who passed by. Lately, he's better, most of the time. Until he can't help it.

"An hour," Anna says. "Then right back here, all right?"

"Yes, ma'am," Sander says, and Clara looks at him to see if he's being sarcastic, which he is not. It's a whole new world for her, Sander can tell.

The park: The newborn Sander, soft, defenseless, feels every green leaf, every flower, every shaft of evening sunlight penetrate into him. A bright chattery mountain stream runs the length of the park, and on either side are tangled thickets of birds and flowers. Here, though, is the picnic area: bright grass, wooden tables, barelegged couples lying next to each other on quilts, touching.

"The world is ending," Clara says.

"It is," Sander says. It's nothing he wants to talk about.

"When?"

"Soon," he says. "I don't know. People said it was going to happen a couple of years ago, but then it didn't."

"But you still believe it."

"I believe in Jehovah," Sander says. "People make mistakes. They interpret His word, they add and subtract. People are people. Jehovah doesn't change."

"The end of the world—that's a terrible thing to believe," Clara says, and sits down on a bench. Sander sits on the same bench, not quite as far from her as he can get. He feels so full of desire and fear—it might spill out. Yet he speaks what he believes.

"It's God's love at work," he says. "He's given us a chance to redeem ourselves. To mean something."

"But only through Him."

"Only through Him," Sander says. She's right there on the bench. Perhaps he could kiss her. People have certainly kissed her before.

"Have you ever touched a baby's head?" she asks.

"I don't know."

"Sure you have," she says. "That soft spot, up on top of their head, the place they're so vulnerable. Or the way they smell—not the powders and the ointment but just the smell of a baby."

"Sure," he says, and he's almost certain he has.

"Fontanel," she says, remembering. "Or what about this, the flowers and all, the green grass and the rain. There's so much that's pretty about the world."

"It'll go on."

"Without us."

"Without most of us," he says.

"Then it won't really exist," she says. "Without somebody to touch it, see it. Without somebody to breathe that smell of baby."

Sander is amazed. It's something he's known all along, this passing sadness, the beautiful dream of the world, only to have it all end. Clara has put her finger on it.

"It doesn't make sense," she says.

"It doesn't have to make sense," he says. "You don't have to understand it. That's for faith to do."

Her eyes swim up to him from someplace deep under the surface.

"You do believe," she says.

"I do," he says, and in that moment he does.

"Okay," she says, and gets up off the bench and starts down the path into the woods, in a fury of thought. Sander follows. It's what he does, in his chinos and black shoes: he's a follower. Small birds scatter and chirp as they pass. Sunlight glints on the water of the creek. The world, he thinks, this generous world. He is looking at a bird by the water to see if it is a dipper when she stops short and he runs into her, *bang*, almost knocks her down.

"Sorry," he says. "Sorry, sorry. I wasn't looking."

"It's all right," Clara says.

But Sander doesn't hear. The after-print of her body on his is too strong, just the accidental touch—he doesn't get touched enough. Not nearly enough.

"Faith," she says. "Where do you get it? Where can I buy some?"

Sander doesn't know. Just now he's nowhere near his God, dazzled by the sunlight, the girl. He says, "It's work sometimes."

"Just sometimes?"

"All the time," he says. "And half the time it doesn't come, and you're just nowhere. Sorry."

"No, that's okay," Clara says. She takes his hand and says, "Thank you. Thank you for being honest."

"Oh," Sander says, and blushes.

"I'm not supposed to do that, am I?" she says, dropping his hand.

And Sander almost catches the moment, almost manages to hold on. "It's all right," he says. "No harm done."

Clara's there at Fellowship again on Wednesday night and on Sunday, dressed modestly in her own way—long skirt and combat boots, a navy woolen beanie on her head instead of the lace frill favored by the hens. Sander barely sees her. The chicks are so delighted to have a new face among them that they surround her. At one point, a long wistful look as Clara searches out Sander's eyes and smiles at him: What's to be done? They have me.

On Monday, they go walking again, with his mother's blessing.

Clara wants to talk about Hell and why they don't believe in it. This is where she comes in: A God who doesn't hate His people. Come to me or not. Sander explains, but his mind is on the body. Her body, his. It's a warm afternoon, almost hot, and girls in swimsuits and cutoff jeans are lounging in the shallows of the creek, sitting on fallen logs and letting their feet dangle in the rushing water, laughing, drinking beer. This wide world of pleasure, and Sander with his blinders on. When he can manage it.

"I tried this before, when I was twelve or something," Clara says. "I was Catholic for a year. I was confirmed and everything. Catherine," she says. "That was my confirmation name."

"I don't know how that works."

"It's like being baptized again, kind of. My mom had me baptized when I was a baby, but then when I was trying to be a Catholic . . . I don't know. It just seemed like the thing to do."

"You change your name?"

"You get, like, an extra name, from a saint. They're supposed to help you after that. They have their specialties."

"What does St. Catherine do?"

"I don't know, exactly—I just thought it sounded cool. Clara Catherine. Also, she has a torture thing named after her."

"Which one?"

"The Catherine wheel," she says. "They tie you to it and then they break your bones."

"Nice!" Sander says, which makes her laugh, a coarse, cawing laughter that sounds at home in the woods. Animal cry, he thinks.

"The Catholic boys were worse than the regular boys," she says. "All they want is blow jobs, blow jobs, blow jobs."

Sander feels it rising but he can't make it stop, and even the trying to stop it makes it worse, and then he's blushing, a hot and awful mess, and Clara sees it—how could she miss it?—and the pause in her face makes it worse, the hot blood pulsing through his face.

"I'm sorry," she says.

She walks off ahead of him, to give him a chance to recover. So she is considerate. He follows, every footstep throbbing in his face. Slowly, slowly, it subsides. It's hot anyway in the afternoon sun, and his face is engorged. Just thinking the word, *engorged*, and he blushes more. Engorged, engorged.

She's waiting a ways down the path, by the creek, in the shade of a big cottonwood, sitting on a log and taking her boots off.

"I'm hot," she says. "It's the turtleneck. I'm going to take a dip, just for a second. Come in the water with me?"

"No, thanks," he says immediately, then immediately regrets it. The stream here falls over a tumble of rocks into a deep, nearly still pool, shoulder-deep at least. The bank is smooth round pebbles.

She stands, all modesty in her long sleeves and skirt, and takes the hem of her skirt in her hand and walks out into the still water, raising the skirt as she goes so it won't get soaked. It still gets wet in places, water darkening the gray cloth. Between the water and the hem of her skirt, Sander glimpses the cool white outline of her thigh, the palpable flesh. Just an inch or two. If she wades out any deeper . . . but she stops, and looks back at him. Is she laughing at him? Or just smiling?

"Come in," she says. "It feels great."

Yes, he thinks, oh, yes. But what's he going to do? Take his pants off? Also, this is sin, and he knows it. This is the lure of the flesh. This is the moment they have been warning him about, all of them.

"Come on," she says.

"I can't," he says. "I shouldn't."

"All right, then," Clara says, and turns her back to him, turns her face up to the sun. For a moment, Sander thinks she will dive in all the way. He feels it himself: the plunge, the beautiful clear cool water. Instead he sits on the log and feels sorry for himself and tries not to look at Clara, who is not looking at him, who doesn't care if anybody sees her or not. He looks everywhere—the sky, the stream, the trees—but always back to her. The shape, even under her clothes, the curve of her hips. Sander is hopeless. Sander is lost.

Clara wades out of the water toward him, dropping the hem of her skirt as she goes until the only bare part of her is her pretty feet, which is the last thing Sander finds to stare at. She sits next to him on the rough log. Sander wishes he could find a way to make it smoother for her.

"I get it," she says. "You're not supposed to enjoy yourself or something. But I don't understand why."

"God wants other things for me," he says.

"You can't have both?"

"I don't know," he says, while inside his mind he searches frantically for God to guide him. Even the name of God sounds like a fraud to him, a lie he's telling himself.

"I'm really asking," Clara says. "I want the things you want. I want to feel like a whole person, you know? Just at peace with things. But then I'm, like, there's nothing wrong with pleasure. I'm in the water and it's clean water, you know? I don't see what's wrong with it."

Sander says nothing, but stretches out his hand and lays it on the damp fabric of her skirt, just at her knee. Clara looks at his hand and then at his face, with a deep sadness, almost exhaustion. She takes his hand from her knee and gives it back to him.

"That's not what I want from this," she says. "From you."

"Okay," Sander says.

"We should get going," she says, and laces up her big black boots.

And Sander follows—down the path through the woods, across the bridge and home again, where his mother waits in the kitchen —but only a ghostly part of Sander. The real person is still back in the woods, still wondering where God was, why God did not stop him from making a fool of himself. All through dinner, all through the night, he wonders. Where is the holy part of him? He can't find it, only sin. He seems to be made of sin, to contain nothing but dirty desires, tits and asses.

All week, his mother looks at him as if she knows something, as if she suspects him, and maybe she's right to. Clara's white thigh torments him, the ease as her body enters the stream, the dazzle of sunlight on water and pale skin.

She isn't there at Fellowship. He looks from face to face and doesn't see her. Then back to his mother, who has seen him searching, who knows, who is disappointed in him. This much good remains in Sander: he's sad for the sake of Clara's immortal soul that he drove her away. His greed and sin have pushed her back into the darkness. He sees again what a trap and a contrivance the world is, a tangle of sin and pain. And Sander's God is nowhere near. He searches and searches within himself.

Then she arrives, and Sander fills with an unreasonable happiness. All is not lost, not yet. She takes her place in the women's section and kneels and prays, modest in her long skirt, a gray scarf over her head. She's naked under her clothes, though. Sander knows this. Maybe God will find a way for them. Maybe they will marry. Maybe there is a godly way. Sander is filled with lust and virtue at the same time, seeing her in bridal white, the tattoo snaking up her neck. Sander in a good suit, with a good haircut . . .

A commotion at the back of the room. Everybody looks: it's Clara's father, in undershirt and ponytail and intelligent-looking glasses.

"Come on, girl," he says to Clara. "We're done here."

"I don't want to."

"That doesn't matter. It's time to go."

He takes the scarf from her hair, not quite roughly, grips her arm and pulls her to her feet. Sander needs to rescue her, Sander needs to help.

Instead it's his mother who walks over to them.

"Let the girl stay," Sander's mother says. "For the sake of her soul."

The father laughs the same loud cawing laugh as his daughter. The same. Everything is being taken from Sander.

"Y'all sound crazy as a shithouse mouse," the father says. "Two years, when she turns eighteen, she can believe whatever bullshit she wants to. But for now I have to take care of her. Steer her in the right direction. Come on, honey."

He keeps his grip on her arm, up by the shoulder, and pushes her toward the door. Clara looks back in a kind of panic, seeks out Sander's face, implores him. But he sits rooted to his chair, suddenly heavy. This is the last he will ever see of her. He knows it and still cannot move. Then she's gone, and an electric hush falls over the room. Nobody says anything.

A week later, they drive by Clara's house on the way to a different neighborhood and see the windows empty and open. Nobody lives there now. Sander feels it as just one more thing. One more nothing. None of this matters. Everything that matters to him is gone. His mother pulls to a stop a few blocks farther on, and Sander takes the big valise of pamphlets, walks behind her. The sun shines down on his black suit. Still eight weeks of summer left.

A Small Sacrifice for an Enormous Happiness

FROM *A Public Space*

FROM HIS BALCONY, Nikhil waited and watched the street as hyacinth braiders tied floral knots, rum sellers hauled bags of ice, and the row of elderly typists, who'd seemed elderly to him since he'd been a boy, struck the last notes of their daily work. Beside him on the balcony, his servant, Kanu, plucked at the hair that grew from his ears.

"Keep a lookout for babu," Nikhil shouted to Kanu. "I'll check on the tea."

Kanu was so old he could neither see nor hear well, but he still accepted each responsibility with enthusiasm.

The tea was ready, as were the sweets, the whole conical pile of them—the base layer of pistachio mounds, the center almond bars that Nikhil had rolled by hand himself, and on the top three lychees from the garden, so precariously balanced, a single misstep would have upset their delectable geometry.

When he returned to the balcony he saw Sharma walking up the cobbled lane, his oiled hair shining in the late afternoon light. The typists greeted him with a verse from a Bollywood number —Sharma's boxer's jaw and darling eyes reminded the typists of an emerging movie star—and Sharma shook his head and laughed.

Kanu limped downstairs to let Sharma in, and Nikhil waited in the living room while the two of them made their way up.

"And what is the special occasion?" Sharma said, eyeing the pile of confections with a boyish grin.

Nikhil refused to say. He allowed Sharma to have his fill, watching with satisfaction as his fingers became honey-glazed from the offering.

Afterward, when they lay on the great divan—hand-carved and older than his mother's ghost—Nikhil breathed deeply to calm his heart. He feared the words would be eaten in his chest, but he'd been planning to tell Sharma for days, and there was no going back now. As evening settled, the air between them became heavy with the sweetness of secrecy, but secrecy had a short wick.

"My dearest, fairest boy," he said. "I want our love to increase."

Sharma raised his eyebrows, those lines thickly drawn, nearly fused. Who better than Sharma to know Nikhil's heart? Who but Sharma to take it all in stride?

"I desire to have a child with you," Nikhil said.

Nikhil had trouble reading Sharma's expression in the waning light, so he repeated himself. His fingers were shaking, but he took Sharma's hand anyway, gave it a squeeze.

"I heard you the first time," Sharma said.

A rare cool wind had prompted Nikhil to turn off the ceiling fan, and now he could hear the rum sellers on the street enunciating prices in singsong Urdu.

He touched Sharma's face, traced the line of his jaw, unsure still of how his lover had received his news. Likely, Sharma was still mulling—he formed his opinions, Nikhil believed, at the pace the street cows strolled.

Nikhil waited out the silence as long as he could. "Listen," he finally said. "The country is changing."

"A child diapered by two men," said Sharma. "Your country is changing faster than my country is changing. What about the boys from Kerala?"

They had learned about a schoolteacher and a postal clerk who'd secretly made a life together. Unfashionably attired and chubby cheeked, they seemed too dull for the news. A few months ago, locals threw acid on their faces. Even in the black and white of the photographs, their scars, along the jaw, the nose, the better half of a cheek. Ten years since man had landed on the moon, and still.

"We are not boys from Kerala. We are protected."

No ruse better than a woman in the home, Nikhil had argued over a year ago, and eventually Sharma had agreed to a marriage of convenience. Kanu, who had loved Nikhil through his child-hood and even through his years of chasing prostitutes, had ar-ranged for a village woman who knew about the two men's rela-tionship but would never tell.

Nikhil rummaged through his almirah and returned with a gift in his hands. "You close your eyes now."

"Oh, Nikhil." But Sharma closed his eyes, accustomed now per-haps to receiving precious things.

Around Sharma's neck, Nikhil tied his dead mother's necklace. It had been dipped in twenty-four carats of gold by master artisans of Agra. Miniature busts of Queen Victoria decorated its circum-ference. A piece for the museums, a jeweler had once explained, but Nikhil wanted Sharma to have it. That morning, when he'd visited the family vault to retrieve it, he'd startled himself with the enormity of what he was giving away, but what better time than now, as they were about to begin a family?

"Promise you'll dream about a child with me."

"It is beautiful, and I will wear it every day, even though people will wonder what is that under my shirt."

"Let them wonder."

"You are entirely mad. Mad is what you are."

Nikhil was pulled back to the divan. Sharma, lifting Nikhil's shirt, placed a molasses square on his belly, teasing a trail of sweet-ness with his tongue. Nikhil closed his eyes and allowed himself to be enjoyed. Down below, the rum sellers negotiated, the prices of bottles fluctuating wildly.

Afterward, they retired to the roof. Their chadors cut off the cold, but Nikhil still shivered. When Sharma asked what the matter was, Nikhil kissed the spot where his eyebrows met. There was an-other old roof across the street, where grandmothers were known to gossip and eavesdrop, but he did not care. Let them hear, he thought, let them feel this wind of enormous change.

The next morning, while Sharma washed, Nikhil said, "I want you to toss the idea to your wife. Get Tripti used to the matter."

Sharma dried himself so quickly he left behind footprints on the bathroom's marble floor. "Toss the idea to my wife. Get her used to the matter," Sharma said, before he changed into his work-ing clothes, leaving Nikhil to brood alone.

Tripti would have few issues with the arrangement of a child, Nikhil believed. After all, at the time of her marriage to Sharma,

her family was mired in bankruptcy, her father had left them nothing but a reputation for drink and dishonesty, and she herself—insofar as he recalled from his sole meeting with her, at the wedding
—was a dour, spiritless creature who deserved little of the bounty
that had been provided her. What little else he knew was from Kanu's reports. Extremely pliable, Kanu had first said. Then, closer
to the wedding: A little stubborn about the choice of sweets. She
wants village kind. On that note, Nikhil had wilted—let her have
her desserts, he'd said, the wedding paid for, and the matter removed from mind.

The next few days, when Sharma was away at the village and
at the foundry, Nikhil paced around the house, overcome by the
idea of a child. He'd always dreamed of becoming a father but
had never believed it would be his due until this year's monsoon,
when, in the middle of a deluge, his forty-two-year-old sister had
given birth to a girl. The rain had been so fierce no ambulance
could ferry them to the hospital, so the elderly women of the family assumed the duties of midwifery and delivered the child themselves. The first moment he saw his niece he nearly believed in
God and, strangely, in his own ability—his *right*—to produce so
perfect a thing.

He couldn't bring Sharma to his sister's house to meet his new
niece, so the next week he'd spent their Thursday together sharing photos; if Sharma experienced the same lightness of being,
he didn't let it show. All Sharma said was, "Quite a healthy baby
she is."

It was true. She'd been born nine pounds two ounces. The family had purchased a cow so that fresh milk would always be available.

Nikhil convinced himself that Sharma had opened his heart to
the idea of fathering, but the exuberance of this conclusion led
to certain practical questions. Sharma's wife would be the carrier
of the child, but where would the child live? In Sharma's house
in the village, or in Nikhil's house here in the city? If she lived in
the village, which Nikhil admitted was the safer option, how would
Nikhil father her, how would she receive a proper education?

These questions consumed the hours. When he went to check
on his tenants, he was distracted and unable to focus on their
concerns. A leaky toilet, a broken window, the group of vagrants

who'd squatted outside one of his properties—all these matters seemed trivial compared to his imagined child's needs.

The next week, the afternoon before he would see Sharma again, he stepped into a clothing store on Rashbehari Avenue to calm his mind. It was a shop he'd frequented to purchase silk kurtas for Sharma or paisley shirts for himself. He told the attendants he needed an exceptional outfit for his niece. They combed the shelves and found a white dress with a lacy pink bow. He imagined his daughter wearing it. From his dreaming he was certain a girl would come out of their love—Shristi was what he'd named her —Shristi enunciating like a princess, Shristi riding her bicycle up and down Kakulia Lane.

Early on, they'd agreed Nikhil would avoid the foundry, but he was feeling so full of promise for Shristi that he did not deter himself from continuing down Rashbehari Avenue toward Tollygunge Phari, nor did he prevent himself from walking to the entrance of Mahesh Steel and asking for his *friend.*

Sharma emerged from the uneven music of metalworking with a cigarette between his lips. His Apollonian features were smeared with grease. His hands constricted by thick welding gloves, which excluded the possibility of even an accidental touch. When he saw Nikhil, Sharma scowled. "Sir," he said, "you'll have the parts tomorrow."

Though he knew Sharma was treating him as a customer for good reason, the tone still stung. Nikhil whispered, "See what I have brought." He produced the perfect baby girl dress.

"You have lost your soup," Sharma whispered back. Then, so everyone could hear, "Babu, you'll have the parts tomorrow. Latest, tomorrow."

Nikhil tried again, "Do you see the collar, the sweet lace?"

"You should go to your home now," Sharma said. "Tomorrow, I'll see you."

But that Thursday Sharma failed to visit. Nikhil and Kanu waited until half past nine and then ate their meal together by lamplight.

Thursdays because it was on a Thursday that they had met three years ago, that time of year when the city is at its most bearable, when the smell of wild hyacinth cannot be outdone by the stench of the gutters, because it is after the city's short winter, which manages, despite its brevity, to birth more funerals than any other time of year. In the city's spring, two men walking the long road from Santiniketan back to Kolkata—because the bus has broken and no one is interested in its repair—are not entirely oblivious to the smells abounding in the wildflower fields, not oblivious at all to their own smells.

He supposed he had fetishized Sharma's smell from the beginning, that scent of a day's honest work. The smell of steel, of the cheapest soap. The smell of a shirt that had been laundered beyond its time. The smell of his night-bound stubble. He allowed his hand to linger on Sharma's wrist, pretending he was trying to see the hour. An hour before sunset. An hour after. He did not remember exactly when they parted. What did it matter.

What mattered were the coincidences of love. The day he saw Sharma for the second time he counted among the small miracles of his life.

Sharma was drinking tea at the tea stall on Kakulia Lane. He was leaning the weight of his body on the rotting wood of the counter, listening to the chai wallah recount stories. Later, he would learn that Sharma had landed a job at a nearby foundry and that this tea stall was simply the closest one, but in that moment he did not think of foundries or work or any other encumbrance, he thought instead of the way Sharma cradled his earthen teacup, as if it were the Koh-i-noor.

Oh, he had said, did you and I . . . that broken bus . . . What an evening, yes?

A question that led to Thursdays. Two years of Thursdays haunted by fear of discovery, which led to a wedding, because a married man who arrived regularly at Kakulia Lane could not be doing anything but playing backgammon with his happenstance friend. What followed was a year of bliss. He considered this time their honeymoon. They were as seriously committed as any partners who'd ever shared a covenant, and shouldn't that show?

Sharma did visit the following Thursday, though the matter of his absence the week before was not raised. Instead of their usual feast at home, they ate chili noodles doused with sugary tomato sauce at Jimmy's Chinese Kitchen, along with stale pastries for dessert. Sharma was wearing Nikhil's family necklace under his shirt, with just an edge of the queen's image peeking out from the collar. Seeing his gift on his lover's body released Nikhil from his brood, and for the first time that night, he met Sharma's gaze.

"You're cross with me," Sharma offered.

It wasn't an apology, but Nikhil was warming to the idea of a reconciliation.

"Anyway, Tripti and I have been discussing the issue of the baby."

Tripti and I. He so rarely heard the name Tripti from Sharma's lips, but that she could be in league with him, discussing an *issue?* Unjust was what it was.

"It's in part the physical act. We eat our meals together. We take walks to the bazaar or to the pond. But that, no, we do not do that."

"Don't worry," Nikhil said. "I shall do the deed. I shall be the child's father." While it was unpleasant to imagine the act of copulation itself, he'd studied the intricacies of the reproductive process and believed his chances were excellent for a single, well-timed session to yield its fruit.

"But you can barely stand the smell of a woman."

What passed over Sharma's face may have been described as amusement, but Nikhil refused to believe his lover wasn't taking him seriously—not now that he'd opened his heart like a salvaged piano. "Sharma," Nikhil said. "It shall be a small sacrifice for an enormous happiness."

"Oh Nikhil, do you not see that we are already happy? Anything more might upset what we have. We should not tempt the gods."

Nikhil ground away at the pastry in his mouth until the memory of sweetness dispersed. The things Sharma said. As if there were a cap on happiness in this world. It was Sharma's village religion talking again, but there was something more. He sensed in the way Sharma held his hands in his lap, the way he kept to the far side of the bed when they retired for the night, that Tripti had wormed something rotten into him. He was vulnerable that way, Sharma was.

When Nikhil awoke the next morning, Sharma had already departed, but in the bathroom, which he'd lovingly reconstructed from Parisian prints, with a clawfoot tub and a nearly functioning bidet, he found Sharma's stubble littering the marble sink. Sharma had always been fastidious in the house, taking care to wipe away evidence of his coming and going, and the patches of facial hair offended Nikhil. He studied their formations, searching for patterns. When nothing could be discerned, he called for Kanu to clean the mess.

Only one train went to Bilaspur, a commuter local. For two hours, Nikhil was stuck next to the village yeoman, who'd gone to the city to peddle his chickens and was clutching the feet of the aging pair he'd been unable to sell, and the bleary-eyed dairyman, who smelled of curd and urine. The only distraction was the girl with the henna-tinged hair who'd boarded between stops to plead for money, whose face looked entirely too much like the child he envisioned fathering.

When he reached the Bilaspur terminus, he was relieved to see the rows of wildflowers on either side of the tracks, to smell the bloom of begonias planted by the stationmaster's post.

It wasn't difficult finding Sharma's home. With money from the foundry and regular gifts of cash from Nikhil, Sharma had purchased several hectares of hilltop land and built a concrete slab of a house, garrisoned with a garden of squash, cucumber, and eggplant, and with large windows marking the combined living and dining area. Nikhil found the structure too modern, but that was Sharma's way—he had never swooned over the old colonials of Kakulia Lane.

From inside the house, Nikhil could hear the BBC broadcast, which was strange given Tripti didn't understand English. Nikhil tiptoed toward the open living room window, and from there he spied. Sharma's wife was holding a book on her lap, mouthing back the words of the BBC announcer.

"BER-LIN WALL," she said. "DOWNING STREET."

She had a proud bookish nose—adequately sized for the resting of eyeglasses—a forehead that jutted too far forward, reminding Nikhil of a depiction of Neanderthal gatherers, and the slightest of chins, which gave to her appearance a quality of perpetual meekness. Her sari was stained with years of cooking. Her only adornments were the bright red bindi on her forehead and the brass bangles that made music whenever she turned a page.

There were certain topics Nikhil and Sharma had left to the wind, foremost the matter of Sharma's marriage. In the beginning, Nikhil experienced a shooting pain in his abdomen whenever he thought about Sharma and Tripti coexisting in domestic harmony, though over the past few months that pain had numbed; the less he'd thought of Tripti, the less she existed, but here she was now — the would-be mother of his child. He rapped on the grill of her window.

"Just leave it there," Tripti said without looking up from her book.

It was the first time she'd ever spoken to him. Her voice, which was composed of rich baritones, seemed rather forceful, and her demeanor, that of the lady of a proper house, left him feeling uncertain about his next move. At last, he said in a Bengali so refined it could have passed for the old tongue of Sanskrit, "Perhaps you've mistaken me for the bringer of milk. I am not he. Madam, you know me but you do not know me."

The words had sounded elegant in his head, but when spoken aloud he flushed at their foolishness.

She looked up to study his face, then his outfit, even his shoes now rimmed with the village's mud. "I know who you are," she finally said. "Why don't you come inside?"

He had not planned beyond this moment. He had allowed his feet to step onto the train at Howrah, imagined a brief meeting, a quick exchange at the doorstep, ending with a mutually desirable pact.

"I can't stay long," he said. Sharma would be home in another hour, and Nikhil had no wish to see Sharma in the same vicinity as his wife.

While he settled into the living room, Tripti puttered around the kitchen. The house was decorated with woodcarvings and paintings of gods and goddesses. Parvati, the wife of Shiva, smiled beatifically from a gilded frame, and her son the remover of obstacles was frozen inside a copper statuette. From the plans Sharma had gloated over, he knew a hallway connected the three bedrooms of the house — one for Tripti, one for Sharma, and the last a prayer room — and he wondered now who slept where, how their mornings were arranged, what politics were discussed, what arguments were had, where the laundry was piled.

Tripti brought two cups of tea and a plate of sweets. "Homemade," she said. He'd been raised to fear milk sweets from unfamiliar places, but out of politeness, he took the first bite — a little lumpy, only mildly flavorful.

"Sharma is always praising your cooking," he said, but it was a lie. They never bothered to discuss Tripti's cooking; in fact, Nikhil had teased that they were lovers because of his talents in the kitchen. Still, it felt appropriate to compliment this woman, and he continued in this fashion, standing to admire the Parvati painting, which he described as "terribly and modernly artful."

"Nikhil Babu," she interrupted. "Are you here to discuss the matter of the child?"

He sighed with relief. Until that moment, he'd been unsure about how to broach the subject.

"You know," she said. "We discuss our days. We may not be lovers, but we are fair friends."

He experienced what felt like an arthritic pain in his shoulder, but it was only the collar of his jealousy. At least they were not *best* friends.

She pointed to the book on her coffee table, an English language primer. "Unfortunately, it's just not on our horizon. You see, I'm going to university. I shall be a teacher."

"University," he said. "But you did not even finish eighth grade."

"That is true, but at Bilaspur College, the principal is willing to accept students who display enormous curiosities."

He found it improbable that she would be able to absorb the principles of higher learning, but he had no particular wish to impede her efforts. Education was a challenge he understood. "You want to improve yourself? Wonderful. If you are with child, I will have tutors come to you. Not professors from Bilaspur College. Real academics from the city."

But it was as if she had not heard him at all. She submerged a biscuit in her tea and stared out into the garden.

"Whose happiness are you after, Nikhil Babu?" she said. "Yours and yours only?"

He found himself grinding his teeth. The great bane of modernity. Though the country had opened itself to the pleasures of the other world—cream-filled pastries, the films of Godard, a penchant for pristine white-sand beaches—he did not care for the consequences, the dissolution of ordering traditions, with whose loss came poor speech, thoughtless conduct. A village woman addressing him without the slightest deference.

"Perhaps you should enroll in a school for proper manners," he said.

Tripti eased her teacup down. He followed the geometry of her sloping wrist, but there was no break of anger in her face.

"Listen," he said. But how could he explain that his want for a child had become rooted in his body, in the bones of his hands and the ridge of his knee, where just that afternoon the girl on the train who'd emerged from the rice fields to beg in the vestibules, whose outstretched palm he would normally loathe—there was no way to lift the country by satisfying beggars—had touched him. Had he not smiled back and touched her hair?

"If you're planning to catch the last train back," she said, "it's best you go now."

He chewed another of Tripti's lumpy sweets. When properly masticated, it would have the consistency to be spat and to land right between Tripti's eyes. But Tripti had turned away from him and resumed her studies. Soon he was all chewed out; he had to show himself out of the house.

By the time he reached the train station, the six o'clock was arriving at the platform. He squatted behind the begonias by the stationmaster's post and waited to see if Sharma was aboard. With the afternoon's disappointment, he felt he deserved to see Sharma's face, even if only covertly. See but remain unseen. In that moment, he could not have explained why he did not peek his head out of the tangle of flowers, though a glimmer of an idea came, something to do with the freedom of others—how, in this village of Sharma's birth, unknown and burdened, Nikhil could never be himself. Sweat pooled where his hairline had receded. How old the skin of his forehead felt to the touch.

As passengers began to disembark, those who were headed for the city clamored aboard. He looked at the faces passing by but did not see Sharma. The first warning bell sounded, then the second, and the stationmaster announced that the train was nearly city bound.

He saw Sharma as the crowd was thinning out. He was walking with someone dressed in the atrocious nylon pants that were the fashion, and perhaps they were telling jokes, because Sharma was doubled over laughing. In all their evenings together, he couldn't recall seeing Sharma laugh with so little inhibition as now, so little concern about who would hear that joyous voice—who would think, What are those two doing? He watched Sharma walk along the dirt road toward his house, but it was an entirely different progress; he was stopping to inspect the rows of wildflowers on the path, to chat up the farmer who'd bellowed his name.

He kept watching Sharma's retreating form until he could see nothing but the faint shape of a man crossing the road. It was then he realized that the city-bound train, the last of the day, had left without him; he sprinted into the stationmaster's booth and phoned his house. It took several rings for Kanu to answer. "Yello?"

"Oh, Kanu," he said. "You must send a car. You must get me. I am at Bilaspur."

The connection was poor, but he could hear Kanu saying, "Babu? What is happening? What is wrong?"

There was no way to express how wounded the afternoon had left him, and he knew the odds of securing a car at this hour, so he yelled back into the phone, "Don't wait for me, Kanu. Make dinner, go to bed!"

He asked the stationmaster if there were any hotels in the village. A room just till the morning, he said. The stationmaster shrugged and pointed vaguely in the direction of the dirt road.

There were no hotels, he soon discovered. Either he would sleep underneath the stars or he would announce himself at Sharma's house to spend the night. He was certain he couldn't do the latter —what a loss of face that would be—but the former with its cold and its unknown night animals, seemed nearly as terrifying.

He paced the town's only road until he grew hungry. Then he headed in the direction of Sharma's house, following a field where fireflies alighted on piles of ash. He had no wish to be discovered, but in the waning daylight that would soon turn into uninterrupted darkness, he felt as anonymous as any of the mosquitoes making dinner of his feet.

When he reached the entrance to Sharma's house, he could smell the evening's meal: lentil soup, rice softened with clarified butter. He could see the two of them together in the kitchen. Sharma was slicing cucumbers and Tripti was stirring a pot. The way Sharma's knife passed over the counter seemed like an act of magic. Such grace and precision. Soon, he knew the lentils and rice would be combined, a pair of onions diced, ginger infused into the stew, the table set, the meal consumed. He watched, waiting for the first word to be spoken, but they were silent partners, unified by the rhythm of their hands.

They moved into the dining room with their meal, and he crawled to the open kitchen window. Sharma had left his mother's necklace on the kitchen counter, next to the cheap china atop the stains of all meals past. What he was seeing couldn't be dismissed: Sharma had treated his greatest gift as if it were nothing more than a kitchen ornament. Nikhil's hand snaked through the window to recover the heirloom, and he knocked over a steel pan in the process.

Sharma rushed to the kitchen and began to yell "Thief, stop" as if it were a mantra. Nikhil scurried down the hill, the necklace secure in his grip, and when he paused at the mouth of the town's only road and turned back, he thought he saw Sharma's hands in the window, making signs that reminded him of their first meeting, when in the darkness those dark fingers had beckoned. Nikhil almost called back, but too much distance lay between them. Whatever he said now wouldn't be heard.

Arcadia

FROM *Granta*

"THERE'S ROOM FOR EXPANSION," Otto said over breakfast, reading the thin-paged free newspaper the organic people sent out to all the farms. He tapped an article with his thick finger, and Peter noticed that Otto's nail was colored black with nail polish, or a marker. Or maybe it was only a blood blister.

"We draw a leaf or some shit on our label," Otto said, squinting at the page. "Even if it just kind of looks like this. People wouldn't know the difference."

Heddy simmered slices of lemon at the stove, poking at the pan with a chopstick. She'd changed into a sweater dress and her legs were rashy. Every morning since she found out she was pregnant, she'd been drinking hot lemon water. "It corrects your pH levels," she'd explained to Peter. She used the hot water to wash down all her prenatal vitamins, big dun-colored pills that smelled like fish food, pills that promised to soak the baby in minerals and proteins. It was strange for Peter to imagine their baby's fingernails hardening inside her, its muscles uncoiling. The unbelievable lozenge of its heart.

Heddy pursed her lips sideways at her brother. "That's kind of stupid, isn't it?" she said. "I mean, why don't we just get certified, the real way?"

Otto fluttered his hand. "Got a few thousand lying around? You're certainly not contributing."

"I'm broadening my mind." She was starting her first semester at the junior college in town.

"You know what broadens after that?" Otto said. "Your ass."

"Fuck you."

"Yeah, yeah. I had to hire more people and that costs."

Peter had seen these new workers: a bearded man and a woman, who'd moved into one of the trailers a few weeks ago. They had a young boy with them.

"It all costs," Otto said.

Heddy narrowed her eyes but turned back to the pan, intent on fishing out the lemon.

"Anyway," Otto continued, "we can still say 'natural' and all the rest."

"Sounds good," Peter said, trying to be enthusiastic. Otto was already shuffling the pages, on to something new. He seemed to like Peter as much as he liked anyone. When he found out that Peter had gotten Heddy pregnant, it was his idea that Peter move in and work for him. "I guess she's eighteen," Otto had said. "No longer my worry. But if I see so much as a bruise, I'll end you."

Heddy put her hand on Peter's shoulder: "He's teasing," she said.

Peter had moved into Heddy's childhood bedroom, still cluttered with her porcelain dolls and crumbling prom corsages, and tried to ignore the fact of Otto's room just down the hall. Otto managed the hundred and fifty acres of orchard surrounding the house. The land was near enough to the North Coast that great schooners of fog soaked the mornings with silent snow. When it rained, the creek outran its banks, a muddy, frigid surge that swamped the rows of apple trees. Peter preferred it up here, the thousand shades of gray and green instead of Fresno with the sameness of heat and dust.

By the time he and Otto had finished breakfast—eggs from the chickens, fried in oil and too salty—Heddy had gone up to their bedroom and come down with all her things, her raincoat already zipped, a canvas backpack over her shoulder. He knew she'd already packed it with notebooks, a separate one for each class, and her chunky cubes of Post-its. No doubt she'd devised a color-coded system for her pens.

Otto kissed her goodbye, making a lazy swat at her ass as he headed out to turn the heater on in the truck, leaving Heddy and Peter alone in the kitchen.

"Heddy's off to Yale," she announced. She tightened her raincoat hood and grinned at him from the circle within. With her face isolated by the hood, she looked about twelve, the blooms of color on her cheeks tilting even more cartoonish. She slept through most everything—the dogs, the rooster, thunderstorms —and it seemed like proof of her greater moral center, something Peter could imagine existing as whole and real in her as a red apple. An innocence coupled with a strange knowingness: when they had sex, she kept looking down to watch him go inside her.

"You look pretty," Peter said. "Done at four, right?"

Heddy nodded. "Home around five," she said. She loosened her hood, pulling it back to expose her hair, the tracks from her comb still visible.

Peter and Otto spent the day in near silence, the seats of Otto's truck giving off vapors of leather. Otto drove the orchard roads, stopping only so Peter could dash out in the rain to open a gate, or chase down the ripple of an empty candy wrapper. No matter how much time they spent together, Peter couldn't shake a nervousness around Otto, a wary formality. People liked Otto, thought he was fun. And he was fun, the brittle kind of fun that could easily sour. Peter hadn't ever seen Otto do anything, but he'd seen the ghosts of his anger. The first week Peter had moved in, he'd come across a hole punched in the kitchen wall. Heddy only rolled her eyes and said, "He sometimes drinks too much." She said the same thing when they saw the crumpled taillight on the truck. Peter tried to get serious and even brought up his own father, dredging up one of the tamer stories, but Heddy stopped him. "Otto pretty much raised me," she said. Peter knew their mother moved to the East Coast with her second husband, and their father had died when Heddy was fourteen. "He's just having his shithead fun."

And they did love each other, Otto and Heddy, living in easy parallel habitation, as if the other person was a given, beyond like or dislike. They surprised Peter sometimes with their sentimentality. Some nights, they watched the movies they'd loved as children, colorized films from the fifties and sixties: orphans who could talk to animals, a family of musicians that lived in a submarine. The movies were oddly innocent—they bored Peter, but Otto and Heddy loved them without irony. Otto's face went strangely soft during these movies, Heddy on the couch between Otto and Peter, her socked feet escaping from under the blanket. Peter heard them talking, sometimes: they carried on long, sober conversations, their voices sounding strangely adult, conversations that trailed off whenever Peter came into the room. He'd been surprised that neither Heddy nor Otto cared that much about nudity, Otto striding naked down the hall to the shower, his chest latticed with dark hair.

When Peter talked to Otto, it was only about yield. How many tons of almonds per acre, what kind of applications they'd make to the soil in a few weeks, after harvest was over. When they drove past any of the workers in their blue rain ponchos, up in the trees on ladders, or gathered around chubby orange water coolers, Otto would honk the horn so they jumped. One man held up his hand in silent greeting. Others shielded their eyes to watch the truck pass.

They were mostly seasonal pickers, moving from farm to farm, and a few students on leave from fancy colleges. The students accepted produce and a place to live as trade, an arrangement that Otto found endlessly amusing. "They got college degrees!" Otto crowed. "They email these fucking essays to me. Like I'm going to turn them down."

The new guy Otto had hired was different. Otto didn't even ask him if he'd work for trade. He had already asked for advances on his salary, accompanied by careful lists of his hours written on the backs of envelopes. Peter knew Otto had let the guy's wife work, too. Nobody seemed to care who watched their boy, except for Peter, who kept his mouth shut.

Around noon, Otto pulled the truck off into a grove of stony oaks. They left the doors of the truck open, Peter with a paper bag between his knees: a sandwich Heddy had made for him the night before, a rock-hard pear. Otto produced a bag of deli meat and a slice of white bread.

"The kid from Boston asks if he can take pictures while he harvests," Otto said, folding a slice of meat into the bread. "What for? I ask him." Otto paused to chew, then swallowed loudly. "For his website, he says to me." He rolled his eyes.

"We should get a website," Peter said, unwrapping the pear. "It's not a bad idea."

It had actually been Heddy's idea. She'd written about it in her notebook. Heddy's notebook wasn't expressly secret, but Peter knew he wasn't supposed to read it. It was for her self-improvement.

She wrote down business ideas for the farm. Kept itemized lists of the food she ate, along with calorie counts. Wrote down what days of the week she would wear her teeth-whitening strips, what days she would jog around the orchards, ideas for baby names. She'd written the beginnings of bad, sentimental songs that confused him, songs about pockets full of rain, men with no faces. One page she'd filled with his name, over and over in ballpoint pen. It took on a new life, his name, repeated like that. The inane embroidery.

"A website," Otto said, stuffing the ham into his mouth. "Freeman Farms on the web. Get one of the college kids to do the thing. With photos. Apples you'd want to fuck."

Otto laughed at his own joke. Under the far grove of trees, Peter could see the workers, clustered together for their lunch. Since it had stopped raining, some of them had hung their dripping ponchos in the branches, for shade.

Otto and Peter spent the rest of the afternoon in the office. Otto had Peter handle the phone calls to their accounts. "You sound nicer," he said. After Peter finished up a call with the co-op in Beaverton, Otto jabbed a chewed-up pen in his direction.

"Go find out who's gonna make our website," he said. "I want flashy shit, too, blinking lights and video and everything." He paused. "Maybe a place for a picture of us, too. So people can see who they're doing business with."

"That's a good idea."

"It makes people feel safe," Otto said. "Doesn't it? To see a face."

Heddy had taken his car to school, so Peter drove Otto's truck out to the trailers, the passenger seat full of the cartons of extra eggs from the chickens. The workers lived in five aluminum-sided mobile homes, the roofs tangled with wires and satellite dishes, yards cruddy with bicycles and a broken moped. He could tell which cars belonged to the college kids, who needed even their vehicles to be blatant with opinions: they were the cars scaled with bumper stickers. Otto had let the college kids pour a concrete slab by the road a few months ago; now there was a brick grill and a basketball hoop, and even a small garden, scorched and full of weeds.

As he approached, Peter saw a boy out in front of the first trailer, the boy from the new family, bouncing a mostly deflated ball off the concrete. He must have been eleven or twelve, and he stopped playing to watch Peter's truck approach. There was a shadow on the boy's shaved scalp; as Peter pulled up to the trailer, he realized it was a kind of scab or a burn, black with dried blood, thin and delicately crackled. It covered a patch of the boy's head like a jaunty cap.

A woman—the boy's mother, Peter assumed—opened the door of the trailer and stood on the concrete-block stoop, not closing the door fully behind her. She was in slippers and men's pants, cinched at the waist with a belt, and a ribbed tank top. She was younger than he would have guessed.

"Hi," Peter said, stepping out of the car. He ran his fingers through his hair. It made him uncomfortable whenever Otto sent him to talk to the workers. Peter was twenty, the same age as some of the college kids. It wasn't so bad talking to them. But the real workers, the older men—Peter didn't like giving orders to them. Men who looked like his father; their red-rimmed eyes, the hunch of the manual laborer. Peter had harvested garlic in Gilroy during high school summers, had driven in the morning dark with his father, the cab stinking of the magenta grease they used on their Felcos. He remembered the way the group went quiet when they saw the foreman's truck, how it was only after the truck had fully retreated that they turned the radio up again, like even the meager pleasure of listening to music was something that had to be hidden.

"Otto said we could finish at three," the woman said, picking at her shirt hem. She was kind of pretty, Peter saw as he walked over to her: long black hair she'd braided, the blurry edge of a badly done tattoo creeping over her shoulder. She reminded him of the girls in Fresno. "It's after three," she said.

"I know," Peter said, sensing her worry. "It's fine. Otto just wanted to know if someone knew about computers. Like, how to make websites. I'm supposed to ask around."

"I know computers," the boy said, picking up the ball. The ball was marbled in a trashy pale pink, and the boy pressed it between his hands so the ball bulged.

"Zack, baby," the woman said. "He doesn't mean you."

"I know a lot," Zack said, ignoring his mother.

Peter didn't know what to say. The kid seemed sick or something, his eyes unfocused. "Otto wants a website for the farm," Peter said, glancing from Zack to the woman. "I'm Peter, by the way," he said, holding out his hand.

The woman let the door shut behind her, walked over, and shook his hand. "I'm Steph," she said. She seemed to get shy then. She put her hands on her son's thin shoulders. "Matt's my husband," she said. "The beard?"

"Otto likes him a lot."

"Matt works hard," Steph said, brushing lint off Zack's T-shirt. "He's at the store."

"Does he know anything about computers?"

Zack said, "Matt's dumb."

"We don't say that, baby," Steph said. She shot Peter a look, gauging his expression, then tried to smile. "Matt's not great with computers. One of the younger people might be better," she said, nodding her head at the trailers with the hammocks strung up in the yard.

"I'll ask them," Peter said. "Oh," he remembered, "I have eggs for you." He walked back to the car and got a carton from the passenger seat. "From the chickens," he said.

Steph frowned. It took Peter a moment to understand.

"Just extras," Peter said. "It's not payment or anything."

Steph smiled then, taking the carton, and shrugged. "Thanks," she said. The tattoo on her shoulder was a kind of vine, Peter saw as she came closer, thick and studded with black leaves. Or maybe they were thorns.

Zack let the ball drop to the concrete and reached out for the eggs. Steph shook her head at him, softly. "They'll break, honey," she said. "It's best if I hold them."

Zack kicked the ball hard, and Steph flinched when it hit the metal siding of the trailer.

Peter backed away. "I'm just going next door," he said, waving at Steph. "It was good to meet you."

"Sure," Steph said, cradling the eggs to her chest. "Say goodbye, Zack."

Steph couldn't see, like Peter could, how Zack's face had tightened, a look of concentration fleeting across his face. Zack let one hand rise up to graze the edge of his wound. He scratched, and a quick filament of blood streamed down his forehead.

"He's bleeding," Peter said, "Jesus." Steph let out a harsh breath of air.

"Shit," she said, "shit," and she huddled Zack in her other arm, still clutching the eggs, and started pulling him toward the house. "Inside," she ordered, "now. Thank you," she called over her shoulder to Peter, struggling to get Zack up the steps, "Thanks a ton," and then the two of them disappeared inside, the door snapping shut.

Heddy came home breathless from her day; kisses on both of Peter's cheeks, her bags tossed on the counter. She used the office computer to look up a video on the Internet that showed her how to cover her books using paper shopping bags, then spent half an hour at her bedroom desk, dreamily filling in the name of each class, smudging the pencil with her fingertips.

"That's the only way to get a realistic shading," Heddy explained. "Like it?" she asked Peter, holding up a book.

"It's great," Peter said, naked on top of the bedcovers, and Heddy's eyes scatted down to study her drawing again. He had planned to tell her about his day, about Steph and Zack. That horrible wound. But it would make her sad, he thought, and she cried so easily now. Worried even when she had a bad dream, as if the fear would pass through her blood somehow and affect the baby.

"*Le français,*" Heddy said, slowly. "I got to pick a new name," she said. "For class. I'm Sylvie," she said. "Isn't that pretty?"

"It's nice," Peter said.

"I got to pick second from a list. The girls who had to pick last got, like, Babette." She erased something with great concentration, then blew the remnants away. "I have to get special shoes," she continued, "for salsa class."

"Salsa class?" Peter sat up to look at her. "That's a class?"

"I need a physical education credit," she said. She smiled a mysterious smile. "Dancing. Good to know, for our wedding."

He shifted. He wished suddenly that he was wearing underwear. "Who do you dance with in this class?"

Heddy looked at him. "My classmates. Is that okay?"

"I don't want some asshole bothering you."

She laughed. "God, Peter. I'm pregnant. Think I'm safe."

He decided not to tell her about Steph and Zack.

"We're going to make a website for the farm," Peter announced, lying back against the pillows.

"That's great," she said. He waited for her to say more. To say it was her idea, not his. He sat up and saw she was still bent over her books.

"A website," he repeated, louder. "One of the workers knows how to make one. He can set it up so people can order off it."

"That's wonderful," she said, finally smiling at him. "I've always thought we should have one."

"Well," he said, "I had to convince Otto. But everyone else has one. It makes sense."

"Exactly," she said. She left her books on the desk to come to the bed, to lay her head on his chest. Her scalp was pure and clean through her parting. Her weight against him felt nice, the press of her tight belly, and he kissed the top of her head, her hair that held the cold of the air outside and smelled like nothing at all.

Peter propped the front door open with a brick and lugged cardboard boxes of canned food and plastic bags of bananas from the car to the kitchen table. He'd been in charge of grocery runs since Heddy started school. Rainfall was the heaviest it had been in twenty years, everything outside crusty with wet rot, and on the way to the house Peter stepped over a neon earthworm in the wet grass. The worm was slim, the color of bright new blood.

Peter cleaned out the refrigerator before putting the groceries away, throwing out the expired tub of baby spinach he'd bought on the last run, the leaves matted into a wet stink. He was still learning how to buy the right amount of food.

He could hear Otto moving around in the office. Otto had been working with one of the college kids to build the farm website. They had figured out the domain name, and there were some photos up already, a form to submit orders that was almost finished. The college kid spent a lot of time out on the porch, talking on his cell phone, his fingers pinched girlishly around a cigarette.

Peter watched now as the college kid walked back to the trailers through the gray rain. In the distance, greasy smoke was rising from the brick grill. He thought of Steph. Peter had seen her a few times, working alongside a man he assumed was Matt. She hadn't acknowledged him. Peter hadn't seen Zack outside the trailer again, even on sunny days.

Peter bought a notebook for himself on the grocery run. He'd meant to write in it, like Heddy did. Record his ideas, his thoughts about the world. He splayed it across his knees and waited with a pencil, a glass of water. But there was nothing he wanted to say. He wrote down what Otto had told him about living well on an acre, what plants to buy. What trees could grow from cuttings. What sort of drainage you'd need. He would need to know these things when he and Heddy got their own place. He let himself imagine it: no trailers crudding up the property. No Otto leaving commas of pubic hair on the toilet seat. Just him and Heddy and the baby. He put the notebook aside. The water in his glass had gone stale. He picked an apple from the bowl on the table and flicked open his pocketknife, making idle cuts in the apple's skin. It would be hours before Heddy came home.

Soon he started carving designs, words. It pleased him to get better at it, to let whole sections drop cleanly under his knife. He carved his own name over and over in loops he linked around the core. Liking the reveal of wet flesh against the red skin. He lined up the finished apples in the refrigerator, where the rotting spinach had been.

He napped on the couch and dreamt about Heddy dropping a glass, the two of them watching it explode blue and low on the ground. He jerked awake. It was dark already. Otto came into the kitchen and flicked on the light. He opened the refrigerator and burst out laughing.

"You are losing your mind."

Peter looked up from the damp couch. Otto swung two apples by their stems, Peter's cuts withered and browning, wrinkled at what had been their sharp edges.

"Do you work only with apples? Or is there room for expansion? I'm talking oranges here, pears," Otto said. "I'm so proud you're keeping busy."

Peter got up when he heard the car outside. His shirt was wrinkled but he tucked it in as best he could.

"It's freezing," Heddy said, hurrying through the door without a coat on. Her hair was dripping onto her shoulders, her raincoat bunched in her arms.

"Look," she said. She held out the raincoat. "Mold," she said, flinging it to the floor. "Crazy, huh?"

She didn't wait for Peter to answer.

"I'll have to get a new one," she said, kissing him quickly. She tasted like chlorine. She'd started swimming after class in the school exercise center. "Low-impact exercise," she called it. She said it was good for the baby. Peter tried not to think about her body exposed to strangers in her swimsuit with the high-cut legs. How the seat of her swimsuit sometimes wedged itself into her ass. She got home later and later these days.

"How was swimming?"

"Fine," Heddy said. Her hair was dripping all over the floor and she didn't seem to notice.

"You've always sucked at swimming," Otto said to Heddy. He tore one of the plastic bags of bananas open with his teeth. He tried to peel a banana, but just mushed the top. Heddy reached over and grabbed the banana from Otto.

"It's easier to open it from the bottom," she said, pinching the banana at its stubby end so the peel split cleanly under her fingers.

Otto narrowed his eyes at her, snatching the banana back. "Thanks, genius," he said. "Glad to know you're learning so much. *Voulez-vous coucher avec moi* and all that shit." He laughed, then turned to Peter. "Sam fixed the home page," he said. "All the pictures load now."

"Good," Peter said. "I told the co-op they could start ordering online in a week or so. They seemed happy."

Heddy ignored both of them, kicking her raincoat in the direction of the trashcan. Peter watched her while Otto kept talking. Each time she parked on campus, it cost ten dollars, and Peter knew she kept meaning to buy the parking pass that would save her a hundred bucks. Last week she told him, finally, that the pass was no longer a good deal. She seemed to feel this had been a great failure on her part, the failure to buy the parking pass in time.

Heddy set water to boil for her tea, cleaning her fingernails with the nails of her other hand, and then arranged herself at the table to do her homework. She'd gotten a bad grade on her first French test, and had seemed perplexed and hurt ever since. Peter didn't know how to help her.

Otto was telling Peter some story about one of the workers, some RV they wanted to park on the property.

"And I tell him, sure, be my guest, if you can even drive that thing," Otto said.

"Can you guys go outside?" Heddy said, finally looking up at them. "Sorry," she said. "I just—I have to call someone for school. On the phone."

It was cold on the porch, the air gusting with the smell of wet earth. Peter hunched into his coat. Otto was still talking, but Peter wasn't listening. He looked up at the sky but couldn't orient himself. When he tried to focus, the stars oscillated into a single gaseous shimmer and he felt dizzy. Even on the porch he could hear Heddy inside on the phone. She was speaking halting French to someone she called Babette, and she kept breaking into English to correct herself. He felt ashamed for suspecting anything else.

"I know," Heddy said. "She is *très mal.*" Her accent was clumsy, and he felt bad for noticing. Through the windows, Peter saw her pacing the kitchen, her familiar shape made foreign by the pocked glass.

Otto paused his monologue to study Peter.

"Where's your head at, brother?" Otto said. "You look like you're off in space."

Peter shrugged. "I'm right here."

Inside, Heddy said a final *"Bonne nuit."* Peter watched as she gathered her books and headed up the stairs, her shoulders a little hunched. Her rear was getting bigger, a humble sag that moved him. She turned out the lights as she left, like she forgot anyone was even out there.

Peter had thought it was coyotes, the whooping that woke him up. He stood at the window of their bedroom, feeling the cool air beyond the glass. The ragged calls filtered through the dark trees and had that coyote quality of revelry—his father used to say that coyotes sounded like teenagers having a party, and it was true. He hadn't spoken to his father since he'd left. But Peter had Heddy now. A house of their own that they'd live in with their baby, the curtains for the nursery that she'd want to sew herself.

The idea pleased him, and he glanced over. Heddy was still sleeping peacefully, her mouth open. The salts she liked to dissolve in her baths were still in the air, and a dark stain spread across the comforter from her wet hair. There was something new in her face, though, some cast of resignation, since the bad grade in French. At least she was still going to classes. She made a face

when he'd asked about registration for next semester, as if even
that was uncertain, though classes would end a month before her
due date.

A dog had been killed a while ago; Heddy swore it had been a
coyote, so Peter knew he would have to go downstairs to make sure
the three dogs were tied up, that they hadn't left any of their food
uneaten. He pulled his boots from under the bed and found his
hat. Heddy turned over but didn't wake up.

The dogs were fine, up on their hind legs when they heard Peter coming. They whined and pulled their chains, dragging them
heavily on the ground.

"You hear the coyotes?" he asked them. Their food bowls were
empty and silver, smelling of their breath. "You scared?"

The noise came again, and Peter stiffened. The coyotes were so
human-sounding. He whooped back, crazily.

"Ha," he said, scratching the dogs. "I'm scary too."

But the noises doubled then, and Peter could make out, in the
mass of the cries, what sounded like whole words. He could see,
far off in the orchard, car headlights turn on abruptly on one of
the dirt roads, casting a smoldering wash of light on the surrounding land.

"Fuck." Peter looked around. Otto's truck was gone; he was
probably in town. Peter hurried to his own truck and started the
ignition, then jumped out to untie one of the dogs, an Australian
shepherd that Heddy had named, to Otto's disgust, Snowy.

"Up," he said, and Snowy leapt into the cab.

Heddy had taken the truck to school, and it smelled like wet
clothes and cigarettes, the radio turned up full blast to the staticky
dregs of the country station. She hadn't told him she'd started
smoking again. Peter knew she wasn't supposed to smoke—pregnant women couldn't smoke. But suddenly he wasn't sure. Because
Heddy wouldn't smoke if it could hurt the baby, he told himself.
So maybe he had it wrong. Peter fumbled with the volume knob,
turning the radio off, and took the ranch roads as fast as he could
without headlights.

The strange headlights he had seen were still on, but the car
wasn't moving. As Peter got closer, he slowed the truck, but he
knew whoever it was had heard him. His heart beat fast in his
chest, and he kept one hand on the dog.

Peter was close enough that his own truck was lit now. He parked and felt around under the seat until his hand closed around a short piece of broken rebar. "Hello?" Peter called from the truck. The headlights of the other vehicle hummed steadily, and specks of bugs swooped in and out of the twin columns of light.

Peter climbed out of the truck, the dog following.

"Hello?" he repeated.

It took him a moment to understand that the other truck was familiar. And before he had understood it fully, Otto walked out from the darkness into the bright room made by the headlights.

He was drunker than Peter had ever seen him. He wasn't wearing a shirt. He looked to the air around Peter's face, smiling. Like an athlete in the stadium lights.

"Peter," Otto said. "You're here."

Behind him, Peter saw two women giggling in the orchard. He could see that one was naked, a plastic camera on a strap around her wrist. He noticed the other woman's T-shirt and see-through lavender underwear before realizing, in a sickening moment, that it was Steph, her dark hair sticking to her face.

"Steph and I made a friend," Otto slurred. "Come on," he said to Steph and the woman, impatient. "Hurry up."

The women held on to each other and stepped gingerly through the grass toward the trucks, the woman with the camera plumper than Steph. They were both wearing sneakers and socks.

"I know you," said Steph, pointing at him. She was drunk, but it must have been something else besides alcohol. She couldn't quite focus on Peter, and she smiled in a strange, fanatic way.

"Hi," said the plump girl. Her hair was blond and worn long with jagged edges. "I'm Kelly. I've never been to a farm before."

Steph hugged Kelly, her small tipped breasts pressing into Kelly's larger ones. She said loudly into Kelly's ear, "That's Peter."

Otto kept licking his lips and trying to catch Peter's eyes, but Peter couldn't look at him. Snowy ran up to the women and they both shrieked. Steph kicked at the dog with her dirty tennis shoes as he tried to nose her crotch.

"Don't kill 'em," Otto said to Snowy. "I like 'em."

"Come on, dog," Peter said, patting his leg.

"You aren't going, are you?" Otto leaned against his truck. "Help me finish this," he said, the bottle in his hand sloshing.

"Don't go, Peter," Steph said.

"I told them they'd only drink the best," Otto said. He held out a bottle of grocery-store champagne to Peter. "Open it for the girls."

The bottle was warm. Snowy was agitated now, circling Peter's feet, and when Peter twisted the cork and it shot into the dark, Snowy yelped and took off after it. Steph took the bottle from Peter, the bubbles cascading down her arms and frothing into the hem of her underwear. Kelly clicked the shutter.

"See?" Otto said. "That was easy."

"Steph," Peter said. "Why don't I drive you back to your house, okay?"

Steph took a long drink from the bottle. She regarded Peter. Then she let her mouth drop open, bubbles and liquid falling down her front. She laughed.

"You're a disgusting girl," Otto said. Snowy came to sniff at his boots, and Otto gave him a heavy kick. The dog whimpered. "A disgusting girl," Otto repeated.

"Hey, shut up," Kelly said, meekly.

"Fuck you," Otto said, smiling hard. "Fuck. You."

Peter started to move toward his own truck, but Otto came over and pushed him back, one hand steady on his chest.

"Come here," Otto said to Steph, his hand still on Peter. "Come on."

Steph turned her back on Otto, pouting. Her buttocks through the netted underwear were shapeless and crisscrossed with impressions of the ground.

"Oh fuck off," Otto said. "Come here."

Steph laughed, then took shaky steps toward Otto. He caught her and shoved his mouth against hers. When they pulled apart, he clapped at her ass. "Okay, now kiss him."

Peter shook his head. "No."

Otto was smiling and holding Steph by the hips. "Kiss him, babe. Go on."

Steph leaned over so her chapped lips brushed Peter's cheek, her body pressed against his arm. The shutter clicked before Peter could back away.

"Listen," Peter said. "Why don't you guys go somewhere else?"

"Really?" Otto laughed. "Go somewhere else. Interesting suggestion."

Peter hesitated. "Just for tonight."

"I own this fucking property. You are on my property right now."

"Otto, go home. This isn't good."

"Good? Don't you work for me? Don't you live in my house? You fuck my sister. I have to hear that shit." He pushed Steph away. "You think you know her? Do you even realize how long Heddy and I lived out here alone? Years," he spat, "for fucking *years.*"

Heddy was still asleep when Peter came into the bedroom, the room navy in the dark. He took off his clothes and got in bed beside her. His own heartbeat kept him awake. The house was too quiet, the mirror on Heddy's childhood vanity reflecting a silver knife of moonlight. Could a place work on you like an illness? That time when it rained and all the roads flooded—they'd been stuck on the farm for two days. You couldn't raise a baby in a place like this. A place where you could be trapped. His throat was tight. After a while, Heddy's eyes shuddered open, like his hurtling thoughts had been somehow audible. She blinked at him like a cat.

"Stop staring at me," she said.

He tried to put his arm around her, but she'd closed her eyes again, nestling away from him, her feet soothing each other under the sheets.

"We need to get our own place."

His voice sounded harsher than he'd meant it to, and her eyes startled open. She started to sit up, and he saw the shadowed outline of her bare breasts before she groped for the blankets and pulled them tight around her. It struck Peter, sadly, that she was covering her breasts from him.

He took a breath. "I could get another job. You could be closer to school."

She said nothing, staring down at the covers, pinching at the fake satin border.

He suddenly felt like crying. "Don't you like school?" he said, his voice starting to unravel.

There was a silence before she spoke. "I can just work here. For Otto." She started to turn from him. "And where am I ever going to speak French anyway?" she said. "You think we'll take the baby to Paris?" She laughed, but it was airless, and Peter saw the tired hunch of her shoulders and understood that they would never leave.

*

The next morning, Peter woke to an empty room. Heddy's pillow was smoothed into blankness, the sun outside coming weak through the fog. From the window, he could see the dog circling under the shaggy, emerald trees and the trailers beyond. He forced himself to get up, moving like someone in a dream, barely aware of directing his limbs into his clothes. When he went downstairs, he found Otto on the couch, his shoes still on, fumy with alcohol sweat. A pastel quilt was pushed into a corner, and the couch pillows were on the ground. Otto started to sit up when Peter walked past. In the kitchen, Heddy had the tap running, filling the kettle.

"And on the couch, you'll notice my dear brother," Heddy said, raising her eyebrows at Peter. There was nothing in her voice that indicated they'd talked the night before, just a faint tiredness in her face. She shut off the faucet. "He smells like shit."

"Morning, Peter," Otto said, coming into the kitchen. Peter worked to keep his gaze steady and level on the tabletop as Otto pulled up a chair.

Heddy padded toward the stairs with her mug of lemon water, glancing back at them. Otto watched her go, then went to the sink and filled a glass with water. He drank it down, then drank another.

"I'm in hell," Otto said.

Peter didn't say anything. A band of pressure built around his temple, a headache coming on.

Otto drank more water in huge gulps, then opened the cupboard. "Do you forgive me?"

"Sure."

Otto closed the cupboard without taking anything out. He turned to look at Peter, then shook his head, smiling. "Shit. 'Sure,' he says. Listen," Otto continued. "I'm meeting these guys today who've been emailing. They want to work. You have to meet them too."

The headache was going to be a bad one, a ghosted shimmer of the overhead light starting to edge into Peter's vision. "I don't think I can," he said.

"Oh, I think you can," Otto said.

Peter couldn't speak, so Otto went on. "So we'll meet here. Or do you want me to tell them we'll meet in town?"

Peter pulled at his collar, then let his hand drop. "I guess town," he said.

"Easy," Otto said. "Wasn't that easy?"

They finished their breakfast in silence. The room got soggy with quiet, the air pressing in, a stale vapor that seemed a hundred years old. Heddy stooped to kiss Peter goodbye, her bag over her shoulder. Peter forced himself to smile, to kiss her back.

"Lovebirds," Otto called, and Peter looked over, just as Otto held up his hands to frame Heddy and Peter.

Heddy stood and Peter noticed she had put on slashes of dark eyeliner that made the whites of her eyes brighter. The faint smell of cigarettes lingered in the air where she had just been. Her hair was pinned up off her neck. She had on a light jacket instead of her old raincoat. She looked like a new person, like no one he knew.

Hog for Sorrow

FROM *Bomb*

LUCY AND KIT sat waiting side by side on a black leather couch, before a long glass window that looked out over Tribeca, the winter sun in their laps. Kit stole sideward glances at Lucy, who hummed, twisting her hair around her fingers in a compulsive fashion. Her hair was long and lionlike with a slight wave to it, gold with yellowy shades around her face. Kit couldn't look at her for very long. She cringed and recoiled, as if faced with a bright light. Lucy was too radiant.

A low glass table stood before them. Fake potted plants flanked the sofa, their waxy leaves coated with dust. Lucy crossed and uncrossed her legs. Her eyes were quick and green, flitting about the room like birds. She wore a blue mini-dress with a white collar and peep-toe black heels. On her lap sat a chestnut leather purse with a brassy curved handle. Lucy was both plump and long limbed. "A tall cherub," she had once said of herself with a laugh of self-hate. She mocked herself constantly, but with a certain joy. Her joy had a tough edge to it and seemed wonderfully defiant considering the pleasureless nature of their business. Kit was captivated by her. It seemed magical and impossible that one could laugh so heartily while waiting to be handled by a perfect stranger.

At the far end of the room, Sheila sat at a steel desk, staring at the bright page of a catalogue, poised with her red pen. She booked all of their appointments sulkily, sighing whenever the phone rang. Kit and Lucy considered her a bitch, though she rarely said a thing. "She does it all with her eyes," Kit had quietly remarked. They spent much of their time on the black couch talk-

ing shit about Sheila, leaning near one another and giggling con-
spiratorially.

Lucy removed a gold-tone compact from her purse and clicked
it open. She patted powder onto her chin and gave her mouth
a glance. It was pale pink and without lipstick, open slightly, her
teeth and tongue peeking through. When her client arrived, she
ate a green Tic Tac, biting down on it. He was a short, swarthy guy
with a newspaper under his arm.

Lucy rose and clacked across the room with the steady grin of
an assassin. It was her third appointment that day but she was an
enduring faker, tossing her hair and sucking in her stomach. The
man twinkled as he handed Sheila a white envelope full of money,
which she counted and placed in a small drawer, then led them to
their room with a crabby smile, one hand extended.

Once she was alone, Kit raised her butt off the sofa and pulled
her stockings up. Sheila returned to her desk and groaned. She
circled something in her catalogue and Kit's client called to say he
would be fifteen minutes late.

"But he's already fifteen minutes late," Kit said.

"Well," Sheila said, without looking at her, "there was some sort
of emergency. I told him you would wait."

"Yeah, I remember that."

Kit walked to the bathroom. The walls were gray with one
frosted window and a big beige air freshener that hissed vanilla
perfume every ten minutes. She yanked the window open and a
great wind came into the room. Snow rushed onto the black tile
floor. Kit lit a half-smoked joint from her purse. She kept several
on hand at all times in a battered Altoids tin.

She took a squinty suck and held the smoke in, liking the long
burn, then leaned her head into the wind and exhaled, snow pricking her face. She peered down at the neon-white streets below, car
tops mounting quietly with snow. Kit shivered. She took another
long toke and thought of the miserable year she'd spent at Ben-
nington, where she had barely attended class, watching snow fall
from her dorm window. She had been bored there. All anyone
wanted to do was get plastered and sleep around. It was a lot like
being a prostitute, she thought, only she had never gotten paid.

Kit took another tug of smoke. She stubbed the joint lightly in
the tin and licked her index finger, daubing the orange ember.
With one hand, she pushed on the window until it clapped shut,

then walked to the oval mirror. Kit stared at herself like a doctor who—right away—sees something very wrong. She wore a sleeveless black dress that she had bought in high school for her aunt's funeral. Her body hadn't changed much since then. She still had narrow legs and a lean, gloomy face, half-moon shadows under her eyes. There was a pubescent look about her, a Peter Pan shapelessness. She flickered between boy and girl.

Kit returned to the black couch, reeking of pot, and began eating a flattened corn muffin from her purse. Sheila shot her a look of amazement and Kit glared back at her. She took another bite of the greasy yellow muffin and a man walked in. He removed his collared black coat and looked pensively about the room, tugging off his leather gloves. "Hi," he said. "I'm Ned."

Kit smiled, her mouth packed.

He stared at her and she tensed with embarrassment, knowing that he was comparing her face to the one he had seen on the Internet, a photo in which she sat posed on the arm of a beige sofa with the stricken look of a woodland creature in captivity. Kit hated to have her photo taken. The fact of one moment being yanked from all the other moments scared her. It was the same fear when people stared at her, much as Ned was doing. Her fear looked fresh and clearly he found this attractive. She seemed unaccustomed to it—unable to hide it—which suggested that she had not been a prostitute for very long.

To Kit, Ned looked a little desperate. Like someone on *Judge Judy*, fighting for old furniture. She watched as he counted out ten twenties on Sheila's desktop, then wiped his nose with the back of his hand. Sheila led them to a square bedroom with scuffed white walls and brown carpeting. Once she'd shut the door, Ned removed his suit jacket and the two sat on the edge of the bed.

"What was your name? Tammy?"

"It's Tonya," she said, crossing her legs. "So what are you into?"

"I'm not going to touch you." Ned pressed his temples. "But I'd like you to get undressed."

Kit nodded absently. Her eyes were bloodshot and her thoughts floated somewhere near the ceiling. Ned leaned his face toward her neck, as if about to plant a kiss there, but instead took a sniff.

"Your hair smells like pot," he said. "And like that big piece of cake you were eating."

Kit turned in alarm. "It was a corn muffin."

He smiled oddly. "You should be careful, eating all the muffins you want. You'll get fat."

"No I won't," she frowned. "Not if I tried. No one in my family is fat." It was absolutely true. They were a bunch of beanpoles with long feet and sunken faces. Ugly, Kit thought. But uglier was his smile and his warning. His wish for her not to eat. For her to remain locked in a single state of attractiveness, like a woman in a painting, with no body fat or smells, nothing to say.

Kit could smell Ned too. Strong cologne with the scent of his underarms screaming behind it, a bright, beer-like tang. She tried to imagine the women who loved his smell. A wife. Daughters. Possibly girlfriends. These women were lurking in the private lives of even the ugliest men she saw. Ned was neither ugly nor handsome. He had the sort of face that there had to be hundreds of. A pale white oval with a slight shine. Small eyes and a largish nose.

"I bet you drink a lot too," he said, still smiling foolishly.

"Not really."

"Youth is an incredibly buoyant medium," he mused. "What you can do at twenty you can't do at forty."

"So you're forty?"

"About that."

Kit undressed. She lay on the bed with shining eyes, like some dog awaiting the strange and particular abuse of its owner. Ned stripped down to his boxers and stood alongside the bed, staring down at her.

"You are so stoned," he said.

"Not so much," she said.

"Yes you are. You're barely here at all. It's like you're dead."

Kit felt a flash of panic pass through her eyes and knew he'd caught it. Ned was right. She was completely stoned. And because of this, certain things in the room appeared huge. The pink-flowered Kleenex box. The pump bottle of generic lube. Ned's oily, egglike head.

Kit was arranged face-down on the bed. She shut her eyes and Ned rocked into the quiet space between his hands. "I think you like this," he said, which was what they all said.

She fell into a partial sleep. Dreamless brown darkness closed around her. She heard her heart beat. It was like a fist pounding at the bottom of a swimming pool. Ned groaned. He came onto her buttocks and she woke, a dull hate glowing inside her. She stood and wiped off her butt cheeks with a tissue. "Are you married?"

He nodded.

"Does she know you come here?"

"I think she does."

"And it doesn't bother her?"

"She has a very good life," he said. "She's not gonna go and fuck that up." He lay down on the bed next to her.

Kit refrained from pointing out that he had not answered the question. He went on to say that his wife didn't work. She took care of his daughter. He talked about her in a frank and vulgar manner, like she was an animal who had eaten out of the same can for years. He said she was really interested in astrology. He said all women were. He said his wife kept a dream journal and he laughed gently, slightly like a madman. "Who cares about dreams?" he said. "They don't mean anything."

Ned said he was a dentist and Kit wondered how he handled all that revulsion. He complained about his practice and boringly recounted the events of a cocktail party in which he had humiliated a fellow dentist in front of several beautiful women. "That took a bite out of his swagger!" he said. And Kit laughed obediently, which felt like the worst kind of sex.

Kit and Lucy walked to the train at dusk, snow swirling past their faces. The sky was a pearly gray, the moon dimly visible. The two walked along a narrow path of brown slush, bookended by white humps of snow. In their boots and coats, they looked like the children that they were. Each bundled and waddling, their tight dresses and biscuit-colored stockings buried underneath. Lucy wore a long tweed coat with big glossy black buttons, Kit a brown leather bomber jacket and sagging wool-knit hat. They hooked arms, steadying each other.

"He, like, reprimanded me for eating a corn muffin."

"What an asshole."

"It was like he wanted me to be dead. Like I was interfering with my potential hotness by living." Businesspeople passed swiftly in black coats. "I hate this neighborhood," Kit sneered. "I hate every single person."

"Are you okay?"

"No. I'm freezing. And I hate these tights." She wiggled with discomfort. "I hate this dress."

"Well," Lucy grinned, "they need you to remind them that they want to fuck you."

Kit laughed. They stopped in front of the train station and looked at each other. "Do you wanna come over?" Lucy asked. There was snow in her eyebrows.

Kit couldn't help but smile sheepishly at the offer because, until that moment, they had only ever spent time together in diners or on the black couch. "Yeah," she said. "I do."

Lucy's apartment was small and lit like a bar, one long room with yellow light in every corner. There was an old clawfoot tub next to the stove and a mattress on the floor by the wall. Kit stooped to pet a brown rat terrier with a silvery snout. He rolled under her hand with a guttural moan, groveling with delight. "That's Curtis," Lucy said.

"It's like a dirty-sock sex club in here," Kit laughed.

"I know." Lucy smiled without embarrassment. "Curtis pulls them out of the hamper. I should probably throw some of them away," she said, lifting a white ankle sock off the floor. "That way I would be forced to do laundry more often." She jammed the little white sock into an overfilled wicker hamper. "I won't go until I'm completely out of clothes. Hate it too much."

"Seriously, I could look anywhere and see socks."

"Do you want anything?" Lucy asked.

"Anything?"

"Well. Beer or water."

Kit laughed. "I'll take water."

"Help yourself, okay? I've gotta take him down." Lucy Velcroed a little red coat onto the dog and left.

Kit ran tap water into a Charlie Brown Christmas mug. She roamed around the room, sipping water and snooping vaguely. Apart from the strewn socks, Lucy's apartment was relatively bare. There were tall Mexican candles on the floor by her mattress, a tiny cactus on the windowsill. And on the floor there was an old mint-green record player with brown accents. Lucy's possessions looked misplaced, but because there weren't so many, the wrongness of their arrangement had a childish charm.

Kit spotted several photos of a younger-looking Lucy, tacked by the bed in a crooked cluster. In one she sat in an auto rickshaw, in another she stood handling fruit in a marketplace. Kit approached the images intently. She sat cross-legged on the bed and stared up at them.

The door flung open and Curtis raced inside. He leapt onto Kit's lap and squirmed on his back in ecstasy, biting her fingers gently, his wet paws paddling. Kit stroked his underside, her eyes fastened to the photographs.

"He likes you," Lucy said.

"Does he not like a lot of people?"

"No. He likes pretty much everyone."

Lucy hung her coat on a hook by the door. She pulled off her boots and stockings, then fetched a can of beer from the fridge and tapped the top of it with her fingernail. She turned to Kit, who still sat staring at the photographs. "In India I just went around buying things. You can spend a quarter in like a half-hour," she said, cracking the can open. "It was so beautiful there. Every single person was doing something. It was such a sensory overload, but way softer than America."

"I want to travel," Kit said. She looked at Lucy. "I sort of feel like I have to do it now, while I'm still cute. Like if I wait till I'm old and ugly it won't happen."

"You might be right," Lucy said and took a swig from the silver can. "But I'm really looking forward to being old and ugly."

"What do you mean?"

"I mean it'll be nice to be left alone. I want to get a little house somewhere with grass out front for Curtis. There's no grass here. I mean, there *is* grass but you aren't allowed on it, not with a dog, anyway. It's like walking through some holy museum." She stooped to pet Curtis. "Sucks."

Kit smiled.

"What?"

"Nothing. I just like when you talk about how much something sucks."

"Fuck you."

"I'm serious! That's always how I know I like someone. They'll be going on about their own hell and it should be tedious to listen to, but for some reason it's not. Something about their face or the way they're joking about their unhappiness is so . . . attractive."

"I know exactly what you mean. It's like perfume."

"Right."

Kit set the mug down on the floor and hugged her bony knees to her chest. Curtis trotted over. He lowered his snout into the mug and began lapping.

"He does that," Lucy said unapologetically and smiled at the animal. She knelt beside the record player and put the Modern Lovers on. The record turned and crackled. Jonathan Richman sang *Roadrunner, roadrunner* in his hot, sloppy way and Lucy began to dance, shouting along with the words.

"You're so retro," Kit marveled, staring up from the bed.

"I know, right?" Lucy said, catching her breath. "The record player was my grandmother's but all the records are mine." She began to sing again, gaily shaking her hips and shoulders. Lucy was a silly dancer, but in the way only someone who is confident of their sexiness can be. She flailed about like she had no respect for anyone or anything, whipping her gold lion hair from side to side.

"You're a good singer," Kit said.

"Fuck you."

"I'm not kidding! You're really good."

Lucy rolled her eyes and threw herself back into the air. Jonathan sounded more like a loud talker than a singer to Kit. *I'm lonely and I don't have a girlfriend but I don't mind.* He made her wish she were in a band.

Lucy tired herself out dancing to the next few songs and the two wound up lying on her mattress. They talked about dropping out of college, how it had been the easiest decision in the world. Lucy had studied dance at Sarah Lawrence, which surprised Kit.

"What was that like?"

"It was like being abused. Routinely. By people I had no respect for." She sighed. "What did you go for?"

"Writing," Kit said.

"That makes sense." Lucy smiled. "So when did you know you were a writer?"

"I don't know. About ten, I guess. But I didn't consider myself a real writer. I had one skill and that was to lie in bed," she laughed. "I loved being alone in my room. I mean, that was the real love. I just wrote because there was nothing else to do. It didn't feel special."

"So were you a slow kid or a fast kid?"

"Well I was both."

"Me too."

Kit raised herself up on both elbows and crawled over to her bag. After some digging she brought her Altoids tin onto the floor and surveyed its sooty contents. She returned to the bed with a crooked smile, a joint pinched between thumb and forefinger.

"I can't smoke pot," Lucy said.

"Oh. I thought maybe you just didn't like to at work."

"No, I never do. Some people get all focused and brilliant when they're high but I don't."

"Well I can only focus on like, cleaning my bathroom," Kit said. She lit the joint and dragged on it.

"I can only focus on hating myself," Lucy said. "It's like I can feel every cell and every pore and I'm hating them one by one. Then I put giant signs on them like CRAZY, FAILED, FAT."

Kit laughed and smoke leaked from her mouth. She set the joint down in the open tin, coughing into her fist. She imagined saying: *I love that you're fat. I love everything about you.* It was the absolute truth. But she said nothing and strained not to look at Lucy. She heard her heart beat. She began branding herself. LESBIAN. LOSER. WHORE.

"So you never get paranoid?" Lucy asked.

"I definitely get paranoid."

"Like how?"

"I just get scared I'll say what I'm thinking or do something insane. Like tell someone what a shit they are or like, assault them."

"You want to assault people?"

"No! I mean, not really. It's just this fear of losing it. I mean, I have that fear anyway. 'Cause you hear about people doing crazy things out of nowhere. And the slight possibility that I could be one of those people, that someone else could be inside me . . . it's the loneliest feeling. Like what if I didn't know myself?"

"You aren't one of those people."

"How can you be sure?"

"I just am."

Kit smiled. This was one of the nicest things anyone had ever said to her. *You aren't crazy.*

Curtis curled beside Lucy and laid his chin on her breast. She began rubbing his ears and he went limp, collapsing into a state of bliss.

"How old is he?"

"I think five or six. I got him two years ago with my boyfriend. We were totally wrong for each other." She smiled, shaking her head. "I mean, I loved him but we argued constantly." Lucy looked down at Curtis. He was asleep. "I wonder what it's like to hear people fighting in another language your whole life."

"You hear the tones," Kit offered. "You understand. There's probably only one language."

"That seems true." Lucy began stroking Curtis and he roused for a second, then went soft again. "I wish I knew what his life was like before I got him. It's so strange. Dogs are the repositories of stories we can never know."

"That's probably part of the pleasure of looking into their eyes." Lucy nodded.

"He's very cute," Kit said.

"You think so?" Lucy said in disbelief. "I mean, I think so, but no one else does. I got him from a shelter. He was scheduled to be killed the next day."

The dog raised his head and yawned. Up close, Kit could see that he had an underbite and one gluey eye, both of which truly were cute.

"He destroyed my sofa," Lucy said and Kit tried to imagine where a sofa could have fit in the apartment.

"That sucks."

"Yeah. He also hates when I talk on the phone. And when I masturbate."

"Oh God. What does he do?"

"He just stares at me with this totally disgusted look and then pouts for the rest of the day. Actually, he also does that when I cry."

"He doesn't want to see you become an animal."

"Exactly."

The next morning, Kit got a call from Sheila. Ned had made an appointment to see her that afternoon.

"I can't believe it," Kit said.

"The corn muffin guy?" Lucy asked.

"Yeah."

"I guess he liked you."

"It really didn't seem that way."

It was Lucy's day off. She padded around the apartment in a short silk robe. Pale blue, with a pattern of multicolored fish, the sash tied loose at her waist. It was a tiny garment, her thighs on full display, a flash of her bum here and there. She made coffee and fried eggs over toast, humming all the while, feeding scraps to Curtis with her fingers. "You can come over later if you want," she said and tucked a blond strand behind her ear.

"All right," Kit said, smiling slyly. She squatted in the tub, washing her armpits and vagina. Lucy handed her a pink disposable razor. She opened a window and poked her head out. It was oddly warm. Shrunken gray mounds of snow hugged the sidewalk below. Dirty water dripped from the eaves.

"I can't believe how warm it is," Lucy said.

"And people still say global warming isn't happening."

"Yeah, well, American stupidity is accelerating at the same rate."

Ned arrived in a mute daze. He wore a flat, melancholy expression and seemed barely to register Kit's face as she waved from the black leather couch. Sheila led them to the same awful room and Kit sat tentatively on the edge of the bed. Ned removed his coat and sat beside her. He stared at the brown carpet and said nothing.

"Are you okay?" Kit asked.

Ned grunted slightly. With averted eyes, he rolled her onto her stomach and hiked up her dress. Kit sat up and pulled her dress off the rest of the way, then lay flat on her front like a routine sunbather. She heard his belt fall to the floor. Ned began jerking off and Kit thought of other things. Lucy dancing. The dog. Donuts on a plate. She studied the nicks and scuffs on the white wall, her head on its side. Ned's breath quickened. He gasped and Kit sat up, turning to make sure he had come.

Ned stood naked with his arms at his sides. He was crying.

Kit stiffened. Goose bumps raised over her body. She considered dashing out of the room naked, but Ned lurched toward her. He sank his hot face onto her breasts and sobbed for what felt like minutes, then withdrew his face with sudden embarrassment.

Ned moved to the edge of the bed with his back to her and Kit didn't ask what was wrong. She didn't want to know.

"My kid is sick," he said. "Six fucking years old."

Kit said nothing. She eyed the shininess between his shoulder blades.

"I can't see her. I don't know what to say to her." Ned looked over one shoulder desperately, his eyes flashing. "What do you think I should say to her?"

"I don't know." Kit crawled over to him and forced her hand onto the small of his back, patting it. "What does she have?"

"Leukemia," he said, as though Kit were an imbecile.

Her hand hardened on his back but she continued to pat him, almost harshly. "It's okay," she said uselessly. "It'll be okay."

Ned turned sharply. "You don't know that. No one does. No one knows what it's like . . . to cease."

Kit removed her hand from his back. She stared into space. "I bet it's like a drug experience," she said finally. "Especially if you're at a hospital and your insides are failing you. Like you probably have odd sensations. You feel really warm or you hallucinate. Then just drift off."

"Not everyone goes peacefully. People die screaming." He had his arms folded.

"You're right."

"My uncle died screaming. He didn't want to die."

"How did he die?"

"Bone cancer."

They leaned back on the bed and each looked at the other's feet. Hers were long and bare. He wore red and black argyle socks. Kit looked at them awhile and then through them, at nothing, her thoughts wild. She was angry. She hated Ned for dragging some dying little girl into the picture, for crying all over her breasts. She looked down at her knobby knees, the brown beauty mark near her crotch. I'm like Lucy's dog, she thought. *I don't want to see him become an animal.*

Kit considered her own animal self. A wild thing looking out a window. A wild thing made to be a doll. For a moment she loved herself deeply, whoever she was. It was hard to know in the awful white room. She felt as if a circus tent were draped over her existence.

Ned uncrossed his arms. "I've upset you," he said and touched her leg gently. It was jarring and repulsive. He had never touched her this way.

"No. I'm not afraid of death," she declared. "I'm glad the human experience ends. I mean, what if it didn't? What if you were just stuck here forever? That would be scarier than death."

He seemed to consider this peacefully, folding his arms again. "So what are you afraid of?" he asked and a slight smile tugged one side of his face. It was as if he had just remembered she was a prostitute.

"Swallowing glass," she said.

"Why?" he asked.

"Because they can't do anything about it. Glass doesn't show up in X-rays. It just takes one tiny piece and you die a slow, painful death."

"Jesus."

"A bartender told me that."

They were quiet awhile.

"I like that you don't wear makeup," he said finally.

"Yeah. I don't think women should," she said. "It looks so clownish."

"No. Some women should *definitely* wear makeup. But not anyone your age. Makeup on a youngster is redundant."

"You think I'm a youngster?"

"Well you are."

Kit stared at him, glinting with hate.

"Look at you," he said. "Your skin."

"What?"

"It's so *new*," he said and touched her cheek softly, letting his fingers rest there. "Youth is a class all its own," he continued. "You all look alike." He took his hand away. "But the fat breaks down—the glow. And you're left with a kind of specificity. You fall into racial stereotypes." He pointed to his own face. "And now you can't tell what I was. I was this beautiful kid."

Kit averted her eyes. She folded her arms over her breasts.

"How old are you, anyway?" he asked. "Twenty-something?"

"I'm nineteen."

Ned smiled greedily. "What's that like," he said sarcastically, "being a teenager?"

"Everyone wants what you have so they try to control you."

Ned looked surprised. He went silent and Kit turned to him, her eyes fierce. "Do you like watching two women together?" she asked.

"What?"

"There's another girl here and if you paid us both double, you could watch us."

"Watch you what?"

"You know."

"Are you a dyke?"

"No. I just think you would like her."

Ned pondered a moment. He got up and reached into his coat pocket, withdrawing a business card. He placed the white card on Kit's bare abdomen and broke into a smile.

Kit saw several other men that day and felt nothing. By nightfall, she stood in the bathroom getting high, staring meditatively out the window. Ned remained in her mind, the weight of his face on her breasts. *He is a hog for sorrow,* she thought. *And maybe I am too.* Kit had never envisioned this life for herself. *This is really happening,* she thought. Any awful thing seemed possible. She was afraid of the concrete and cars down there below, of the opportunity she had always to hurl herself out the window. Kit didn't really want to die, but the fact of having a choice was frightening.

A flood of bothersome memories surged up as she put her pot away. She remembered her mother saying, "Your job should take a little piece of you that you don't mind giving." Kit believed that she had such a job. *It's just my body,* she thought. And it didn't seem like a lot to give away until she considered that it was all she had. *This pussy is my only currency.* It was a sickening thought.

Outside, the moon was huge with white fog in front of it. A twitchy streetlight shone on the hoods of cars. Kit walked carefully over silvery areas of ice. She stopped to peruse the bright aisles of a deli and bought an expensive bar of chocolate wrapped in gold foil.

On the train, Kit sat by the window and remembered that she had offered Lucy's body to Ned and to herself. She imagined telling Lucy this and pictured her repulsed response. Kit broke off a cube of chocolate and sank into a whirling rabbit hole of panic. She almost missed her stop, loading chocolate into her mouth with a fixed look of dread. She walked to Lucy's apartment haltingly, pausing whenever the image of Lucy's disgusted face reemerged in her mind.

Lucy arrived cheerily at the door, barefoot in a black-and-white-checked dress with triangle pockets. They sipped cans of beer on her bed and Kit rolled a joint, which proved tricky since her hands were clammy. She puffed on the loose roll and they talked. Because Kit was nervous, there was an odd theatricality to what should have been mundane chatter. Eventually a silence grew between them. Kit mopped her forehead with her sleeve. She crawled over to her bag and ate the last corner of chocolate, then blurted her proposal.

"And he wouldn't touch us?" Lucy asked.

"No. But he *will* say really degrading things. I actually . . ." Kit stared into space. "I think I really hate this person."

"Why? Because he doesn't respect you?" Lucy said mockingly.

"No. Because he's crazy."

"Look," Lucy said. "Crazy people have one tactic, to convince you that *you're* crazy. So you can't let them."

Kit nodded. "You're right," she said. "I don't know why I even care. It's the weirdest things that bother me about him. Like how he thinks dreams are meaningless." She looked at Lucy. "He thinks his wife is stupid for analyzing them."

"He's probably just a rich guy who went to too much therapy. Those types are really against any sort of prodding of the brain." In a mock-deranged male voice, Lucy said, "It means nothing. I kill women every night. It means nothing!"

Kit laughed. She considered telling Lucy about Ned's dying daughter but quickly decided not to. She couldn't bear to paint him as a tragic figure.

"If he's paying us double, I'll totally do it," Lucy said and Kit smiled, dropping her head, letting hair fall in front of her eyes.

Later they lay in the dark, Curtis sprawled between them. "I feel weak and depressed from that chocolate," Kit said. Lucy groaned softly, nearly asleep. She had hung Christmas lights on her fire escape and they cast a gem-like glow over the bed. Kit raised herself up on both elbows and studied Lucy. Her plump face in the colored light, wreathed with hair and shadows. Kit held her breath. It felt dangerous to watch such a beautiful person sleep. Lucy could wake at any moment, she thought, and there would be no mistaking the unflinching blaze in her eyes.

Kit lowered her head back onto the pillow. She felt slightly gleeful that Lucy was willing to touch her, even if it was for money. It seemed, somehow, like a far-off compliment. She closed her eyes and Lucy's body beamed in her thoughts. She thought of other girls too. All the girls who'd turned her on wildly and never knew.

She rolled onto her side, sweating. Her crotch thumped like a big, wet heart.

Curtis stirred, as if in response to Kit's rising body temperature, the zinging nerves between her legs. He shimmied under the covers and stationed himself between Lucy's feet.

In the morning Kit felt like a criminal. Lucy tromped around in her skimpy robe, Curtis following close behind.

"I made eggs," Lucy said, gesturing toward the stove.

"Great," Kit said, reaching a slender monkeyish arm out for her clothes, which were scattered by the bed, much in the manner of Lucy's socks.

Lucy twisted a strand of gold hair around her pointer finger. "I used to think you didn't eat. 'Cause you're like, *emaciated.*"

"I know. I look exactly like my mom. She's built like a broom."

"My mom's built like a refrigerator."

"Oh come on."

"She *is.*"

They were both sitting on the black couch when Ned scheduled their appointment for the following week. Sheila responded with a look of mild revulsion as she penciled it in. Kit pretended to ignore the look but took it to heart. Later on, she called the number on Ned's business card, which in the right-hand corner had a cartoon tooth. It was smiling and had a set of its own teeth. She held the card with her thumb over the tooth while arranging for him to fork over the extra amount in cash. "If you screw us over in any way," she said, "I won't see you again."

Kit saw a number of men that week and avoided Lucy. She paid off one of her credit cards. She learned that Sheila designed clothes when a small green dress appeared on the arm of the black couch. Sheila asked in an oddly sweet tone if Kit would model it for her. She was smiling but a look of scorn remained in her eyes, pulsing dimly. "I need to see it on someone small," she said.

The dress fit Kit remarkably well and she couldn't help admiring it, but this only depressed her. It meant Sheila was something other than an asshole. She was an artist.

Kit bought herself a handsome leather-bound journal that day. She put an aqua mason jar full of sharpened pencils on the windowsill by her bed. Then she tried to write but couldn't. Ragged stray thoughts circled in her mind. Kit didn't want to sit alone with her life, with the memories of a hundred male voices. She didn't want to fuss over how to describe their faces. Instead she walked around her apartment, smoking pot from a glass pipe with the stereo on. She played Nico, who sounded like a prostitute to her, used and woeful. *These days I seem to think a lot about the things that I forgot to do.*

In the morning Kit grabbed the leather journal and jotted down her dream, which felt remotely like a tribute to Ned's wife. She wrote in a panic, the dream whirling and vanishing. It felt deeply important as she raced on, snatching bits of the fleeing dream. Then she set her pen down and read the frayed, mystical prose with satisfaction. It seemed to be proof of something. That she had an inside. *I exist,* she wrote and instantly felt foolish, scribbling over the words.

Next she stood at the stove brewing espresso in a small steel pot, then went straight back to bed and sipped from her mug, a brown-tone afghan up over her shoulders. She watched hours of reality TV, which felt sleazy. *This is the pornography of our lives,* she thought.

Kit wondered if Ned's daughter was dead yet. She hated to think of him sobbing alongside a hospital bed with a little girl on it. *What is the difference between me and her?* she thought. *Between a daughter and a whore? Possession,* thought Kit. *His daughter belongs to him.*

But they were girls in the same sea, she felt. Both their values had been established in relation to Ned's sperm. It was gold when his daughter was conceived. It had taken a long, holy swim to the womb. But with Kit, his sperm had just been trash, just some muck on her ass. It was a weirdly gratifying epiphany. *I am the receptacle,* she thought. *His daughter is a deity.*

Time passed crudely. Kit had several dreams of leaping out of windows and becoming a ghost. She didn't believe in the afterlife, but in her dreams it seemed so obvious. Even when she woke, it was true for a moment. Kit was deeply curious about death. *We only know how to go from one place to another,* she thought. *How does it feel to go from one place to nowhere?* Her thinking stopped at the point. She could only wonder. *Death is the one thing you can't write about,* she thought.

On the day of their appointment with Ned, Kit woke in a sweat. She forgot her dream instantly, but felt certain it had been a nightmare. *I was being chased,* she thought. Kit hauled herself into the shower and then got high in the kitchen, waiting for her coffee to brew. She set her glass pipe down and called Lucy.

"What the fuck?" Lucy answered.

"Hi."

"*Hi?* You've been ignoring me for days."

"I'm sorry. I've been really busy."

"Whatever."

They met on the street. Lucy in her tweed coat and a pair of oversized amber frames with rose-hued lenses, her bright hair blowing in the wind. Kit leaned up against a brick wall, squinting. She wore dark slacks and waxy brown combat boots. Lucy removed her sunglasses and they exchanged subtle looks of terror.

"Your eyes," Kit said.

"What?"

"They're so green."

"Oh I know. I get startled in the mirror sometimes. 'Cause they change."

"I've noticed that."

"The Irish thought they were fairies," Lucy said nervously. "If they had a baby with green eyes, they thought that the fairies had come and swapped it with one of their own." She nodded as if encouraging herself. "So they basically murdered their green-eyed babies—threw them down a well, hoping the fairies would return their human baby."

"Scary."

"I know."

Upstairs they whipped past Sheila and headed straight for the bathroom. Kit changed into her same black uniform and Lucy removed her coat, revealing a silk camel-tone dress with opalescent buttons down the back. She beamed with anxiety. What was pink came soaring up to the surface of her face like a sunset.

Ned sat waiting on the black couch. He wore a gray felt hat with a top crease. As they approached, he removed the hat and bowed his head. Then a foolish smile came across his face. Ned seemed to be mocking the prospect of his own politeness. He was no gentleman and clearly found this hilarious.

Sheila led them to a large room with one mirrored wall and a creaky king bed. The three of them got naked and it all felt very clinical. The room was a bit cold. Ned seemed giddy. It was as if his depression had receded, he glittered temporarily while aroused. He stood alongside the bed and motioned to it until the girls climbed on. "You're an odd couple," he said, waving his finger at them. "One big and one skinny. But that must be part of the turn-on." He grinned. "Calm down. I'm kidding."

A pained smile transformed Lucy's face. She was posed like a mermaid on a rock, yellow hair half covering her breasts. Kit made a concerted effort not to stare.

Lucy's kisses were muscular with no feeling behind them. She broke into breathy counterfeit moans and Kit cringed. Their teeth clicked. Kit felt a bit the way men must feel, she supposed, when they realize that the prostitute they've purchased is miserable to be near them. She wasn't sure why she had expected it to be any other way. *I'm just another creep who wants to touch her,* she thought. *A little creep hiding behind a bigger one.*

Afterward the sky outside was a gray peach. They rode the train to Lucy's apartment with amazed expressions. Once home, Lucy lit the candles by her bed. It was as if someone had died. Kit searched her face for disgust, but there was only hurt. Lucy sat on the floor beside Curtis, mechanically stroking his muscles.

They ordered Chinese food and stood in the kitchen, eating lo mein from takeout containers. Lucy's glazed look of pain dissipated. She hummed and Kit hated her a little bit. For pretending to be unmarked by the last few hours. And by every other terrible hour of her life. Curtis hopped madly at their ankles. His cries were comically bad, as if a blade were being driven into his body.

"Is he okay?" Kit asked.

"He's fine," Lucy said. "Those are the screams of a manipulator." She scraped brown slop from a can into a little blue bowl and set it down on the floor. Curtis trotted over with a look of slack-jaw joy. He bent down to eat.

"He appears well behaved when he's eating," Kit said.

"Everyone does," Lucy said.

Kit set her lo mein by the sink. "Am I your only friend?" she asked. "I don't mean that in a bitchy way. I don't have any others."

Lucy stared at her. "In a way you are. I used to have a lot of friends."

Kit had never had a lot of friends. But she'd had a few that she didn't have now. *Becoming a whore is like getting very sick,* she thought. *You don't want people and they don't want you.* Only she did want people. A little.

"Ned's daughter is dying of cancer," Kit blurted.

"He told you that today?"

"No. Before. I should have told you. I just didn't want you to feel sorry for him."

"I wouldn't have."

"Really?"

"I don't feel anything for these people," Lucy said dryly.

Kit reached into her bag and felt around. She wondered what Lucy *did* feel. Outside an ambulance wailed by, its twirling red lights passing over the ceiling. She lit a joint and stood with it burning between her fingers. "I don't know why I get high," she said. "My mind is so inherently trippy."

"Maybe you should quit."

"Maybe." Kit let herself stare at Lucy. It was a quiet, burning stare. Her eyes blazed, pouring with feeling. Lucy continued to eat, as if she did not notice. But she did.

PATRICIA ENGEL

Campoamor

FROM *Chicago Quarterly Review*

NATASHA IS MY GIRLFRIEND. Sometimes I love her. Sometimes I don't think of her at all. When I met her she had a broken leg. I was visiting my friend Abel, who sells mobile phone minutes and lives down the hall from her in a building behind the Capitolio. I heard her crying, calling for anyone. I thought it was an old woman who'd fallen but when I pushed the door open I saw a girl, maybe twenty-five, standing like an ibis on one leg, leaning on a metal crutch, her other leg bent and floating in a plaster cast. The stray crutch lay meters from her reach across the broken tile floor.

She looked angry even though I was there to help her. I stepped into her apartment, saw she was alone, picked up the crutch, and handed it to her. She slipped it under her arm and thanked me. I asked her how she got around. Her place was on the fifth floor and there was no elevator.

"I've been up here for two months."

"Alone?"

"My mother lives here but she works during the day."

I asked her name and she told me Natasha, embarrassed the way we of our generation are to have Russian names.

"It's okay," I told her. "My name is Vladimir."

When I returned a week later to buy more minutes for my phone from Abel, I knocked on Natasha's door and it cracked open. Later she admitted there was no lock and no money to buy one so at night she and her mother pushed a dresser in front of it. She was sitting on a sofa with ebony legs, upholstered in a ripping flesh-colored silk, bulges of cushion tissue and bone frame exposed. Her casted calf was propped on a pillow mound atop the glass coffee table. She sat surrounded by books and said she only ever got up to go use the bathroom and to make herself something to eat.

"Don't you get lonely up here, Natasha?"

She shrugged.

"How did you break your leg?"

"It was stupid. *Un mal paso.* I was dancing with a bad dancer. He made me slip."

I was standing so she had to look up at me, trying to decide if she should let herself smile.

"I'll come and see you again," I told her. She said nothing but I could see in her eyes she liked the idea. And so I kept coming, every time I needed a new phone card, and sometimes in between, and Natasha would invite me to sit on the sofa beside her and would offer only a few sentences. I could see she was depressed in that dark apartment, subject to the shadows of the Capitolio and the noise of its endless restoration, drills and hammers on stone, with not even a television to keep her company because theirs had burnt out years ago and there was no money and no man to take it to be fixed.

I asked Abel what he knew about her. He's a writer like me. We met at the university where we both studied journalism. Abel writes small pieces for *Granma* and for an anonymous underground newspaper that gets published on USB sticks and passed around Havana once a month. He also sells black market phone cards. He says I need a side *negocio.* I don't even have a government job. This is why I never have money.

"If I get a job, I won't have time to write my novels," I say.

"What novels, Vladi? You haven't written even *one.*"

Abel said Natasha had an older sister who died from an infection and a father who left for Santo Domingo and was never heard from again. Her mother works as a cashier at the Carlos Tercero shopping center. He said Natasha reads a lot of books though she didn't study in the university, and until she broke her leg she had worked as a *niñera* taking care of the children of a military family in Cubanacán.

"What about the guy she was dancing with when she broke her leg? Was he her boyfriend?"

"*¿De qué hablas,* Vladi? She wasn't dancing. Nata never goes out

with anyone. She broke it when she fell down the stairs. A neighbor found her on the landing between the second and third floor."

Natasha didn't have anyone to take her to have her cast removed
so I offered. We left her crutches at home and I carried her down
the stairs all the way to Dragones for the *botero* lines. We found a
shared taxi going down Zanja in the direction of the clinic and
sat together in the back of that green Ford, our legs pressed together as other passengers climbed in beside us. It was somewhere
around La Rampa that I decided I wanted to kiss her. We passed
Coppelia and she looked out the window past me, licking her lips,
saying when she could walk on her own she'd go there for her
first ice cream of the summer. I kissed her mouth. The woman on
Natasha's other side looked away. The driver watched us from the
mirror. Natasha's lips were still but she didn't pull away. I kissed
her many more times and when I paused she stared at me but we
were quiet until we arrived at our stop and again I carried her,
from the road into the clinic.

When the doctor liberated her leg from the plaster, it was pale
and thin compared to her other calf, which was golden and muscular. Natasha was embarrassed. The doctor made her practice
walking. She was uncertain and wobbled and held my arm tight.
The doctor said she had to be careful. Her ankle would be delicate
for some time. She should not walk on Havana's cobblestones and
uneven roads alone, he said. "You take care of her," he told me
as we left that day. Natasha held my arm like a security bar and I
watched her every step in and out of the taxi back to the Capitolio. When we came to her building she walked on her own to the
corner in front of the Teatro Campoamor where some men were
stealing sheet metal from the barricades.

"Let's go in," she said, and I followed her, because I was just
meeting this Natasha of enthusiasm and with wildness in her
eyes. We walked past the street thieves, the walls of garbage, and
into the theater through a gap that had been ripped through the
wooden door blocks. Everyone knew a famous eccentric squatted
on the theater's upper floors. From Abel's apartment you could
see the guy's laundry hanging from string across what used to be
theater balconies. Natasha led me in and we were at the base of
the old theater's concrete horseshoe, overgrown with plants, even
trees, and I thought of my grandmother's old stories about the

place, where she'd come to hear her first *zarzuela* when Havana
was still grand and beautiful, before its shredding and abandonment and exodus.

Here, the balconies were lined with pigeons and the orchestra
seats, long looted, were occupied by a clan of bony cats. Natasha,
still holding me for support, slipped both her arms around me,
pressed her chest against mine, and kissed me. We were there so
long I managed to lift up her shirt and slide my hands under her
skirt into her panties, but then we heard voices from somewhere
in the theater and Natasha lost her balance, so I helped her cover
up and took her home.

I have another girlfriend named Lily. She lives with her daughter in the apartment her husband left them in three years ago, in
the building next to mine just off Línea in Vedado. I live with my
parents. They didn't see the point of having more than one child.
They didn't have the room for a bigger family. They sleep in the
one bedroom in our apartment. I sleep on a mattress in a corner
of the living room that my mother also uses to give therapeutic
massages to private clients though she was educated in Moscow to
be a physicist. My father is a cardiologist. He's hoping to get sent
on a doctor exchange to Angola or Brazil so he can defect and get
us out of here.

Lily doesn't care for books. She thinks it's funny that I want
to write them. She wants to fuck almost all the time, even if her
daughter is in the next room, and even if her daughter walks in
halfway through because she's hungry, Lily doesn't want to stop.
She got sterilized so she says she's making up for all her condom
years. She's thirty-five. I'm twenty-seven. Lily's face is hard from
sun and smoking Hollywoods and her hair is thin and limp like
thread. Her body is lumpy; her stomach, a rumpled pillowcase.
Somehow she's still beautiful. Sometimes even more beautiful
than Natasha who is lean and pointy, sharp shoulders, elbows, and
hips, a smooth face as if carved of clay. Sometimes when I'm with
Lily, I miss Natasha desperately. Other times I get a feeling of re-
venge. I speak to her in my mind as I lick Lily's body and say, *You
see, Nata, you don't own me after all.*

I am with Lily when Natasha thinks I am writing. This is why she
doesn't call or come looking for me. She wants me to be produc-
tive. I don't even have to convince her to give me the time and

space. She read some pages I wrote a long time ago even though I said they were new. She thinks I'm talented. She believes I can be a great writer. I told her the novel I am writing is about love and mystery and the agony of existence. In my mind, my book is all these things but the truth is I haven't written more than a few sentences. Natasha says it will be the greatest novel ever written. She says they will publish it everywhere and I will be invited around the world to talk about it and be given medals and honors and will meet important people who will think me brilliant. I have already told her I love her so I know she thinks she will be coming with me on all these journeys.

Natasha has no money for books but she is friends with all the dealers at the Plaza de Armas who let her borrow their used copies for a week or two and then she returns them with a smile and a pastry or a candy or even just a kiss on the cheek. They like Natasha because she will sit for hours with them in the shade of the plaza and talk about Barnet or Padura and tell them the man she loves is also a great writer and one day soon his novel will be the most sought-after title on the island.

Here in La Habana Vieja, with her newly borrowed books tucked into her bag, Natasha is tough, confident of her steps, no longer afraid she will twist her ankle. When a shirtless boy of ten or eleven approaches her slowly, eyeing her, then, just as they pass each other on the sidewalk, the boy reaches behind her and slaps her ass with an open palm, Natasha is quicker than he anticipates, grabbing his wrist before he can run off, holding him in place as he kicks and tries to flee, but Natasha slaps him with her free hand, demands to know where his mother is, and vows not to release her grip until the little *cochino* takes Natasha to his *mami* and confesses his crime. Here, Natasha doesn't need me.

Lily doesn't have to work because her husband sends money from Tampa. He works for a moving company and is saving to bring Lily and her daughter over or maybe just enough to come back and live better. Sometimes she gives me a bit of *fula* and I use it to take out Natasha. We go to Coppelia, wait in line for whatever disgusting flavor they have that day. Sometimes we go to a movie at the Yara or to Casa de la Música and Natasha presses close against me in the crowd as we watch a band perform. Then I take her home and while her mother sleeps, Natasha sneaks me into her room. She always pretends she's making a great sacrifice by taking me to bed, like she's a saint and I'm a devil, not like she's enjoying it though she doesn't hide her faces or conceal her moans. But she makes me work for it every time. Not like Lily who never wears underwear, who doesn't have to be convinced of anything.

"When are you going to let me read your book?" Natasha asks every now and then when we're in bed together. It's enough to make me want to get up and leave.

"You know I'm a perfectionist. I don't want anyone to see it until it's ready."

Her friend, who works at a *papelería,* stole some notebooks for me because Natasha asked her to. I don't have a computer. Not even a typewriter. I had one but the ink ribbon ran out and I can't find replacements anywhere. I write in notebooks. Natasha thinks I have dozens full of my writing but it's more like three or four. In my mind I see stories I want to write, I hear the sentences, see each phrase come together like pearls on a string, but when it comes time to write them they evaporate and I'm left in the four corners of my room, my mother working on some fat, naked body under a towel, or I'm in Lily's apartment, her daughter talking to one of the dolls her father sent from Florida; Lily, cooking a meal, humming some old tune, smelling of me under her clothes. If I were a better writer, a *real* writer, I would know how to make Natasha or Lily my muse. But I can't even do that.

Natasha's mother is small and fat in the way of most mothers around here. My own mother has stayed thin by kneading people's bodies all day and my father hates this because he says people think he can't afford to feed her, which is mostly true. He earns too little. It's Mamá's job that lets us eat beyond the Libreta de Abastecimiento, buy imported food at the markets, African fish and Chinese chicken. Natasha's mother is shaped like a *frijol,* with curly hair dyed tomato red, a woman who looks like a meal.

She tells Natasha not to read so much. She tells her that instead of babysitting, she should work on stealing one of the husbands who employ her so that she can blackmail him into sending her away to Miami or Madrid. Natasha can't help confessing these things to me. In the beginning, I could hardly get her to speak, but now I can't keep her quiet. She wants me to know all her secrets. I hush her with kisses, try to silence her with caresses, opening her legs, letting her feel me, but she wants to talk, every time. I tell her I love her, but that sometimes only fills her with suspicion.

"How can you love me when there's still so much you don't know about me?"

"We don't need to know everything about each other, Nata. I love the you I know."

This is the wrong thing to say.

"What do you mean there are things we don't know about each other?"

Nata thinks herself too intellectual to be jealous so I know she won't allow herself to ask me about other women since I've given her no evidence.

"We have our whole lives to discover each other," I say. "But we only have an hour until your mother gets home from work."

Natasha's mother thinks I'm too poor for her daughter. But she likes that I come off as ambitious. Writers and artists and musicians can do well for themselves in this country if they make a name abroad. That's what Natasha tells her mother. I'm going to be famous and Nata is going to be my pillar and raise our children. Just as soon as I finish my novel we will get married, she tells her mother. That line came from me.

Once my mother said, "I don't think I approve of you having two girlfriends like you do."

"Why not?"

"Infidelity is an antiquated model, Vladi. One shouldn't be so greedy. Just pick one."

"I wouldn't know which one to pick."

"That's easy. Pick the one without the husband."

Later that night, as my mother soaked her tired body in the bath and my father washed the evening's dishes, I asked him if he'd always been faithful to my mother in their thirty years of marriage.

He looked at me as if I'd done something terrible of which I should be very ashamed.

"Never ask a man a question like that."

But later he came around to my corner as I lay on my mattress staring at the ceiling, my notebook beside me, turned to a blank page, and stood over me.

"The answer is yes."

He paused, looked around the room and back at me.

"Do you believe me?"

"I will if you want me to."

"It's the truth."

"Okay, *viejo*. I believe you."

It has been years, but they say the end of the Capitolio restoration is in sight, the National Assembly will soon be able to move in, and for this reason, the Cuban government has decided to buy up the properties of those living around it for the purpose of creating more government office space. This is what the officials said when they came to see Natasha and her mother about being relocated. The compensation would be generous, they said. *Fifty thousand dollars generous.* I couldn't believe it. Until last year, one couldn't even buy or sell their own house, and now the government is playing real estate games? But Abel's family got the same offer, and the other families in the building too.

"Fifty thousand dollars is more than a person can earn in a lifetime in this country," Abel says. "Where do you suppose the government is getting all that money?"

"Who knows? Will you take the offer?"

"We don't have a choice. When the government says you go, you go."

Nobody has figured out Abel is the one who wrote the article for the USB newspaper telling everyone the American prisoner was being held in the back of a green house in Marianao next to Ciudad Libertad, right where Batista himself fled Cuba forever. He got that info from a neighbor who befriended one of the guards who said they were treating the old guy pretty good because he would be the ticket to get the Five Heroes back to the island and that's exactly how it was. Abel scooped everyone.

Natasha's mother cries at the thought of leaving her home. We leave her to her tears and walk down to the Campoamor, where we still like to go to be alone though we're not really alone because of the birds and cats and people who hide away in its mezzanine corners even while blocks of concrete fall off the walls and ceilings.

We sit together near what used to be the stage, where great

performers once sang, where elaborate sets and intricate costumes were worn. Natasha's leg has grown supple and her ankles are almost identical in girth when I measure them with my fingers.

Here in the Campoamor she is again that girl of the ripped sofa, who looks at me as if I pulled her out of darkness. Not the hard-edged girl I see walking on the street when she thinks she's alone and doesn't know I'm watching.

Here in the Campoamor I love only her.

She starts another one of her confessions. How her mother used to scold her for not going out enough, saying she'd never meet a nice man that way, would never get married, and would die alone in that apartment by the theater. Her mother said she had to get out into the world; the man of her dreams wouldn't just show up and knock at her door.

"And look what happened," Natasha says, "Mamá was wrong."

I kiss her. But Natasha has more to say.

"Vladi, what if I didn't have a broken leg the day we met? What if I were paralyzed. Would you still have wanted to get to know me?"

"Of course."

"But what if I couldn't move my body an inch and I couldn't touch you or kiss you or make love to you and I couldn't feel anything. Would you still have fallen for me?"

"Nata . . ."

"Tell me the truth, Vladi. I won't be mad."

"How can I separate your body from your mind and your heart when I love it all, Nata?"

Of course she is unhappy with this answer. She doesn't say so but her brows drop and she stares at the ground.

"You read too many books, Nata. You're always thinking the worst things."

"Maybe you don't read enough. That's why you're always complaining you're blocked."

"I read plenty," I lie. "If I'm blocked it's because I'm stuck on this *maldito* island."

"You would leave me if you had the chance. I know it."

Again, a look of sorrow that makes me want to splash her face with a bucket of water.

"You're the one about to be fifty thousand dollars richer. Maybe you're about to leave me."

I don't really believe this but when Natasha starts the game of punishing me for no reason I can't help but play along.

She smiles, feeling confident once again.

I wonder if it's because she's young that she behaves this way. I wonder if ten years from now, she'll grow into a woman more like Lily.

When we go back to Natasha's place, her mother has calmed, sitting on the sofa. "Come, children," she says when she sees us enter. "Sit with me."

Natasha goes to her side and I sit on a chair across from the two of them. Natasha's mother sighs and tells us she has come to a decision.

"We will accept their money and move when they ask us to," she says. "I will buy another apartment. Smaller. Perhaps further up in the hills, in Nuevo Vedado or La Víbora. I won't spend more than fifteen thousand on it. I have a plan for the rest."

"What plan, Mamá?"

"Ten thousand will get an instant visa to the U.S.," Natasha's mother says. "Twenty thousand will buy two."

"We're leaving?" Natasha asks her mother.

She shakes her head and points to Natasha and me.

"No. You and Vladi are."

It used to be that $10,000 would buy you a spot on a powerboat shuttling across the Florida Straits in the middle of the night. Now ten thousand will cover a visa's full bribe to completion at the U.S. Interests Section. No lines, no endless delays of two or three years and nonsensical denials; instant approval and processing of paperwork. A ticket off this rock called Cuba into the sky and the new unknown.

I explain this to my parents who watch me over their dinner of pork stew. I already ate at Lily's. That she feeds me is the main reason my parents don't give me much grief about seeing her. But tonight I only speak of Natasha and how her mother has offered me a way out of this country on the condition that I marry her daughter. It's not enough for Nata to have a *marido*, even if I promise to be forever faithful. She says her daughter deserves an *esposo*, bound by law and paper.

Natasha thinks our getting married is the easiest part of all this. The difficult thing will be to leave her mother here alone.

"It's not how it used to be," her mother said. "You will be able to come back and visit as much as you want and still have the opportunities that La Yuma offers."

"But why don't you come with us?" Natasha asked her but her mother insisted she's too old to start over.

Then she relented a bit and said, "When you and Vladi have children I will join you over there and help you take care of them."

For my father, there is no question.

"Go, *mi'jo!* What are you waiting for? Another revolution? Go!"

My mother is not so easily convinced. It's from her that I've inherited my skepticism.

"Do you love Natasha?"

"Yes." Tonight I have no doubts.

"Do you love this country?"

"Yes," I say, though of this I am not so sure.

Later, I go back to Lily's and tell her everything. She knows about Natasha. She knows to be discreet. But sometimes in bed I make the mistake of telling Lily I love her and then I regret it even though it's true, for that moment. I don't want to make Lily feel bad. She gives me so much when at times it feels as if Natasha only takes from me.

When Lily and I are in bed it's as if she cares only for my pleasure.

"Lily," I tell her, "you are an amazing woman. Your husband is a lucky man."

"What about your Natasha? Do you fuck her the way you fuck me?"

"She won't let me."

But Lily never asks if I love Natasha. Not even tonight.

"You know if you go over there to La Yuma, you will have to work very hard. My husband tells me all the time how much he has to struggle just to survive. Nothing is free. You have to pay for the roof over your head, every ounce of electricity and water you consume. Every time you flush your toilet. You have to pay for the air you breathe."

"I know what it is to work, Lily."

"You? You've never even had a government job. Do you know what I did before I had my daughter? I cleaned toilets at the Calixto García Hospital. Do you know what happens in hospital bathrooms? The worst kind of waste you can imagine. I cleaned it all with my bare hands because most of the time we were short of gloves. Tell me, what work is it that *you* do?"

"I write."

"You haven't written five pages in the year I've known you."

"It takes some writers a year to write a perfect sentence."

"You can live on your invisible words here, Vladi. Not over there."

I think of Natasha. She once told me her first memory was of her sister dying. Natasha was three and her sister, Yulia, five. Their parents had taken them to a swimming pool near la Marina Hemingway, and within hours Yulia was burning with fever, a raw wound blossoming around a small cut on her elbow. They thought the bacteria would only take her arm but she died her first night in the hospital. They brought Natasha to say goodbye though she was already gone. She remembers the sight of her sister, hard, purple, and swollen. I told this to Lily once and it is the only time I've seen coldness wash over her face, her voice hollow as she said, "Children die all the time, Vladi. It's nothing unusual."

My father had a girlfriend as a teenager, long before he met my mother, the daughter of a once-wealthy family from Camagüey who owned property all over the island, which was seized by the revolution except for one house on the edge of Miramar that the family was permitted to keep and live in. As it was forbidden to have American dollars, the girl's father hid the hundreds of thousands of bills he'd accumulated, lining all the paintings with money, stuffing stacks under floorboards, between walls, burying piles beneath rose beds in the garden.

There was so much money he could not hide it all and the man was so tormented by his fortune, terrified he would be discovered and imprisoned or executed, that one day he took all the dollars and made a pile of them behind the walls of the backyard, careful so nobody would see, and set it ablaze. There, the family watched as their fortune and inheritance burned, leaving nothing but scorched earth and the smell of smoke and ashes, which cleared with the afternoon rain.

"What is the lesson here?" my father asked his son when he finished the story.

I did not have an answer.

Was the lesson that one should not get attached to money or that one should not trust the government?

Was the lesson that if the man had held onto those dollars long enough, there would have been a time when it could have bought freedom for all of his descendants?

"Tell me the lesson, Papá." I wanted to know what I was supposed to learn.

"I don't know, Vladi. You're a smart boy. I was hoping you could tell me."

Sometimes in my notebook I write suicide notes. Not because I want to die but because I think it's an interesting exercise to see what sorts of things I have to say about my life, and also because I want to test myself, to see if I really have to write the last letter of my existence, to whom would I address it: to my parents, to Natasha, or to Lily.

Dear Natasha, You make me fucking crazy. You still hide your body from me when we are naked. You talk and talk and talk. But then you go quiet and I love you more than ever and I want to rip you open like the sofa so I can love every bit of your bones. You are my conscience and this is why I so often want to escape you.

Dear Lily, I remember when you saw me on the sidewalk and asked me to help bring your shopping bags to your apartment. Within minutes you were sucking me off as if you'd been waiting for me all your life. You make it hard to leave you. On the street we are strangers but in your home, you know me best.

Dear Mamá y Papá. You raised me not to want what I don't have. You didn't give me a sibling because it was impractical and this is why I hate practical things. In my corner of our home I found solitude and have learned I never want to be alone but alone is the only way I know how to be.

There are new barricades up around the Campoamor so until it is dismantled by road scavengers, Natasha and I can't get in. On my way to see her, I ask one of the construction crew working on the Capitolio what plans there are for the theater, restoration or demolition, but he doesn't know.

"It's been rotting for over fifty years," he says. "For all we know, it will rot for fifty more."

I stop by Abel's place. He's out of phone cards so he can't refill my minutes. We sit in his room where he shows me on his computer the piece he's working on for this month's contraband USB press, talking about how the government is displacing people yet again, not to make room for ministries and offices, like they say, but to sell entire buildings to foreign companies for luxury hotels and condominiums.

"You think that's what's really happening?" I ask.

"There are always money motives behind the official story," Abel says.

He's been telling me for a while about all the foreign investors and enterprises coming to the island, looking to get a claw in before anyone else; technology executives, car manufacturers, even the exiled rum heirs trying to get back in the Cuba-future game, and compensated for what was taken from them so long ago.

"What is your family going to do with the money?"

"My parents are going to buy a place in Playa. They want to get away from the noise of the city. My sister is going to live with her boyfriend. I might find an apartment of my own around here if I can. What about Natasha and her mother? What will they do?"

"They don't know yet," I say, because Natasha's mother has sworn us to secrecy. She doesn't want others to get the same idea and start a situation where you have to pay a bribe just to pay another a bribe.

When I go to her apartment Natasha is waiting for me, the door wide open. She sits on the sofa and I sit close to her, ease her horizontal so that we are two long bodies locked together by ankles and elbows.

Her mother has made the appointment for each of us. The first $500 went to getting us scheduled for the same day with the same employee.

But before that, another appointment. The filing of papers for a civil marriage. Natasha says it's not a real wedding. It's just a legal decision.

"So we won't really be married?"

"We will be, but not in the eyes of God."

"Since when do you believe in God?"

"Since we decided to get married. A civil wedding is bad luck. We need to have another wedding in a church. We can do it in Miami. With a party and everything."

"We won't have any friends to invite. We don't know anybody over there."

"Ay, Vladi," she says, and turns her body over so that we are nose to nose.

When we arrive in Florida, Natasha's mother's second cousin, whom she's never met, will meet us at the airport and let us live in a room he made out of the garage until we get organized and find our own place. Since I've known her, I've told Natasha I know how to speak a little English. When we get to the United States she will see I've been lying.

She says the first thing we will buy when we have enough money is a computer for me so I can transfer all my notebooks to a hard drive and finish my novel. A big American publisher will distribute it. It will tell the truth about *everything*, she says. I don't know where she gets these ideas, this certainty.

Before I came here to be with Natasha, I was with Lily. We were naked on her bed, the metal fan in the corner of the room blowing hard over our sweaty bodies.

"If I didn't have a husband, maybe we could be something, Vladi."

"Maybe."

"When it's time for you to leave, don't say goodbye."

"I won't."

We took a shower together before I left her and sometimes I wonder how it is that if Natasha knows me as well as she thinks she does, she can't sense Lily on me, read on my face that I've made love all afternoon the way I read it on hers after we're together.

Natasha, I think. Who are you? Who am I? Who are we really?

But then it's as if she feels my distance and it's Natasha who begins to strip me, pulling me on top of her and I ease into her, support my arms on the wooden edges of the torn sofa where I fell in love with her, my eyes fixed on the black orb of the Capitolio cupola blocking the sunset just beyond the window, and next to it, the Campoamor, its clandestine residents and starving animals receding into a pond of gray and blue shadows.

DANIELLE EVANS

Richard of York
Gave Battle in Vain

FROM *American Short Fiction*

TWO BY TWO the animals boarded, and then all of the rest of
them in the world died, but no one ever tells the story that way.
Forty days and forty nights of being locked up helpless, knowing
everything you'd ever known was drowning all around you, and
at the end God shows up with a whimsical promise that he will
not destroy the world again *with water,* which seems like a hell of
a caveat.

Dori must find something reassuring in the story. Dori is a pre-
school teacher and a pastor's daughter, and she has found a way to
carry the theme of the ark and the rainbow sign across the entire
three days of her wedding, which began tonight with a welcome
dinner and ends Sunday afternoon with brunch and a church service where, according to the program, her father will give a sermon
titled "God's Rainbow Sign for You." The bridesmaids' dresses are
rainbow, not individually multicolored, but ROY-G-BIV-ordered,
and each bridesmaid appears to have been mandated to wear her
assigned color all weekend; the red bridesmaid, for example, wore
a red T-shirt to the airport, a red cocktail dress to dinner, and now
red stilettos and a red sash reading BRIDESMAID for the bachelorette party. When assembled in a group, Dori's bridesmaids look
like a team of bridal Power Rangers.

Rena is not a bridesmaid but has been dragged along for the
festivities thanks to the aggressive hospitality of the bridal party.
She has worn black to avoid stepping on anyone's color-assigned

toes, and Dori, of course, has worn white, and so all night Rena has been waiting to judge Dori for the look on her face when someone spots the two of them and the rainbow bridal party and takes them for brides-to-be, but so far they have only been to bars where the bartenders greet everyone but Rena and the green bridesmaid, the other out-of-towner, by name.

There is a groom involved in this wedding, though Rena believes his involvement must be loose; she can't imagine JT is on board with this ark business. Rena has known JT for five years. When they met, most of what they had in common was that they were Americans, but far away from home, that could be enough. JT was on his way back to the States after a Peace Corps tour in Togo; she was on her way back from Burkina Faso. The first leg of their flight home was supposed to take them to Paris, but it had been diverted, and then returned to Ghana, after the airline received a call claiming that an agent of biological warfare had been released on the plane. They landed to chaos; no one charged with telling them what happened next seemed sure what information was credible or who had the authority to release it. The Ghanaian authorities had placed them under a quarantine that was strictly outlined but loosely enforced. Had the threat been legitimate, it would have gifted the planet to whatever came after humans. Instead, they'd been stuck on the grounded plane for the better part of a day, then shuttled off for a stressful week at a small hotel surrounded by armed guards, something, JT pointed out, a lot of tourists pay top dollar for.

As two of the three Americans on the flight, JT and Rena found each other. The third American was a journalist of some renown, and so even after the immediate danger was contained, the story of their detention was covered out of proportion to its relevance. Reuters picked up none of the refugee camp photos Rena spent months arranging into a photo essay but did pick up a photo she'd taken of JT in his hotel room. His face was scruffy from several days without shaving and marked with an expression that was part fatigue, part cockiness, just a hint of his upper lip peeking from atop the loosely secured paper mask he'd been assigned to wear. It ran a few months later on the cover of the *Times* magazine, with the text overlay reading *It's a Small World After All: America in the Age of Global Threat.*

In December's deluge of instant nostalgia, the photo made more than one best-of-the-year list. Rena had not lacked for freelance jobs since its publication. Aesthetically, it was not her best work, but JT, handsome, tanned, and blond, was what the public wanted as a symbol of the boy-next-door on the other side of the world. Boy-next-door, Rena knew, always meant white boy next door. When there is one natural blond family left in America they will be trotted out to play every single role that calls for someone all-American, to be interviewed in every time of crisis. They will be exhausted.

Rena was present in the photo, right at the edge, a shimmery and distorted sliver of herself in the mirror. Most people didn't notice her at all. One blogger who did misidentified her as hotel staff. In her line of work, it was sometimes helpful not to be immediately identified as an American, to be, in name and appearance, ethnically ambiguous, although her actual background—black and Polish and Lebanese—was alchemy it had taken the country of her birth to make happen.

It was clear to Rena by the second day of their detention that nobody was dying. Dori phoned daily but stopped worrying about JT's physical well-being somewhere around day four, at which point she took a sharp interest in Rena. JT as JT had talked at length about life as an expat, mostly his life as an expat, but JT as Dori's ventriloquist dummy wanted to know about Rena's childhood, her future travel plans, her dating life. In some ways, Rena has Dori to thank for the fact that she and JT became close enough to sustain a friendship once the crisis was over. Rena guessed where the questions were coming from and wished that she had something to defuse the situation, to reassure Dori, but then and now, she had nothing. She had built the kind of life that belonged to her and her alone, one she could pick up and take with her as needed, and so there she was in JT's tiny hotel room, unattached and untethered and unbothered. To a girlfriend on a different continent, she might as well have been doing the dance of the seven red flags.

Dori is simple but she is not stupid, and since arriving in town for the wedding, Rena has wanted simply to level with her, but Dori will not give her the chance. Dori greeted her warmly and apologized extravagantly for JT's failure to ask her to take the wedding photos; Rena can't tell if Dori is being passive-aggressive or really doesn't know the difference between wedding photography and photojournalism. Dori has left aggressive-aggressive to the yellow bridesmaid, who materializes to interrupt every time Rena finds herself in private conversation with JT. Dori has negotiated her anxiety with perfect composure, but Dori has not womaned up and simply said to Rena did you ever fuck my fiancé, in which case Rena would have told her no.

What had actually happened was that Rena and JT spent most of the hotel days playing a game called Worst Proverb, though they could never agree on the exact terms, and so neither of them ever won. JT believed the point of the game was to come up with the worst-case scenario for following proverbial advice. Over the course of the week, he offered a dozen different hypotheticals in which *you only regret the things you don't do* and *if at first you don't succeed, try, try again* came to a spectacularly bad end. Rena thought the point of the game was to identify the proverb that was the worst of all possible proverbs, and make a case for its failure. She'd run through a number of contenders before deciding on *in the land of the blind, the one-eyed man is king*. The land of the blind would be built for the blind; there would be no expectation among its citizens that the world should be other than what it was. In the land of the blind, the one-eyed man would adjust, or otherwise be deemed a lunatic or a heretic. The one-eyed man would spend his life learning to translate what experience was his alone, or else he would learn to shut up about it.

The fourth bar on the bachelorette party tour is dim and smells of ammonia, with a faint aura of gasoline courtesy of the auto shop next door. The bridal party is seated around a wobbly wooden table playing bachelorette bingo, a hot-pink mutant hybrid of bingo and Truth or Dare. The bridesmaid in blue has unclasped her bra and pulled it from under the arm of her tank top. She holds it in the air and strides to deposit it atop the table of a group of strangers at a booth against the far wall. The blue bridesmaid is two squares away from winning this round of bridal bingo, and this is one of the tasks between her and victory. The prize for winning bridal bingo is that the person with the fewest bingo squares x'ed out has to buy the winner's next drink. The winner never actually needs another drink. Rena has bought four winners drinks already tonight, but everyone is being polite about her lack of effort.

Dori is seated across from Rena and is, in infinitesimal increments, sliding her chair closer to the wall behind her, as if she can get close enough to merge with it and become some lovely, blushing painting looking over the spectacle. Dori claims to have been drinking champagne all night, which has required that she bring her own champagne bottle into several bars that don't serve anything but beer and well liquor, but for hours the champagne bottle has been stashed in her oversized purse, and she has been drinking ginger ale out of a champagne flute. When Dori last ordered a round of drinks, Rena heard her at the bar, making sure some of the drinks were straight Coke or tonic water, for friends who were past their limits. Because she is the prettiest of all of her friends, Rena assumed she was the group's ringleader, but now she can see that this is not true. Dori is the caretaker. Dori turns to Rena, keeping one eye on her friend striding across the bar with the dangling lingerie.

"Sorry this is getting a little out of hand. I guess you've seen worse though. JT says you used to photograph strippers?"

Rena imagines Dori imagining her taking seedy headshots. Her photo series had hung for months in an LA museum, and one of the shots had been used as part of a campaign for sex-workers' rights, but Rena isn't sure the clarification will be worth it.

"Kelly used to dance, you know," Dori says. "She was the first adult I ever saw naked."

"Kelly?"

"In the yellow. My cousin's best friend. She used to steal our drill team routines for the club. We used to watch her practice, and sometimes on slow nights she would sneak us in to drink for free."

"I didn't think you were much of a drinker."

"You haven't heard the rumors about pastors' daughters? Thankfully, I'm not much of anything I was at sixteen. Except with JT. I thought we'd be married practically out of high school."

"Why weren't you?"

"He went to college. Then he went to grad school. Then he went to Togo."

"Where were you?"

"Here," Dori says. "Always here."

There is a shrieking and then deep laughter from the other end of the bar. The blue bridesmaid, whose left breast is now dangerously close to escaping her tank top, has been joined by reinforcements, and they are dragging over a man from the table across the bar.

He is muscled and burly, too big to be dragged against his will, but plays at putting up a fight before he falls to his knees in mock submission, then stands and walks toward their table, holding the bra above his head like a trophy belt. He tosses the bra on the table in front of Dori and tips his baseball cap.

"Ma'am," he says to Dori's wide eyes, "excuse my being forward, but I understand it's your bachelorette party, and your friends over here have obliged me to provide you with a dance."

For a moment Rena thinks this might be orchestrated, this man a real entertainer, Dori's friends better at conspiracy than she would have given them credit for, but then the man wobbles as he crouches over Dori, gyrating clumsily while trying to unbutton his own shirt, breathing too close to her face and seeming at any moment like he might lose balance and fall onto her. Dori looks to the bartender for salvation, some sort of regulatory intervention, but the bartender only grins and switches the music playing over the bar loudspeakers to something raunchy and heavy on bass. The bridesmaids begin laughing and pull dollar bills from their purses. Before they close a circle around the table, Rena sees her chance. She is up and out the door before anyone can force her to stay.

It's a short dark walk back to the hotel, where the bar is closed and its lights are off, but someone is sitting at it anyway. Rena starts to walk past him on her way to the elevators but realizes it's one of the groomsmen. Michael from DC. He was on her connecting flight, one of those small regional shuttles sensitive to turbulence. He is tall and sinewy, and before she knew they were heading to the same place, she had watched him with a twinge of pity, folding himself into the too-small place of his plane seat a few rows ahead of hers.

"Early night?" Rena asks as she walks toward him.

"Let me tell you, you haven't lived until you've been to a bachelor party with a pastor present."

"Cake and punch in a church basement?"

"Scotch and cigars in a hotel penthouse. Still boring as all get out. JT and I were roommates in college and he used to tell me he was from the most boring place in the country, but I didn't believe him until now."

"So you thought you'd liven things up by sitting at an empty bar with a flask?"

"You never know when something interesting might happen."

"At least you got to change out of your rainbow color. Or were you guys not assigned colors?"

"We only have to wear them tomorrow."

"Men. Always getting off easy."

"Easy? Do you know how hard it is to find an orange vest?"

"Ooh, you're orange. Have you spent much time with your bridal counterpart?"

"Only met her briefly."

"See if you can get out of her what she did."

"What she did?"

"You have seven color choices, you don't put a redhead in orange unless you're angry at her. Girl is being punished for something. Must be some gossip."

"So far most of the gossip I've heard at this wedding has been about you."

"I only know one person here. Whatever you've heard isn't gossip, it's speculation."

"Fair enough," he says. "You want to finish this upstairs? Less to speculate about."

So, now there will be something to gossip about. Maybe it will put Dori's mind at ease if Rena appears to be taken for the weekend. Michael tastes like gin and breath mints, and he is reaching for the button on her jeans before the door is closed. Rena affixes herself to his neck like she is trying to reach a vein; she is too old to be giving anyone a hickey, she knows, but she is determined right now to leave a mark, to become part of the temporary map of his body, to place herself briefly along his trajectory as something that can be physically noted, along with the smooth and likely professionally maintained ovals of his fingernails, the faint appendectomy scar, the very slight paunch of his unclothed belly. She clasps a fist in his hair, which is thick and full, but they are at that age now, a few years older than the bride and groom, youth waving at them from the border to an unknown territory. Rena can tell that if she saw Michael again in two years, he would be starting to look like a middle-aged man, not unattractive or unpleasant looking, but it has snuck up on her, that time of her life when age-appropriate men remind her of her father, when you go a year without seeing a man and suddenly his hair is thinned in the middle, his beard graying, his body softer. So she is saying yes please to right now, to the pressure of his palm along her arm and his teeth on her earlobe, and she is surprised by how much she means it.

Sleeping in someone else's bed doesn't stop the nightmares. Rena observes this almost empirically—it has been a while since she has spent the night with anyone and a very long while since she slept soundly. It is her job to go to the places where the nightmares are. It is not a job a person takes if full nights of sleep are her priority. Plus, weddings are not easy. Rena has missed a lot of weddings by being strategically or unavoidably out of the country. The only time she was actually in a wedding, she was the maid of honor. It was her little sister Elizabeth's wedding, autumn in Ohio, a small ceremony, a marriage to a man both of them had grown up with, Connor from the house around the corner. Connor who used to mow their lawn and rake their leaves and shovel their snow. Rena's dress was gold. Her mother worried about the amount of cleavage and her grandmother said *her baby sister's getting married before her, let her flash whatever she needs to catch up.* For a week before the wedding, her sister had been terrified of rain, and Rena had lied about the weather report to comfort her, and the weather turned out to be beautiful, and her sister turned out to be beautiful, and Connor turned out to be the man who, a year later, suspected Elizabeth of cheating because he'd seen a repairman leave the house and she'd forgotten to tell him anyone was coming that day, and so he put a bullet through her head. She lived. Or someone lived: it was hard to match the person in the rehab facility with the person her sister had been.

Rena has not been to visit Elizabeth in three years. Her mother says Elizabeth is making small progress toward language. She can nod her head yes. She can recognize again the names of colors. Rena's sister was a middle-school drama teacher, a job she had chosen because pursuing a theater career would have taken her too far away. When Elizabeth was in college, Rena had come to see her in *Antigone* on opening night, and though the show was not only in English but staged, at the director's whim, to involve contemporary sets and clothing and a backing soundtrack of Top 40 pop, Elizabeth told her afterward that she had memorized the

play both in English and in its original ancient Greek, which she
had taken classes in to better get a feel for drama.

There had been signs. Rena had been too far away to see them,
her parents maybe too close. Connor had threatened her before,
but her sister did not say she was afraid of Connor. The whole week
of the wedding, her sister said she was afraid of rain. All of her
adult life people have asked Rena why she goes to such dangerous
places, and she has always wanted to ask them where the safe place
is. The danger is in chemicals and airports and refugee camps and
war zones and regions known for sex tourism. The danger also
sometimes took their trash out for them. The danger came over
for movie night and bought them a popcorn maker for Christmas.
The danger hugged her mother and shook her father's hand.

That Rena wakes up screaming sometimes is something JT knows
about her, the way she knows that he is an insomniac and on bad
nights can sleep only to Mingus. There was a point at the hotel
when they stopped sleeping in their own rooms and then when
they stopped sleeping in their own beds, and even now she cannot
say whether what they wanted was the comfort of another body
in their respective restlessness or the excuse to cross a line, only
that they never did cross it, and that tonight, before JT's wedding,
she does not want to wake to a strange man holding her while she
cries. It is 4 a.m. according to the hotel clock. She dresses in the
bathroom and leaves, closing the door quietly behind her. Her
room is one floor down and she is ready to pass the elevator and
head for the staircase when she sees JT in the hallway. All week
he has been put together—clean-shaven, with his hair gelled and
slicked into place—but the JT she sees now looks more like the
man she met, like he has just rolled out of bed. He seems as surprised by her as she is by him, and his face relaxes for a moment
as he grins at her and raises an eyebrow.

"Where are you coming from?" he asks.

"Where are you going?" she asks. She is fully awake now and
taking in the scene. It is four in the morning. There is a wedding
today. The groom is standing at the elevator with a duffel bag.
Something has gone wrong.

"I can't do this," he says.

Rena thinks of Dori, surely sound asleep by now, Dori with two
years of wedding Pinterest boards, Dori almost certainly rescuing

herself from the sweaty machinations of the would-be stripper and then making her friends feel better about having upset her.

"You can't just leave," Rena says. "You have to tell her yourself."

"I'm going to call her," he says. "I'm going out of town for a little bit."

Rena moves herself between JT and the elevator to look him in the eyes. He does not seem or smell drunk, only sad, and that he should be sad, that he should treat this decision as a thing that is happening to him, enrages her to the point that it surprises her. She speaks to him in a fierce whisper.

"When I met you we were trapped across the world, and you told me you were calm because you'd learned not to take for granted that anything was safe. You don't get to be scared of a woman you've been with since you were teenagers."

"I was scared," he says. "You were calm. You were so fucking calm, and that was what I liked about you. For a while I thought you were so brave, and sometimes I still do, and sometimes I think it's just that there's nothing in your life but you, and you have no idea what it means to be scared that what you do might matter."

Rena flinches. She imagines slapping him, first imagines slapping the him inches from her face and then closes her eyes and imagines slapping the him from the photograph, slapping the useless mask right off of him. He wants this fight. People would come out of their rooms to see her shouting in the hallway, see a parting quarrel between old friends or old lovers or JT and a woman nursing an old wound. Excuses would be formulated; they would all calmly and quietly go back to sleep. JT is giving her a reason to give him a reason to stay. Rena does not stop him. She walks past him to the staircase and hears the elevator ding before the door closes behind her. The window in her room faces the parking lot, and she sees JT cross through the lot under the flush of the lights and disappear into his car. She sees the car flicker to life before he drives off, and she watches for quite some time but he does not come back.

Rena falls asleep with the curtains still open, and in the morning the sun through the windows is dusty and insistent as the banging at the door wakes her. Her body, groggy from sex and drinking, is temporarily uncooperative, but the noise continues until she is able to rally herself to open it for Dori and Kelly the Yellow Bridesmaid.

"JT is gone," says Kelly.

Rena lets the other women in and pretends not to notice them scanning the room for any indication of her duplicity. She reminds herself that she is unhappy with JT and that this is not her fight.

"I ran into him in the hallway last night," Rena says. "I didn't think he would really go through with leaving."

"Did he say where he was going?" Dori asks.

"That seems like the wrong question."

"To you, maybe."

"Ohio," says Rena. The word has rounded its way out of her mouth before she has time to consider why she is saying it. But now that she has said it she keeps going. She invents an overseas friend with an empty cabin, a conversation about JT's need to get his head together.

"Okay," says Dori. "Okay."

She sends Kelly downstairs to stall the guests and gives Rena fifteen minutes to get dressed.

The address Rena has given is a three-hour drive from where they are in Indiana, mostly highway. Dori buckles herself into the driver's seat, still, Rena notices belatedly, in her pre-wedding clothes —white leggings, a pale pink zip-up hoodie, and a white T-shirt bedazzled with the word BRIDE.

"I really am sorry," Rena says.

"You didn't tell him to leave, right?"

This is true, so Rena lets it sit. She is quiet until Billie Holiday's voice from the car radio becomes unbearable.

"What do you want?" Rena asks.

"From you?"

"From life."

"Right now I want to go find my fiancé before we lose the whole wedding day."

"Right."

At a traffic light, Rena's phone dings and Dori reaches for it with a speed that could be habit but Rena recognizes as distrust. The text, of course, is not from JT.

"Michael?" Dori says. "Michael, really?"

Rena grabs the phone back: *Hey*, says the text. *You didn't have to take off last night.*

Dori's relief at knowing where Rena spent the night is palpable. She turns to Rena with the closest approximation of a smile it seems possible for her to manage at the moment and asks, "So what was it like?" Rena understands her prying as a kind of apology. They are going to be friends now; they are going to seal it with intimate detail the way schoolgirls would seal a blood sisterhood with a needle and a solemn touch.

"It was fine," Rena says. "Kind of grabby and over pretty quick. We were both a little drunk."

"I had to teach JT. It took a few years."

"Years?"

"God, I did a lot of faking it."

"Maybe it wouldn't have taken as long if you hadn't faked it?"

"That, darling, is why you're single. If I hadn't faked it, he would have moved on to a girl who did."

"So she could have waited a decade for him to not marry her on their wedding day?"

They are at the turnoff for the highway, and Dori takes the right with such violent determination that Rena grips the door handle.

"My wedding day's not over yet. We could have JT back in time to marry me and get you and Michael to the open bar."

"There's an open bar?"

"We're religious. We're not cheap. Besides, my mother always says a wedding is not a success if it doesn't inspire another wedding. There's a bouquet with your name on it. Cut Michael off of the gin early and teach him what to do with his hands."

Dori is technically correct about the timeline; it is early, the sun still positioning itself to pin them in its full glow. In the flush of the early morning light, Dori looks beatific, a magazine bride come to life. Rena has no idea in which direction JT actually took off, but it is possible that he has turned around, that he will turn around, that their paths will cross, the light hitting Dori in a way that reveals to him exactly how wrong he has been, and Dori will crown Rena this wedding's unlikely guardian angel. Until Toledo, there will still technically be time to get back to the hotel and pull this wedding off, but Rena saw JT's face last night, and if she knows anything by now she knows the look of a man who is done with someone.

As for Michael, it doesn't really matter what she says about him; Dori is spinning the story that ends in happily ever after for everyone, the one where two years from now Rena and Michael are telling their meet-cute story at their own wedding. But Rena can see already everything wrong with that future. As a teenager, she prized her ability to see clearly the way things would end. She thought that if she saw things plainly enough, she could skip deception and disappointment, could love men not for their illusions but for their flaws and be loved for hers in return. She did not understand how to pretend. In her early twenties a series of men one by one held her to their chests and kissed the top of her head if they were gentlemen and palmed her ass if they were not and told her that she deserved better than they could give her. But what did it matter what she deserved, faced with the hilarity of one more person telling her glibly that better was out there when she was begging for mediocrity and couldn't have that?

Rena pressed herself against the emptiness, flirted with cliché: nights fucking strangers against alleyway walls, waking to bruises in places she didn't remember being grabbed. Though it had been almost a year of this by the time her sister was shot, her friends were happy to make retroactive excuses, to save themselves the trouble of an intervention that might only have been an intervention against a person being herself. So, more rough strangers, years she let make her mean. If she was not good enough for the thing other people had, who could be, if she did not deserve love, who should have it, if she could not find in a mirror what was so bad and unlovable in her, she would have to create it. She learned how to press the blade of her heart into the center of someone else's life, to palm a man's crotch under the table while smiling sweetly at his wife, to think, sometimes, concretely and deliberately, of her sister, punished for a thing she hadn't done, while raising an eyebrow in a bar and accepting a drink from a man who didn't bother hiding his ring. All the things she was getting away with! All the people who couldn't see beauty or danger when it was looking right at them, when it had adjusted itself and walked out of their upstairs bathroom after tucking their husband's penis back into his boxers, when it was under the hotel bedcovers while their boyfriend checked in on video chat. It was, if she is honest with herself, only because the circumstances were so strange that she didn't sleep with JT, that she didn't, one of those nights they

woke up together, look him in the eyes and part her lips and trail
her fingers down his bare chest and wait for what came next. It
hadn't been knowing Dori existed that kept her from it.

Rena thought for years that the meanness in her would be hers
forever, except first, the hard mean thing about her started to
sparkle; she began to advertise trouble in a way that made her the
kind of woman friends did not leave alone with their boyfriends.
Then, the rage she'd spent a decade fucking to a point softened
into a kind of compassion. Men seemed more fragile to her now,
and because it was impossible to entirely hate something for being broken, she forgave even those men who'd left her teary-eyed
and begging for their damage. No wonder they had sent her off
—who wants to be loved for the hole in their chest when there is
a woman somewhere willing to lie and say she can fix it, another
prepared to spend decades pretending it isn't there? She was, she
wanted to tell everybody, so full of forgiveness lately, for herself
and for everyone else. Her heart, these days, was a mewling kitten,
apt to run off after anyone who would feed it, but try telling that
to anyone who had known her the last decade, to anyone who had
lived through all of her tiger years and wouldn't hold a palm out
to her without wanting the chance to be destroyed. It was a lovely
daydream Dori was having for her, but if Rena went to Michael's
door speaking of her kitten heart, he would only hear kitten, he
would only think pussy.

The awkward conversation fades into the comfort of nineties pop
—God bless XM radio, the mercy of Dori changing the station before Billie broke open what was left of their hearts. Songs they
have forgotten but now remember loving keep them company as
they press through the landscape of rest stops and coffee shops
and chain restaurants, slightly above the speed limit, so that things
look even more alike than they might otherwise. By a little after
ten they are at the edge of Indiana and Dori needs to pee, so they
pull over at a rest stop off the turnpike. Rena follows her into the
travel plaza to buy a bottled water and a packet of ibuprofen, her
mouth still dry and her head faintly pulsing. The warm smell of
grease activates her hangover, and by the time Dori exits the ladies' room, Rena is grabbing breakfast at the McDonald's counter.
There must be some law that any chain in an airport or rest

stop is required to be just slightly off-brand: Rena's hash brown tastes congealed and suspiciously like grape soda, and her breakfast sandwich is dry and slightly oblong. Dori has a Coke and a sad parfait, which is so sad that she has downed the Coke before making it more than a few spoonfuls into breakfast. When she gets up to refill the soda, she walks by a man a few tables away, hunched over his own pitiful breakfast, the bottom of his gray beard dotted with a drip of coffee he doesn't seem to have noticed. His face breaks into a full smile as Dori walks by, and on her way back he calls, "Who's the lucky man?"

Dori freezes. For a moment her grip on the soda is so shaky it seems clear that she will drop it, that she will stain the offending bride T-shirt beyond wearability, which will at least solve the problem of future commentary. But she keeps the soda in hand and composes herself as she turns back to the man with the beard, who has dabbed off the coffee with a napkin while waiting for her reply.

"All of Toledo," she says with a smile.

"Huh?"

"Bride's our band name. I'm the drummer. Show tonight."

"Yeah?" he says. His smile is still just as affable and natural; it is not the wedding that excited him but the chance to congratulate a stranger's happiness, and this endears him to Rena. She walks over to join the conversation Dori and the stranger have started regarding their imaginary band. He was in a band in college. The band was called Cold Supper. His name, fittingly, is Ernest.

"We never made it so far as the tour part," Ernest says. "Got out of the garage at least, played a few local shows. But never the road."

"Believe me, the glamour of the road life doesn't stop," says Rena, holding up the soggy second half of her sandwich.

Ernest smiles and pulls out a phone to show them a picture one of his old bandmates posted a few months earlier. A younger, skinny and long-haired version of himself plays the guitar. He has not played in years, ten or fifteen, but he has a lucky pick in his wallet, which he shows them too. It is smooth to the touch and dips in where his thumb has pressed against it and has faded to the yellow of a smoker's teeth. Ernest insists on an autograph on the way out, promises to tell his niece in Toledo about their made-up show in a made-up bar, and so they provide him the autograph on a paper napkin, renaming themselves Glory and Tina. He waves them good luck on their way out. Rena flushes with shame. Ernest and his earnestness, his guitar pick, his poor niece in Toledo.

In the car Rena can't bring herself to close her door or click her seat belt, even as Dori starts the car and the bells ding.

"I have to tell you something," she says. "I have no idea where JT went. I made the cabin thing up."

Dori is still flushed with guilt and exhilaration from the life they made up inside. It takes a minute for her face to catch up with her feeling, for her eyes to start and her delicate features to scrunch together.

"You made it up?" she says. "What the hell address did you give me?"

"My sister's old house."

"Who lives there now?"

"Some people who sued their realtor because they didn't know when they bought the place that someone was shot there."

"Who was shot there?"

"My sister. By her husband. Two days before her first wedding anniversary. She's alive. She can't talk. Or maybe she can now. I don't visit."

"So this is your fucked-up cautionary tale? It's a good thing JT left me now because if he hadn't he would shoot me when he got sick of me?"

"I wasn't thinking that. I wasn't thinking anything, and I said the first thing that came to mind."

"The house where your sister got shot was the first thing that came to mind when I asked if you knew where my fiancé was?"

"It's always the first thing that comes to mind," Rena says, and she is too relieved by the honesty to be ashamed.

Dori pulls the car out of the rest stop lot and Rena prepares for the long silence on the way back. Dori will be too proud and polite to say what happened; she will only say they didn't find him. She will send guests home with tulle-wrapped almonds and be front and center at her father's sermon Sunday, by which point Rena will be on a plane home, home being a city she hasn't yet lived in, two weeks in a short-term sublet while she looks for a real rental, her belongings in a pod, making their way across the ocean. But two exits later and many exits too early for that future, Dori gets

off the highway. Rena isn't sure which set of signs they are following until they get there.

Waterworld. As advertised in highway billboards, except the
billboards make it look giant and fluorescent, while in person it
is somewhat sadder, a slide pool one direction, a wave pool in another, and off to the side, vendors and a carnival stage with no
show in progress. It is fifteen dollars to get in, but the real cash
cow is the entryway gift shop, where now that they are here Rena
supposes it would be rude not to buy a bathing suit. Dori buys a
pink suit and a pair of blue Waterworld sweats. She is luminous. It
is the first time all weekend Rena has seen her in real color.

"I'm sorry," Rena says, which she realizes only then that she
didn't say earlier. Dori doesn't answer, and Rena follows her pool-
side, where they lock their phones in electric blue lockers with the
paint scratched and peeling. KING SUM, someone has carved into
theirs, and there is no explanation or response. On the other side
of the lockers, there is a whole tangle of slides, the tallest of which
has a long line, but it is the one Dori wants and so they wait.

In order to go down the slide you must first go up, and halfway
through their waiting they have come to an uncertain staircase,
alarmingly slippery in places, spiraled and winding around a cylin-
der. The higher they go the more Rena feels something like fear.
Once she spent some time in Mexico, in the city where Edward
James built unfinished or intentionally incomplete sculptures in
the middle of a series of waterfalls: stairs leading nowhere, a lack
of clarity about what was nature and what was built, a wildly unsafe
tourist trap. This staircase should feel safer but does not, and by
the time they reach the top Rena is giddy with relief at the thought
of going back down. She seats herself at the start of the slide with
something like genuine joy.

It is a fast ride to the pool below. At the third turn is a water-
proof camera, the kind that projects the photo down to a booth
where the operator will offer to print and frame it and sell it to you
at an outrageous markup. Dori and Rena, riding together, two to a
tube, down through a series of sharp turns, are sprayed with water
that seems to be coming from every direction and then dropped
into the pool, which stings first with impact and again with chlorine. Rena surfaces with an unexpected lightness, which she sees
mirrored in Dori's smile. It occurs to her this might be the least

terrible idea anyone involved in this alleged wedding has had in the last forty-eight hours.

Dori insists on checking out their picture after they towel off, so she heads for the photographer while Rena retrieves their phones.

Rena has three texts from Michael:

Did I do something wrong last night?
Did you kidnap the bride?!
Hey, I don't know what's up, but get your perfect ass back here—there's an open bar waiting for us.

There are five texts from JT:

Where did you guys go?
Why did you think I was in Ohio?
Tell her I'm here
Tell her I'm sorry
Wedding is on! Where are you?

Wedding is on! JT has doubled back after all. He has come back to the place where whatever his decision is, it always stands. When Dori makes her way to the lockers, Rena hands her the phone. For a minute Dori's face is soft. She reaches for her own phone and reads through whatever amended case JT has made for himself there. She tugs on a strand of her wet hair. Then she turns to Rena and shrugs, turns the phone off, and shoves it back into the locker. She holds out to Rena the photo of the two of them. Dori's hair is whipping behind her, her smile open-mouthed and angled away. Rena is behind her, staring at the camera, laughing and startled. Dori has chosen a hideous purple-and-green airbrushed paper frame reading WISH YOU WERE HERE.

"This is going to be hilarious someday," Dori says. "I hope."

Rena stashes her phone in the locker with Dori's. There is still nothing at the carnival stage, and so they share cheese fries and cotton candy and make their way to the wave pool, where they rent inner tubes. Rena floats and thinks of the last time she did this, which must have been twenty years ago, must have been with her family when this was the kind of day trip they would have all found relaxing. When Rena would not have looked at the water and thought of E. coli, of hantavirus, of imminent drought, of a recent news story of a child who drowned in a pool like this because his parents sent him to the water park alone for daycare and no

one there was watching for him. When it was still her job to keep
Elizabeth's swimmies on, when there was still Elizabeth's laugh,
when there were still seas to be crossed, when the whole world was
in front of her. Wish you were here. Wish you were here. Wish you
were here.

Ugly

FROM *Yale Review*

THE COMPANY WAS SENDING me to Monroe for six weeks. Of
course, professionally it was a good thing, a sign of their regard,
their trust, and that was a relief. Because I was always afraid that
one day—and it might be soon—they'd realize that I didn't belong. That my place at Verdance, a company that manufactured
herbal remedies, was really stolen and its relinquishment might
be demanded, and with perfect justice, at any moment. My background was neither in science nor in business. I've never had any
idea whether what they called "the product," or "the products,"
or sometimes, foreswearing articles altogether, "product" really
worked, or if I'm involved in the sale of snake oil. I take on faith
the CFO's assertion that we—by "we" I mean the company of
course—are making a handsome profit.

My background was in literature, and my time spent attending
to niceties of language made me unhappy every time I had to say
the sentence "I work for Verdance in Human Resources." What
was a human resource? I couldn't rid myself of the idea that the
phrase had about it a tincture of slavery. And Verdance . . . a ridiculous name that the founders took a boyish pride in . . . "It's like
Verd . . . from verdure, you know everything green, but we add a
dance to it, so we make our business a dance."

I have left English literature behind me. It's been five years
since I told everyone I was quitting. I stopped just short of finishing my PhD. The problem was my dissertation. I'd set my heart
on a topic but I couldn't find anyone willing to be my adviser. I
wanted to focus on three poems about roses, Thomas Carew's, Ed-

mund Waller's, and William Blake's, using the poems to examine larger questions—questions of time, desire, beauty, death—and see how the image of the rose could illustrate the cultural differences these questions raised.

I was told that my topic was both too small and too large. Three short poems, but three large historical periods. The Renaissance people wouldn't venture into the part of the seventeenth century that moved into the eighteenth, and the Romantics felt they had no access to the earlier periods.

And in the end, after months of fruitless arguing with intransigent professors, I began to feel it wasn't worth it. Where would I end up, if I finished my dissertation? An underpaid peon at a third-rate institution God knew where, fighting with other overqualified, underpaid cohorts for the scraps left on the table of the dying liberal arts? Which, I had begun to fear, would no longer be economically viable at the end of a decade. Fifteen years, I reckoned, at the very best.

I gave it up, with a little sadness, but not without a riven heart. Sometimes, coming in and out of sleep, lines of the poems still come to me. "Ask me no more where Jove bestows / When June is past, the lovely rose . . . Go lovely rose / Tell her that wastes her time and me, / That now she knows, / When I resemble her to thee, / How sweet and fair she seems to be . . . O Rose thou art sick. / The invisible worm, / That flies in the night / In the howling storm."

I began working for Verdance as a "technical writer," translating scientific or New Age scientific jargon into readable prose. But I got bored with that quite early on, and I was glad that they transferred me to Human Resources because I was told I had "really good people skills." What they meant was that I was good at calming some people down and revving others up. That I could settle office conflicts somehow, I don't really know how, better than anyone else in the department, and that when some workers had to be warned that they weren't "quite up to scratch," I seemed to be able to encourage them without making them seem overwhelmed.

They had sent me to Monroe because of what they called a "productivity lag." What they meant, in English, was that the Monroe branch wasn't making as much money as the others, their orders weren't up to the three other locations: Scottsdale, Arizona; Ashland, North Carolina; and what they liked to call "our mother ship," in Danbury, Connecticut, where I worked, commuting every day to my apartment in the city. When I got back from Monroe I'd be moving from the Lower East Side to a place on West End and Eighty-Ninth; it would save me at least forty-five minutes a day in travel. I'd be moving in with Hugh. We were talking seriously about marriage now; we'd been talking about it in a desultory, slackish way for almost two years, the way you might talk about buying a refrigerator with an icemaker in the door, something you'd quite like but didn't really require.

The higher-ups—Jason, Josh, and Jonathan—were reluctant to say what they really believed: that the productivity lag was a result of their generosity, their flexibility, their willingness to allow people long parental leaves and the option of working from home. "The problem is, it's a kind of demographic bottleneck," Jonathan said, or it might have been Jason. "For some reason they all started reproducing at the same time, and so there's just not enough product being handled. We need someone to go out there, not exactly lower the boom, but you know give them kind of a reality check."

"You mean you want me to tell them Santa Claus is dead."

"Something like that," Josh said. He was the one with the sense of humor.

"No, nothing like that," Jonathan said. "It's just . . . we need to readjust."

"In this market, they should be more amenable to adjustments in the workplace," said Jason, who was the most wedded to management jargon.

"It's not going to be nice," I said.

"It would be better if you had kids yourself. I mean, the weird thing is, almost nobody here *has* kids . . . what is it in the Midwest? I guess there's nothing to do in the cold winters but fuck. Haven't they heard of birth control? The only one here with kids is Brianna, and let's face it, that would be a nightmare in the people skills department."

"I could try to reproduce in the next two weeks," I said.

I could see Jonathan looking hopeful for a moment. Then he laughed. "I get it," he said.

"If you can make this happen, there's a big bonus in it for you, Laura," Josh said. "And with the new place you're moving into, I'm sure you can use the extra cash."

I wanted to say no, but I didn't have a leg to stand on. It would only be six weeks. "How big a bonus?" I asked.

"It depends on how successful you are. But let's just say, even if you do a shitty job, you'll be well rewarded."

I'd never been to the Midwest; I was one of those New Yorkers that made a reality of the Steinberg cartoon. The fact is, I'd never wanted to go. And certainly, Monroe wasn't a place that Hugh would ever think of going. I could hardly even believe Missouri was a real place. It was one of those states, like Wyoming, that seemed improbable. I knew it was called the "Show Me State." Its capital was St. Louis. I liked *Meet Me in St Louis*. But I wasn't going anywhere near St. Louis. Monroe was four hours from St. Louis . . . and I was pretty sure I wouldn't get there more than once, if ever.

Hugh didn't want me to go, but the prospect of the bonus pleased him mightily; he really wanted to spend money on good furniture. We spent our evenings trawling sites for contemporary Italian couches, the way some couples might have trawled porn sites looking for some specialty that would appeal to both their appetites—the woman wanting bondage, the man wanting her to dress like a French maid. I admitted that my taste in furniture was far less developed than Hugh's; he is, after all, an architect, and it was a fairly recent thing that I had enough money to even consider anything more demanding than Ikea. I found the things that he particularly admired rather off-putting . . . they didn't seem like they really belonged in a house; I thought they'd be better in a space capsule. One couch that Hugh was particularly taken by—it was by an Italian designer and it cost $8,000—was the color of tomato juice and shaped like some sort of bean, only it didn't look the slightest bit organic. I thought if you opened it up you'd find a surveillance system, microphones, speakers, lots of wires . . . I said I found it slightly inhuman. Hugh pointed to the description in the website that said it was "ironic." When I read it more closely I told him that the word was *iconic,* not *ironic,* and I guess that was why he was willing to give it up. Everything else he liked was so charcoal and black, so low to the ground, that I couldn't imagine taking a nap on it, or—finally the argument that swayed him—making love on it with any kind of confidence. But I promised Hugh that we could use whatever money I made on a bonus to buy some wonderful furniture, something that excited us both.

I might not have had the most cultivated taste in interior design, but the place the company had arranged for me to live, Brook-side Corporate Housing, lowered my spirits dramatically when I opened the door. It was obvious what whoever had designed it had in mind: it was meant to offend no one and to absorb the great-est possible abuse. The linoleum was gray, the living room carpet-ing was gray and smelled of something that was clearly meant to cover something up—and of course I was busily wondering what that something might have been. The couch was upholstered in a gray-blue tweed; the armchairs matched. The coffee table was supposed to look wooden, but it was clearly not made of wood. I remembered something called "particleboard," and I didn't want to imagine what the particles might be.

I spent as little time there as possible. I had breakfast at a café that sold the *New York Times;* if I asked for an extra shot, the cap-puccino was almost up to New York standards. I lingered longer than I should have, because I dreaded going to work every morn-ing. I didn't like the job I'd been sent to do, and I didn't quite know how to do it.

The third morning, after my coffee, I noticed an antiques store next to the café. Wanting to kill time before the inevitable arrival at the office, I stood in front of the window. I wasn't someone who'd spent time in antiques shops, but my eye fell on a vase that stood on a bare wooden table. It was a deep rose color, and its surface was almost iridescent, entirely unornamented; nothing got in the way of its allowance of a play of lights. The shape was classi-cal: almost an urn. It occurred to me that I might feel better about Brookside Corporate Housing if I had one nice thing of my own there. The anonymity of the place was nearly total—except for my clothes and toiletries I'd brought nothing with me, not even books: I'd downloaded everything I wanted to read on my Kindle.

I heard the tinkle of a bell and noticed that the shopkeeper had opened the door. She wasn't a good advertisement for the beautiful things in her window; I try not to judge people on their looks—it's a skill I've cultivated in Human Resources—but I had rarely seen someone who seemed to take so little care with her appearance. I could see right away that nature had not been kind; she had the kind of oily hair that would never look clean, and al-though I guessed she was in her fifties, her face was covered with an acne that would have anguished a teenager. Perhaps it had an-guished her, and she had understood that there was nothing much she could do to make herself look good, and she had given it up. But she could have done something better than the clothes she had selected: orange running shorts, an orange tank top, orange knee socks and sneakers. Whatever her dermatological misfortune was, it affected the skin on her arms and legs, which was mottled and unsmooth.

"Take the plunge, why don't you?" she said. I was surprised at her voice; it was low and velvety and the accent was cultivated, Eastern, upper class.

She stepped into the store to let me in. I followed; how could I not? It would have been horribly rude, and besides, I really was interested in the vase.

Inhibiting my entrance was a large, elderly, and overweight golden retriever; a few feet behind him, making himself comfortable on a ratty-looking divan, was an equally ancient chocolate Lab. I thought it probably wasn't a good marketing ploy; probably people wanting fine things didn't want to be stepping over dogs and knowing they'd have to take a clothes brush to whatever they were wearing after they got back home.

She turned on the lights and I saw that what she had was of a very high quality. There didn't seem to be a pattern to the placement; easy chairs were next to desks and dining tables situated themselves too close to china cabinets. I tried to call up and make sense of some words I had never used but that I thought might be of use here: *hutch, tallboy, armoire, étagère.* The room was large and dim, and the rows of tables receding into the foggy distance gave the impression of a forest just at nightfall; some sense of adventure beckoned, but there could, as well, be the chance of doom.

"I was interested in that pink vase in the window," I said.

"Lusterware," she said. "German immigrants specialized in it. Early twentieth century." She hopped into the window with an agility that surprised me. She put the vase in my hand. I was enchanted by the way the light played differently on the surface indoors.

"Luster," she said. "Isn't it a great word, *luster.*" It's a particular kind of light, not exactly a shine, something slightly thicker.

"It is a wonderful word," I said.

She ran to the computer and typed something out with a remarkable speed, printed it out, and handed the page to me.

Lusterware. *Pottery* or *porcelain* with a *metallic glaze* that gives the effect of *iridescence,* produced by metallic *oxides* in an *overglaze*

finish, which is given a second firing at a lower temperature in a
"muffle kiln," *reduction kiln,* which excludes oxygen.

"How much?" I asked.

"Twenty dollars."

"Are you sure?"

"I'm always sure. It's what I do. It's my business. What's yours?"

I told her part of my reason for being in Monroe. "I live in a
pretty awful place; I just wanted to have one beautiful thing to
look at."

"One beautiful thing," she said. "Everybody should have one
beautiful thing."

I was feeling that I much preferred being with this strange
woman than going to the office.

"Lois," she said. "I'm Lois."

"Laura," I said.

"Laura," she repeated, nodding. "It's a good name. It's a sensible name. So many names now aren't sensible."

"I know what you mean," I said. "I'm so glad I wasn't named
Tiffany or Ashley."

"Or Brittany. Spelt Britni."

I realized that I hadn't laughed since I'd left New York.

"You have wonderful things here," I said.

"Take a look around." The room with its rows of tables seemed
like a forest, this place, the demesne of chairs, seemed like the
overcrowded province of some resentful, fussy aunts. I began to
find it difficult to breathe; I could feel my lungs constricting. And
then, with no notice, my lungs felt rich and light, and a ridiculous
line of poetry came to me. "My heart leaps up when I behold a
rainbow in the sky."

It wasn't, of course, a rainbow. It was a small, graceful chair,
upholstered in a light green. Its arms were curved and elegant,
and I saw that there was a pattern of leaves carved into the wooden
jointure of the back and cushion. So many of the chairs Hugh and
I had looked at were either engulfing or unwelcoming. I was curious to see if this lovely thing was comfortable.

Immediately I knew that I would have to make it mine. It fit me
so well; it was neither too hard nor too soft; I wouldn't fall asleep
when I was reading, but I wouldn't have to shift around to make
myself comfortable. But before that moment, I had had no idea
of buying a chair; I could perfectly well sit in the anonymous but

comfortable furniture in corporate arms, and it would be a problem to move it when I would be leaving in what would be, after all, a matter of weeks.

Lois came into the room and joined me.

"That's a real beauty," she said. "A real beauty. 1870s. Maybe 1880s. I'd be glad if she was yours."

She jumped up and grabbed me by the hand. Hand in hand (her hand, as I imagined, was sweaty and clammy, and I didn't like my proximity to it), but at last she dropped my hand as she made her way to, and I could see her running to, the computer. She typed something out and ran back, the old dog following her more quickly than I thought he could. She handed me what she'd just printed out.

Description

American Victorian Eastlake upholstered cherry armchair. Aesthetic influence, having a padded, arched back flanked by carved, scrolled stiles, supported on a wide rail cut-out with a large carved sunflower nested beneath a serpentine-shaped, scrolled vine terminating with opposing anthemions, fitted with two rail arms, padded between arched ends respectively; embellished with Greek key above a short beehive, turned support and scrolled acanthus, and a trapezoidal padded seat with a teeded front rail supported on blocked double ogee molded legs, fitted with small wooden castors and flared rear legs which are continuous from the stiles.

Dating is from the 1880s to the 1890s. The back and seat are each covered with a pale green damask fabric pattern with a field of small palmate leaves accompanied by scrolled tendrils. The finish is in good overall condition with a warm, dark reddish-brown finish having a few minor scratches, but which is probably original. The upholstery on the seat needs to have the prints retied. Measures 35" tall and 25" across the arms.

"I don't know what your background is, but have you heard of John Ruskin?" Lois said.

"Of course," I said. "I'm a failed English PhD." For some reason, I told her about my dissertation. She didn't seem interested.

"Well the people who made these chairs were American disciples of Ruskin and Morris." They didn't do a lot, but what they did was fine. "She's a real beauty," Lois said. "I'd be happy if she was yours."

"How much?" I asked, my heart beating stupidly fast.

"Three hundred. But we'll have to take it to a friend of mine for a little repair."

"But I'm only here six weeks."

"He'll do whatever I tell him. If we take it over, he'll do it while you wait."

"Okay, Lois, I really love it."

It occurred to me that maybe she wanted me to bargain with her. But I had no impulse. I wanted to take her home. I was already calling it "her." But after all, I knew that She was mine.

"We'll take this other chair with us, it needs to be resprung, and oh God, so much, it needs so much."

I guess I was lonelier than I thought because I accepted her invitation with what I hoped wasn't a too obvious eagerness.

"Help me hump this one into the car," she said, pointing to a chair she'd placed near the door. This one was small—Lois said it was called a slipper chair—perfect for a rather reserved, perhaps easily intimidated wife of a judge or surgeon sometime between 1925 and 1960. The upholstery was a pale pink brocade, but the seat and the back looked like someone had taken a box cutter to them with a particularly brutal hand.

We drove for ten miles or so, and Lois spoke to me as if we had known each other for years, referring to people by their first names only, so I had no idea who she was talking about. I gathered they were relatives, and so I tried to assuage her worries about their health, their financial well-being, their fragile sprits—even though I had no idea of the real circumstances. But she took no comfort from anything I said, rejecting any hopeful note as simply out of the question. When she wasn't speaking, she was whistling through her teeth something that I thought dated from the First World War. "Wait Till the Sun Shines, Nellie," "Daisy Daisy," "Down by the Old Mill Stream."

She drove to the back entrance of a warehouse and beeped her horn in what must have been a coded pattern because in a minute a bald man in overalls with a reddish toothbrush mustache came out of the metal door, accompanied by a springer spaniel.

The dog jumped on Lois, and she bent down so he could lick her face. From the pocket of her shirt she took three small dog biscuits, for which the dog seemed grateful, but not surprised: it was clearly a part of their routine.

"Hey, Rusty," Lois said. I wasn't sure if she was talking to the man or the dog, although the dog was white with tannish spots, so I was betting on the man.

And in fact it was he who responded. "Well aren't you a sight for sore eyes. What have you brought me from your treasure trove?"

She opened the back of the station wagon and lifted the chair into the driveway.

"You just don't understand how people can abuse a lovely thing like this," he said.

"They didn't deserve to have it. Ever. Not for one minute."

I'd heard people speak that way about children or animals that had been badly treated, but I'd never heard the words applied to furniture. I understood, but for Lois and Rusty the chair was, if not a living thing, then something with a life.

She didn't bother to introduce me, and I saw no way to introduce myself, so I just followed behind her, and looked over her shoulder as she and Rusty looked through swatches, bringing a few to the chair then stepping back from it until they finally both agreed on one that was very like the original.

"That's it, that's it," Lois said.

"No question about it. We're on the money this time, girlie," he said.

They high-fived each other. It had been a long time since I'd seen two people so happy.

The place smelled wonderfully of new wood and hot glue and steamy fabric. My eye traveled to the part of the warehouse where people were cutting and sewing and nailing and gluing with the peaceful, rapt expression that comes over someone when he's doing something he knows he's good at, that he believes is of real use.

That night, after Lois had dropped me off and I ate my lentil salad in front of the TV, it occurred to me that neither of them had said a word about money. Not a single word.

No one at the Monroe headquarters of Verdance seemed to have the slightest interest in seeing me outside of work. It wasn't that they weren't friendly; they were excessively friendly. But they probably sensed that my presence there wouldn't be good for any of them, and besides, they all seemed to have small children. Which was the problem, of course, the reason I was there. I understood that they were busy and tired, I understood why none of them had so much as invited me for a coffee. I didn't mind being alone so much, not really; I was enjoying being able to read at night and watch BBC mysteries on my laptop. But I was delighted when Lois called and asked if I'd be interested in a wonderful set of Spode dishes that she needed to get rid of and would give me at "a ridiculous price, just because I like you. And the pattern is called 'old rose' and I remember what you said about that dissertation of yours that you never wrote."

I certainly knew that she was odd, and that the offer for the dishes was odd. I knew it was odd, that everything about it was odd. Why would she think I wanted a set of china? And didn't she know that people didn't just tell people that they liked them, and that they were giving them a good deal because of that? Or if they did say that, that the other person wouldn't believe them, not either part of the sentence, either that the salesperson liked them or that the deal was really good? But there was something uncanny about Lois—she might have been a figure in a children's tale, the trickster, the woman coming from nowhere who knows everything and knows just what everyone should do.

Then I wondered if she knew something about me that I didn't know about myself, that I had always wanted a set of matching china, good china, real china, but had never had access to that particular truth.

She indicated a set of dishes displayed in a glass-fronted cabinet, and once again my heart leapt when I saw them. Roses, the pattern was of roses, vivid, but delicate, strong blossoms, a deep pink, and leaves and stems a clear and lucid green. Roses, what I had wanted to write about, what I had given up. Roses that had been put into poetry so that they would last forever, and now roses would be on my table; I would be eating off roses that, like the roses in the poems, would not die. And I could have them, they would be mine. Immediately, the possibility of a whole new life opened for me. Openhearted Thanksgivings, the grieving newly widowed, bipolars whom nobody was sure when to invite, people from exotic foreign countries who'd never had cranberry sauce. My whole family: all the little fissures healed. They weren't major fissures, not anything moral or political or religious—none of us was particularly political or religious, but we simply had different interests. Or maybe it's better to say we just weren't that interested in one another. My brother and his wife and three children all seemed devoted to, if not based on, computers; my sister had moved to Montana and was raising designer dogs—some mix of poodle and something else not so smart, I can never remember exactly what. I don't even know exactly what my parents are interested in. They watch a lot of television. They go on cruises: my mother keeps saying how she'll never get over the Alaskan landscape, but my father said once was enough for him. "You've seen one moose, you've seen them all," he'd said. I think that hurt her.

But I knew we would all be livelier than ever around the table with my wonderful new dishes. Of course I didn't have a table yet, and I knew this wasn't the kind of pattern Hugh would like, but I could let him buy some kind of postmodern, off-center table and convince him that putting a pattern of rose china on it would be "incredibly ironic."

"Are you sure?" I asked Lois when she offered me the whole set —service for twelve—for $300.

"I wouldn't have made the offer if I weren't sure."

"But how will I get it back to New York?" I asked. Then I remembered somewhat guiltily that Hugh had agreed to drive out and drive me back to New York in a month. I realized how far that thought was from my mind. I tried to make a joke of it, to myself, really more than Lois. "A month seems like a lifetime away," I said.

"So you'll only be with us another month," she said.

I felt ridiculous that those words made me so sad.

"It will take me quite a bit of time to pack these properly," she said. "Can I bring them by your place tomorrow?"

"Lois, you don't have to do that. I'll be glad to come by and get it."

"No biggie," she said. "I want the excuse to visit the chair."

The apartment was so entirely blank, so impervious to improvement, that it was impossible to have the slightest even reflex anxiety about having a guest.

She set the large box down on my counter. She was wearing her usual outfit of running shorts, T-shirt, knee socks, and sneakers. She told me she ran marathons, but it was so incongruous with everything else about her that I couldn't keep the idea in my head. Everything about her suggested the opposite of healthiness, of health.

"Where do you want me to put these?" she asked, her eyes flicking every surface like the eyes on a Felix the Cat clock I'd had as a child.

I pointed to the closet.

"Sit in the chair," I said. "It will be glad to see you."

She rested her hands on her thighs, leaned back, and sighed deeply. She closed her eyes.

"I feel so bad for you," she said.

I couldn't think of any reason for her to feel bad for me. I hadn't told her anything about my life, and besides, I had been unusually unmarked by tragedy.

"Life's been good to me, Lois," I said.

"That's as may be," she said. "It's as may be. But I know about you: you care for the look of a thing. And this place is, well, it must be terrible. So unlovely. No one who had anything to do with this place cared for the look of a thing. It must be terrible."

"Well Lois, I'm only here for another month."

"But a month of living among unlovely things is like a month of bad food. You're being poisoned. Seriously poisoned. Thank God you have the chair. When you look at it, well, it's like drinking spring water after you've had nothing but junk food."

I didn't know what to say. I felt exposed, and simultaneously understood; at once violated and protected.

"Would you like to move into the basement apartment I own? I sometimes rent it out. It's downstairs from where I live. Just one big room. A studio. On the lake."

"Oh, Lois, really it's too much trouble. Only a few more weeks."

"Four weeks of poison. Is that something you want to do to yourself?"

"The company's already paid for this," I said.

"I wouldn't charge you," she said. "I'm going to use it for storage from now on anyway, I'm sick of dealing with tenants. I'd be happy for you and your chair to move in."

"But I don't have any furniture," I said.

"Jeez Louise, what business do you think I'm in?"

"May I think about it Lois?" I said. "Just for a day or two."

She stood up and slapped her hands on her thighs. She looked at me with a curious patience, and I felt the possibility of a large leisure in which to make my choices.

But in the morning after I woke up and sat on the scratchy

tweed couch looking at the parking lot and counting the dents in the wall-to-wall carpeting, I knew that I'd made up my mind.

We agreed to meet at the house after I was through with work and she'd closed the shop. I could see the lake after I'd turned off the main commercial street, which was clearly trying to revivify itself by attracting a new, younger clientele: there was a bicycle shop, a yoga studio, a Thai restaurant. Next to the Thai restaurant I was happy to see a plumbing supply store, huge, the size of a fire-house, plain, responsible, like a slightly unimaginative bachelor uncle who had never moved away.

From the outside, the house was undistinguished: two stories, white stucco, small, serious-looking windows trimmed in serious black. I walked down a small flagstone path to the front door; on that side of the house, the house facing the lake, the windows were larger and untrimmed.

Lois came to the door. Her hair was wet from the shower, but it still looked greasy, and her skin was more mottled than usual, probably because of the water's heat. She was wearing her usual shorts, T-shirt, and knee socks. This time they were lime green. "This is it," she said, and showed me into a room that was almost breathtaking in its plainness. The walls were white, the floors slate-gray, the cabinets were a plain light pine, the countertop and the three stools beside it matched its wood.

I was simultaneously alarmed and thrilled by the emptiness. I wanted some time to understand what I was feeling so I turned my back on Lois, and focused on the view of the lake.

I had never thought much about lakes. I'm a born and bred New Yorker, you remember, and when people like me thought about a body of water it was only the ocean. You could even take a subway to it. But lakes—they were irrelevant. Maybe they had something to do with motorboats or water skiing, the kind of thing done by people you would never know.

The lake was so close to the door of the apartment that it could have been its front lawn. There were ten paces' worth of grass and there it was. Even closer than a lawn, it spread itself like a lap, and as I thought of the word *lap,* meaning something to sit on, to be comforted by, and a gentle sound of water, I felt immediately comforted and accommodated, and I knew that I would stay.

"I'll just bring a few things from the shop for you," Lois said. "It will be all ready for you to move in tomorrow at this time."

She was, as she said, in the furniture business, but the way she "furnished" my apartment was simply perfect. She provided only what I absolutely needed: a simple platform bed whose wood matched the cabinets and counter, a plain pine table with apple-green legs, and a chair of matching apple green. At the center of the empty space, which because of its very emptiness served as an almost theatrical backdrop, we placed my chair, just the right distance from the window so that I could sit, surrounded by nothing, and look at the lake.

Sitting in my chair and looking at the lake became the most important thing in my life. The house faced east, so I didn't get to see sunsets, only sunrises, which might have been disappointing, but it wasn't. Like the dishes Lois had sold me, getting up to see the sunrise suggested to me the real, the very real, possibility of an entirely new way of living. I never let myself say a new way of life.

I would wake early, sometimes as early as five, and sit by the window. I watched for the last star . . . the morning star; I watched the moon disappear, and the sky gradually lighten. What I liked best were the moments before the sun was actually visible: the dimness, gradually taking on color, as if it were some porous paper drinking color in: first silver, then gray-blue, then the dramatic pink and yellow. When the full sun struck the lake, it was almost disappointing: a diva showing off, silencing the gentle chorus.

Twice, Lois invited me to the movies to the "film society," where classic films were shown to an audience of which I was the youngest by at least thirty years. We saw *Jules and Jim, The Bicycle Thief,* and *Strangers on a Train.* We ate at a pub near the film society; Lois always ordered a hamburger, but left three-quarters of it behind, and nibbled only three or four of her fries. The hamburger always came with lettuce, tomato, and onion, and she always removed it and put it on her plate. I wondered why she didn't tell the waiter to hold the lettuce and tomato, but I didn't like to ask.

And five or six times, I realize now, I stopped by Rusty's shop. It was open till nine. He had said to come any time, and I took him at his word. I'd just drop in, bringing sweets or cheese and crackers, and everyone seemed glad to see me, no one suggested it was odd. It was soothing to be there, with the good smells, and the serene industriousness, and NPR playing in the background, and the dog—whose name I never learned—moving from one warm spot to another, circling to find the perfect spot for his latest naps. I thought that what they were doing was a wonderful way to make a living, and the words *make a living* seemed more literal than metaphoric. The words that came to me were *innocent, beneficent,* and I was pleased at the slant rhyme—an atavistic pleasure, but I welcomed the old taste. After a while, I realized that I'd begun fantasizing about apprenticing myself to Rusty, calculating how long I could live on my savings before I needed to earn money again. I knew that was ridiculous, and I banished the thought whenever it rose up.

I was proud of the way I was living. Having so few objects around me, I became newly interested in the desire to live modestly, which I think also had something to do with the lake, so modest in its largely uninterrupted wideness. The rare swell, the occasional constellation of waterfowl, but mostly just the expanse of calm, even water. A meadow of water, where all creatures might safely graze.

I cooked for myself every night; sometimes I'd make a big soup and have it for a first course several evenings in a row. I spent time at the farmer's market that had just opened for the season, and I bought early asparagus and tender spring onions, and waxy new potatoes; I splurged on artichokes, which I cooked simply, steaming them with just a spoonful of oil and a little salt. I downloaded three versions of the Bach Cello Suites: Casals, Rostropovich, Yo-Yo Ma, and I played them over and over trying to hear the differences; after a while I told myself I could. It made me very happy to listen to classical music on the local NPR on my way to and from work; I called and made a one-time donation; I even believed them when they said it was "awesome." They asked if I would like to make an ongoing contribution; I said I would be leaving the area soon, and saying that, I felt quite sad. One morning I read the label on a container of cut-up cantaloupe I'd bought at the supermarket. *Living up to your life,* it said, and with a deep quiet pleasure I told myself I was doing just that.

I was almost embarrassed at my clichéd response to the coming of spring, or I would have been embarrassed if I had mentioned it to anybody, but I never did. Each evening, the increasing minutes of light seemed tremendously valuable, like a legacy I'd been left from an aunt I'd never known existed. I would eat my dinner in front of the window, and watch as the sky sipped in the last silver light. I hoped no one would ask me how I was, because I would have found it hard to explain why I was so happy.

But then it was over, quickly, and for good. As if the power company had just turned off the electricity and suddenly everything went dark. But no, it wasn't like that—it was that suddenly someone turned the lights up, and I could see that I'd been wandering around in some half-lit twilit state, mistaking things for other things, mistaking myself for another person.

I guess it was the sight of Hugh's headlights in the driveway. He'd come to drive me home, but a week early so we could relax together. He was driving his parents' BMW and the lights seemed unsuitably, even offensively bright. When he turned off the ignition the lights went on inside the car and I could see him flip the visor down and look at himself in the mirror. I could see the pleasure he took in his own reflection—that he was so well put together that he didn't even need to comb his hair—and I was ashamed for both of us.

He was going to stay with me for a week. I was grateful; it would be a great help transporting everything.

Standing in the doorway, I felt a tremendous shyness. I realized it wasn't just shyness. It was reluctance. I didn't want him here, here in my place. My place but, of course, it was really Lois's.

"The view is just spectacular," he said, looking around for a place to leave his jacket. When we embraced, I was surprisingly aroused by his smell and the texture of his beard. It was six o'clock and he usually needed a shave by five.

"What's the décor? Heartland minimalist . . . with a little heartland hideous thrown in," he said, plopping himself down in my beautiful chair.

I didn't like the idea of his sitting in my chair. I knew he'd say something insulting about it. Why hadn't I realized that it was a mistake for me to buy furniture that I knew he wouldn't like? Well, I realized it too late, and little beads of panicked sweat formed at my hairline like seed pearls.

"How'd you come by this monstrosity?" he said.

Monstrosity. Anyone would say he'd gone too far. It might not be his taste, but certainly he could see that it was well made, and, on its own terms, admirable. I don't know, even now, why I didn't defend myself. My chair. My right to my own taste. My right to deviate from the tyranny of high postmodern. And why did I say what I said next, the plain false words of the last-minute betrayer.

"It belongs to my landlady."

"The famous Lois," he said. "Even the name is ugly. I can't wait to clap eyes on her."

My panic intensified. I would not allow Hugh to "clap eyes" on Lois. I would do whatever was necessary to keep them apart.

But that turned out to be impossible. No sooner had I resolved in my mind to keep them apart than there was a knock on the door and Lois's habitual, "Yoo-hoo!"

I wondered later if she deliberately dressed her worst as a test: of me, of Hugh. She'd just come from a run, so not only her face, but her bare legs were blotched. She was wearing lime-green nylon running shorts, a peacock-blue sleeveless T-shirt, exposing her arms, also blotched, and raspberry-colored socks that seemed to have been chosen deliberately to match her running shoes. I was hoping I had just imagined it, but I thought I saw Hugh visibly shudder at the sight of her. And I was convinced she knew I had betrayed the chair, denied my connection to it, passed it off like a bastard child, pretending it was my mother's, that I had never in fact given birth.

"Welcome to our fair city," she said, extending her sweaty hand to Hugh.

He didn't take her hand, but he did, to his credit, offer coffee.

"No thanks. Got to jump into the shower. I reek."

"I'll bet you do," Hugh said, after she'd run out the door, closing it firmly behind her. It was, after all, her property.

He pressed the button of the coffee grinder with what seemed to me an unnecessary force. He slammed the drawer where I kept the silverware; he banged the cups onto the counter. He pulled the stools out, making what I knew was a deliberately unpleasant sound against the slate floor.

"It's an act of aggression, it couldn't be anything else," he said.

"Aggression?" I said, not knowing what he was talking about.

"Looking that ugly. Appearing in the world like that. Forcing people to have to see you in that way, forcing them to have to experience ugliness. It's like those crazy people with TB who sneeze on people in the subways just so they'll get infected too."

Ugly. It was a terrible word, and yet it sounded so inoffensive . . .

it was so short and it ended in an *ee* sound, so it appeared not to be too serious, too dangerous. It wasn't the opposite of *beautiful,* because beauty suggested something eternal, whereas the claims of ugliness were much more modest; ugliness would go away, somehow, would be made to seem irrelevant by the sheer passage of time. I had first met Lois when I said I wanted one beautiful thing. I hadn't used the word *ugly;* I don't know what word I'd used when I was thinking to myself about the problem with where I lived. When she had come to the place I was staying at corporate housing, the words she used were *unlovely* and *lowering.* But *ugly?* We hadn't said it . . . maybe because it would have coated the inside of our mouths . . . by which I really mean our minds, with a sticky, nasty-smelling paste.

"Hugh, that's really going too far. Lois has no idea of hurting people. She's kind of in her own world, but it's a benign world . . . she does have an aesthetic sense, a real one, but it just doesn't extend to her own appearance."

"Oh, my God, my darling, I must get you away from here. They've infected you with softening of the brain." And he scooped me up—I literally felt scooped, as if he were something metallic and clearly shaped and I was something formless, like flour, or sugar or salt—and threw me down onto the bed.

I shouldn't have let him make love to me, as I shouldn't have said that the chair was Lois's, but as he touched me and traveled over my body with his hands and mouth, I realized how starved I'd been for this kind of attention, the attention of his body—let's call it by its right name, sex—and I gave in, there was nothing in me that wanted not to give in, to hold back. Even as I was giving in, I remembered an aunt of mine who had been widowed young and after a decade remarried. She said to me, "I didn't even realize I'd missed it"—she never gave the "it" a name—"but then when I had it again, it was all very clear. What I'd been deprived of."

Making love to Hugh, I was no longer the person who spent days in Rusty's workshop, or hand-washed my new china, or sat in my beautiful chair to watch the sun rise. And lying in his arms, I had no doubt which one was the real me. Perhaps I had been infected with brain softening. Perhaps I had gone flaccid, flabby, and I would return now to the taut, hard, muscular self, shedding the false fat that covered my true skeleton.

The next week was so busy that I hardly had time to think. I had, all these weeks, been working out a plan so that the people who were in the office least could stagger their flex time; and the people who worked at home would have to come into the office at intervals that would ensure their productivity. Everyone would have to give up a little, but the relinquishments were fair and even: no one, I hoped, could feel ill-done-by or ill-favored. First I presented it to their Human Resources person, who had kept me at a great distance all the weeks I'd been here, almost cowering when she saw me, and disappearing into her office, almost slinking there, when I'd asked her to consult. I could see that she thought my plan was good; for the first time in my presence, her spine straightened, she looked me in the eye. She gave me a high-five —something I loathed, something, though, it didn't matter. I had to make a presentation—oh the bullet points, the flow charts—to everybody in the company, and no one challenged me. There was a lot of nodding when I said, "Look, we all have to work together because no one wants the company to go under. If this happens, we're all out of a job." Then I had long private conversations with each of the people most affected. And, to my astonishment, no one suggested that what I offered was unacceptable, problematic, harsh.

I made my report to Jason and Jonathan and Josh, and they were so pleased that if they could have leapt off the computer screen to embrace me, I was sure they would. They offered me what seemed a ridiculously large bonus, and I had no impulse to refuse. What surprised me, driving home, back to my lake abode, was how pleased I was at the thought of all that money. It made me feel lighter, younger . . . I drove faster than I ever had. I was happy to be giving up my Toyota Camry rental; I was looking forward to driving Hugh's parents' BMW.

I hadn't talked to Lois in all the time that Hugh had been there. And I didn't want to. I wanted to leave right away. We had planned to rest up for two days after my last day of work, but I burst into the apartment, told Hugh the news about my bonus, and said, "Let's go. Let's go right now. Let's get out of here. I'll just leave Lois an envelope and avoid all the messy farewells."

"I love you . . . I love you . . . let's get out of Dodge," he said.

There wasn't really much for me to pack up. I had decided I would leave the dishes and the chair. There wouldn't be a place for them in my New York life. Lois would resell them to someone more appropriate, she'd make a little more money, and they could live in a home where they belonged.

Hugh was running the engine. I told him I wanted to check the place one last time.

It was just before seven; the light over the lake was silvery, and the clouds were beginning to be underlit: peach and mango, and a dark gray, like the kind of eye shadow you would only wear in a city, the kind that magazines call smoky. I looked back. There was my chair, framed by the dim emptiness. But it was not my chair, and I wondered if it ever really had been. "You are beautiful," I said to it. "You are very beautiful. You are fine, you are good, you are full of goodness and I am not. You don't belong with me. You wouldn't want to belong to me. You should be grateful that you aren't mine."

The Midnight Zone

FROM *The New Yorker*

IT WAS AN OLD hunting camp shipwrecked in twenty miles of scrub. Our friend had seen a Florida panther sliding through the trees there a few days earlier. But things had been fraying in our hands, and the camp was free and silent, so I walked through the resistance of my cautious husband and my small boys, who had wanted hermit crabs and kites and wakeboards and sand for spring break. Instead, they got ancient sinkholes filled with ferns, potential death by cat.

One thing I liked was how the screens at night pulsed with the tender bellies of lizards.

Even in the sleeping bag with my smaller son, the golden one, the March chill seemed to blow through my bones. I loved eating, but I'd lost so much weight by then that I carried myself delicately, as if I'd gone translucent.

There was sparse electricity from a gas-powered generator and no Internet and you had to climb out through the window in the loft and stand on the roof to get a cell signal. On the third day, the boys were asleep and I'd dimmed the lanterns when my husband went up and out and I heard him stepping on the metal roof, a giant brother to the raccoons that woke us thumping around up there at night like burglars.

Then my husband stopped moving, and stood still for so long I forgot where he was. When he came down the ladder from the loft, his face had blanched.

Who died? I said lightly, because if anyone was going to die it was going to be us, our skulls popping in the jaws of an endangered cat. It turned out to be a bad joke, because someone actually had died, that morning, in one of my husband's apartment buildings. A fifth-floor occupant had killed herself, maybe on purpose, with aspirin and vodka and a bathtub. Floors four, three, and two were away somewhere with beaches and alcoholic smoothies, and the first floor had discovered the problem only when the water of death had seeped into the carpet.

My husband had to leave. He'd just fired one handyman and the other was on his own Caribbean adventure, eating buffet food to the sound of cruise-ship calypso. Let's pack, my husband said, but my rebelliousness at the time was like a sticky fog rolling through my body and never burning off, there was no sun inside, and so I said that the boys and I would stay. He looked at me as if I were crazy and asked how we'd manage with no car. I asked if he thought he'd married an incompetent woman, which cut to the bone, because the source of our problems was that, in fact, he had. For years at a time I was good only at the things that interested me, and since all that interested me was my work and my children, the rest of life had sort of inched away. And while it's true that my children were endlessly fascinating, two petri dishes growing human cultures, being a mother never had been, and all that seemed assigned by default of gender I would not do because it felt insulting. I would not buy clothes, I would not make dinner, I would not keep schedules, I would not make playdates, never ever. Motherhood meant, for me, that I would take the boys on month-long adventures to Europe, teach them to blast off rockets, to swim for glory. I taught them how to read, but they could make their own lunches. I would hug them as long as they wanted to be hugged, but that was just being human. My husband had to be the one to make up for the depths of my lack. It is exhausting, living in debt that increases every day but that you have no intention of repaying.

Two days, he promised. Two days and he'd be back by noon on the third. He bent to kiss me, but I gave him my cheek and rolled over when the headlights blazed then dwindled on the wall. In the banishing of the engine, the night grew bold. The wind was making a low, inhuman muttering in the pines, and, inspired, the animals let loose in call-and-response. Everything kept me alert until shortly before dawn, when I slept for a few minutes until the puppy whined and woke me. My older son was crying because he'd thrown off his sleeping bag in the night and was cold but too sleepy to fix the situation.

I made scrambled eggs with a vengeful amount of butter and Cheddar, also cocoa with an inch of marshmallow, thinking I would stupefy my children with calories, but the calories only made them stronger.

Our friend had treated the perimeter of the clearing with panther deterrent, some kind of synthetic superpredator urine, and we felt safeish near the cabin. We ran footraces until the dog went wild and leapt up and bit my children's arms with her puppy teeth, and the boys screamed with pain and frustration and showed me the pink stripes on their skin. I scolded the puppy harshly and she crept off to the porch to watch us with her chin on her paws. The boys and I played soccer. We rocked in the hammock. We watched the circling red-shouldered hawks. I made my older son read *Alice's Adventures in Wonderland* to the little one, which was a disaster, a book so punny and Victorian for modern children. We had lunch, then the older boy tried to make fire by rubbing sticks together, his little brother attending solemnly, and they spent the rest of the day constructing a hut out of branches. Then dinner, singing songs, a bath in the galvanized-steel horse trough someone had converted to a cold-water tub, picking ticks and chiggers off with tweezers, and that was it for the first day.

There had been a weight on us as we played outside, not as if something were actually watching but because of the possibility that something could be watching when we were so far from humanity in all that Florida waste.

The second day should have been like the first. I doubled down on the calories, adding pancakes to breakfast, and succeeded in making the boys lie in pensive digestion out in the hammock for a little while before they ricocheted off the trees.

But in the afternoon the one light bulb sizzled out. The cabin was all dark wood and I couldn't see the patterns on the dishes I was washing. I found a new bulb in a closet, dragged over a stool from the bar area, and made the older boy hold the spinning seat as I climbed aboard. The old bulb was hot, and I was passing it from hand to hand, holding the new bulb under my arm, when the puppy leapt up at my older son's face. He let go of the stool to whack at her, and I did a quarter spin, then fell and hit the floor with my head, and then I surely blacked out.

After a while, I opened my eyes. Two children were looking down at me. They were pale and familiar. One fair, one dark; one small, one big.

Mommy? the little boy said, through water.

I turned my head and threw up on the floor. The bigger boy dragged a puppy, who was snuffling my face, out the door.

I knew very little except that I was in pain and that I shouldn't move. The older boy bent over me, then lifted an intact light bulb from my armpit, triumphantly; I a chicken, the bulb an egg.

The smaller boy had a wet paper towel in his hand and he was patting my cheeks. The pulpy smell made me ill again. I closed my eyes and felt the dabbing on my forehead, on my neck, around my mouth. The small child's voice was high. He was singing a song.

I started to cry with my eyes closed and the tears went hot across my temples and into my ears.

Mommy! the older boy, the solemn dark one, screamed, and when I opened my eyes both of the children were crying, and that was how I knew them to be mine.

Just let me rest here a minute, I said. They took my hands. I could feel the hot hands of my children, which was good. I moved my toes, then my feet. I turned my head back and forth. My neck worked, though fireworks went off in the corners of my eyes.

I can walk to town, the older boy was saying, through wadding, to his brother, but the nearest town was twenty miles away. Safety was twenty miles away and there was a panther between us and there, but also possibly terrible men, sinkholes, alligators, the end of the world. There was no landline, no umbilical cord, and small boys using cell phones would easily fall off such a slick, pitched metal roof.

But what if she's all a sudden dead and I'm all a sudden alone? the little boy was saying.

Okay, I'm sitting up now, I said.

The puppy was howling at the door.

I lifted my body onto my elbows. Gingerly, I sat. The cabin dipped and spun and I vomited again.

The big boy ran out and came back with a broom to clean up.

No! I said. I am always too hard on him, this beautiful child who is so brilliant, who has no logic at all.

Sweetness, I said, and couldn't stop crying, because I'd called him Sweetness instead of his name, which I couldn't remember just then. I took five or six deep breaths. Thank you, I said in a calmer voice. Just throw a whole bunch of paper towels on it and drag the rug over it to keep the dog off. The little one did so, methodically, which was not his style; he has always been adept at cheerfully watching other people work for him.

The bigger boy tried to get me to drink water, because this is what we do in our family in lieu of applying Band-Aids, which I refuse to buy because they are just flesh-colored landfill.

Then the little boy screamed, because he'd moved around me and seen the bloody back of my head, and then he dabbed at the cut with the paper towel he had previously dabbed at my pukey mouth. The paper disintegrated in his hands. He crawled into my lap and put his face on my stomach. The bigger boy held something cold on my wound, which I discovered later to be a beer can from the fridge.

They were quiet like this for a very long time. The boys' names came back to me, at first dancing coyly out of reach, then, when I seized them in my hands, mine.

I'd been a soccer player in high school, a speedy and aggressive midfielder, and head trauma was an old friend. I remembered this constant lability from one concussive visit to the emergency room. The confusion and the sense of doom were also familiar. I had a flash of my mother sitting beside my bed for an entire night, shaking me awake whenever I tried to fall asleep, and I now wanted my mother, not in her diminished current state, brittle retiree, but as she had been when I was young, a small person but gigantic, a person who had blocked out the sun.

I sent the little boy off to get a roll of dusty duct tape, the bigger boy to get gauze from my toiletry kit, and when they wandered back I duct-taped the gauze to my head, already mourning my long hair, which had been my most expensive pet.

I inched myself across the room to the bed and climbed up, despite the sparklers behind my eyeballs. The boys let the forlorn puppy in, and when they opened the door they also let the night in, because my fall had taken hours from our lives.

It was only then, when the night entered, that I understood the depth of time we had yet to face. I had the boys bring me the lanterns, then a can opener and the tuna and the beans, which I opened slowly, because it is not easy, supine, and we made a game out of eating, though the thought of eating anything gave me chills. The older boy brought over Mason jars of milk. I let my children finish the entire half gallon of ice cream, which was my husband's, his one daily reward for being kind and good, but by this point the man deserved our disloyalty, because he was not there.

It had started raining, at first a gentle thrumming on the metal roof.

I tried to tell my children a cautionary tale about a little girl who fell into a well and had to wait a week until firefighters could figure out a way to rescue her, something that maybe actually took place back in the dimness of my childhood, but the story was either too abstract for them or I wasn't making much sense, and they didn't seem to grasp my need for them to stay in the cabin, to not go anywhere, if the very worst happened, the unthinkable that I was skirting, like a pit that opened just in front of each sentence I was about to utter. They kept asking me if the girl got lots of toys when she made it out of the well. This was so against my point that I said, out of spite, Unfortunately, no, she did not.

I made the boys keep me awake with stories. The younger one was into a British television show about marine life, which the older one maintained was babyish until I pretended not to believe what they were telling me. Then they both told me about cookie-cutter sharks, who bore perfect round holes in whales, as if their mouths were cookie cutters. They told me about a fish called the humuhumunukunukuāpua'a, a beautiful name that I couldn't say correctly, even though they sang it to me over and over, laughing, to the tune of "Twinkle Twinkle, Little Star." They told me about the walking catfish, which can stay out of water for days and days, meandering about in the mud. They told me about the sunlight, the twilight, and the midnight zones, the three depths of water, where there is transparent light, then a murky, darkish light, then no light at all. They told me about the world pool, in which one current goes one way, another goes another way, and where they meet they make a tornado of air, which stretches, my little one said, from the midnight zone, where the fish are blind, all the way up up up to the birds.

I had begun shaking very hard, which my children, sudden gentlemen, didn't mention. They piled all the sleeping bags and blankets they could find on me, then climbed under and fell asleep without bathing or toothbrushing or getting out of their dirty clothes, which, anyway, they sweated through within an hour.

The dog did not get dinner but she didn't whine about it, and though she wasn't allowed to, she came up on the bed and slept with her head on my older son's stomach, because he was her favorite, being the biggest puppy of all.

Now I had only myself to sit vigil with me, though it was still early, nine or ten at night.

I had a European novel on the nightstand that filled me with dimness and fret, so I tried to read *Alice's Adventures in Wonderland,* but it was incomprehensible with my scrambled brains. Then I looked at a hunting magazine, which made me remember the Florida panther. I hadn't truly forgotten about it, but could manage only a few terrors at a time, and others, when my children had been awake, were more urgent. We had seen some scat in the woods on a walk three days earlier, enormous scat, either a bear's or the panther's, but certainly a giant predator's. The danger had been abstract until we saw this bodily proof of existence, and my husband and I led the children home, singing a round, all four of us holding hands, and we let the dog off the leash to circle us joyously, because, as small as she was, it was bred in her bones that in the face of peril she would sacrifice herself first.

The rain increased until it was deafening and still my sweaty children slept. I thought of the waves of sleep rushing through their brains, washing out the tiny unimportant flotsam of today so that tomorrow's heavier truths could wash in. There was a nice solidity to the rain's pounding on the roof, as if the noise were a barrier that nothing could enter, a stay against the looming night.

I tried to bring back the poems of my youth, and could not remember more than a few floating lines, which I put together into a strange, sad poem, Blake and Dickinson and Frost and Milton and Sexton, a tag-sale poem in clammy meter that nonetheless came alive and held my hand for a little while.

Then the rain diminished until all that was left were scattered clicks from the drops falling from the pines. The batteries of one lantern went out and the light from the remaining lantern was sparse and thwarted. I could hardly see my hand or the shadow it made on the wall when I held it up. This lantern was my sister; at any moment it, too, could go dark. I feasted my eyes on the cabin, which in the oncoming black had turned into a place made of gold, but the shadows seemed too thick now, fizzy at the edges, and they moved when I shifted my eyes away from them. It felt safer to look at the cheeks of my sleeping children, creamy as cheeses.

It was elegiac, that last hour or so of light, and I tried to push my love for my sons into them where their bodies were touching my own skin.

The wind rose again and it had personality; it was in a sharpish, meanish mood. It rubbed itself against the little cabin and played at the corners and broke sticks off the trees and tossed them at the roof so they jigged down like creatures with strange and scrabbling claws. The wind rustled its endless body against the door.

Everything depended on my staying still, but my skin was stuffed with itches. Something terrible in me, the darkest thing, wanted to slam my own head back against the headboard. I imagined it over and over, the sharp backward crack, and the wash and spill of peace.

I counted slow breaths and was not calm by two hundred; I counted to a thousand.

The lantern flicked itself out and the dark poured in.

The moon rose in the skylight and backed itself across the black.

When it was gone and I was alone again, I felt the dissociation, a physical shifting, as if the best of me were detaching from my body and sitting down a few feet distant. It was a great relief.

For a few moments, there was a sense of mutual watching, a wait for something definitive, though nothing definitive came, and then the bodiless me stood and circled the cabin. The dog moved and gave a soft whine through her nose, although she remained asleep. The floors were cool underfoot. My head brushed the beams, though they were ten feet up. Where my body and those of my two sons lay together was a black and pulsing mass, a hole of light.

I passed outside. The path was pale dirt and filled with sandspur and was cold and wet after the rain. The great drops from the tree branches left a pine taste in me. The forest was not dark, because darkness has nothing to do with the forest—the forest is made of life, of light—but the trees moved with wind and subtle creatures.

I wasn't in any single place. I was with the raccoons of the rooftop, who were now down fiddling with the bicycle lock on the garbage can at the end of the road, with the red-shouldered hawk chicks breathing alone in the nest, with the armadillo forcing its armored body through the brush. I hadn't realized that I'd lost my sense of smell until it returned hungrily now; I could smell the worms tracing their paths under the pine needles and the mold breathing out new spores, shaken alive by the rain.

I was vigilant, moving softly in the underbrush, and the palmettos' nails scraped down my body.

The cabin was not visible, but it was present, a sore at my side, a feeling of density and airlessness. I couldn't go away from it, I couldn't return, I could only circle the cabin and circle it. With each circle, a terrible, stinging anguish built in me and I had to move faster and faster, each pass bringing up ever more wildness. What had been built to seem so solid was fragile in the face of time because time is impassive, more animal than human. Time would not care if you fell out of it. It would continue on without you. It cannot see you; it has always been blind to the human and the things we do to stave it off, the taxonomies, the cleaning, the arranging, the ordering. Even this cabin with its perfectly considered angles, its veins of pipes and wires, was barely more stable than the rake marks we made in the dust that morning, which time had already scrubbed away.

The self in the woods ran and ran, but the running couldn't hold off the slow shift. A low mist rose from the ground and gradually came clearer. The first birds sent their questions into the chilly air. The sky developed its blue. The sun emerged.

The drawing back was gradual. My older son opened his brown eyes and saw me sitting above him.

You look terrible, he said, patting my face, and my hearing was only half underwater now.

My head ached, so I held my mouth shut and smiled with my eyes and he padded off to the kitchen and came back with peanut-butter-and-jelly sandwiches, with a set of Uno cards, with cold coffee from yesterday's pot for the low and constant thunder of my headache, with the dog whom he'd let out and then fed all by himself.

I watched him. He gleamed. My little son woke but didn't get up, as if his face were attached to my shoulder by the skin. He was rubbing one unbloodied lock of my hair on his lips, the way he did after he nursed when he was a baby.

My boys were not unhappy. I was usually a preoccupied mother, short with them, busy, working, until I burst into fun, then went back to my hole of work; now I could only sit with them, talk to them. I could not even read. They were gentle with me, reminded me of a golden retriever I'd grown up with, a dog with a mouth so soft she would go down to the lake and steal ducklings and hold them intact on her tongue for hours until we noticed her sitting unusually erect in the corner, looking sly. My boys were like their father; they would one day be men who would take care of the people they loved.

I closed my eyes as the boys played game after game after game of Uno.

Noon arrived, noon left, and my husband did not come.

At one point, something passed across the woods outside like a shudder, and a hush fell over everything, and the boys and the dog all looked at me and their faces were like pale birds taking flight, but my hearing had mercifully shut off whatever had occasioned such swift terror over all creatures of the earth, save me.

When we heard the car from afar at four in the afternoon, the boys jumped up. They burst out of the cabin, leaving the door wide open to the blazing light, which hurt my eyes. I heard their father's voice, and then his footsteps, and he was running, and behind him the boys were running, the dog was running. Here were my husband's feet on the dirt drive. Here were his feet heavy on the porch.

For a half breath, I would have vanished myself. I was everything we had fretted about, this passive Queen of Chaos with her bloody duct-tape crown. My husband filled the door. He is a man born to fill doors. I shut my eyes. When I opened them, he was enormous above me. In his face was a thing that made me go quiet inside, made a long slow sizzle creep up my arms from the fingertips, because the thing I read in his face was the worst, it was fear, and it was vast, it was elemental, like the wind itself, like the cold sun I would soon feel on the silk of my pelt.

The Chicane

FROM *Washington Square Review*

WHEN THE FILM with the French actor opened in the valley, I went to the second showing of the night. It was a hip romantic comedy, but it was not memorable in the way his first film had been, the bawdy picaresque that made his name.

More than thirty years ago, my aunt Lauryn had been hired to accompany him on interviews and serve as interpreter. She was a student at the university in Madrid, taking a junior year abroad from her home in the States, in the American Midwest.

Lauryn was lively and funny, a passionate girl with evenly tanned skin. The actor remained in character, and when she wrote him a month later to say that she was late, she did not hear anything back. On the day she miscarried, her best friend thousands of miles away had "a bad feeling" and called the concierge of Lauryn's building in Madrid; otherwise Lauryn would not have survived the overdose.

She rallied with the help of her mother in Chicago, during lengthy conversations she relied on every night. One year later, she met someone who adored her. She had moved to Lisbon to translate medical documents while she completed her last college courses. Macario was next.

Macario was in line at the door when the Banco de Portugal opened at nine o'clock. Inside, he took a seat in the partitioned office of a personal banker while the banker secured the key to the strongbox. The personal banker escorted him to the vault, and the two men stood together as Macario unlocked the strongbox and added to its contents a tape cassette in a navy felt bag. He closed the box, and let the banker accompany him upstairs, and to the door.

The bank was in Lisbon, and the trip in from Estoril had taken three hours. Another driver would make the trip in four, but Macario had raced cars for a living, and though semi-retired from the circuit, drove with speed and aggression still. Racing was how he had first met Lauryn, an American girl studying languages abroad, who cut classes to go to the track. She looked Latin, not Midwestern, and when he saw her at the finish line, he was pleased to find that she was fluent in Portuguese.

When Lauryn brought him home to meet her mother a couple of months later, Hillis wished her husband were alive to help. She was tired from losing her husband not yet a year before, and she made a decision to wish for her daughter's happiness if she could not count on Lauryn's judgment. The wedding was held in Lisbon, with a brief honeymoon at the Ritz. Hillis did not make the trip, but sent a surpassingly generous gift.

The house Macario rented for them in Estoril faced the sea. Chalet Esperanza had been built in the sixteenth century; its terraces poured bougainvillea to the ground. The newlyweds drank coffee in the morning on the bedroom terrace, close enough to the sea to spot starfish on the beach at low tide. Macario brought his bride a tiny poodle—mostly poodle—that had hung around the track for several days. The pit crews had fed it, but no one had showed up to look for it. Lauryn named the dog Espe; she bathed it and bought the dog a wardrobe of collars. Macario took that summer to get to know his bride.

Lauryn wrote to Hillis about the blissful days they woke to. She told her mother that she walked to the market earlier than the tourists, said she was not herself a tourist since her wedding to Macario. She said she rid herself of the flat Chicago *a*—she noticed this the few times she spoke her native language. She was where she was meant to be, she said, living a life that made sense.

She was learning the history of the coastal towns, visiting the landmark churches, thriving in Estoril's moderate summer instead of the humid heat of Illinois. She said she liked to linger in Parede, a small beach where the high iodine content in the water was said to be good for the bones; there were two orthopedic hospitals in the town. Lauryn told her mother she thought she might visit one and read to the patients in the children's ward.

Some days she went to Tamariz, the beach beside the Estoril Casino and Gardens, or to Praia dos Pescadores for the fish market, or to the baroque Church of the Navigators to pray that Macario would always return to her but not to the track.

The Circuito Estoril at the Autódromo was a tricky course on the Formula 1 circuit with its bumpy straights, constant radius corners, heavy braking zones, and a tricky chicane. The month they had the chalet, July, was a month when only motorbikes raced. Unless Macario and Lauryn extended their stay, his racing pals would not be around to tempt him back onto the course.

Each felt the other was a prize, so where was the need to continue to compete?

Such was Lauryn's thinking, as reported to her mother, and passed along to me. Macario, she pointed out, had filled a trophy case already; did he need to risk his life now that he had a wife, and, soon, a child?

Though Lauryn was twenty-one years old, and I was seventeen, she treated me not like her older sister's child, but as someone who could profit from all that she had learned. Though I could not pick up languages the way that she could, I took in other lessons.

That summer, Lauryn started to wear loose shifts. She no longer tucked in her shirts. She took naps, and was alternately sick and ravenous. She instilled in Macario a lust for dynasty, a word she used ironically, but which he did not.

Then she made the classic mistake of taking the exotic out of its element. She took her husband home and turned him into what she could easily have found without leaving Illinois. Macario did not hold it against her, but Lauryn came to blame him for the same things that drew her to him first.

After the month in Estoril, Lauryn brought Macario home again. She wanted an American doctor, she wanted her mother's help with the baby, she wanted Macario to take a job with the company her father used to run. She wanted an American husband, after all. When their son James was born, Macario pronounced it "Zhime." Portuguese was the language they fought in.

*

The first two years of motherhood were a balm for Lauryn. During the pregnancy she had stopped taking medication to lift her spirits, and she did not take it up again after the baby was born. She attributed her changes in mood to the new responsibilities, to the vigilance required to protect her child and make sure he would thrive. She talked to her mother on the phone or saw her every day. I saw her every few months when I flew in from California to get away from the life that had not yet started for me. I preferred her life, the one she talked about from before the baby was born.

Macario helped with childcare when he came home from the office in the evening. Still, Lauryn said she needed a break from them all, from it all, and booked a flight to Lisbon on her twenty-third birthday.

Macario would not have known there *was* a tape if the chief of police had not been an old friend who told him. It was not generally known that the police taped international calls placed within the capital. So when Lauryn placed the call to her mother in Chicago from a room in the Lisbon Ritz on the last night of her life, the conversation was recorded by police. The chief of police not only told Macario this, he gave him a copy of the tape.

Macario listened to it once, and then put it in his strongbox at the bank. He did not tell Hillis there was a tape of the last conversation she had had with her daughter, or that he had listened to Lauryn as she made less and less sense after taking the pills. But he did tell me.

Hillis and I drank coffee on her terrace on the eighteenth floor of her apartment building, close enough to Lake Michigan to smell diesel fuel. She had mostly quit caffeine when Lauryn died; it fought the medication she had taken since then to calm her. But you could not lose everything at once, she maintained, and continued to drink coffee in the morning, as before. In the years since Lauryn died, she had lost her view from the terrace. It had been largely blocked by the John Hancock building, which she had watched go up from her living room across from the office and residential tower.

Hillis did not want to talk about Lauryn, but she seemed to enjoy my visits when I came back to Chicago from the coast. Though there was not any glamour to the work that I did, my grandmother asked for particulars. In an uneasy near-coincidence, I edited articles for medical publications. It was a job I knew I would leave as soon as something better appeared.

I am sure that if Lauryn had wanted a doctor to come and pump her stomach she would have phoned the front desk of the Ritz Hotel and told them to send one up to her room. She wanted to talk to her mother, and hear her mother tell her from thousands of miles away that James was sleeping in the guest room in his crib, and that it was hard to make out what she was saying—could she speak up?—and that she would feel better when she woke up in the morning, and then ask her mother to stay on the line while she sang herself to sleep.

Macario did not let me listen to the tape; I had to take his word for what was on it when he took me aside at James's tenth birthday party and gave me this ugly gift. Why tell me then? He had no answer when I asked him.

This morning I thought to make a tape recording of my own. I wanted to tell my aunt about the party I went to in Malibu last night. The fellow who answered the door was not the host, but the French actor, the rake who played a rake in his film debut, who seduced my aunt in Madrid so many years before. He had aged pretty well; he still had it, I thought.

I had wanted to play something out, so I trailed him through the house, then asked if he would step outside and show me the night sky. I introduced myself as Lauryn, and spelled out where the *y* replaced an *e*. Did I expect him to flinch? With his arm around my shoulders, he narrated what we looked up and saw. I would not have known if he was right about the constellations. His accent almost worked on me. But when he stopped talking, and leaned in for the kiss, I ducked, and said, "You can remember me as the girl you showed the new moon to."

"But darling," he said, "there's a new moon every month."

Still, I wanted to tell my aunt. The days of tape cassettes were over, but the equipment must be somewhere to be found, and when I was the one who found it, wouldn't I record a tape on which I told her the story? Wouldn't I mail it off to Macario in a suitable felt bag so he could take it to the bank in Lisbon and unlock the strongbox and place it beside the tape of his wife chattering away in the vault.

Tally

FROM *Epoch*

I KNEW A SOBER MAN whose brother had died driving drunk on the high windy plains. The living brother, the sober brother, took to drink straightaway. He was belligerent and incompetent, drunk, and a gentle, almost girlish man, sober. He drank schnapps of every flavor and hue.

It was my job to pour and to tally, to feed a coin now and then into the jukebox when the quiet was too much to bear. Merle Haggard, Garth Brooks, Emmylou. "I got friends in low places" —every variation of that town and time is for me ferried by this one dumb song.

The man, the men—the sober man, the dead man—had a sister, inscrutable as a turtle. She appeared each night and drove her living brother home, for months in the same floral blouse. And then she didn't. She had given up, or gone elsewhere. And so the sober brother drove home wildly, drunk, the long way around, making turns that were not in the road.

One night after several months of this I let myself accompany him home. I drove us out to the turn his brother had missed and we lay in the grass for the stars. I felt pity, yes, and alluring. Enchanted by a grief that wasn't mine. We heard a bird in the dark we couldn't see. *Meteor, meteoroid, meteorite*, we remembered. *Sedimentary, igneous, metamorphic.*

After a time we stood up and he kissed me. In his hair the pods of a seed caught—feathery, silver, like something spit from a galaxy, space junk—luck—that sought and found him.

His place was tiny, the bathtub dragged into the kitchen—the longest clawfoot I'd ever seen. You could lie in that tub without bending, sink beneath the glistening meringue of foam and entirely disappear. He went under. You cannot believe for how long. I couldn't see his face but his eyes showed, drastic, dark, sprung open. One eye disappeared, appeared again. He was winking at me slowly, the minutes slow in passing.

In bed, he moved as if blind. He was precise, and maddeningly patient. Once he whistled—one note—as to a dog.

The body opens, can be opened, a marvel, and still we live.

When he had finished, he filled the bath again. Carried me to it—not a word. Again the soap foamed up, great billowing mounds. It smelled of berries. In my cunt, a burning balloon.

The window glass shook. Water sloshed in the tub. We thought we'd caused it. We had lain in his drunk brother's ashes, in grass where he had gone ahead. It had not been my grief but I had claimed it. The mountains shuddered. The horizon bucked, it buckled—the boulders strewn and the grasses, erratic, the path of the glacier plain. This isn't metaphor. This was an earthquake, a moving ripple—ground I had thought of as solid warped, and returning to liquid again.

Gabe Dove

FROM *Salamander*

I MET GABE DOVE when I was sad and attracting men who liked me sad.

There was the jeweler with goopy eyes, the lawyer who over-texted. Men with lotioned hands, combed beards, tight jeans. Many had allergies. Few ate bread. Inside of two coffees, they were chronicling the history of their itchy and unrested bodies. I listened. I was too weak to protest. All of our hearts had recently been destroyed. They brought me tulips, sent me jokes from the Internet. I think they enjoyed observing somebody sadder than them. They thought me gentle, soft, easy on their hearts.

"Enough of these limpdicks," said Angela, unwrapping a beef sandwich on her desk. I stole a fry. Angela was admin like me, ten years younger, and generally exasperated from repeating her own advice. "You've got to meet someone normal," she said. "Someone from Shelby."

Shelby was Angela's neighborhood. Shelby was where my mom played mahjongg in a hair salon. Shelby wasn't the kind of place I'd go looking for a man. "But these uptown guys," I said, pressing ketchup from a packet. "At least they have money."

"They're snobs," said Angela. She licked a trail of beef juice from her wrist. "Go on—I can't finish. Look. Do you want a good one or not? Or just sleep with someone, why don't you. You've got to break the seal."

I described my latest dream to Angela. Tunnels of blood, winds, the sensation that I'd been murdered. Sure it's sleep, but how is it rest? The fry sagged in my fingers. "It's just that I can't stop thinking about him. I can't stop thinking about—"

"Hold up," said Angela, raising her hand. "Remember? His name is Mr. Fuckbag."

Mr. Fuckbag. Right.

"Practice saying it," she said. "I want you to say it twenty times a day." She put down her sandwich and looked me squarely in the eye. "Fuckbag. Fuckbag. Fuckbag."

I wanted a good one. I was ready. But I knew that these things don't happen right away. You have to go through some months. You have to go through some people. Who knows why, but that's how the universe works: it doesn't cough up your people right away.

In the meantime, there are some opening acts. Some vaudeville.

Some asked about my triathlon stuff. Some did not. A lot were the type who liked Asians. Their googly eyes were too enchanted, too soon. They marveled at my tiny frame, my hairless arms, how they could wrap their fingers all the way around my wrist. They liked me small.

Fuckbag was funny, but I couldn't laugh about this stuff, I'm sorry. Not about Ex.

I'd slept with none of them. I don't know. I could have. But I thought like maybe I would be hurting Ex if I did that, like somehow he would know. *Did you get what you want, Chuntao? Did it solve all your problems?*

Some days I'd say I was working from home. I'd steal Oreos from my new roommates and guiltily replace them, measuring the columns in their crinkly plastic trays. Outside, the sidewalks rippled with people. Sometimes I put on real pants and walked among their swishing hair, their sniffing dogs. But the feeling always came back. The park, the office, the bench under the trees: there was nowhere I could go where I would feel okay.

In my latest dream, Ex lifted my dangling leg and swallowed me like a pill. I bumped along his mute red veins. The rumbling I heard was his voice.

I tried swimming in the river. Coach had said, Stay in the pool, take it easy, don't push. But pushing's the whole point—you want to feel it, don't you? So I did the ninety minutes in the cold and craggy waves. In the river there were no other swimmers: just hunched men in dinghies, a speedboat or two. Lily pads clogging the shores. Floating branches to push out of the way.

But always there was Ex. Even with my face in the water, ears plugged all the way to my brain: Ex was there. It was for Ex that I glossed my nails, for Ex that I curled my hair, for Ex that I tried on twenty scratchy blouses in the litter of the fitting room. I could not decide. What did I want? I wanted him to see. To see me and rethink how things had gone.

Sometimes, in the river, I had this sensation that I was drowning. Ridiculous, I know—I'm an ace, I'm an expert. I was all-state three times. But I tell you: I couldn't breathe. Once I had to stop. I was choking, I had to curl myself over a branch like a kid in her very first lesson, the one who still needs plastic floaties, the one nobody wants to be.

Angela said, "I know him from church." And I guess—because Angela and because church—I was expecting a white guy.

She thumbed his number into my phone. "Gabe . . . Dove," she said. "Don't be surprised if he takes a while. He's a doctor." She nodded approvingly.

Our texts were brief, all logistics. At home I watched an episode of *Spy 25,* but only half. I put on my orange twisty dress. I did my hair.

I waited by the hostess stand. He'd agreed to come to my neighborhood, to a bar called The Vault. It was a nothing place, a comfortable place. The walls were covered with autographed photos of local celebrities: Popovich, Robinson, Duncan doing a lay-up. I commented on the hostess's cool necklace—she always wore the best jewelry. She thanked me and I laughed. I was nervous, I guess because of Angela. I liked Angela. She took the time.

So in walk these guys in baseball caps and shorts. I search their faces but they're going straight for the bar, not for me. Then the revolving door spins and suddenly, in a cold gust of air, there's this guy in a suit. The whole works—tailored cuffs, pressed pants, shiny shoes. All wrong for this bar. He's searching the room, neck stretched, holding the handle of a small suitcase on wheels. He looks like somebody's dad.

"Are you . . . ?" he said. He dipped toward me, extending his hand. "You must be Chuntao. Hello!"

We shook, him sandwiching my hand like I'm some long-lost

friend. "Hi," I said, eyeing the suitcase. "Were you on a trip?" He explained that ha, if only, everybody asks him that, but no—he just doesn't want to ruin his back. I nodded at Gabe Dove. He followed me to the bar, shoes clicking behind me, the suitcase rolling so loudly that I could hear the hostess staring.

He was Asian. Did Angela pick him because of that? Maybe she had that on her mind. Maybe like that would make us more compatible. But what about the rest of me, Angela? What about all that? These were my thoughts as Gabe Dove excused himself to wash his hands.

"I see you're getting back out there," said the bartender, who winked and poured my usual.

"Just pretend you don't know me, please," I said. On the mirrored wall behind the bottles my watery arms were adjusting my ponytail. All that time I'd spent blending my eye shadow—I could have been finishing my show.

Gabe Dove returned. We sipped. Me, my Bud Light, him, brandy on ice. Brandy—like an old person. We discussed my job (admin at Livagon Insurance) and his (ear, nose, and throat). He worked at Veterans. TV was not his thing. Despite his weird suit, he rested his elbows comfortably on the sticky bar, his eyebrows very interested in the stuff I was saying. He had an accent I didn't know, lilting up at the ends of sentences, making them sound like questions. A Rod Seeger song came on, my fave, and I got distracted —Gabe Dove's explaining face, lit green and white by the flashes of a soccer game.

We talked about Angela: her easy laugh, her Bible group, that kidney thing with her mom. We got quiet. That was about all I knew about Angela.

Gabe Dove spun his cardboard coaster. "So. What kind of Asian are you?"

"Chinese," I said. "But I'm from Mississippi. That's where I was born. I was born in the U.S."

"Mississippi!" he said, leaning back. "That's unusual." I myself had never thought it was unusual, but more and more, that was the feedback I was getting.

Gabe Dove searched my face. Finally he said, "So . . . me. I'm from Burma."

"Oh, yeah?" I said.

"Yes. From Rangoon. I was ten when we left."

"Cool," I said, and gulped my beer. I had a feeling there were things I was supposed to know about Burma, that I was supposed to be asking questions. But my brain was Styrofoam, all the way through.

Gabe Dove asked if I'd been to China, seen all that it had to offer.

"Nope," I said. "For so long it was hard to go there. Laws and stuff." That part I knew. Mom used to complain—not because she wanted to go back, but because that era constituted yet another intolerable fact of her life.

"We lived there for a year," Gabe Dove explained. Some border town in Yunnan. He described thick winding streams and lush mountain gorges, obviously thinking I'd enjoy this window into my ancestral country, but in truth, I wanted to slap him. I didn't want his reportage. It embarrassed me.

"It's amazing," he said. "Before that, I'd only known the Myanmar jungle."

"Oh yeah?" I said. "What's in Myanmar?"

"Oh," said Gabe Dove. A concerned expression flitted across his face. "They're the same thing, actually. Burma, Myanmar. Just different names for the same country."

My face burned. "Oh, yeah! Of course." In my lap I squeezed my leg, nails digging in. "Stupid, stupid."

"No no, not stupid!" he said. His eyebrows reached out to me. "It's totally confusing. The history is all screwed up. Lots of people don't know."

I excused myself and went to the bathroom. I sat on the toilet. I'd already drunk too much. My heart knocked hurriedly, like it was trying to get out. I dropped my head to my knees and watched the band of my underwear, breathing penitently into the elastic and the frayed, tiny loops.

I swung open the stall door and blinked into the mirror. My eyes were bloodshot, crazy. I cupped a hand under the faucet and gulped. Slowly I could feel my toes inside my shoes. And I thought, Okay, let's get back out there. Let's show him what you've got. Not quite like I wanted him, but like I wanted to show that I wasn't who he maybe thought I was. I licked a corner of a paper towel and fixed my shadow.

"Sorry," I said when I returned, easing myself onto the stool. "I get the flush." I pointed to my red face.

"Do you?" said Gabe Dove, smiling worriedly. "I don't, but my cousin does. Sometimes he can't hear. I wonder if it has to do with his vestibular." He tapped his fingers on the bar, eyeing me. "Maybe we shouldn't be drinking."

"No, no," I said. "We should." I swiveled toward the wall of bottles, brushing his elbow with mine. The arm inside his sleeve felt solid, assured. And at that moment something shifted in the gravity around Gabe Dove. He adjusted his posture, pressing back, and it surprised me — this quiet weight of him.

I'd never been with an Asian guy. I don't know. They reminded me of my cousins. Too familiar. Wouldn't Mom like to be here, nodding over her glass, endorsing this scene.

And I thought, Why not. He's safe. He's a known quantity. Whatever happens, he can't hurt me much: he doesn't have the power.

It's like Angela said. You've got to break the seal.

I yawned fakely. I stretched provocatively. He suggested that we leave. His white-line hair part communicated that he wasn't the adventurous sort, but as we walked into the sprinkling rain he said, "Want to go back to your place?"

My place. I pictured my bed: three shoved-together couch cushions on the carpet of a bedroom belonging to my colleague's cousin's landlady. No sheets.

"What about your place?" I said.

"I'm down in Shelby," he said. "So . . ."

"I'm in Dale," I said. "West Dale. Way west."

"It's just that I hate the bus," he said.

"Who doesn't?" I said, staring ahead at the sidewalk dampening under our shoes. Not to budge: that was the challenge. I wanted desperately to kiss a man, to remember the dormant powers inside of me, but also to be far from anything that reminded me of my life. So we walked. His suitcase squeaked behind us. I let us shift along in silence, the rain blowing through a triangle of streetlight, pricking my eyelids.

Finally he said, "It's not the greatest place. It's sort of embarrassing."

"I don't care," I said, and I didn't.

We waited for the 64. In the bus shelter was a backlit ad for Pawsh Dog, and Gabe Dove stared at the slender hand brushing the terrier. We gripped the bus loops, swaying with the corners, and I tried not to step on his shoes each time the bus hit a pothole.

By Exit 32 the sign for Fantasy Hair rose up from the earth like
a ghost. Somewhere inside was the ripped card table, the clinking
tiles, Mom's friends talking too fast to understand. I watched my
hands, the little curled hangnails. Generally I tried not to linger
in Shelby.

The home of Gabe Dove was right off the highway, behind the
erected wood sound barrier: a squat, cube building of schoolyard
brick. "Here goes nothing," he said, unlocking the second pad-
lock. His apartment was one long hallway, with doorways slinking
into low square rooms. Two-burner stove. Stacked milk crates for
bookshelves. He kept apologizing. Doctor, yes, but there was all
that debt and helping out the fam.

Gabe Dove gazed into the cabinet, selecting a crystal-cut tumbler and a scratched jam jar. He gave me the tumbler, poured
us Campari, said cheers, and plopped a hand on my shoulder. It
didn't move. I didn't move either. We both let it hang there, as
if we'd just made roadkill of a squirrel and didn't know what to
do. But I tell you: it was nice. The refrigerator humming at my
back, the jittery ceiling fan, and me thinking, I don't have to do
anything. I don't even have to speak, I can just keep lowering this
syrupy red medicine into my mouth. Things will happen.

The first time Ex kissed me, we were below deck on his family's boat. His parents, his sister—their flip-flops above our heads,
dragging around the bar cart. That was the thing about Ex: he
didn't give a shit. It felt wonderful to be around that—he made
me feel bigger, made me want to be somebody. He gripped my
body like every piece of me was worth something immeasurable.
My butt, my back, my neck, my stomach. He tried lifting my shirt
but I tugged it down—I have always been self-conscious about my
breasts. They hang down my front like the breasts of an old lady,
like two bags. Sometimes I wear a bra to bed, thinking it will help,
knowing it won't help. There is nothing I can do. I have consulted
all the forums.

What I do like are my legs—long, muscular, with shapely calves.
Swimmer's legs. Sometimes in store windows I see my reflection
and think, Are those attached to me? I made sure that Ex got a
good long look at them, flexing them in the air, balancing my elbows on the bolted cushions.

I followed Gabe Dove to his bedroom and he closed the door,
as if someone might interrupt us. He flipped off the lights. Then

he removed the whole suit, all at once, belt and pants and tight white underwear, like a fitful toddler, like he couldn't wait to be out of his clothes.

He had a tattoo on his chest: curls of writing, indecipherable, faded to blue.

His breath was herbal. His mouth hard, gyrating, searching in the dark.

Overall I'd say he was blunt and methodical, his limp hands pausing nowhere. Like someone working over me with a mop.

When we were having sex I sort of wished that I wasn't, that maybe this was a mistake, I'm not ready, it would have been better if I'd just kissed him quickly and gone home before I ended up V-legged and jiggling underneath this person: Where was my dignity? Here was the moment I had dreaded and craved. But it didn't feel like things were happening. It didn't feel like much was being accomplished.

Through the rain, through the sound barrier, an eighteen-wheeler grumbled down the highway, the driver suddenly accelerating, as if seizing a lane or waking from sleep.

When it was over, Gabe Dove got me a glass of water. He stroked my hair while I sat on the edge of the bed, sipping. "Sorry," he said. "That was kind of fast." But I wasn't sorry; I had wanted him to hurry up. I wasn't sure what to make of him holding my waist like this, easing the glass from my hand and lowering it to the nightstand. He *thanked* me. "Thank you," he said, bending to kiss my shoulder. "Thank you for being here." For being here? I didn't know what to say.

"Do you want to stay?" he said, lips resting on my skin.

"Do I want to stay . . ." I said I didn't have a toothbrush. Or stuff for my contacts.

"Stay," he said. "In the morning, we can go to this bakery down the street. Their donuts are otherworldly."

And I am telling you that I stayed, on the promise of a maple-glazed donut. I told you: I was sad.

I slept well. In the morning, the unfamiliar cracks in the ceiling made me think I was dreaming. Gabe Dove snored loosely, his hand asleep on my stomach. I saw that he had hair all over: torso, chest, sprouts from his nipples. Despite the clicking of the radiator and the fact that I had to pee, there was, overall, an unmistakably peaceful feeling. His bed was a real bed—thick mattress, solid frame. A pot on the windowsill, with an orchid arching effortlessly.

The body of Gabe Dove shifted. He stuck his nose in my ear. "Hello."

"Hi," I said. Then Gabe Dove burrowed his face in my armpit. I laughed.

I wanted a shower. He brought me a toothbrush on a folded towel, like a ring bearer. The water was extra hot, the pressure strong. I filled the bathroom with steam, wiped my hand over the mirror. I looked dewy, refreshed: wouldn't Coach be proud. Here I go. Taking it easy.

I went to the living room. Papers slopped on the coffee table, paint-chipped trims—what had depressed me the night before now seemed like homey clutter. I made us coffee. Percolation, rich smells. Gabe Dove hummed from the bedroom, folding things.

He emerged, hair wet. We did it again. In broad daylight this time, on the couch. It was more fun this go around. I got into it. I even took off my shirt. Why not? I was never going to see this guy again.

Afterward he searched between the cushions and found me my underwear. "Donut time," he said.

We walked. To my relief Gabe Dove left his suitcase at home, making him seem lighter, more spontaneous. He whistled. I listened. The arm of Gabe Dove was around my shoulder. The streets were desolate, so many parking spots open. Sunday morning: everybody's at church. Only later did I realize that Gabe Dove wasn't, that he must have made a decision about it, that maybe Angela would see him missing from the pews. He led me down the broken sidewalk of a strip mall, to a shop between a laundromat and a Claire's.

Okay: so these donuts. They were good. Crusty and soft—they deflated when you bit in. Sugar smashing on my tongue. I ate four. Gabe Dove kept bringing napkins to our plastic wobbly table. He was grinning, but not from the donuts. He was grinning at me, at something on my face or something goofy I was doing. But I wasn't doing anything. I was eating my donut.

A glistening crumb dangled from his chin, and again I had the urge. I wanted to reach across the table and slap his sticky, dumb expression.

"I've had a great time," he said. "Do you enjoy bowling?"

Gabe Dove. His was a name that compelled you to utter it in its entirety. And in general that seemed true of Gabe Dove: you looked at him and had the feeling you were seeing all of him, all at once.

"Sure," I said. "Okay."

In Mississippi, back in the day, you would never go out with a white guy. Or—as my mom put it—they would never go out with you. She'd see them everywhere—driving to sock hops, slurping milkshakes, tutoring black boys on the weekends for church. You can look but you can't touch. Laws and stuff.

Not that you'd want to, Mom would say, brushing the memory aside with her hand. *So rude. So entitled.*

But I wondered. When she spoke of it, her eyes would gaze at some far-off mountain. What had she wanted? Who? But it didn't matter. She turned nineteen, they selected my father. Arrangements were made.

Years passed. The government changed. They lifted the dam from the river. Now all of Quitman County could have at each other.

And yet, my mom would say. The rivers didn't mix. Not in the way you'd expect. She'd shake her head, gazing again at that invisible mountain. *You still couldn't have them, see.* Or, more accurately, they wouldn't have you.

But Ex's family: they loved me. His mother squeezed my thick hair and marveled at my creaseless eyes. I was this special thing. On the boat his sister and I would compare tan lines like old girlfriends. "Of course she tans," his father said once. "She's a Chinese." His wife laughed, nervous, looking at me. I laughed too, loudly. I let them know it was A-Okay.

One time we docked and tied the rigs, the family yawning from the sun. I followed their strolling bodies to the city center and watched them kneel in a little park with cars zooming all around. They flapped out a blanket. We ate salty cheeses, plush bread, slices of watermelon dribbling to my elbow. It was a wonderful feeling, licking my fingers like that.

But then they started rolling up their jackets. They stuffed their sweaters into purses. I didn't get what was happening, until they lowered their heads onto the grass, onto the makeshift pillows. They slept. I put my cheek on Ex's chest, shutting my eyes against the chirps and swishes of people walking by. I didn't sleep, but I will never forget it: the rise and fall of his lungs, the sun warming my face.

I described the scene to my parents. That night they were in the kitchen, using a calculator to check a pile of receipts. My father coughed into his fist and said it was something he'd never do—he would never sleep in public. Mom rubbed her temples, as if just the image gave her a headache.

Because they had ideas about what could happen. They said people would steal your stuff, would call the cops, call anyone. People would think you were a drunk.

"Gabe had a great time," Angela said, grinning and rubbing her hands together. She described my whole date back to me, but with more sparkle than I would have put in: the colorful bar, the misty rain, the speeding bus driver.

"He's a great guy." I dropped my purse on my desk. "But he looks—how do I put this? He looks like my cousins."

Angela frowned. "He does?"

"I mean, he's so nice. No question. But he looks sort of like my brother." I didn't have a brother, but what did Angela know?

She crossed one leg over the other. She seemed to be inspecting my clothes, the whole outfit I had chosen. "It's not like he can control it," I said. "That's just the way he looks."

Angela leaned back in the swivel chair, her arms behind her head. I had never seen her do that before. That was something our boss did. "Don't you think that sounds a little . . ."

"A little what?" I said.

"Like something you shouldn't say?" Angela bit her lip as if to stop more from spilling out. Great. So here we were. My white friend trying to tell me what's what.

"Uh-huh," I said. "Sure thing."

I kept sleeping with Gabe Dove. I made sure Angela knew.

And at any rate it was fun; it was good to get back into practice. We would meet after work, or sometimes on the weekends. I started saving him a Friday or a Saturday. Sometimes he wanted to have dinner first, or walk along the river, which was nice, sure, but really I wanted to hurry back to his bed, where I could take off my clothes and remember what it felt like to be irresistible.

We kept on for some weeks. Some weeks became months. I

don't know: it was nice. His apartment. His humble body, rounded
at the edges. The way I could let my gut hang out: I didn't care.

One night we'd just finished doing it. I helped myself to his T-
shirt and gym shorts, crawled under the sheet, and put my cheek
on the chest of Gabe Dove. "You know, most people call me just
Gabe," he said.

"Gabe. Gabe. Gabe." I tried it out. "Nah."

He laughed and kissed my hair. "Fine. Have it your way." The
blue loops of his tattoo stretched to my horizon. I tapped it with
my finger. "What does it say?"

"That?" he said, looking down, as if he'd just noticed it was
there. "It's nothing." He shifted underneath me. "I was young."

"Is it a saying?" I said, rippling my fingers over the words. "Is it
some sort of poetry?"

"I'll tell you later." He spoke like someone shooting an arrow
into the ground.

"Is it a lyric from a song?"

"It's a name," he said.

"A name!" The thought excited me. "An old girlfriend?"

The arm around my shoulder went still. It seemed careful not
to move. "Not a girlfriend."

"Someone important?"

"Hey," said Gabe Dove. A hand squeezed my shoulder. "Do you
want to go on a double date? Angela's seeing someone."

I stopped. Okay. It's not like I even really wanted to know. So
I let us turn our attention to this guy of Angela's. Rory, or Rufus.
Some dude she'd met at the pool hall. I didn't exactly want to be
out with the three of them. Gabe Dove was someone I liked enjoying in private, out of sight of anybody else. "Um," I said. "When
would this double date be?"

"I don't know. We can coordinate." I listened to him describe
his schedule at the hospital, the upcoming visit to his dad's. It
made me tired. "I hope it isn't weird for you," said Gabe Dove,
kissing my hair again. "It's just that I'm excited. I feel really comfortable with you."

My stomach turned. Suddenly I wanted to kick him. Pinch him.
Do something to snap him awake. "Hey," I said. "How about you
punch me?"

Gabe Dove stopped the kissing. "Punch you?" he said.

My toes were tingling. They flexed under the blanket. "Yeah."

He propped his head up on his elbow, gazing confusedly into my face. "Like how?" he said. "Like where?"

"I don't know. In the stomach? In the arm?" It was just a punch. Good god, did I have to decide everything?

Gabe Dove frowned. He made a fist, limply, and nudged me in the shoulder. "No, no," I said. "Do it for real." I opened my arms, exposing my belly, the whole of my torso.

"I'm not sure I understand," he said. "I'm not sure I know what you're talking about." He was thinking too much. That was his problem.

"I mean, it's a punch," I said, staring at the ceiling, exasperated. I was matter-of-fact. "Like what do you know about pain?"

Gabe Dove hovered over my face, as if examining something trapped under glass. One eyebrow twitched uncontrollably, and his scrunched-up face was crisscrossed with new lines. On his lip was a thin white scar that I'd never noticed before, from an old piercing or some sort of cut. But all of this was secondary to the hugeness of his eyes, swollen with concern. I thought he might shout, or shake me. But then something passed, like a storm come and gone. His shoulders subsided. He relaxed.

"I'll punch you," he said quietly. "But not now."

Gabe Dove lay down and pulled the sheet over his shoulder, exposing my feet to the cold.

"You'll what?" I said, thinking I'd heard him wrong. "What was that? Gabe?"

"Don't worry," he said, turning away, adjusting his pillow. He switched off the lamp. "You'll see."

I blinked. The radiator, the curtains, the crates of books: all went mute in the dark. It took a minute to notice my hands clenched around the sheet, my heart knocking at my ribs. I watched the back of Gave Dove. His round shoulders, his quiet breathing. Was he asleep? Was he pretending?

In the morning we went for donuts. We walked along the sound barrier and past the tossing circles of the laundromat. But something was different. He didn't sling his arm around me. He didn't kiss me at the crosswalks, or whistle songs from the radio. Instead he followed behind me, silent. The sidewalk moved beneath us like a conveyor belt. I kept thinking, Will he punch me at the bus stop? At the streetlight up ahead? Will he punch me as I'm biting my donut, when I'm least expecting it, a burst of crumbs and sugar spraying from my hands?

He opened the door and I walked in. He closed it. He didn't punch me. I ordered two donuts and waited at the counter beside him. He didn't punch me.

We sat. I chewed my donuts. They tasted like water, like air-filled plastic. I was so excited. I fussed with a paper napkin, wiping each finger and the curved edge of every nail. I was aware of his feet moving under the table. But Gabe Dove's eyes sat unmoving behind square sunglasses that he didn't take off, revealing nothing. "What's wrong?" he finally said.

I giggled loudly. "What do you mean, what's wrong?" I squeezed my hands between my thighs. My fingers were so cold.

"You just seem like not yourself."

"Don't I?" I wanted to laugh. Suddenly everything was funny.

Gabe Dove's mouth maintained its solid straight line across his face. He sucked on the straw of his iced double coffee.

I played along. I kept my laugh to myself. We ate in silence, me watching his every gesture, each cough and shift of weight ripe with possibility.

The next Friday we went to Mermaid Bowling. I waited for it the whole night—through the shoe rental, the weighing of balls, the sitting on our little bench. But it didn't come. We went back to his place. He closed the door. Still nothing. We undressed. We did it in the foyer—I couldn't wait for the bedroom—but afterward he just went to the bathroom and started his electric toothbrush. In bed he turned away again, no cuddling and no punch.

Weeks passed. I waited for it in elevators, across parking lots, at the bus stop of the 64. Any time we were quiet, even for two seconds. Then I realized it might happen in the middle of a conversation. Why not? My voice got jumpy, readying for surprise. Everything I said sounded flirty, more alive.

I bought Angela a box of six cupcakes. No reason. Half carrot and half chocolate, her faves. "Gee, thanks," said Angela, peering under the lid. She lowered it and looked at me. "Is anything wrong?"

"No," I said. "Or, yes. But in a good way."

That day Gabe Dove picked me up from work. We went to a horror movie, *The Chopping Mall*, and I hid behind our popcorn as the lights went dark. Gabe Dove munched, staring ahead, his jaw moving and preoccupied.

I wondered if he'd forgotten. Like maybe it'd slipped his mind. I wanted to ask, but that would ruin the whole thing. So I just had to wait. I had to be patient. During the previews he was quieter than usual: that told me something. He touched my thigh and I nearly jumped out of my skin, laughing. He spooked me.

"Since when are you skittish?" he whispered.

"Since now," I grinned.

The movie was bad and I hugged Gabe Dove's shoulder through all the bloody parts. It felt wonderful to squeeze my eyes, to grip him like that, everything thrilling and safe. I thought about that patch of grass with Ex and his family. It wasn't their boat I wanted. It wasn't the cheese and the wine. It was the napping on the blankets. Closing their eyes wherever they pleased.

What was wrong? I thought in the dark. What was wrong was that I was getting better.

A week later I swam across the entire river. The water gave way beneath my hands; my breaths were deep and easy. I emerged panting onto the shore, seaweed clinging to my legs, aching and glorious. I regretted that there wasn't more water to cross. Even the twigs strewn on the sand looked shiny, invincible. I took my time strolling back, feeling the warm sun dry the droplets from my skin. I was going to be late. It felt wonderful not to give one shit.

I met Gabe Dove on the esplanade. He was sitting on a park bench, suitcase at his side. Atop the suitcase was a flattened paper bag, and Gabe Dove was peeling an orange and balancing the shreds of rind on the bag. I approached him but he didn't look up from his orange. "What kept you?" he said.

I was so awkward sitting down: all jacket sleeves and purse straps and wet stringy hair. I settled myself. I kissed the scruff by his ear. Gabe Dove stretched his arm along the bench but didn't touch me, maybe not wanting to get his orangey hands on my back. "Guess what?" I said. "I swam the whole river today."

"That's great," he said.

"I can't believe it. I have to call Coach. I used to swim for ninety minutes straight, but not lately, thirty's been like all I can do. But after today? Wow." I crossed my legs and admired the smooth lines of muscle forming in my thighs. "Hey," I said. "How about we go to Mermaid's?"

"I'm not sure," he said, twisting toward me. "Truthfully, Chuntao, I don't think that this is working for me."

I blinked. "Working for you?"

He raised his head from the orange and looked at me with steady eyes. "I don't think we're right for each other. I think we have different values."

"Values?" His face: it was the same face. But it was making no sense at all. "What the fuck are you saying?" I said, my voice arriving at my ears like it wasn't my own.

"Well," he said, "if really you want to know, I think you're mostly concerned with yourself, and you don't care about other people, and you don't listen, and you're scared, and you're immature, and you lie, and you have a vision of what you want that's very narrow, and self-serving, and fucked up, and you're willing to use people to get it. People like me."

I couldn't speak. Wind flew in my mouth. "I don't even like you," I yelled. "I never liked you. You're boring and you're predictable and you're bad in bed and you look like my fucking cousins. For fuck's sake!"

Gabe Dove opened his mouth but bit it closed, grimacing as if at some odor. His head tilted. His eyes changed. "How does it feel to be punched?"

There was something happening to my chin. My eyes crumpled and burned. I was crying. My hands were pulling at my face.

"You want to hurt me," I said.

"You want me to be someone else," he said.

"Never, never," I said. But he was right.

I was choking. I couldn't breathe. I leaned over my knees. The grass zoomed in all directions, a thousand blades shifting in blurs and sharp glints. "I feel like there's something wrong with me," I said.

"Could be," said Gabe Dove. Warmth spread across my back. Gabe Dove was rubbing my back.

"Something is wrong with me and I don't know what it is."

Gabe Dove was tracing a circle over my shoulders. He was offering me a cold slice of orange, placing it in my shaking hand.

"Seems so," he said.

*

Years later I checked out a book about the history of China. Seven hundred and forty-one pages, 2.5 inches thick, written by Poverman and Levitsky. I could have gotten the e-version, but I sort of liked the weight in my backpack, like I was on some quest, like I was climbing a mountain. I took it to The Vault—it was now called The Lounge—and sipped Bud Light while reading it on my stool. "That's a big book," grinned the men at the bar. "Does it have any pictures?"

The book: it wasn't my favorite. It didn't really grab me. Opium wars, rebellions, people killing and getting killed. Now, years later, I can only tell you that they happened. Not when or where or who exactly was involved.

But there was a chapter toward the middle, about fighting in Rangoon. *A devastating loss,* it said, *to the people of Myanmar.*

And I thought: No.

It's Burma, guys. Didn't they know?

I lugged the book to the grocery store. I pushed it in my cart, in the seat meant for children. Tubes of cookies tossed beside it. Cheese chunks, plastic-wrapped.

Burma. Two round sounds. Like the name of a woman.

"You sure know a lot about Burma," said my mother in the hospital. She whimpered and scratched the band at her wrist.

Burma, I said aloud down the shaking elevator at Livagon Insurance. I said it through the windshield wipers, blurring the red lights.

What do you know about pain? I'd asked Gabe Dove. And the thing I remember only now is that he didn't ask what I meant. About the punch, sure. But not about the thing I was asking him about.

"You'll see," he'd said. And he turned off the light to show me —to show both of us—the things that he knew.

Let's Go to the Videotape

FROM *Harper's Magazine*

THE FINALISTS WERE HIM and some other people, but really there was just him. Him filming his boy, who was riding a bike for the first time. A red-and-blue Spider-Man one-speed with plastic webbing and Spidey graphics arrayed along the frame. The bike had been this year's Christmas surprise because Gus was five and not so much depressed as departed from faith that the universe doled out her favors equitably. He was, in this way, easy to impress but hard to parent, which often felt to Nick like trying to grow a happy boy in the soil of their misfortune.

Who doesn't film his kid experiencing a threshold moment? It was bittersweet, really. Of course it was. Gus pedaling away on his own, newly aware of his autonomy, which contravened everything Nick had taught him by force of grief, the bond between them fortified by the loss of Nick's wife—Gus's mom—three years ago in a car accident that was still being litigated today.

And so, the film. Possibly the winner of *America's Funniest Home Videos,* on which was: Gus wobbling along on his bike, insisting his father *not let go,* as Nick gripped an iPhone that actually corrected for the tremble in his hand as he *did* let go, despite the screaming woman who'd taken up residence in his heart the instant his wife died—her name was Dread—and Gus, whose fear turned to joy when he realized he wasn't falling, on the contrary he was flying. There was, also, a hint of the disconnect that afflicts people who are filming an event instead of participating in it, so that even as Gus's tire snagged on a rock and he vaulted over the handlebars; as his helmet, which was too big, came down over his eyes like the curtain at show's end; as he popped out of the bush where he had landed and turned around several times because he could not see; as he cried out to his father, Nick beheld this spectacle at a distance, and continued to film.

Later, when they watched the clip at home, they agreed Gus had been pretty scared but also that it was pretty funny. He looked like one of those animals with its head trapped in a bag. Cue the circus music and probably Nick's friends would be amused.

They were. The next morning, six emailed back saying: *Hilarious.* Also: *That kid.* And: *I forwarded this to my sister who teaches kindergarten, and even she thought it was a riot.* By day's end, it had been posted online, subtitled humorously, and had more than five thousand views.

The studio was warm. Sweat dribbled down the host's neck, which someone kept blotting with a paper towel. He two-stepped across the room and worked his face into expressions of mirth. When he smiled, you could see his molars and caps. The audience sat on padded bleachers arranged as if someone had tossed them there. Ten grand, the host was saying, because that was the top prize for the night.

"Shoo-in," Nick whispered, and poked Gus in the ribs.

"Too tight," Gus said, and yanked at his chinos. The audience had been told to dress business casual, which had Nick stuffing Gus into last year's pants and polo, looking at the result and thinking: *big picture.* He would leave the superlative fashion sense to double-parent families and focus, instead, on celebrating his son with five million other Americans.

He pointed at the screen. The first finalist had a walrus rolled on its back like spilled pudding and an animal trainer nudging it in the gut with her foot. The voice-over said, "Yeah? Then *you* do ten sit-ups for a lousy piece of fish." The audience clapped. Second finalist: an older woman making popcorn who took a kernel in the eye. The voice-over said, "Glasses, Granny. The better to *seeeeee* you with." The audience clapped. The man sitting next to Gus let out a hacking laugh, and said, "So true."

"We're up," Nick said.

Gus pulled at his collar. This morning he had asked Nick if the show was really a good idea because one of the kids at school had seen the video online and called him a tard, but Nick, who'd been bullied for stuff like poorly apportioned facial hair in high school, knew that kids who wanted to harass his son would find a way, video or not.

"You're my special guy," he'd said. "And after tonight, everyone will know it." Which probably had not mollified Gus, but which had filled Nick with the kind of anticipation he hadn't felt since his second date with his wife. Before she'd been his wife, though already he could predict their future. Or some of it, anyway: They got married; they had Gus. And after, when Nick took stock of things, he found himself happy to a degree of hubris that attracts wrath the way an especially bright flower attracts a bee.

Subdural hematoma is what the doctors had said. Blunt-force trauma. Nick had been rear-ended by a car doing forty. His seat had lurched forward, then back, which slammed his head into his wife's, who'd been sitting behind him to coddle Gus because Gus got carsick. Weak seats, the industry had said. Regulated poorly. Under the speed limit, the other driver had said. It wasn't clear who had been to blame, but the blame was out there waiting for the law to assign it.

Not long after the accident, Gus had developed a speech impediment. A kind of nasal approach to language Nick barely even noticed anymore, but which the producers thought might ruin their film's big moment. So at 10.4 seconds in, when Gus rose up from the bush, pumping his arms like a newborn bird, and saying, almost yelling, "Daddy, am I okay?" the question was printed at the bottom of the screen in a cartoon font. The voice-over said, "Ahhh, the big questions."

Nick snickered and clapped Gus on the back. And when the audience laughed with more vigor than before, Nick said, "See?" and he beamed—less with pride than relief. Because the hardest part of being a single parent wasn't the logistics or even the exhaustion, but just the solitude of having no one to share his son's life with. The day after his wife died, Gus picked up a pink crayon and drew a circle for the first time. Nick had been so proud, though there was nothing sui generis about the circle or the precocious timing of its drawing. But who could he tell besides his wife? Who would care beyond his friends, whose care was dutiful at best? My boy just used a fork! Used the potty! Zipped his jacket! All these moments relished, extolled, and filed away in a vault of memories no one else would open. When Nick was feeling extra grim, he wondered if these memories were even safe with him as their only safeguard.

He was bad with names and faces and recently had a meeting with several lawyers, one of whom he mistook for opposing counsel because he hadn't remembered spending a half-hour with the man just two months earlier. So it was possible all the milestones Gus had jumped would actually be forgotten and in this way erased from the human script being written every second by every person on earth.

The show was almost over, time for the host to announce the results. Third place: "The Lazy Walrus." No surprise there. First place (Nick crossed his fingers in his lap, embarrassed that he should care so much): "The Existential Biker"! Sent in by Nick and Gus Slocombe from Providence, Rhode Island. Nick threw up his arms. Gus put his palms together, but if he'd meant to part them again, no one could say because the host was on them in seconds, shaking Gus's hand and saying congratulations. And, "How's the bike riding going?" Nick went a little pale. He hadn't known they'd be interviewed, and certainly not that the questions would be directed at Gus.

"I didn't catch that," the host said.

"Haven't tried," Gus mumbled.

"Well then!" the host said. "What are you going to do with the money?"

Nick shrugged. He hadn't really thought about the money. "Pay down some lawyer bills, I guess."

"Well then!" the host said. "How about this father-and-son team."

The morning after the show aired, Nick's inbox was full. He had 257 friends on Facebook and, overnight, 4,478 new friend requests. His timeline flowered with posts, half from women wondering where Gus's mom was in all this. After she died, Nick had shied away from joining any support groups because they contrived relationships among people whose only shared interest was grief. He knew some of his resistance issued from ego and pride but that some of it was rooted in real suspicion of the premise that a shared problem is a problem improved, no matter whom you're sharing it with. He'd have shared any problem with his wife, but that was because her bona fides had been tested and proven. After she was gone, he found himself unwilling to entrust his hurt to anyone but her. But now he was replying to these inquiries with the story of her death, and within a few minutes, he'd been added or invited to multiple groups having to do with widowhood and single parenting and dating as a single parent and head trauma and, by extension, a group advocating better helmets for high school football players.

By the time Gus woke up, Nick had shucked many parts of his inner life and plated them with words he'd never spoken to his friends, let alone put out for public consumption, until it was no wonder his was a hugely appetizing page, not to mention his YouTube channel, where people had come to check out his other videos because "The Existential Biker" was no longer his to air.

Gus shuffled into the kitchen in his pajamas.

"Why aren't you dressed?" Nick said. "Bus'll be here in twenty minutes."

"I'm itchy," Gus said, and lifted up his shirt.

"Cream's in the cabinet," Nick said. They'd been through this before. Anxiety rash is what that was. Best not to be indulged.

"But I don't want to go," Gus said. "Probably they all saw the show."

"I hope so!" Nick said. "You won ten grand. How many of your friends can say that? Is there anything you want me to buy you?"

Gus trudged off to the bathroom.

Nick was a real estate agent. He'd been on the job for years but rarely delegated the menial stuff to the newer guys. He always ran his own open houses. Did his own showings. These were what kept the job fresh. The influx of people and their stories, which were always about running to or running from. Divorce, marriage, death of a child, birth of a child. Today he was showing a five-bedroom colonial for $1.8 million to a couple exiled from New York City who kept saying, "All this for one point eight?" He loved buyers from New York. They'd pay $1.8 million for a shoebox *plus* shoehorn and feel lucky for it.

Normally he liked to choreograph how his clients moved through a home—sequencing and narrative were the name of the game here—but today he was so distracted by his phone buzzing news of activity on his social media, he let them wander on their own.

"It works," he said, when asked about the fireplace. "Baseboard," he said, when asked about the heat. He thumbed the keypad on his phone, writing: *Me, too! Like I have any idea how to collage.*

The man tapped him on the shoulder. "I remember those days," he said with a yawn.

Nick put his phone away. "Do you have any more questions about the house?"

The man looked up at the crown molding squared around the room. "When it felt like nothing else existed in the world but you and her. All I can say is: enjoy it."

Nick shook his head, then smiled. Maybe the Internet really was his new girlfriend. "I was on TV last night," he said. "Me and my boy. *America's Funniest Home Videos.*"

"Yeah? 'Unexpected foul-ups involving children'?" The man mimed air quotes.

Oh, right. Nick had almost forgotten. In addition to their skewed value judgments, his New York clients had also been so abraded by one another, they were never charitable, just mean. But Nick's spirits were robust. "We won," he said. "So lots of people are getting in touch." And he held up his phone.

"Enjoy it," the man said, though now his voice was less ominous than sincere.

Nick's phone buzzed again, but this time he didn't even try to be discreet. Just grinned and checked his messages and a voice-mail he hadn't noticed from his son's school saying he had to come pick up him right away.

Gus's lip was split down the middle. Swollen.

"Dad, what are you doing?" Nick positioned his phone and hit the record button. "Evidence," he said. "I'm gonna nail those little shits."

The way Gus had told it, he'd been surrounded by some of the older kids. "Am I okay?" they sneered, knocked him down, and said, "Guess not!"

"You're taking karate," Nick said. "And I'm buying you a BB gun. Two of them so you can leave one in your desk."

"It's okay," Gus said. "Probably I deserved it. Think I cut one of them in line or something."

"Almost done," Nick said, and zoomed out to capture a look on his boy's face that was pathos itself. Gus's lower lip pushed out beyond the upper in a pout he could not help. "I can call their parents," Nick said. "Of course. Now tell me again, what happened to you?"

"I fell," Gus said.

Nick stopped recording. "Don't you want me to help?" he said.

But Gus began to cry. And Nick knew he wouldn't call anyone.

That night, he put him to bed with the same bear Gus had slept with every night since his mom died. A proxy mom is what it was, with ears shorn of their fur because Gus chewed on them in his sleep. Did he need a therapist? Nick often wondered if he could mitigate his son's grief and hurt just by loving him or if his love would always be deficient for being compensatory.

Later, at the computer, he wrote: *Thanks. My kid's a looker, right?* Because he'd uploaded the video of Gus's busted lip, which had garnered 457 likes in five minutes. Ten minutes after that, someone had reposted it with a title that read: *Oh, life.* Nick had been added or invited to multiple groups having to do with parents of kids who were routinely bullied. He joined them all.

I wouldn't worry too much about that.

Sounds like you're doing an amazing job.

Gus is lucky to have you.

They all grow up despite us.

I totally agree.

Hang in there.

For the rest of the night, Nick gorged himself on the support offered up by Hajib Kumari and Stephanie Lustig, Joanna Schwartz and Jerry Stanwick. He was so touched all these people had taken the time to think about him and Gus, he stayed up late with his computer and woke up on the couch well after Gus had made his own breakfast and left for school.

Nick figured Gus must have been feeling sanguine about his prospects for the day, else he would not have left on his own. But he still felt badly and resolved to make it up to him at dinner. He was still mulling this over when the phone rang. It was his lawyer, which rarely boded well, except today was a different story. "They want to settle," he said, without hello.

This was the car company. A monolith that probably controlled 40 percent of the market, was being sued every day, and whose lawyers on retainer cost more than Nick would earn in his lifetime.

"Settle?" He said the word like he didn't know what it meant while picking up several Cheerios that were adrift on the couch. For a moment, he stopped hearing his lawyer as he realized with shame that Gus had taken his breakfast right next to him as he slept.

"Bad publicity," the lawyer said. "People are hashtagging about Gus and your story and it's gotten back to them. We should have done this years ago."

"How much?"

"You can quit your day job, if that's what you mean."

Nick agreed to the terms, then went online to share the good news. He got a few likes. Shawnie Davis posted a picture of the sun cresting over the horizon at dawn.

"How's my guy?" Nick said, and tousled Gus's hair. "Sorry about this morning, but you shoulda woken me up!"

"You were tired," Gus said. He put his backpack on the floor. It seemed heavier than a backpack should be for a five-year-old.

"Anything happen today?" Nick said. He'd already looked Gus over and surmised nothing had happened, which was what gave him the courage to ask.

"Mrs. Saffron said since everyone's been talking about our movie, we should all make our own."

"That's great. You got any ideas? Maybe like a dinosaur movie or something?"

"Can I use your phone to make it?"

Nick flipped through everything on his phone and decided it was fine. "Let me know if you need anything," he said as Gus went to his room.

When he hadn't come out an hour later, Nick put his ear to the door. "Take twelve," Gus said. So Nick backed away.

He microwaved them fish sticks for dinner but with a side of cheesy polenta he'd made thanks to a recipe posted by someone who thought maybe Nick needed some new ideas for how to nourish his kid. Gus said it was good, but he was obviously distracted and wanted only to return to his movie. Nick spent the evening online.

On Fridays, all the parents got a newsletter that recapped the week's highlights. This week had been all about multimedia and the kids' projects, so in the letter was a link to the school's YouTube channel where all the videos had been posted. Nick decided to make an event of it. Gus was still at school, and Nick was taking the day off. Maybe he'd take every day off from now on. He hadn't decided. He made some popcorn and cracked open a Dr Pepper.

"Let's go to the videotape!" he said and laughed. One of the kids had filmed his stuffed animals having a dance party. Another had filmed a tutorial about how to make a sandwich with one hand, since he was using the other to hold the phone. Gus's video was seventh, but after watching four of the others Nick just skipped ahead. At first the picture was black because Gus had his finger over the camera, but then suddenly there he was, front and center. He was sitting on his bed, filming himself.

"I'm Gus," he said. "I'm five."

Nick felt his chest expand. He was so proud of his son and knew what a big step this was for him given how self-conscious he was about his speech. You could barely even detect the problem. Gus enunciated. Focused. Looked right at the camera and seemed to project a confidence that was less put on than newly acquired. Nick smiled. Maybe he really was doing something right. He could not possibly love this boy any more than he did already.

"Okay, lemme get my stuff," Gus said, and moved out of the frame. And then: "Vroom! Vroom!" as he sped two Matchbox cars across his bedspread, which was checkered in pictures of cars from multiple decades. Nick had often overheard Gus yapping about the cars and had thought it wonderful that his son showed an interest in something age-appropriate because such things were telltale of a boy whose psyche was generally untrammeled by the grief galloping through their lives.

"This was our car," Gus said, holding up a yellow 4×4. "You can't see it, but there's me, Mommy, and Daddy inside."

Nick sat up so quickly he upended the bowl of popcorn on his lap.

"And this is the other car." A VW Bug. Tiny in comparison. Harmless. Gus opened his arms, then crashed the cars into each other. Once and then many times, all without saying a word, which was somehow more ghastly than if he'd added sound effects. Then he got back in frame. "And that's how my mom died," he said.

Nick was shaking his head. His son had recorded a narrative he'd never shared with his father, and now the school had made it available to every parent at Grayson Elementary?

"I don't remember much except I wasn't feeling well so Mom had to sit in the back with me and now she's dead and I'm not."

Nick was on the phone to the school in seconds. He'd sue them too, if he had to. He felt like driving over there and strangling whoever answered. But the principal was contrite and reassured him they'd take the video down immediately and with apology. He'd signed a release at the beginning of the year, she said, but also: she understood. "I'm a single parent, too," she added. He hung up. And then he refreshed the page every five seconds, during which intervals more and more people had commented on the video. Wasn't the school's site private? Who were these people? Gus needed counseling, they said. Gus was neglected. Gus was crying out for help.

Nick turned off the computer. But later, Ray Murtagh recommended a child psychiatrist renowned for treating orphaned children. And Caitlyn Donner posted links to studies about the positive effects of antidepressants on children. But then Heather Gonzales posted links to studies refuting other studies about the positive effects of antidepressants on children. Nick was grateful for the community and put off by the community, and wished with an aggression he had not felt in some time that his wife were here to relieve him of having to make all the decisions. How dare she have left him alone.

"What's up, bud?" Nick said. Gus was back from soccer and limping slightly.

"I fell," he said.

Nick eyed him skeptically.

"It's soccer," Gus said. Which was true.

"I made a Bolognese," Nick said. "Like Hamburger Helper, but with eggplant and portobello mushrooms."

He had intended to broach the subject of the film once they were at the table. "Romano or Parmesan?" he said.

Gus shrugged.

"What's wrong?" Nick said.

"They took my movie down."

Nick looked away, knowing instantly that he was going to lie about his part in this. "They did?" he said. "I saw it. It was great."

"They didn't think so," Gus said. He'd skewered a mushroom with his fork and was using it to carve a path through the pasta.

"I'm sure that's not it," Nick said. "It was a good video. It's how you feel. You're sad about Mom. I am, too. Though of course you know it's not your fault, right, bud? I mean, we've talked about this a lot." Except they'd never talked about it, though Nick had always meant to.

Gus pulled out a flash drive from his pocket and spun it around. "They said it wasn't appropriate."

"Do you know what *appropriate* means?"

"Sorta."

By now, Nick had shrunk so low in his chair, it was a wonder he hadn't actually moved at all. He wanted to strangle the principal all over again, though what he really wanted was just to know what to do. When he'd been a kid, it was all G.I. Joe and ThunderCats. And here was Gus with a flash drive. Nick held it up to the light as if examining a gemstone. So many decisions and judgment calls to be made about how to pass his son through a world that had evolved beyond his capacity to understand it.

"You are more than appropriate," he said.

"Okay, Dad."

"No, no," Nick said. "I mean it. Come on," and he went to his computer, where he popped in the drive, turned up the volume, and enlarged the movie.

Gus's face took up the whole screen. He said: "I feel bad a lot of the time. I think about what if I didn't get sick. Or if we were going to the store instead of the zoo. If my mom is out there like people say. If she misses me."

Nick gripped the armrests of his chair. This was like looking into the well of Gus-related joys that had kept him afloat since his wife died but seeing now that those same joys had sunk his boy into self-recrimination and despair.

"See?" he said. "You're amazing." But now he was sinking, too. "I know," he said. "How about we post this to my page? Would that make you feel better?"

Gus put his forehead on the desk.

But Nick had already hit upload. And watched the friends roll in.

KYLE McCARTHY

Ancient Rome

FROM *American Short Fiction*

WE MIGHT AS WELL begin with the homes. The condos, the
townhouses, the penthouses, the classic sixes and sevens. Let's begin there and with the servants that cook and clean them, though
"servant" is not the term used. The wealthy prefer "housekeeper."

This one time, I was called for an emergency paper intervention, dispatched on twenty-four hours' notice to Seventieth and
Park, where Isabel Shear led me past her snowy-white bedroom, a
capacious boudoir whose proportions easily exceeded my Brooklyn
studio, and into her office, a tidy little space by the back staircase
dedicated solely to the serious intellectual work of eighth grade.

The assignment that had caused Isabel Shear so much grief read
as follows: *Compare the impact of the cult of domesticity on an upper-class
woman, a working-class woman, and a slave during the last years of the
Roman Empire.* If you send your child to a top Manhattan independent school, she will complete essentially this assignment for the
next twelve years of her life. Note the nod to historical relevance,
the dutiful attention to women and minorities. Note, too, that Isabel must complete this assignment using only primary documents,
because Trinity wants to train her to be a real historian. How many
primary documents from 100 AD, do you think, discuss the house-
keeping practices of slaves?

I see, from the Word document glowing on her wispy Mac, that
upper-class women have given Isabel no trouble at all: she knows
exactly how they were oppressed. Working-class, too, Isabel has
managed, but when it comes to the part of her outline labeled
SLAVES she has only three question marks. Following my gaze, she

says, "Yeah, I've been having trouble with that part, 'cause, like, slaves don't have homes."

"Slaves have homes," I say.

"No, they don't." She seems offended by the suggestion. "They're slaves. How can you have a home if you're a slave?"

"Why don't we look at the primary documents?"

We stare blankly at Marcus Aurelius's *Meditations*.

"See," I say uncertainly. "Even if these slaves had to live in a bad part of the house, maybe a place that you or I would not *want* to call home"—I think confusedly of my own apartment, the chipped tile, dank shower, and two-burner stove—"it was still their *home*, they still took pride in it. They had domestic feelings."

"No, they didn't." Now there is real bitterness in Isabel's voice, as if I have deliberately led her into a tautology, as if I, and not her teacher—no doubt a freshly minted PhD who had dreamt of seminars at Wellesley, not first period at Trinity—had assigned her this impossible task. "How can they be domestic if they don't even have a home?"

A light knock, followed by the soundless entrance of a Filipino woman in lavender sweats. "You can put it here," Isabel says, pushing aside her laptop. Down glides a tuna steak on a scalloped white plate, some kind of green reduction drizzled over its charred flesh. Isabel says not a word. Specifically, she does not say the word *thanks*.

The woman steps back. Our eyes meet. I try to convey subtle irony, an intimation of *here we both are, serving this thirteen-year-old*. Absurdly, I hope I will be recognized by her as a comrade, conscripted into this lucrative, absurd work.

"You want something to drink?" she says. "A sandwich?"

Aghast, I shake my head. "Oh no, I'm fine, really. I'm great." A big smile, but she has already turned away.

I did not do well on my SATs. I did fine—to be frank, I probably did better than you—but I did not rocket them out of the park. In my defense, I never got tutored, I didn't buy a practice book, I took them only once. Any extra effort would have struck me as gauche. During my teenage years I conceived of my intelligence as a natural phenomenon, like the sea. The sea does not *try* to get better. The sea *is*. The extent of my preparation was to add a banana to my morning cereal. Then bubbles for three hours, then talking shit in the parking lot. "How easy was that math?" I boasted to my best friend, Lacie, and then we went to get high near the Stop & Shop where they carried the vegan moon pies we loved.

What I did, rather than ace my SATs—I will tell you this, because you probably want to know, because you probably will ask, as most of my clients eventually ask, especially after I assure them that it's *okay* not to be good at standardized tests, that I, in fact, am not good at standardized tests, they say, "Not to be rude or anything, but how did you get into Harvard, then?"—is that I wrote a play, a play in which the biblical Eve kills the biblical Adam, then travels forward in time to counsel a young heroin addict named Jane. Never mind that I knew nothing of heroin or addiction; never mind that I had not, until that year, ever read the Bible. I had a vision. At the climax of the play, Eve lifts her shirt and presses Jane's palm against her ribs. "You didn't come from Adam," she intones. "You came from me."

Obviously, it was a smash success. An empowering tale that, to a certain kind of middle-aged, second-wave feminist—a woman possessed of a slow-simmering anger, say, a woman sure that something still wasn't right, that something was in fact wrong with today's females, the ones who said they weren't feminists, who were applying to medical school in record numbers, putting off childbearing in record numbers, giving blow jobs and getting boob jobs and joining sororities in record numbers—to that kind of despairing older woman, to those English teachers and underemployed actors who had agreed to judge the Young Playwrights competition, my play was pure vindication, the raising of the banner they'd seen so dispiritingly flag. They gave it all to me; I won everything there was to win. Briefly, and too young, I felt invincible.

Not that I say all this to my clients. Instead, I murmur that I "liked to write" back in high school, that I "got some attention for it."

The first time I told Isabel this, she said, "So you were angular."

"What?" Even as I spoke it dawned on me: What other word would mean the opposite of well-rounded?

"A freak who is freakishly good at one random thing." She sighed. "Admissions people love them."

Angularity may have gotten me into Harvard, but it also had the unfortunate effect of turning me into a writer. My blood, infused once with praise, sang for more.

But how? Once you hit eighteen slinging two decent lines of

dialogue together is little more than a party trick. In the years after graduation, as I wrote and failed to get money for my writing, I began to weigh my Ivy League degree, thinking of all the anxious elites who believed in its talismanic power enough to pay for it. So I pumped up my scores and queried a host of tutoring companies.

That was how I found myself, at seven thirty at night, gliding upward in a mirrored box steered by a solemn youth with acne and a garnet bow tie. That first time, Isabel had answered the door herself, a tiny girl in tiny green shorts, dwarfed by a darkly glowing hall of gold and onyx. "Let's go up to my office," she said, which surprised me. Usually, apartments do not have *ups;* usually, teenage girls do not have offices.

I asked, "Should I take off my shoes?" and she said, "Sure." But I had only asked to be polite. I hate taking off my shoes in my students' houses, especially if I'm not wearing socks. It makes my feet feel dirty, polluted from the world of subways and streets. Here the doorknobs shone, the walls were shadowed by delicate spindly sculptures, and the carpet was so soft that my toes—my profane toes—curled with delight. As we drew back into the house the texture kept changing underfoot, raised nubs, soft pile, ridged geometric designs, all of it clean and fluffy and fresh. Up and up we went, two flights of stairs, down a long hall filled with glossy black-and-white photos of her family, portraits so artful they seemed like magazine spreads, as if the Shear family were a celebrity family, as if we were passing their Annie Leibovitz shots from *Vogue.*

Finally we reached the modest white cubby where Isabel did her work, a small room tricked out with a laser printer, a MacBook Pro, a stray iPad, and a curated row of tiny international souvenirs, which—more than the Frank Stella hanging in the bathroom, more than the drawer of chilled Pellegrino or the courtside tickets to the US Open—would come to represent to me all the mysteries of the way the very rich raise their children.

There was a tiny koala bear, a geisha in red and gold, a snowball with the Leaning Tower of Pisa inside. There was a Big Ben, a noseless Sphinx, a penguin with its flippers out. They were not what a child would have picked—they were kitsch, but carefully curated kitsch, ironic nods to the idea of souvenir, a symbol not so much of these places—Australia, Japan, Italy, Egypt—as of the idea of travel as consumption. A joke, in other words, much too elaborate for Isabel to understand.

I was distracted by her lips. Were they artificially plumped? Hard to believe. Maybe she was just suffering a mild allergic reaction to, say, gluten, which she definitely and in defiance of her mother ate (*Isabel ate a bagel and went into a GLUTEN FOG right before her PSATs,* Rachel Shear had written in her first and only email to me). I had seen Isabel with packages of peanut butter crackers—she was, after all, thirteen and hungry and not yet completely brainwashed by fad diets. Regardless. Though she was in every other sense a child, though she had tiny child limbs that squirmed as she sat at her desk and a washboard for a chest and a delicate stem of a neck, her lips were somehow adult, big and fat and swollen, Botox lips, Angelina Jolie lips, definitively sexy lips.

She had a habit, when I talked, of leaning back in her chair with her legs up, her head tilted and her mouth slightly agape, her eyes dreamy and soft. She looked like a soft-porn star when she did this. But her complete lack of awareness as she assumed a posture of sexual abandonment only revealed how completely, how utterly, she was still a child. Right?

On the corkboard over her desk she—or a decorator—had tacked photos of her from all the bar and bat mitzvahs she had attended over the past year, a kaleidoscope of Isabels dressed and coiffed like a Barbie doll, gleaming in dozens of configurations. There she was, with her friends, always posing, fixing the photographer with an empty-eyed pout.

There was another photo of her, black and white, a professional headshot—she was trying to become an actress—and again her hair hung in soft coils, her makeup was flawless, her eyes dark and inky as she gave that dead, sexed-out stare, and she looked nineteen, I mean she looked legal, up there on the corkboard, but when she was before me, copying out her medieval history textbook word for word, wearing mesh shorts and an old T-shirt, she looked like she might still enjoy Truth or Dare, might still enjoy a bedtime story.

I don't mean to sound shocked. All thirteen-year-old girls want to be seventeen, unless they want to be ten again. No thirteen-year-old wants to be thirteen—they are always straining forward or back. But I was one of the ones who wanted to go back, to be ten; in fact, sometimes I think I could have been ten forever, that I would be happy, still, playing touch football with the boys, riding my bike, inventing elaborate dares with Lacie, keeping scientific records of rocks, having sleepovers, reading chapter books in bed until lights out at nine thirty, and then bounding forth each morning, sweet-smelling and hungry and happy and confident of the day.

Yes, I would go back to ten, in a heartbeat I would, but I also mistrust this nostalgia of mine, for I belong to the generation who hit puberty just as *Reviving Ophelia* hit the bookshelves. At once, female adolescence went from *a time of transition* to *a time of doom,* an apocalyptic meltdown of personality. Mary Pipher, PhD, described the brilliant, vivacious girls she had known, how in the teenage years they stopped speaking in class and started cutting themselves, little red slices on the skin. Across the nation, in suburbs everywhere, mothers read this book, and their daughters read it, too. Maybe this is why I want to go back, because I snuck *Reviving Ophelia* from my mother's nightstand and learned how I was going to lose myself, that my childhood was Eden but I had to leave, that in this poisonous late-twentieth-century misogynist culture, anorexia and suicide and rape and self-hate were the inevitable wages of womanhood.

And now here I was, fifteen years later, locked in a little white room with a little white girl who was rushing, as fast as she could, toward the time when she would have to be a woman every day. Fine. Fair enough. But usually, when little girls try to be women, their inept experiments with eye shadow and cheap dresses from H&M mark them as babies, only playing pretend. Isabel had an army of hairstylists and makeup artists—the very best in New York, no doubt—to turn her into a starlet, an ingénue, a little Lolita. I couldn't stand it.

I remember the woman who played the heroin addict in my play. She was a skinny white woman with a long orange ponytail named Catherine, and the woman who played Eve was an older black woman with a round moon face named Melanie. One day, as we were all sitting around the table, I gave a little speech about the play. I meant it to be a feminist speech, a rousing speech, a we-are-all-oppressed-as-hell speech, but Melanie, when I finished, said, "I don't know. I've always really liked being a woman. It doesn't seem so bad to me."

I still remember the shame I felt. She was right: my life wasn't so bad. It was hard to say—or it seemed to me at the time hard to say —exactly why being female was so awful, exactly how I had been oppressed—I mean, I still talked a ton in class, I hadn't tried to kill myself, not even once—and also, even though I knew nothing about her life, nothing except that she was an actor, a middle-aged black woman who did regional theater in Philadelphia, I thought or sensed or assumed that her life had been harder than mine, that if she liked being female then what reason could I possibly have to complain?

But, as I said, I knew nothing about her, and because I was six-teen, a sixteen-year-old girl who had not properly washed her hair in a month, who wore baggy men's corduroys from Goodwill and giant hoodies in colors like dune and umber; because I undoubt-edly spent a lot of that rehearsal, when I was not talking about oppression, wondering whether Jonah, my high school boyfriend, was not asking me to have sex because he was a good kid or be-cause he just didn't want to have sex; because when you are sixteen it is actually medically impossible to think of anyone except your-self for longer than thirty seconds—because of all these things, I probably did not think too much about her, about Melanie, I mean. I wanted to have sex, I felt I was ready, we were ready, we were sixteen, we were in love, we had been dating for a year, but I needed him to ask. I needed him to want it, want it so badly that he would do the thing you were never supposed to do, the thing that we had been warned about, again and again, in health class: put pressure on me. Pressure. Boys must not pressure girls, girls should not pressure girls. No one must pressure anyone to do any-thing, ever. But I wanted him to pressure me; I wanted to have sex without choosing, fully, to have sex; I wanted to avoid responsibil-ity, just a little bit, for my wanting.

The day that Isabel turns in her paper about the slaves, we do not celebrate or linger. It is on to the Sermon on the Mount. Christian-ity sneaks up on us, as it snuck up on the Romans.

We read each line, then discuss. I gloss over the bad news about rich people, because I am sensitive, and whisk her ahead to the part about the light, about not keeping your light hid. She consid-ers, says: "So, Jesus is just like, worship me, worship me."

"Yeah, pretty much."

"Oh my *God*. He's like Beyoncé or something. He's bigger than Beyoncé."

She contemplates this for a minute and then her face screws up. "Wait, can you imagine if you *were* Beyoncé?" She clamps her hand over her mouth, agog. "If you actually *were* her?"

Until this moment, it has never occurred to Isabel that Beyoncé is an actual person. Until this moment Beyoncé has been a behemoth, an empire, a brand. There is too much Beyoncé for Beyoncé to be contained in one person.

Of all the mementos from bar mitzvahs on Isabel's desk, the one that fascinates me the most is a small yellow box of candy. Isabel's face is on it. Smiling in a white satin gown, she gestures like Vanna White at the gumdrops, a perfect sugar princess.

This is what the rich do, after they have bought epic pieces of property and priceless art, after they have grown bored of travel and the ballet and a box at the baseball stadium. They buy their way closer to celebrity, and then they buy themselves a simulacrum of it. Yet they never quite believe their own pose. Nothing excites Isabel so much as Beyoncé, I think, because Beyoncé has something that Isabel cannot buy.

Later, when Jonah and I finally did have sex, when I said, "All my friends think it's weird we haven't had sex yet," and he said, "Oh, do you want to have sex?" in a jovial, sporting tone, as if I had suggested we take up an obscure but hypothetically enjoyable hobby, and then when we had finally gotten naked in his basement bedroom, when he had torn the foil packet of the Trojan condom that I had made him buy, when we had actually started to *do it*, we could not stop laughing. The whole procedure seemed unwieldy and faintly absurd. We could not muster the requisite solemnity. "Ow, ow, you're hurting me," I gasped, but I was giggling. I guess I was nervous. I guess we both were.

It's hard for me to imagine Isabel finding anything funny about sex. It's too hooked in to glamour for her, too connected to looking a certain way.

When her teacher returns her paper in two days, it will be branded a B+; this will prompt her mother to decide that I don't understand Isabel's needs, that it is simply "not working out." We don't know it yet, Isabel and I, but we are on our last session together. After tonight we will never see each other again.

We move on to the adultery section of the Sermon on the Mount. Most people forget it's there. "So," I try to explain, "Jesus is saying that before you weren't allowed to commit adultery, but now, you can't even think about it. Thinking about it is as bad as doing it."

Her mouth is open, her eyes are far away. We forge on.

"Wait, what does that mean?" she asks.

I scrutinize. I stall. Finally I say, "So, if you stop sleeping with your wife, you can't divorce her, and if another man wants to marry her, he can't, because you will still be married to her, even if you're not sleeping with her anymore." For some reason I feel wildly unsure whether Isabel knows what *sleeping with* means, even as I know that she does, that she probably knows more words than I know, words for acts I cannot even imagine, acts that probably involve cell phones.

She is paying attention now. She says, "Are you a feminist?"

"Yes," I say. "Are you?"

She hesitates. "Yes." She looks both bashful and proud. "But I don't do any feminist work."

"Me neither," I tell her, and we grin at each other, like two housewives who've just admitted that we don't iron the sheets.

Later, though, I keep thinking about it: feminist work. What is feminist work? For some reason the only two answers that come to mind are escorting women past antiabortion activists and answering phones at a domestic violence shelter. But obviously that can't be right. I feel like I do feminist work. I feel like feminism is more about being than doing, but maybe this is a cop-out. I think of the column my friend Maddy ran in our college newspaper called Ask a Feminist. Nobody had any questions, so she made them up: *Dear Maddy, Is it feminist to carry a Nalgene bottle? Sincerely, Confused in the Co-op.*

She replied, *Dear Confused in the Co-op, A Nalgene bottle aids in hydration, and insofar as it is a feminist principle to stay hydrated and generally healthy, yes, it is feminist to carry a Nalgene bottle.*

Back then I thought this hilarious, but now its faith touches me. From this perspective, my whole life is a feminist work. All those dark leafy greens in the crisper, the yoga class I went to last Tuesday, even the fact that I live alone, have lived alone for six years now, in a little household of one, washed the dishes and taken out the garbage and written my godforsaken manuscript all by myself, for six years, all alone, is a feminist work. Maybe I am a feminist work.

I imagine explaining all this to Isabel, grabbing her by the shoulders before she can grow into those images on the wall, those photos of her older self, and saying, *Who cares? Go live your life! Go muck stalls, go farm potatoes, go smoke pot in the parking lot of a Stop & Shop* . . .

"Hello?" Isabel says, peering at me. "You look totally spaced out."

She's right. I am spaced out, floating, realizing that I don't know anything about her. I try to imagine if I were Isabel. If I actually *were* her.

"Hello?" she says again. "Anybody home?"

ERIC PUCHNER

Last Day on Earth

FROM *Granta*

WHEN I WAS YOUNG, seven or eight, one of my father's German shorthaired pointers had puppies. These were marvelous things, trembly and small as guinea pigs and swimming all over each other so they were hard to count. Their eyes, still blind, were like little cuts. After a few days my father decided we needed to dock their tails. He shaved them with an electric razor, then sterilized some scissors and had me grip each puppy with two hands while he measured their tails and snipped them at the joint. It was horrible to watch. The puppies yelped once or twice and then went quiet in my arms, as still as death. I didn't want my father to see what a wimp I was, so I forced myself to watch each time, trying not to look at the half tails lined up on the porch, red at one end so they looked like cigarettes.

When it was time to dock the last puppy's tail, my father handed me the scissors. It seemed important to him that I do it. *Don't think too much,* he told me. When it came time to snip, though, I couldn't stop thinking and did it too slowly and there was a sense of cutting through something strong, like rope, except it was tougher than rope and gave me a curled-up feeling in my stomach. The puppy began to yelp and thrash around and I made a mess of the thing, snipping several times without finding the joint so that my father had to cut the tail shorter than all the others. He was upset. These were expensive dogs, and you couldn't sell one that wasn't perfect. Still, my father loved me back then and didn't make a big deal of it; he was planning on keeping two of the pups anyway, so he named her Shorty. He could do that in those days—turn his disappointments into a joke.

During hunting season, my dad went shooting once or twice a month, squeezing Shorty and Ranger into the back seat of his Porsche and driving out to a game farm in Hampstead County. I used to get up at the crack of dawn to see him off. He must have known I liked helping him because he always asked me to carry something out to the car: his first aid kit or his decoys with their keels sticking down like ice skates or once even his Browning 12-gauge shotgun in its long-handled case. But it was his Stanley thermos that seemed magical to me because my father's breath, after he took a sip from it, would plume like smoke. My mother hated coffee—"motor oil," she called it—and so I connected it with being a man. Often my dad didn't return until after dark, his trunk lined with pheasant, which he'd carry into the house by the feet. They looked long and priestly with their perfect white collars, red faces arrowed to the ground. It made me feel strange to look at them, and a little scared.

After we moved out to California, my dad stopped hunting, which meant there was no reason to keep Shorty and Ranger in shape. There was an old horse corral on the property we'd rented, and my dad set up their pen inside it. Despite the creeping shade of an avocado tree, the dogs spent much of the day in the hot sun, snapping at flies, whimpering, and getting fat. The corral was a good ways from the house, and eventually I stopped really thinking about them. The whimpering made me sad for a while, and then it didn't. I was fifteen by then. My dad kept saying he was going to find a home for them, but then he moved out himself and left my mom to take care of us—me and the dogs.

"We're going to the animal shelter," my mom said one afternoon. She was sitting at the kitchen table, holding a glass of white wine. I'd never seen her have a glass of wine before six o'clock. I inspected the bottle on the counter—it was half-empty, sweating from being out of the fridge.

"What?"

"I told your father that if he didn't come get the dogs this morning, I was taking them to the shelter. I've been asking him for six

months. It's past one and he isn't here." My mother took a sip
from the glass in her hand.

"They'll put them to sleep," I said.

"You don't know that for sure."

"No one's going to adopt some old hunting dogs. How long do
they try before giving up?"

"Seventy-two hours." My mom looked at me, her eyes damp and
swollen. "Your father won't deal with them. What am I supposed
to do?"

My mother couldn't even get rid of a spider without ferrying it
outdoors on a piece of paper. Then again, the dogs were unhappy,
perhaps sick, and I certainly wasn't going to be the one who got up
at six in the morning to run them up and down the driveway. I had
no interest in dogs or hunting. The only time I ever got up early in
summer was to go surfing, and I groused so much that my friends
usually regretted taking me.

My mother poured herself another glass of wine, which spilled
when she lifted it. She'd begun to wear contact lenses again, something she hadn't done in a long time, and her eyes looked naked
and adrift without her glasses. On the kitchen counter was a book
called *Unlocking the Soul's Purpose.* I wished my sister were here to
see her—my mom, drunk and strange-eyed in the kitchen—but
she lived in Africa, doing something for the Peace Corps I hadn't
bothered to understand. She was nine years older, too worried
about puff adders hiding in her laundry to care much about our
parents' troubles.

I handed my mom a dishtowel. "Dad's going to go apeshit," I
said, hoping the swearing might upset her.

"Ha. Believe me. That doesn't even begin to describe it."

"Maybe he's tied up at work," I said.

"Your father doesn't have a job, remember?"

"He's starting his own business."

My mother laughed. "With his girlfriend?"

"It's a savings and loan," I said, ignoring this.

"Caleb," my mother said. "He's two million dollars in debt."

I smiled at her. "That's money he's *invested,*" I said patiently.
"Venture capital."

My mother got up to put her glass in the sink. My dad had
told me all this a couple weeks ago, the last time we talked on the
phone, but it was just like my mother not to understand. "Your

mother's an idiot," my father said when I told him she'd described him as "unemployed," and what shocked me more than the word itself was how sincere he was—how calmly diagnostic, as if he were trying to make sense of his own hatred. As soon as he said it, I had a feeling like when you drink a Coke too fast and burp it into your head. There was something about her, something needy and timorous and duty-bound, and it had driven my dad away. And now he would be furious about Shorty and Ranger—furious at me, too, for failing to stop her.

When they realized they were going in the car, Shorty and Ranger skittered around the driveway before hopping into the back seat. It made me both happy and sad to see they could still muster some excitement. My mother shut the door quickly, as if she couldn't bear to look them in the eye, and I remembered that she was the one who'd always groomed and bathed them when my dad wasn't running them up and down the yard, talking to them in a dopey, dog-brain voice that occasionally made me jealous. "Buster," she called Ranger sometimes, which is what she also called me, at least when I was little.

"We should do something for them," I said, "before we take them to the shelter." I needed time to think.

"Good idea," my mom said, looking relieved. "Where's the happiest place for a dog?"

"The beach?"

She smiled. "Of course. The beach. My God, I don't think they've ever been."

I climbed into the front seat while my mother shut up the pen. The dogs watched me eagerly from the back seat. Shorty's muzzle, I noticed for the first time, had begun to go gray. "You're not going to die," I told them, though they didn't seem worried. Already a plan had begun to hatch in my brain. My mother, trying to unhook the orange whistle from the door of the pen, dropped it in the dirt.

"Do you need me to drive?" I asked her when she got in the car.

"Don't be ridiculous. You haven't even finished driver's ed."

She managed to back the Mercedes successfully down the dirt road, even with the FOR SALE sign covering half of the rear window. My mother did not have a job—hadn't, in fact, graduated from college because she'd become pregnant with my sister—and despite my efforts at denial the new reality of our lives was begin-

ning to sink in. Selling the Mercedes was not going to be enough
to support us. The house had a tennis court and a swimming pool
overlooking the canyon, and though I didn't know how much the
rent was, I knew it was much more than we could afford. We'd
given notice for the end of the month, but only now, watching my
drunk mother back out into the street, did it occur to me she had
no idea what we were going to do.

But I wasn't too worried. Not because I had any sentimental illusions about my parents getting back together. They hated each
other, that was clear, and I was happy that no more dinners were
going to be ruined because of it, my mother locking herself in her
room to cry. But my father wasn't going to leave me high and dry.
He'd told me as much after the separation. He'd take me in, if I
wanted, just as soon as he found a bigger place. He was looking
in Corona del Mar, trying to find a house on the beach. I could
surf every morning if I wanted to. The name itself—Corona del
Mar—sounded like a foreign country to me, a place you sailed to
in a dream. Very soon he'd zoom up our driveway in his Porsche,
bearing pictures of our new house, grinning in the way he used to
when the trunk was full of birds.

At Grunion Beach my mother opened the glove box and fished
out her old sunglasses. They were white and mirrored and hope-
lessly out of style, the kind you saw on the ski slopes with little
leather side shields on them.

"How do I look?" she asked me.

Poor, I wanted to say. I pretended to drink the coffee I'd made
her buy me at 7-Eleven. It tasted terrible, but I didn't care. I liked
the warmth of it in my hand. We let the dogs out of the car, and
they ran down the dusty trail before splashing into the water and
then galumphing back out when a wave caught them. This was not
the beach where I surfed. Homeless people came here, and spear
fishermen in scuba gear, and strange, well-dressed men with brief-
cases who looked like they'd walked through a mirror in London
or Hong Kong and ended up at the beach by mistake.

It had taken some sly work to steer my mother here, and now I
told her I had to use the bathroom. Instead I headed for the pay
phone and called my father, my heart stamping in my chest. I'd
never been there, to my dad's apartment, but I knew the address
from all the letters my mom had to forward—*Now I'm his collection*

agent too—and I pictured the phone ringing just a mile or so up the street, wondering if his girlfriend would answer. I'd tried sometimes to imagine what she looked like: tall-booted and glamorous and at home in the front seat of a Porsche, the opposite of my mother in every way.

When the machine came on and my father's voice asked me to leave a message, I was almost relieved. I explained what was going on, that he needed to come find us as soon as he could.

"Mom wants to murder Shorty and Ranger," I told his answering machine.

Down on the beach, my mother was absorbed in her Slurpee, sucking on the straw with her eyes closed. I'd been astonished to see her buy anything for herself at 7-Eleven, let alone a Slurpee, which she used to say would "rot my liver." Shorty and Ranger sniffed around for dead things, looking happier than I'd seen them in a long time. It was a beautiful afternoon—sunny and cool, with a breeze like a can of perfect ocean smell—and it was hard to imagine anything being killed.

"I haven't been to the beach in years," my mom said. She slipped off her sandals and dug her feet into the sand, and you could see the warmth of it spread across her face. Her sunglasses, when she tipped her head back, looked like a piece of the sky. "Believe it or not, we used to have a great time together. You and me. Ocean City, remember? We used to bury each other in the sand, like mummies. Your sister too. Even your father got a kick out of it." She shook her head, as if the fact that we didn't go to the beach together anymore was my fault. "I should have come down here more often."

"You still can," I said. "You can come here whenever you want."

She looked at me. "Do you really believe that?"

"Why not?"

"That I can skip down to the beach whenever I want, just for the hell of it?" She seemed angry, though it was hard to take her seriously with the Slurpee in her hand. "Nice try, but I'm going to have to get a job."

I smiled. "Like what?"

My mother lifted her ridiculous sunglasses. "You don't think I have any skills or talents?"

I shrugged. No, I didn't really think she did. She had an okay singing voice, nothing to write home about, and sometimes she could solve math problems without a calculator—but I couldn't really think of anything else, anything special about her.

"I see," she said, slipping her sunglasses back on. Her lips, damp from the Slurpee, looked thin. She gazed down the beach, where Shorty and Ranger were sniffing at a giant bullwhip of kelp. "Remember when your father made you dock Shorty's tail?"

"Not really," I lied.

"I was glad you couldn't do it," she said, ignoring me. "It gave me hope for you."

I took another sip of coffee. The taste almost made me gag, but I decided right then to force myself to like it. Shorty and Ranger looked up from the kelp they were sniffing, distracted by a guy scanning the beach with a metal detector. He was wearing those stupid headphones that beachcombers wear, moving his machine back and forth like a blind person's cane, so tan it was hard to make out his face. He waved at us, smiling, and my mom tugged the hem of her dress over her knees. I had never talked to a beachcomber before and lumped them in the same category as men who collected lost balls from the gully near the golf course, folks my dad called "bottom feeders." I hoped Shorty and Ranger might scare him off, but the man walked up to them boldly and let them sniff his hand.

"Fine dogs," he said to me, taking off his headphones.

He was wearing a madras shirt unbuttoned at the chest, exposing a tussock of gray hairs. I'd heard the term *salt-and-pepper mustache* before, but this was the first time I'd seen one in real life. In another context—if he had been holding a tennis racket, say, instead of a machine for grubbing up lost change—you might even have called him handsome.

"German shorthairs?"

I nodded.

"Did you raise them yourself?"

"They're my father's," I said.

"Used to have a GSP myself. Frisky, her name was. She had hip dysplasia, so the name was perhaps ill-chosen." The man glanced at my mother, and I had the feeling that he was speaking to her somehow and not me, the way you might try to speak to a ventriloquist by talking to his dummy. He looked down the beach. "Where's your paterfamilias, if you don't mind my asking?"

"My what?"

"Your father."

I glanced up at the parking lot. "I don't know."

The man nodded, as if turning this over in his mind. He waved the detector in our direction, and it beeped so loudly that Ranger barked. "Sorry," he said, frowning. "Are you wearing a ring?"

My mother shook her head.

"It's attracted to you nonetheless."

She blushed. The man asked if we had a spot of water on us —"feeling a bit sponged out here today"—and astonishingly my mom lifted her Slurpee and offered him a drink. The man's mustache, when he handed the cup back to her, was red.

My mom laughed. She lifted her sunglasses again and perched them on her forehead. How different she looked without them: tired and sun-stamped, the corners of her eyes mapped with little lines. She was forty-five years old. Something in the man's face seemed to relax.

"We don't want to interrupt your beach hunting," I said.

"Not at all. I was just going to take a little breather." My mom sucked noisily at her straw, and the fact that she wasn't completely herself—that she was a bit drunk—seemed to dawn on him for the first time. "It's me, possibly, who's interrupting something?"

"Caleb and I were just discussing my talents," my mother said, narrowing her eyes. "Namely, how I don't have any."

The man regarded me gravely. The idea of her talentlessness seemed to offend his cosmic sense of justice. "Nonsense. Everyone has a God-given talent."

"Well, He skipped me. Didn't He, Caleb? I'm pretty much useless." My mom smiled at me, but there was a hardness to her eyes that I'd only ever seen directed at my father.

"I don't believe you," the man said. "Not for one second." He looked at me, then back at my mother, as if trying to figure out what he'd walked into. "You mean to tell me there's *nothing* you've ever done that made people go: 'Hello, look at her, I'm impressed'?"

My mother cocked her head. "In college, I could walk on my hands," she said finally. "At parties they'd chant JP, JP—that was my nickname—and I'd walk around like that. Once I even walked to class that way, just for kicks."

"There you go," the man said, vindicated.

I looked at my mother. I knew for a fact that she couldn't walk on her hands. She couldn't even keep up with her exercise video,

Aerobics for Beginners. I had never heard her lie before, about anything, and it gave me an ugly feeling.

My mother glanced at the sieve hanging from the man's belt.
"And your talent, I gather, is finding hidden treasure?"

"I have a certain knack," the man said, and winked at her in a
way I didn't like.

"How does that thingamajig work?"

The man unstrapped his arm from the machine, which looked
like one of those crutches old people wear except with a wire vin-
ing up the shaft to a fancy-looking control box, and handed the
contraption to my mother. Then he slipped the sunglasses gently
from her head and pinched the headphones over her ears and
positioned himself behind her, gripping her hand with his own,
leaning into her as if he were teaching her to hit a golf ball. The
man showed her how to sweep the coil over the sand, back and
forth. My mother laughed at something, and there was a look on
her face I hadn't seen in a very long time, not since my parents
used to get dressed up for parties and my father would tell her, in
a voice I didn't recognize, how "radiant" she looked. She smiled
as the man showed her how to work the knobs and buttons, asking him to repeat himself for no reason. She seemed to hang on
every word. Though I had the sense, too, that she was trying to
prove something to me, that the real her had stepped out of her
body like the harp-toting angel in a cartoon and was watching me
the whole time. I looked away. Shorty and Ranger were panting in
the sand, exhausted from chasing waves, and I felt suddenly short
of breath, too, and a little sick, as though I might throw up. A tire
squeaked in the parking lot—my heart leaped—but it was just a
lost Jeep turning around. Where the hell was he?

When I turned back to my mother, the beachcomber was still
gripping her hand. She caught my eye suddenly and stepped away.
Her dress was rumpled. She took off the headphones and handed
the metal detector back to the beachcomber.

"How much does it cost?" she asked politely.

"Seven hundred," he boasted. "You can get cheaper ones, but
not with a zero-to-ninety-nine target ID."

"What a rip," I said.

The man turned to me and frowned, studying me for a second.
"Tell that to the guy who found the Mojave Nugget."

"The what?" my mom asked.

"Mojave Nugget. 4.9 kilos of solid gold." The man hitched up his pants. "You wouldn't believe the treasures lurking underfoot. Friend of mine, just last week, found a diamond ring, and no river rock either. One and a half carats."

I snorted.

"Pardon me?" the man said.

"Mojave Nugget. Jesus Christ. Don't be a moron."

"Caleb!" my mother gasped.

"Will you please just go look for pirate treasure somewhere else?"

The man was about to speak, to put me in my place, but my face seemed to make him reconsider. He straightened his shoulders. Gallantly, he handed my mother her sunglasses and then started back toward the water before stopping a few feet away to slip his headphones on, as if to show everything was fine. My mother wouldn't look at me; she put her sunglasses back on and plopped down in the sand again.

"Does it feel as good as you thought it would?" she asked after a while.

"What?"

"Calling someone an idiot."

I nodded, though it didn't feel good at all. My mother busied herself with her feet, swishing sand over them until they disappeared. I'd never heard her sound so disgusted with me. She yawned, and the disgust in her face seemed to shrink back into sadness.

"Okay, buster," she said to Ranger, checking her watch.

I glanced at the parking lot. "It's only three o'clock."

My mother stared at her missing feet, then at me. I remembered burying her in the sand in Ocean City, how my sister and I would cross her arms over her chest like a pharaoh's. It seemed like something from a different life.

"Here," I said, kneeling beside my mother and beginning to dig a trough.

"What are you doing?"

"Burying you in the sand."

My mother yawned again. "God, I'm so tired," she said. "Must be the wine. I feel like I could sleep right here."

I dug with two hands. The idea was to keep us here till my father showed up—keep us here, at least, until I could get ahold of him. The sand was less hot the deeper I plowed, each layer cooler than the one above it, and the coolness under my fingernails versus the warmth against my wrists was such a specific, one-of-a-kind sensation that I came unstuck from time for a second. I could half hear the shrieks of Ocean City, half smell the whiff of my mother's sun lotion, half see the smile on my father's face as he smeared the lotion into her back and made her hum like a girl. His wet hair was swooped back and perfectly parted—he carried a folding comb, one that popped out like a switchblade, even to the beach—and I found him incredibly dashing. One time, walking back to the car on the hard part of the beach where the surf had retreated, he stopped to show my sister and me the print of his sneaker tread in the sand, a perfect impression, complex as a tiny fortress. Embossed in the middle of it was the word SADIDA. My father found this to be a marvelous thing. *Sadida,* I said to myself, because it sounded strange and marvelous to me too. And then my mother made a shoe print next to my father's—she was wearing sneakers as well, her old Tretorns—and we stopped to admire this, too, the four of us laughing for no reason, and I remember making the long drive back to Baltimore, feeling bored and lucky and spanked all over from the sun, and thinking *Sadida Sadida Sadida* as we chattered over the Botts' dots on the highway.

Now my mother lay down in the trough I'd dug, looking up at me in her sunglasses, and I started to push sand over her legs and arms and torso. I buried her as best I could. Shorty and Ranger watched me work. When I was done, she was a mound of sand with a head sticking out. Her cheeks, like mine, were dusted with freckles.

I let her lie there in her sunglasses, tucked to her chin, until I wondered if she'd fallen asleep. "Mom," I said, but she didn't answer. Then I jogged up the path to the parking lot, Shorty and Ranger trailing behind me as if I were leading them to the next great happiness. They waited by the phone as I rummaged in my pockets. I had another quarter, I was sure of it, but all I could find was a dime and a nickel. I checked the change slot: empty. I was fifteen years old—practically a man, or so I believed—but I felt suddenly like I might cry. I don't believe in psychic powers or anything like that, so I can't explain the certainty I had that afternoon, staring at the rusty phone and its rain-warped Yellow Pages dangling from a cord: a feeling beyond all doubt that my father was home, that he'd been there all day, that he was busy working and hadn't gotten my message.

I peered over the rocky berm to where I'd left my mother on the beach, but couldn't see her face. She was just a lump of sand. The beachcomber, too, was nowhere to be seen. I felt as strange as I've ever felt.

I checked under the rear fender of the Mercedes and found the little magnetic box where my mom kept a spare set of keys and loaded Shorty and Ranger into the back seat before climbing behind the wheel, blinded by the leathery heat. There was a map in the glove compartment, tearing along the folds. I looked up my dad's street. The Mercedes started right up, no problem, and though I lurched a bit in reverse, I managed to get out of the parking space well enough and coax it onto the road. I spaced my hands at nine and three o'clock on the wheel, as I'd been taught to do. The big car seemed to glide along, responding to my thoughts. I'd dreamed about it so often that it was like I'd been driving for years. I pulled onto Palos Verdes Drive North, making sure to keep a three-second space cushion between me and the car ahead. I couldn't help thinking how easy—almost disappointingly natural —it was, this adult thing that all my life had seemed like magic.

I found my dad's street and turned down it, bucking over a speed bump that sent Shorty and Ranger tumbling from the back seat. At first I thought I had the wrong address. I'd been expecting a condo complex, but this was a stucco apartment building shaped like a box and propped up on stilts. It looked like it might try to creep away in the middle of the night. SAXON ARMS was written on the front in medieval-looking script. Parked under the building, squeezed between two of the stilts, was my father's Porsche.

I let the dogs out of the back seat and we walked around to the other side of the building, their collars jingling, and climbed the stairs. One of the apartments had a BEWARE OF DOG sign, emblazoned with the picture of a snarling pit bull, taped inside the window. I stopped at my dad's door and knocked. It was not a long flight of stairs, but my heart was going as if I'd run all the way from the beach.

"Caleb!" my dad said when he saw me, nearly dropping the CD in his hand. He was wearing sweatpants and one of those pleated Cuban shirts with tiny buttons where there weren't any button-

holes, which I'd never seen him wear before. He hugged me in the
doorway, and I could smell the coffee on his breath mixed with the
chemical newness of his shirt. Music played behind him; he was a
jazz fan—Fats Waller, that old stuff—and I realized how much I
missed hearing its delirious ruckus around the house. Shorty and
Ranger barked, excited to see him, and my father bent down to say
hello, closing the door most of the way behind him.

"Did you get my message?" I asked.

"I did," he said, glancing behind him. "Just now. I've been on
my office phone all morning." He cleared his throat. "Wow. Look
at you. How the hell did you get here?"

"I drove."

"You have your license already?"

I nodded. My father eyed me carefully—suspiciously, I thought
—and then treated me to the rare abracadabra of his smile. "Ser-
ena's taking a shower. She's been lying out on the patio. The
woman can sunbathe through an earthquake."

The idea of her lying out in the middle of a Tuesday, instead
of dealing with bills or laundry or groceries, seemed exotic to me.
Scattered on the welcome mat was a pair of pink flip-flops. My
dad bent down to collect them, grumbling under his breath, and
Ranger slipped into the apartment. "Ranger, heel!" my father said,
jogging after him. Shorty and I followed into what looked like the
living room, though it was hard to say since the only furniture
was a futon folded up into a pillowless couch. Nearby, tucked into
one corner, was a kitchen area with a little stove and a microwave
whose door was open and some *Vogue* magazines stacked on the
counter next to a Carl's Jr. bag. One of the cupboards had the
sticker of a Teenage Mutant Ninja Turtle on it. I searched around
for the office he was talking about.

"I've got my eye now on a house in Manhattan Beach," he said
without looking at me. He grabbed Ranger's collar and pulled him
away from a ficus plant in the corner, glancing at the closed door
beyond the kitchen. I could hear pipes moaning inside the walls.

"What about Corona del Mar?"

"It's like Club Med down there now. Anyway, those cliffs? Whole
town's sliding into the ocean."

My father turned down the music, then glanced again at the
closed door of the bedroom. He hadn't thanked me for bringing
Shorty and Ranger, but I chalked this up to my appearing out of

the blue. Shorty found the Carl's Jr. bag on the counter and tried
to pull it onto the floor, pawing her way up the cupboard.

"Down, girl!" my father said and yanked Shorty's collar, hard
enough that she yelped. The dog skidded over to me, crouched
on her hind legs. "No one cleans up around here. It's dog heaven.
Didn't you bring their leashes?"

"I thought you'd want to save them from the shelter."

"I do, bud. I do." My dad's face softened. "But they're pointers.
I can't keep them cooped up in here. They're run-and-gun dogs."

"Mom's going to kill them."

"It's me she wants to kill," he said proudly. He looked at Shorty
and then glanced away again, as if he couldn't meet her eye. "Does
she talk about me?"

"Mom?"

"We lived in an apartment about this size, in New York. This was
before your sister was born. The boiler didn't work right, or maybe
the landlord was just a prick, but we could see our breath in that
place. Your mother stole some bricks from a construction site—a
pregnant woman!—and heated them in the oven. We slept with
hot bricks at our feet."

"Can't you keep them for a little while?" I said. "Till the house
is ready?"

"I wish I could, bud, but they're not allowed in the building.
Not even shih tzus. It's in the lease."

The pipes in the wall squeaked off, and my dad excused himself
and disappeared into the bedroom. I could hear him talking to
his girlfriend behind the door, the muffled sound of their voices
—I imagined her naked from the shower, dripping all over the
carpet—and after a while I had the ghostly sensation, watching
the dogs sniff around the kitchen, that we weren't in my dad's
apartment at all. From outside drifted the sounds of a nearby pool,
the echoey shrieks and splashes, and I thought about when Shorty
and Ranger were puppies, soon after my father had docked their
tails, how he'd trained them to swim. We'd had a swimming pool
in Baltimore and I remembered how he'd waded into the shallow
end with them one at a time, cradling them in one hand and then
lowering them into the pool that way, holding them until they got
used to the water. They looked small as rats to me, their tiny heads
poking above the surface. My father had them swim to me as I
knelt on the deck—how scared I was that they'd drown!—but they

made it to me eventually, trembling as if they'd just got back from the moon, and my father took them again and whispered something in their ears, clutching them preciously in both hands.

Eventually, my dad emerged from the bedroom with his girlfriend, who was fully dressed and drying her hair with a towel. She was pudgier than my mother, and not as tall, and had one of those dark tans like she'd stepped out of a TV set that had the contrast knob turned all the way to the left. She'd done up her shirt wrong, and I could see her belly button, deep as a bullet wound, peeking between buttons. She hugged me with one arm.

"I've heard so much about you," she said nervously, then laughed. She stepped back from me. "God, listen to me. That's just what I'm supposed to say, isn't it?" She noticed the dogs and went over to say hello to them, squatting down so they could sniff her hand. She scratched Ranger affectionately, just above the tail, and his hind leg began to bounce. "Aha. The way to every dog's heart."

My dad frowned at her, trying to send her a message across the room, but she didn't seem to notice.

"I thought they'd be more ferocious," she said.

My father snorted.

"Don't they kill birds?"

"Right," my father said. He smirked at me. "They have these little dog guns, and they shoot them out of the sky."

His girlfriend reddened. "How am I supposed to know? I grew up in Burbank."

She went out to the porch to hang her towel on the railing, and I heard a dog bark in a neighboring apartment. The one with the sign in the window, it sounded like. Shorty and Ranger began to bark as well. My father glanced at me, then cocked his head toward his girlfriend and gave me a secret look. He'd always been a mystery to me, a man of ingenious surprises, but now I knew exactly what he was going to do: roll his eyes. And that's precisely what he did. He rolled his eyes, one man to another, the only people in the world with half a brain.

At the beach, I parked the Mercedes and headed down to the water, Shorty and Ranger jingling behind me. I was jingling too, my mom's keys in my pocket. The three of us jingled down the path.

My mother was right where I'd left her, buried up to her neck. It was four in the afternoon. A cool breeze stirred the sand, and you could walk now without stepping on the sides of your feet. I stopped a couple feet away, wondering if I should let her sleep, but then Shorty dawdled over and began to sniff her face. My mother started, then yelled at me to take off her sunglasses.

"Why?"

"I'm afraid to move."

I knelt down and did as my mother asked. There was something caught in her eyelashes: a perfect jewel, glittering in the sun.

"We can't afford to lose it," she said.

She shut her eye very slowly, like an owl, and I reached down with two fingers and plucked the crumpled contact lens from her lashes. Tweezed between my fingers, it really did look like a diamond. I cupped my other hand around it, trying to protect it from the breeze. My mother took some time getting to her feet, but I didn't complain. Anyway, this was our life now.

She found a Kleenex and we wrapped the lens up like a tooth and stuck it in her purse. My mother stared at me with one eye screwed shut, covered head to toe in sand. She looked less drunk, as if popping out of the ground had refreshed her somehow. Ranger bared his teeth and growled.

"He doesn't recognize you."

"Good," she said strangely. She brushed the sand from her arms and legs as best she could, and squinted one-eyed down the beach.

"He's gone," I said.

She nodded. The breeze had sharpened to a wind, and the waves were getting blown out, dark patches flickering across the water and misting the tops of them. You could smell the salt in the air, stronger than before. My mother bent down and rubbed her legs, which were covered in goosebumps.

"It's getting chilly out here," she said. She closed both eyes for a moment, as if she were feeling woozy. "Can I have some of your coffee?"

I went over and grabbed the cup of cold coffee from the sand and handed it to her. She took a sip and grimaced.

"You really like this stuff?"

"No," I said. I handed her the sunglasses.

"You might like it in a couple years."

I tried to imagine what I'd look like in a couple years, and where we'd be living, and how the hell my mother would manage to support us. I tried to imagine this, but I couldn't. I looked toward the water and could see the curve of the earth, way out where the ocean faded into a strip of white, a lone barge out there shimmering on the horizon, still and dainty as a toy, and for a moment the wind at my shirt seemed to blow right through me.

My mother poured the dregs of her Slurpee out, and the dogs sniffed over to the damp spot in the sand, bumping noses. My mom watched them for a while, pink already with sunburn, her glasses reflecting a smaller version of the world, as if the beach and crashing waves and vacant lifeguard stand were as far away as that boat on the horizon, and I could see why Ranger had barked at her. She looked unrecognizable to me, too.

"Why did you say that to that beachcomber?" I asked.

"Which part?"

"That you can walk on your hands?"

My mother looked at me humbly. Then she walked toward the water where the sand was firmer. She got down on all fours and jumped her legs up so she was standing on her hands, bent like a scorpion's tail, the skirt of her dress hanging down around her. You could see her underwear—plain as a man's briefs—but at the moment I was too astounded to care. She walked that way for a few steps, teetering along on her hands and scaring up a puff of kelp flies. A wave foamed between her fingers, dampening the ends of her hair, but she didn't stop. I had the sense that this was the only time I'd ever see her do this. After today, we wouldn't have the chance. But she could still do it now, she could surprise me with a useless talent. The sun flashed behind her, flickering between her legs, and someone watching from down the beach might even have mistaken us for two kids. She teetered on like that, on the verge of falling, while Shorty and Ranger barked and splashed around her, wagging their stubby little tails, no idea what was next.

Novostroïka

FROM *The Atlantic*

DANIIL IVANOVICH BLINOV climbed the crumbling steps of the city council. The statue of Grandfather Lenin towered over the building, squinting into the smoggy distance. The winter's first snowflakes settled on the statue's shoulders like dandruff. Daniil avoided Grandfather's iron gaze, but sensed it on the back of his head, burning through his fur-flap hat.

Inside the hall of the council, hunched figures pressed against the walls, warming their hands on the radiators. Men, women, entire families progressed toward a wall of glass partitions. Daniil entered the line. He rocked back and forth on the sides of his feet. When his heels grew numb, he flexed his calves to promote circulation.

"Next!"

Daniil took a step forward. He bent down to the hole in the partition and looked at the woman sitting behind it. "I'm here to report a little heating problem in our building."

"What's the problem?"

"We have no heat." He explained that the building was a new one, this winter was its first, someone seemed to have forgotten to connect it to the district furnace, and the toilet water froze at night.

The woman heaved a thick directory onto her counter. "Building address?"

"Ivansk Street, number nineteen thirty-three."

She flipped through the book, licking her finger every few pages. She flipped and flipped, consulted an index, flipped once more, then shut the book and folded her arms across it. "That building does not exist, Citizen."

Daniil stared at the woman. "What do you mean? I live there."

"According to the documentation, you do not." She looked at the young couple in line behind him.

Daniil leaned closer, too quickly, banged his forehead against the partition. "Nineteen thirty-three Ivansk Street," he repeated.

The woman considered an oily spot on the glass with mild interest. "Never heard of it."

"I have thirteen, no, fourteen citizens, living in my suite alone, who can come here and tell you all about it," he said. "Fourteen angry citizens bundled up to twice their size."

She shook her head, tapped the book. "The documentation, Citizen."

"We'll keep using the gas, then," Daniil said. "Just leave the stove on for heat."

The woman raised her eyebrows; Daniil seemed to rematerialize in front of her. "Address again?"

"Nineteen thirty-three Ivansk Street, Kozlov City, Ukraine. U.S.S.R. Mother Earth—"

"Yes, yes. We'll have the gas-engineering department look into it. Next!"

Was it fourteen now? Had he included himself in the count? Careful to avoid the ice patches on the sidewalk on his way home from work, Daniil wondered when he had let the numbers slip. Last month twelve people were living in his suite, including himself. He counted on his fingers, stiff from the cold. In the bedroom, first corner, Baba Olga slept on the foldout armchair; second corner, on the foldout cot, were Aunt Lena and Uncle Ivan and their three children; third corner, Daniil's niece and her friend (but they hardly counted, since they ate little and spent most of their time at the institute); fourth corner—who was in the fourth corner? Wait, that was himself, Daniil Blinov, bunking under Uncle Timko; in the hallway, someone's mother-in-law or second cousin or who really knew, the connection was patchy; on the balcony camped Cousin Vovic and his fiancée and six hens, which were not included in the count but who could forget them? Damn noisy birds. That made thirteen. He must have missed someone.

Daniil's name had bounced from waitlist to waitlist for three years before he was assigned to his apartment by the Kozlov Canning Combine, where he worked as a packaging specialist. The ten-story paneled *novostroïka* had been newly built and still smelled of mortar. His suite was no larger than the single room he had shared with his parents in a communal apartment, but he could call it his own. The day he had moved in was nothing short of sublime: he walked to his sink, filled up a glass of water, took a sip, and lay down on the kitchen floor, his legs squeezed into the gap between the stove and the table. Home was where one could lie in peace, on any surface. He felt fresh and full of hope. Then came a knock at the door. Daniil's grandmother burst into the apartment, four sacks of grain and a cage full of chickens strapped to her back. She spoke rural Ukrainian, which Daniil barely understood. She said something about her farm burning down and a neighbor who had it in for her. The exchanges between Daniil and his grandmother had never been long. And so Baba Olga stayed. Two. Two was all right. Until two became fourteen.

Daniil stuffed his hands back into the damp warmth of his pockets, climbed the narrow set of stairs up to his floor. The familiar smell of boiled potatoes and sea cabbage greeted him.

"Daniil, is that you?" Aunt Lena yelled from the kitchen.

Daniil cringed. He had wanted to remain undiscovered by his relatives for a few seconds longer. He opened the closet to hang his coat, and a pair of gray eyes stared back at him, round and unblinking. Daniil started. He had forgotten Grandfather Grishko, the fourteenth member of the Blinov residence, who slept standing, as he used to do while guarding Lenin's mausoleum. Daniil closed the door softly.

"Come look, we get barely any gas," Aunt Lena said. She wore a yellowed apron over a floor-length fur coat. Its massive hood obscured her face. "Took me three hours to boil potatoes." She turned the knobs to maximum; the elements quivered with a faint blue. "Did you go to the city council? They should look into it."

"It seems they already have," Daniil said. "They're just better at turning things off than on."

Aunt Lena's daughter jumped out from under the kitchen table, singing, "May there always be blue skies!" She air-fired at the light bulb hanging from the ceiling. Aunt Lena tickled the nape of the child's neck, and she retreated back under the table.

"What did they tell you at the council?" Aunt Lena asked.

"The building doesn't exist, and we don't live here."

She brushed a strand of hair off her forehead with a mittened hand. "I guess that makes sense."

"How?"

"I had a talk with the benchers last week." She was referring to the group of pensioners who sat at the main entrance of the building, ever vigilant, smoking unfiltered cigarettes and cracking sunflower seeds day and night. "They told me this block was supposed to have only two towers, but enough construction material was discarded to cobble together a third—ours."

A series of barks blasted through the thin walls of the bedroom. A chill colder than the air ran through Daniil. He hadn't approved of the hens, but they were at least useful—now a dog?

Aunt Lena cast her eyes down. "Dasha. Bronchitis again, poor child."

Daniil fiddled with the gas knobs, never having felt so useless.

"What are you going to do?" she asked.

Aunt Lena's daughter bellowed, "May there always be me!"

Cough cough cough cough cough cough cough.

"I don't know."

Uncle Ivan appeared in the doorway to inform them that he needed to get a glass of milk. Everyone evacuated the kitchen and waited in the hallway to give him enough space to open the refrigerator.

The human shuffle complete, Daniil and Aunt Lena resumed inspecting the stove. Aunt Lena's fur hood kept falling over her eyes until she flung it off, releasing a cloud of dust.

"Grandfather Grishko's telling everyone he hasn't seen his own testicles in weeks," she said. "We're tired of the cold, Daniil."

Daniil stroked the smooth enamel of the stove. "I know."

Cough cough cough cough cough cough cough cough cough cough cough.

"And we're tired of hearing about the testicles."

The memo on Daniil's desk unsettled him. It was addressed from Moscow:

In accordance with General Assembly No. 3556 of the Ministry of Food Industry, Ministry of Meat and Dairy Industry, and Ministry of Fish Industry on January 21, 1988, the Kozlov Canning Combine has been ordered to economize 2.5 tons of tin-plate per month, due to shortages. Effective immediately. See attachment for details.

At the bottom of the memo, his superior's blockish handwriting:

THIS MEANS YOU, DANIIL BLINOV.

Attached to the memo was a list of items the combine had canned that year. Daniil read the list with great interest. He mouthed the syllables, let them slosh around his tongue deliciously: sausages in fat; macaroni with beef, pork, or mutton; apricots in sugar syrup; mackerel in olive oil; sturgeon in natural juice of the fish; cubed whale meat; beetroot in natural juice of the vegetable; quince in sugar syrup; beef tongue in jelly; liver, heart, and kidneys in tomato sauce; cheek, tail, tips, and trimmings with one bay leaf; and so on.

The telephone on Daniil's desk rang.

"You've read the memo?" Sergei Ivanovich, his superior, was calling. Daniil turned to look across the many rows of desks. Sergei Ivanovich stood at the doorway of his office, watching Daniil, the receiver pressed to his ear.

"I have, Sergei Ivanovich." Daniil inquired about testing alternative tin-to-steel ratios for containers.

"None of that, Daniil Blinov. Just stuff more food into fewer cans. Use every cubic millimeter you have," his superior said. "You're not writing this down."

Daniil pulled up an old facsimile and set to doodling big-eared Cheburashka, a popular cartoon creature unknown to science.

"Good, very good," Sergei Ivanovich said. "But don't think of pureeing anything."

"No?"

"The puree machine's on its way to Moscow. Commissar's wife just had twins."

Daniil noted the diameter of Cheburashka's head, to make sure the ears matched its size exactly. "Sergei Ivanovich? May I ask you something?"

"If it's quick."

"I was looking over the impressive list of goods our combine produces, and couldn't help wondering . . . Where does it all go?"

"Is that a philosophical question, Daniil Blinov?"

"All I see in stores is sea cabbage."

Sergei Ivanovich let out a long sigh. "It's like the joke about the American, the Frenchman, and the Soviet guy."

"I haven't heard that one, Sergei Ivanovich."

"That's a shame," Sergei Ivanovich said. "When I have time to paint my nails and twiddle my thumbs all day, Blinov, I'll tell you the joke."

Daniil resisted the temptation to roll himself into a defensive ball position under his desk, like a hedgehog. He straightened his shoulders. "Sergei Ivanovich? May I also ask about the pay?"

Daniil watched his superior retreat into his office. Sergei Ivanovich mumbled something about the shortages, surely the pay would come through next month and if not then, the month after, and in the meantime don't ask too many questions. He hung up.

Daniil reached into his desk drawer, produced a new sheet of grid paper and a T-square. He ran his fingers over the instrument, rich red in color, made of wild pearwood. When he was a child his parents had awarded the T-square to him for top marks in school. At the time he thought the pearwood held some magical property, a secret promise.

He set to work drawing diagrams of food products in four-hundred-milliliter cylinders. Chains of equations filled his grid paper. Some foods posed more of a packing problem than others: pickles held their shape, for instance, while tomatoes had near-infinite squeezability. Soups could be thickened and condensed milk condensed further, into a cementlike substance. String beans proved the most difficult: Even when arranged like a honeycomb, they could reach only 91 percent packing efficiency. In the middle of every three string beans hid an unfillable space. Daniil submitted a report titled "The Problematics of the String-Bean Triangular Void" to Sergei Ivanovich's secretary.

For the rest of the day, Daniil pretended to work while the combine pretended to pay him. He drew Gena the Crocodile, Cheburashka's sidekick. He pondered the properties of dandruff, specifically Grandfather Lenin's dandruff. Could a bald man have dandruff? Unlikely. But what about the goatee?

Daniil reached the entrance to his building in late evening. His eyelids were heavy with fatigue, but his feet kept him from going inside. Perhaps it was the hacking coughs, the questions, the innumerable pairs of shoes he'd have to dig through just to find his slippers. With his index finger he traced the red stenciled numbers and letters beside the main entrance. Nineteen thirty-three Ivansk Street. The building was a clone of the other two buildings on the block: identical panels, square windows, and metal entrances; identical wear in the mortar; identical rebar under the balconies, leaching rust. Nineteen thirty-three Ivansk was there, in front of his nose. He blinked. But what if it wasn't? He stepped closer to the stenciled numbers, felt the cold breath of the concrete. Was he the only one who could see it? It was there. Or it wasn't.

"Fudgy Cow?" a voice behind him asked.

Daniil jumped. In the dark he could make out the hunched silhouette of Palashkin, the oldest member of the benchers. He sat in his usual spot on the bench. Palashkin lit a cigarette, handed a candy to Daniil. The chubby cow on the paper wrapper smiled up at him dreamily. Daniil hadn't seen the candy in months. He pocketed it for later.

"What are you out here stroking the wall for?" Palashkin asked.

Daniil shrugged. "I was just on my way in." He stayed put.

Palashkin looked up at the sky. He said in a low voice, "It's all going to collapse, you know."

"Oh?"

"Whispers is all it is now, rumors here and there, but give it another year. Know what I'm saying? It's all going kaput."

Daniil gave the concrete wall a pat, thinking that Palashkin was referring to the building. "Let's just hope none of us are inside when she goes."

"What are you, cuckoo in the head? We're already inside."

"I don't know about you, but I'm outside," Daniil said, now feeling unsure.

"Go eat your Fudgy Cow, Daniil." Palashkin extinguished his cigarette between his thumb and his index finger, stood up, and disappeared into the dark.

Daniil bent so close to the glass partition, he could almost curl his lips through the circular opening. The woman in booth No. 7 (booths 1 to 6 were CLOSED FOR TECHNICAL BREAK), Kozlov Department of Gas, wore a fuzzy wool sweater that Daniil found comforting, inviting. He gazed at her and felt a twinge of hope.

The woman shut the directory with a thud. "What was it, thirty-three nineteen Ivansk, you said?"

"Nineteen thirty-three Ivansk."

"Look, I've heard rumors about it, but it's not on any of the lists. Thirty-three nineteen Ivansk is, though."

"That doesn't help me."

"Don't be hostile, Citizen. You are one of many, and I work alone."

"I know you know nineteen thirty-three Ivansk exists. It exists enough for you to fiddle with the gas when you feel like it," Daniil said.

"What are you accusing us of, exactly?"

"Us? I thought you worked alone."

The woman took off her reading glasses, rubbed the bridge of her nose. "Refer to the city council with your questions."

"I was there last week."

"So?"

"So nothing," he said.

"Refer to the factory in charge of your apartment assignment."

"What do you think they know? The whole combine is in a state of panic." He was referring to the problem of the string bean.

"Best wishes with your heating problem," she said. "Next!"

Cough cough cough cough cough cough cough.

Daniil entered his apartment to find every square centimeter of shelf and bed space covered in stacks of red bills. His relatives had squeezed themselves into corners to count the money. No one looked up when he came in.

Daniil backed out of the apartment, closed the door behind him, stood on the landing until he had counted to thirty, then came back in. The red bills remained. *All right,* he thought, *so the hallucination continues. Run with it. Let the mind have its fancy.*

The children's shrieks and snivels and coughs rang from the kitchen, but their voices seemed warped and far away, as though they were coming from a tunnel.

Uncle Timko, the only grown-up not counting bills, sat cross-legged on Daniil's bunk, hacking away at a block of wood with a mallet and chisel. "Your grandfather's disappearing testicles saved the day, Daniil."

"I can't stand lamenting them anymore," Grandfather Grishko said. He assumed his straight-as-a-rod Honor Guard pose, co-cooned in a bed comforter. "Back in my district, they had quite a reputation. The girls would come from far and wide just to—" He said a few things Daniil chose to block out of his hallucination.

"The *children!*" Aunt Lena said from somewhere under her fur.

Grandfather Grishko tossed a red stack at Daniil. He leafed through the crisp bills, half expecting them to crackle and burst into pyrotechnic stars.

"This is my life's savings, Daniil," his grandfather said. "I've been keeping it for hard times, and hard times have arrived. Take the money. Don't ask me where I've been stashing it. Put it in for heating, bribe someone, anything."

Daniil mustered a weak thank-you.

Uncle Timko held up his mangled block of wood. "Does this look like a spoon or a toothbrush?"

"Neither."

"It's supposed to be both."

"You're getting wood chips all over my sheets."

Uncle Timko ignored him. "Spoon on one end, toothbrush on the other. A basic instrument of survival."

Four hours later, they finished counting the bills. The sum of Grandfather Grishko's savings, along with the money the other relatives had scrounged up, turned out to be a hefty 8,752 rubles and 59 kopecks.

Daniil calculated what 8,752 rubles and 59 kopecks could buy. He took the rabid inflation into account, recalled the prices he'd seen at the half-empty state store the week before. Daniil looked from the stacks of bills to the expectant eyes of his family.

"We've got enough here to buy one space heater," he declared. He held up a finger to stop the dreamers in the room. "If I can find one."

Daniil found another memo on his desk, this one addressed from Sergei Ivanovich:

TO FILL UNFILLABLE STRING-BEAN TRIANGULAR VOID, ENGI-NEER TRIANGULAR VEGETABLE. DUE FRIDAY.

Daniil rubbed his temples. An irresistible desire to stretch came over him. He wanted his body to fill the office, his arms and legs to stick out of the doors and windows. He wanted to leap and gambol where wild pearwood grew. His great parachute lungs would inflate, sucking up all the air on the planet.

The phone rang.

"Is that a Fudgy Cow on your desk?" Sergei Ivanovich stood in his office, on tiptoe, squinting again.

"Just the wrapper, Sergei Ivanovich."

"I haven't had one in months."

The line filled with a heavy silence.

"I should get back to the triangular vegetable, Sergei Ivanovich."

"You should." Sergei Ivanovich kept the receiver pressed to his ear. "Daniil Blinov?"

"Yes, Sergei Ivanovich."

"Was it good?"

"The candy? A little stale."

Sergei Ivanovich let out a moan before catching himself. Daniil's superior glanced at his own superior's office, to find himself being observed as well. He hung up.

Daniil placed the wrapper in his drawer, beside the T-square and the drawings of the entire Cheburashka gang. He turned to the diagram lying on his desk: a tin can containing exactly seventeen black olives. Seventeen was the maximum capacity, provided the olives were a constant size. The ones in the middle were compacted into little cubes, with barely any space for brine. *Good,* thought Daniil. *No one drinks the brine anyway.*

The heater was set to a lavish High. Its amber power light flickered like a campfire. Fourteen figures huddled around the rattling tin box and took turns having the warm air tickle their faces. Some even disrobed down to their sweaters. A bottle of *samogon* appeared from its hiding place, as did a can of sprats. Daniil felt the warmth spread to his toes, to his chilliest spots. Aunt Lena took off her hood and Daniil noticed that her normally pallid cheeks had gained a lively red. Grandfather Grishko sat on a stool like a king, legs spread, chewing on a piece of *vobla* jerky he claimed predated the revolution.

A knock came at the door.

Everyone fell quiet. Daniil ignored it.

Another knock.

Aunt Lena poked Daniil's arm.

Daniil took another swig of home brew, slid off his chair (which Uncle Timko immediately occupied), and opened the door.

Two tall men stood in the dark, narrow hallway before him, holding a coffin.

Daniil teetered where he stood. "Uh, hello." His relatives crowded behind him. "If you're here to collect me, I'm not ready yet."

"We need access to your apartment, Citizen," the man on the right said.

"Why?" Daniil asked.

The man on the left rolled his eyes at the man on the right. "God dammit, Petya, do we have to give an explanation at every landing?"

"An explanation would be nice," Daniil said.

"The guy on ten croaked, and the stair landings aren't wide enough for us to turn the coffin around," the one named Petya said. "So we need to do it in people's apartments."

"Yet somehow you got it all the way up to ten." Daniil knew the cabinet-size elevator wouldn't have been an option.

"When the coffin was empty, we could turn it upright."

"And now you can't."

Petya narrowed his eyes at Daniil. "Some might find that disrespectful, Citizen." In agreement, Baba Olga flicked the back of Daniil's neck with her stone-hard fingers. Petya said, "Look, this thing isn't getting any lighter."

"You aren't here to collect anyone," Daniil confirmed.

"As you can see, we've already collected. Now let us in."

Everyone stood aside as the men lumbered in with the coffin, trampling on shoes and scratching the wallpaper.

"Yasha, we'll have to move the cot to make room," Petya said.

"Which one?"

"Pink flower sheets."

"Keep holding on to your end while I set mine down," Yasha said. "Toasty in here, eh?"

"Yes, mind the heater by your feet," Daniil chimed in.

"I'll have to step out on the balcony while you pivot."

Baba Olga lunged at the men. "No, no, don't open—"

A panicked brood of hens stormed the room.

Aunt Lena clutched at her chest. "Sweet Saint Nicholas."

"We'll have to report this poultry enterprise, Citizens."

Daniil opened his mouth to tell them the hens must have flown in from another balcony; then everything went dark.

The heater's rattle ceased. The hens were stunned silent. Through the window, Daniil could see that the neighboring buildings were blacked out as well.

"Electrical shortages," Yasha said. "Heard about it on the radio. Looks like the blackouts are starting today."

"I'm setting the coffin down," Petya said. "I have to set it down, dear God, it's about to slip out of my hands—"

"Slow, slow—"

A delicate, protracted crunch of tin filled seventeen pairs of ears. Daniil had counted. Seventeen, including the man in the coffin. No one said anything for a few seconds. They did not need to see to know what had been crushed.

"Well, looks like we're going to be here awhile," Yasha said. He sat, a shuffle followed, a stale smell of socks wafted through the air. "Wasn't some jerky going around?"

Daniil's head whirled. Seventeen humans in a room, arms and legs and fingers and toes laced together. Plus one bay leaf. The crunch of the space heater replayed in his mind. Seventeen olives. *Cough cough cough cough.* Daniil would die just like this, stuffed and brined with the others, their single coffin stuck in someone else's bedroom. No one drinks the brine anyway. Already the cold was seeping in. A small clawed foot stepped on his. *A little heating problem.* A brush of feathers huddled on his feet, shivering. Daniil took a step forward, and the feathers swished past. In the dark he felt for the coffin, yanked out the crumpled space heater from underneath. The corner of the coffin slammed down to the floor. The children screamed.

Daniil stepped onto the balcony, flung the heater over the ledge. For a second he felt weightless, as if he himself were flying through the air. A hollow crash echoed against the walls of the adjacent buildings.

Daniil stepped back inside, sank down on his bunk. Wood chips scratched between his fingers.

Grandfather Grishko was the first to speak. "Daniil, go down and get it." The whispered words were slow, grave. "We'll get it fixed."

Daniil didn't know what his grandfather was hoping for, but he would do as he was told. Then he felt the cold steel of his uncle's mallet and chisel among the wood chips. He grabbed the instruments and descended to the ground floor. A gruff voice offered caramels but Daniil snatched the man's cigarette lighter instead. Its flame illuminated the red stenciled numbers. Daniil cared for nothing else, but there had to be heating, because heating meant

No. 1933 Ivansk existed and he and his family had a place, even in the form of a scribble buried deep in a directory. He would show them, the ones behind the glass partitions, the proof. Daniil positioned the chisel. The first hit formed a long crack in the concrete, but kept the numbers whole.

JIM SHEPARD

Telemachus

FROM *Zoetrope*

TO COMMEMORATE EASTER SUNDAY, the captain has spread
word of a ship-wide contest for the best news of 1942, the winner
to receive a double tot of rum each evening for a week. The con-
testants have their work cut out for them. Singapore has fallen.
The *Prince of Wales* and the *Repulse* have been sunk. The Dutch East
Indies have fallen. Burma is in a state of collapse. Darwin has been
so severely bombed it had to be abandoned as a naval base. The
only combatants in the entire Indian Ocean standing between the
Japanese Navy and a linkup with the Germans, who are currently
having their way in Russia and North Africa, seem to be us. And
one Dutch gunboat we came across a week ago with a spirited crew
and a crippled rudder.

We are the *Telemachus,* as our first lieutenant reminds us each
morning on the voice-pipe: a T-class submarine—not so grand as
a U, but not so dismal as an S. Most of us have served on S's and
are grateful for the difference, even as we register the inferiority
of our own boat to every other nation's. The Royal Navy leads the
world in battleships and cruisers, we like to say, and trails the Bel-
gians in submarine design.

In the chaos following Singapore's surrender we've been provided no useful intelligence or patrol orders. A run through the
Sunda Strait between Java and Sumatra ended in a hail of enemy
fire on the approaches to Batavia. At our last dry dock the Cey-
lonese further undermined our morale by invariably gazing out
their harborside windows at first light to see if the Japanese had
arrived. We have no idea whether we will find any more ports avail-

able to us now that we've shipped back out to sea. We have no idea whether we will find more torpedoes once we've expended our store. "Heads up there, boys," our captain joked to those of us within earshot of his map table last night. "Is there anything more exhilarating than carrying on alone out on the edge of a doomed world?"

"Sounds like Fisher's childhood, sir," Mills responded, and everyone looked at me and laughed.

They view me as a sorry figure even by the standards of their meager histories. As a boy I was a horrid disappointment, pigeon-chested and gap-toothed, and as grandiose as I was untalented. The only activity for which I was any use at all was running, so I ran continually, though naturally not in competitions or road races but just all about the countryside, in fair weather and foul. It brought me not a trace of schoolboy glory, though it did at times alleviate my fury at being so awful at everything else.

The characterization my parents favored for me was *out of hand,* as in, *What does one do when a boy gets out of hand?* My stepfather inclined toward the strap; my mother, the reproachful look. Her only brother had been killed in the first war, and her first husband had come to a bad end, as well; and my stepfather never tired of pointing out that a disapproving countenance was her solution to most of life's challenges. He said about me that by the time I was out of short pants and he was forced to introduce me at pubs or on the street, friends sympathized.

My father had been presumed lost at sea on a bulk cargo ship that had gone missing between Indonesia and New South Wales. When I asked if he had loved me, my mother always replied that it hurt too much to recall such happiness in any detail. When I pressed for particulars nonetheless, she said only that he had been quick to laugh and that no man had possessed a greater capacity to forgive. When I asked my aunts they said they'd barely known the man, and when I asked if he'd been pleased with me, they said they were sure that had been the case, though they also remembered him not much liking children.

My stepfather viewed my running as a method of avoiding achievement or honest labor and marveled at my capacity for sloth. He pressed upon me *Engineering Principles for Boys* and *Elementary Statistics* and all sorts of other impressive-looking volumes I refrained from opening. He asked if I was really so incurious about the world of men, and I reassured him that I was very curious about the world of men, and he responded that in such case I must bear in mind that the world of men was the sphere of industry, and I clarified that I meant the *adventurous* world of men, that arena of tropic seas and volcanic cataclysms and cannibal feasts and polar exploits. He said that if I wanted to grow up a fool I might as well join the navy, which was precisely what I had already resolved to do.

Mills told everyone when he arrived aboard that he'd been one of those posh boys who'd gone to boarding school where at great expense he'd been provided rotten food and insufficient air and exercise, and so submarine duty oddly suited him. His father had been great with speculation and then it had all gone smash and he had hung himself. Mills remembered his mother sitting in the drawing room during the months that followed with all the bills that she didn't dare to open, since there was no money to pay them, and he remembered thinking that it would be a good thing for her if she had one less mouth to feed. He'd been a chauffeur, a silk-stocking salesman, a shipyard hand, and the second mate of a sailing ship before signing on with Her Majesty's Navy.

As gunner's mates we bunk in the torpedo stowage compartment, between the tubes. He calls me "the Monk" because even in our tiny living space I never bother with pictures or photographs. I carry what I want to see in my head. Everything else feels like clutter.

"Our mate here doesn't know how to take things easy," he says by way of explanation to our fellow torpedomen. He seems to think he panders to my vagaries with a resigned good humor.

Mills was assigned to us at Harwich as a replacement for a mate we'd lost to carbon monoxide poisoning when a torpedo's engine had started prematurely in the tube. He asked me confidentially what sort of boat he was joining, and I recounted our most recent patrol, which I described as three weeks of misery that we'd endured without sighting a single enemy ship. We'd run aground and been unsuccessfully bombed by our own air force. We'd damaged our bow in a collision with the dock upon our return. He said that on *his* most recent patrol they'd surfaced between two startled German destroyers, each so near abeam that their bow wakes had spattered onto the submarine's deck. He and his captain on their bridge had just gaped up at the Germans above them, since they'd been beneath the elevation of the German guns, and too close to ram without the destroyers ramming one another. He said they'd pitched back down the conning tower ladder with the Germans still shrieking and cursing them. He said they'd mostly worked the arctic reaches out of Murmansk, sinking so much German tonnage that the Russians had presented them with a reindeer.

He said he was pining for a nurse he'd met in the Red Cross who, last he'd heard, had been sent to London and now no doubt was pouring lemonade over the wounded in the East End. Her father upon first meeting him had cordially asked, "And who or what are *you*?" and her mother, upon his reply, had remarked only that people had been doing dreadful things at sea for as long as she could remember. He said that every time he'd managed to arrange some privacy with the nurse and attempt a liberty with her she'd begged him instead to "do something useful," though he'd been encouraged by her remark about her father that no man had ever behaved so badly with the ladies and gotten away with it.

Occasionally when he was particularly displeased with the lack of vivacity in my responses he'd say that he didn't suppose I had any of my own experiences to relate, and I'd assure him I had very few, though I had in fact before I left home conceived an intense and inappropriate fondness for a cousin on my mother's side. This cousin's own mother in her house displayed a photograph of herself and my lost father alone under an arbor, peering at one another and smiling, but when I asked about it, the woman appeared faintly stricken and was no more informative than my mother. When I was fourteen and my cousin twelve I lured her into a neighbor's garden and in my overheated state crowded my face in close to hers, alarming her. Bees drowsed above a flower she'd been examining. She turned to fix her eyes upon my mouth, and when I moved still closer she backed farther away. She was chary around me during our visits afterward but also took my hand under tables in dining rooms and once, having run into me unexpectedly in a hallway, put a finger to my lips. In my fantasies I still imagine an unlikely world in which I would be allowed to marry her and she would want to marry me. In the packet of correspondence I received upon arrival in the Pacific my mother noted that my cousin Margery had let on that I was writing *her*, at least, and my cousin in her response to my letters asked apropos of nothing if I remembered a day years earlier during which I had acted very odd in the garden beside my home. When off duty I lie in my berth between tubes five and six and wonder what others would make of someone who can conceive of tenderness for only one other being, and a tenderness improper at that.

That hallway encounter occurred the month following my eighteenth birthday, soon after which I served my first sea duty on the HMS *Resolution,* an elderly battleship that had been hurriedly refitted, and still dreaming of my cousin I stumbled around its great decks on those tasks I was able to execute, grateful for the small mercy of remaining unnoticed. We sailed around the Orkneys in seas so tumultuous that during one gale our captain threw up on my feet. The other excitement about which I was able to write my cousin transpired one calm morning when we all turned out on the quarterdeck to witness the spectacle of the second pilot ever launched from a seaplane catapult. The first had broken his neck from the colossal acceleration. The second had been provided a chock at the back of his head for support.

I detailed for her my impressions of my first submarine, the *Seahorse,* and the way I'd almost fallen overboard when hurrying across the narrow plank onto its saddle tanks while the chief petty officer watched from the bridge, expressing his displeasure at my insufficient pace. How intimidating I'd found its insides, its lower half packed with trimming tanks, fuel tanks, oil tanks, electric batteries, and so on, and its upper all valves and switches and wiring and cables and pressure gauges and junction boxes, and how I'd had to learn from painful experience which valve was likely to crack me on the head over which station, and the revelation that above the cramped wooden bunks were cupboards and curtains. I described how the conning tower became a wind tunnel when we surfaced and the diesels were sucking in air, and how the diesels themselves were a pandemonium of noise in such confined space. I described a rare look through the periscope, as I glimpsed far more clearly than I'd expected a flurry of tumbling green sea that blurred the eyepiece like heavy rain on a windscreen and then swept past.

There was much I chose to spare her. On our first sea trial the piston rings wore away and exhaust flooded the engine room and everyone had to work gas-masked at their stations, sweating and panting and ready to faint. On our second, one of our own destroyers tried to ram us and then, after we'd identified ourselves, reported that it had pursued without success two German U-boats. On our practice emergency dives everyone threw themselves down the conning tower ladder, trampling each other's fingers, and not even shouted orders could be heard above the awful Klaxon. On training maneuvers we lost the torpedo-loading competition, the navigation competition, the crash-dive competition, and the Lewis gun competition. On our second practice torpedo attack everything went according to plan, and when I reported accordingly to our torpedo officer he said, "Are you hoping for a prize?"

With nowhere to go we are headed vaguely toward the Andaman Sea off the west coast of Indochina, diving by day and gasping in relief in the cooler surface air at night. Every few days the captain announces our itinerary. He long ago resolved whenever possible to keep the crew informed, since it is his belief that we have a right to know what we are doing and why, and as security is hardly an issue aboard a submarine.

It is impossible to verify whether the wireless silence has to do more with our forces' standing orders not to give away our positions to the enemy's direction finders, or with the total unraveling of our efforts in the region. The captain finally patched through to HQ Eastern Fleet and was told to stand by and then nothing more. A week later a Dutch merchant ship we raised on the horizon reported its understanding that the Eastern Fleet had abandoned even Ceylon, and fallen all the way back to Kenya. That, the captain announced, for the time being left the decision to us whether to quit the field or to strike a blow with what we had. He was choosing the latter.

The crew is divided about his verdict. On the one hand, as our torpedo officer advised us, at such a dark time perhaps even an isolated victory could do something to buoy morale. It took only one U-boat to sink the *Royal Oak* in Scapa Flow. On the other hand, alone and unsupported, if we were to attack a fleet of any size at all our chances of escape would be infinitesimal. Run into the right ship, he said, and we could find ourselves in all the papers. Run into the wrong one, Mills replied, and we could find ourselves with seaweed growing out of our ears.

The captain has elected to ignore the few enemy merchant vessels we spy, in order to hoard our likely irreplaceable torpedoes for capital ships. When we're surfaced and the circumstances seem safe he has the wireless operators continue to request information. Upon crossing the tenth parallel he announced over the voice-pipe that as far as he knew the entirety of the Royal Navy's fighting strength had now fled the Indian Ocean for the Bay of Bengal.

Despite the limitation of shifts to four hours, with everyone so cramped and hot and miserable it's an ongoing effort of will to recall what we are supposed to be doing or monitoring every waking second of such a long patrol. Even in the head a lapse in focus can have calamitous results, as any mucking up of the sequence of valve operations to empty the lavatory pan will cause its contents to be pressure-sprayed into the inattentive crewman's face.

Because of the chaos in Ceylon we were revictualed with one type of tinned food only: a peculiar soaplike mutton that's been breakfast, lunch, and dinner for the past three weeks. Those who complain are reminded that it all tastes of diesel oil, anyway. We have weevils in our biscuits, as if we're serving under Nelson at Trafalgar.

A bearing seized in one of the engines and the engineers spent three days disconnecting and slinging the piston; the resulting vibration was so severe our conning tower lookouts couldn't see through their binoculars. Now with that addressed we wait for a ship large enough to engage, and those who complain about the uncanny solitude are reminded what the alternative will mean.

In our berths Mills suggests it's a miracle we've made it this far. He came aboard sufficiently early in our Norway patrols to wish that he hadn't, and he often compares the two theaters for their relative miseries: off Norway we couldn't cook on the surface because it was too rough, whereas here it's impossible when submerged due to the heat. He claims we were even more fatuous then. When the French surrendered we were all upset since it meant the end of shore leave for the rest of the summer, and we spent those months living quietly, fed by wireless rumors, and one day intercepted a plain-language signal pleading for rope and small boats from anyone in the vicinity of Dunkirk. As we were many miles north, all we did by way of response was to wonder at the reason for the break in radio discipline, while we sailed about like imbeciles, amazed at such empty seas.

After Dunkirk the expectation was that the Germans would invade from either Normandy or Norway, and the RAF had to concentrate on France, so that left our submarine fleet to provide adequate advance warning of any flotilla from the north. The Royal Navy had a total of twelve submarines to dedicate to that work, including ours. Together we were responsible for 1,300 kilometers of Norwegian coastline, although the good news was that military intelligence had decided we could focus on those few ports from which a sizable offensive force could be mounted. Our orders upon sighting such a formation were to report and then to attack. To report would require us to surface within view of the enemy, which would render the attack part of the directive irrelevant unless their gunners were blind, and the real question would be whether we'd even finish the broadcast. Each submarine had been provided with a padlocked chest of English pounds and Swedish kronor so that those of us bypassed by the invasion could in the event it was successful refuel in Göteborg or some other neutral port and then cross the Atlantic to carry on the fight from the New World.

To evade Luftwaffe patrols, particularly given the onset of white nights, by June we were submerged nineteen hours daily, and gambling that we could recharge our batteries and refresh our oxygen supply between enemy air sweeps. Those who lost that bet were devastated on the surface. At the end of nineteen hours our atmosphere was so thin that matches wouldn't light and even at rest we heaved like mountain climbers. American and German submarines were equipped with telescopic breathing tubes that could breach the water like periscopes, but when we proposed the same for our submarines we were told there was no tactical requirement for such a fitting. Our Treasury feared spending a million pounds to save a hundred million, our captain said bitterly, and its ranks were filled with rows of mincing clerks cutting corners.

As our periods submerged lengthened, our medical officer lectured us in small groups about the danger signs of carbon dioxide poisoning. Night after night just as breathing became all but impossible we were saved by a little low cloud providing just enough cover to surface. With the hatches opened, the boat revived from the control room aft to the engine room, though that didn't do much for the torpedo room, so Mills and I and our mates were allowed to come to the bridge two at a time for fifteen minutes of fresh air.

But we weren't safe even below. In calm weather the Norway Deep is clear as crystal, and we could be seen down to ninety feet, which we learned on our first day off the coast when six dive-bombers took their turns with us before heading home.

Around the solstice some nights never did get fully dark, and in the horrible half-light one after another of our boats was destroyed when it was finally forced to surface: the *Spearfish,* the *Salmon,* the *Sturgeon,* the *Trusty,* the *Truant,* the *Thames.* By July losses totaled 75 percent of those ships engaged. During one of our agonizing waits on the surface two Me-109s dropped out of the clouds and we could hear the *pom pom* of their cannon fire over the watch's screaming as he plummeted down the ladder, and while we submerged a gunner's mate snapped in his distress and beat himself senseless by pounding his forehead against his torpedo tube. He had doubled his jersey up over the steel first, to muffle the sound.

The invasion failed to materialize but we remained on station nevertheless, weathering the autumn and winter storms. During the worst of them we alternated at the watch, poking our faces and flooded binoculars into the wind's teeth, riding up wall after wall of steep and chaotic waves, and maintaining a twenty-four-hour vigilance in case the impossible happened and an enemy funnel coalesced, the captain struggling to keep the sextant dry long enough to snatch a star sight and gain a clue as to our where-abouts. In the heaviest gales the breaking waves poured in over the conning tower and filled the control room below, sparking the switchboards and washing through the entire ship. The hatches had to stand open because when the diesels could no longer draw air they stalled, so a stoker with a great suction hose would squeeze atop the tower beside the watch, absorbing the battering as he pumped the water back out.

One moonless night soon after surfacing I was on watch with the captain and two others, and all around in the darkness ship after ship appeared out of the mist, the hulls of transports rising above us like slabs of cliffs. We had run head-on into a full convoy, ascending inside the ring of their escorts, whose attentions were all trained out to sea. There was no time to dive and attack from periscope depth, nor to estimate the correct angles.

"What's the old rough rule?" the captain whispered, extending his hand toward the first transport. "If the enemy is slow, give him nine degrees of lead, or the width of a human hand at arm's length." With his fist as a gunsight over the bow, he set the fir-ing interval through the voice-pipe, then shouted, "Fire!" At the launch of each torpedo we could feel the ship lurch slightly backward, and before leaving the bridge we watched a huge column of water erupt from one of our targets, followed by a thump. He shouted, "Dive!" and plunged down the ladder, and underwater we heard two more huge, far-off bangs at the correct running ranges, and the entire crew cheered. We went deep for hours, hanging silently, those of us off duty forbidden even to move since the clink of a dropped key could expose us, while we listened to the concussions of the sub hunters' depth charges growing closer, then farther, then closer, until finally the German Navy seemed to run out of explosives.

On my last leave at home after the Norway patrols my cousin Margery insisted on bringing me round to her favorite pub and there a whole series of men with whom she seemed utterly at ease insisted on buying me drinks. "I didn't know you had a favorite pub," I told her, and she said, "Why would you?" She added that I should see her friends, and that her background had not prepared her for the amount some girls could drink. I asked if she had a favorite friend and she cited a girl named Jeanette who had an up-to-date mother who allowed them to smoke in the house. I continually had to repeat myself over the din of the place and when she finally asked with some exasperation why I couldn't speak up, I told her that almost everyone in the crew had what the doctors called fatigue-laryngitis from having reduced our voices to whispers for months in our attempts to outwit the enemy's hydrophones. She apologized, and when I told her it was nothing she took my hand.

One of her friends from a table nearby after a harangue with his mates asked me to settle the matter of whether the English had in fact invented the submarine. "Not hardly," I answered, and he said but hadn't the English always led in naval innovations? Who'd invented the broadside? Who'd converted the world from sail to steam? From coal to oil? And what about turret guns? "What about them," I asked. And Margery chided him that I wasn't allowed to talk shop, and that we needed some privacy to discuss family, thank you.

Once we were left alone she asked how my family *was* getting on, and I told her that my mother had reported she was enduring both my absence and the nightly bombing raids with a puzzling calm. When I asked after her family, Margery reminded me that they all remained greatly concerned about her older brother Jimmy, who was with the RAF and had already lost many friends. She said that now when he returned home on his leaves her mother and sister wore hypnotized looks and their conversations never strayed from speculations about the weather. And that Jimmy had in confidence told her some horrible stories. I suggested that perhaps he shouldn't have, and she responded that she'd known her entire life that the world beyond her home was stunning and heartless, and that all she'd ever heard from her mother about the protection afforded by an adherence to the rules was wrong. While she was speaking she seemed to scan the room first and then to focus on the nearer details of my face.

On our way home in the darkness of the blackout she said that she'd always been fond of me, and I said that she couldn't imagine how fond I'd been of her, and she pulled me into an alley and kissed me, and my chest felt like it did when I was running as a boy, and as her kiss continued her mouth flooded mine with pleasure. When I got hold of my senses I gripped her head and kissed her back. Finally she pulled away and said that we had to get home. While we walked she remarked that *there* was some rule-breaking for you: first cousins, kissing.

We stopped on her front step. She was lit for a moment when someone waiting up for her peeked through a blackout curtain. She said I should take care of myself. I grasped her hands, still dumbstruck and happy. She asked if she could tell me something, and then waited for my assent. She said that during some of the family gatherings we spent seated beside one another at dining tables it had been for her as if the stillness we made together were like a third person who was neither of us and both, and that when she'd felt the most sad and alone it had helped to imagine herself creeping into that third person who was half hers and half mine.

Did I have a sense of what she meant? she asked after a moment. I told her I did, though some part of it had confused me, and I worried that even in the darkness she could hear that. Well, she said, maybe it would come to me, and she said good night, and kissed my cheek, and the next morning I was off to the Pacific.

We sailed for Singapore through Gibraltar with a merchant convoy bound for Alexandria, and left the convoy to stop over in Beirut, which provided our first sight of a camel outside of a zoo, and where we painted our gray ship dark green for its Far Eastern tour, and from there proceeded to Haifa and Port Said and the Red Sea and on to Aden and the Pacific War. The entire time I castigated myself for the inadequacy of my response to my cousin's overtures. Before we'd left Harwich the captain had addressed the crew, announcing that we could all settle back and prepare ourselves for a long journey filled with indescribable discomforts. We'd taken him to be joking.

Our initial view of Singapore was a towering column of black smoke on the horizon. When we docked at the naval base jetty the captain went ashore in his whites to inquire as to where to lodge his men. He found everyone in headquarters burning records, and was told that our allotted accommodation had been destroyed by bombs that afternoon.

While he searched for an alternative we remained aboard. The bombing resumed, and with the harbor too shallow to dive, the hatches had to be kept shut or the splashes from the impacts would swamp us. A few of the torpedomen beside me who I thought were dozing turned out to have fainted from the heat. Everyone else just waited. We were all losing so much sweat the decks were slick underfoot. After an hour of the concussions one of the stokers went wild and tore down all the wardroom pinup girls before his mates restrained him.

Around sundown the captain returned with the news that he'd finally located the rear admiral for Malaya inspecting the chit-book in the rubble of the officers' club, and he'd offered us his house in the hills. A commandeered truck transferred those off duty, and the rest of us had to make do in the boiling confines of the boat.

The next morning black clouds hung over the entire waterfront from the burning oil and rubber dumps and we refitted and loaded any supplies that we could in the chaos. The last provisions aboard were crates of Horlicks malted milk and Australian cough drops. When we cast off, one old woman with a spade was digging herself a private air-raid trench in the garden of the Raffles Hotel. To the east the sky was filled with high-altitude bombers, and once clear of the harbor we submerged, and as we rounded the channel buoy the captain at the periscope reported a convoy of our own troop transports arriving. He could make out the standards of the Argyll and Sutherland Highlanders. The whole ship went silent at the thought of what they were disembarking into.

We chugged three thousand miles west. We started leaking oil. One night I worked my way back to the wardroom, where the chief and the captain were sitting and talking quietly so as not to disturb the sleepers. They invited me to join them, and as they chatted about where they might be this time the following year, and the perversities of women, and the favorite pubs they had known, I fell asleep with my head on the wardroom table, and for days afterward they joked about how much they apparently had bored me. A gunlayer on his watch at last spotted a swallow, and the next afternoon a stoker sighted an old boot, and in the end we made Colombo Harbor in Ceylon. For two weeks no one had spoken except to give or to acknowledge orders.

The captain suggested we use our week in port to become human beings again. Mills responded that he would commence his rehabilitation with a nice, invigorating fuck. Our chief was carried ashore with dengue fever and instructions to rest up and then to report with a clean bill of health and no nonsense. Despite the direness of our situation those of us on liberty took real showers and shaved our beards on the harbor tender and then escaped to the four corners of the city. I found myself at the Colombo Club, which given the circumstances had been opened to enlisted men. I passed the time strolling about the lawns and staring at the women. I listened to their husbands' leisurely comments about sporting events. The captain commandeered a deck chair in the mornings, and after a few drinks took to playing something he called bicycle polo, which always left him limping. A lone Hurricane trailing smoke flew over, circled back, and belly-landed on the club green, after which the pilot climbed out and proceeded directly to the bar. Upon drawing any attention I disappeared. Nights I dreamt incessantly and awoke so soaked with sweat I could smell my room from the hall.

I returned to my running, ascending the steep steps to the top of the cable tram, where I'd arrive bathed in sweat and then come right back down while the natives along the way looked on, amazed. They seemed to think Englishmen were prone to this sort of thing.

I went out drinking by myself. One night I happened upon Mills and our stoker petty officer, and the petty officer slipped on some stairs and rolled all the way to the bottom and then vomited.

Mills said, "You know what they say: 'If that's the navy, all *must* be well with England.'" After I woke in the gutter of a bazaar without my billfold, Mills insisted I go out drinking with them.

We bought rounds for crewmembers of the *Snapper* celebrating a sunk Jap submarine. The Japs had attacked a Dutch merchant ship and then machine-gunned the survivors in the water, so after the *Snapper* sank the sub, the crew beat to death with spanners the two Japs they'd fished out. They said that off the west Australian coast they'd been laboring into harbor in heavy seas when an American submarine had surfaced and ripped right by them like they were standing still. They said that in Australia girls welcomed sailors at the gangways with crates of fresh apples and bottles of milk.

We met Mills's cousin, who'd been left behind in hospital when his ship had fled the port. He'd served as a messcook aboard a destroyer in Manila and loved the Philippines because he'd had multiple girlfriends and Scotch had been seventy-five American cents per bottle. For little more he'd maintained a love shack in the bush, a one-room hut up on stilts. The toilet and shower had emptied below without benefit of pipes and the only running water had been from heaven. All the palm trunks nearby were encircled with steel mesh to keep the rats from stealing the coconuts. In the bar he stripped his shirt to show us his tattoos, including a smiling baby's face over one side of his chest that was labeled *Sweet* and another on the other side that was labeled *Sour* and *Twin screws, Keep clear* on the small of his back.

He loved the story of the *Snapper* crew rescuing the Japs to beat them to death. He'd befriended a sampan man in Manila who'd rowed British officers around the harbor to visit the town or to shoot snipe, and for years the man had told anyone who'd listen that soon the Japanese would invade, and he'd been more accurate than any prognosticator in London. And when the Japanese did arrive they'd crucified him on his boat for ferrying the enemy. Mills's cousin had spied his body as the destroyer fought its way out of the port.

Three more went down with dengue fever before we departed Ceylon: our messcook, which allowed Mills's cousin to come aboard as his replacement; the junior engine-room rating; and a torpedoman. Mills and I showed the new torpedoman his station, and while he peered with dismay at the hideous and antiquated confusion of corroded pipes and valves and levers, Mills advised him that another way of looking at the situation was that hardly any other crew had been granted our abundance of experience and survived.

A merchantman that staggered into harbor turned out to be carrying a mail packet that included letters for both Mills and myself. Mills had heard from his Red Cross nurse, who'd also sent a photograph. He teared up when he showed me. When he noted my response he protested that just because he was no celibate that didn't mean he'd forgotten her.

I received three letters posted over a span of eleven months from my stepfather and the prelate's daughter and my cousin. My stepfather had attached to his note a newspaper clipping of the bomb damage on our street. He wrote that my mother had discovered the neighbors' cat dead in the rubble of the back garden gate, that she had been keenly hurt by my refusal to write, and that she dispatched her regards nonetheless, along with the news of an old classmate of mine also in the navy whose wife had just given birth. He added that when it came to me he often wondered if I would ever reach the top of fool hill.

The prelate's daughter had sent a photograph of herself, too, and confided that she'd shared with her father what we now meant to one another and that he'd asked her to leave his house. She wanted to know what she should now do. She was referring to a night I'd been on leave from the *Resolution* and had encountered her outside a tearoom in Harwich. It had transpired that she was bereft from another sailor failing to meet her as promised, and I had offered to walk her to the navy yard in consolation. She'd dried her eyes and put an arm around my waist and cheered herself with my stories of my own haplessness. We necked next to others in the darkness under the Halfpenny Pier and she opened her skirt to my hands. She whispered how much we liked one another, and it sounded so piteous that I stopped, and she seemed to think we'd gone far enough in any event. She'd saved her chewing gum in her palm and she signaled we were finished by returning it to her mouth. Before we separated on King's Head Street she'd written down my name and posting and her address, and handed me the latter.

Margery wrote that she hoped I was well, and that she now at her family's insistence languished in a remote place where nothing momentous was likely to happen. She wrote that previously her nights in London had been long periods of enforced inactivity in her building's shelter, waiting for the all-clear, and that after one bombing she'd emerged to find a woman's body covered in soot and dust and had stooped to uncover its face. She wrote that in the middle of a memorial service for one of her mother's best friends she'd retired to a dressing room and wept at her own cowardice. She said her family often inquired if she had any word of how I was getting on, and that her little niece had asked her if I sank all of the bad people could I then swim home. She said she recognized our relationship had been at times an unconventional one but she hoped that I wouldn't hold this against her, and that with whomever I chose to share my life I would be happy. She also enclosed a photograph of herself, in a sundress, almost lost in the dappled light and shadow of a willow tree. I began any number of responses to her letter, all of which I kept as insufficient.

When rumors started circulating about our impending patrol I spent mornings looking for myself in the mirror, as if I'd fallen down a well. In the days before our departure a senior medical officer gave us each the once-over. "Here's an interesting phenomenon," he remarked. "Let's have a look at your fingernails." I held out my hand and he indicated the concentric ridges. "Each ridge is a patrol," he said. "The gaps between correspond to the lengths of your leaves ashore." I looked at him. "Purely psychological," he said.

On our last night in Ceylon all the offshore watch returned in various states of intoxication, and the captain sentenced them, somewhat wryly, to ninety days on our own ship in the loathsome heat and overcrowding. "Very good, sir," one of the drunken mates said in reply, and the captain answered that the mate could now make it one hundred and twenty days.

After two weeks in the Bay of Bengal everyone is feeling lethargic and suffering from headaches. Some of the crew haven't shaved during the entire patrol and resemble figures from another century. Running on the surface at night we slip past sleepy whales bobbing like waterlogged hulks. Our medical officer taps out on a tiny typewriter a new edition of his *Health in the Tropics* newsletter, which he titles "Good Morning." This week's tip is: "If you have been sweating a lot, wash it off, or at least wipe it off with a hand towel, since the salt that your sweat has pushed out of your pores will irritate the skin." The only ship traffic we've encountered has been trawlers and junks, and the captain has decided that in such cases we'll just lie doggo and watch them move past. We find our new torpedoman all over the ship, his eyes around our feet, looking for dog-ends. When we're off duty Mills can instantly sleep and I lie awake. Sometimes when I can no longer stand my own company I go to the wardroom. There I find the captain or the chief alone at the table with binoculars slung round his neck and his head on his arms.

Mostly we're immersed in a haze of inactivity. We dove to evade a flying boat sighted by our starboard lookout. A heavy bomber swept directly overhead on a northerly course but did not appear to have noticed us. The 0400 watch reported that three small vessels he couldn't identify had altered course toward our location, then turned in a complete circle for no apparent reason before continuing on their transit.

We are perpetually in one another's way, tormented by septic heat sores, bodies that stink, and endless small breakdowns on the ship. The only clean-off available is a little torpedo alcohol applied to the rankest spots. Wet clothes never dry. Condensation is everywhere. Shoes are furred with mold and our woolens smell worse than the head. The batteries have begun to fume and refuse to charge. The periscope gland leaks. In the night we passed one of our own bombed-out merchant ships, listing miserably. The tinned mutton when opened is now often slimed over, and even the roaches won't touch it. Mills claims he can't imagine this going on much longer, but his cousin says that if this has to be done it's better that we should do it, since we know what we're about, and newcomers would likely cost their friends their lives.

I'm jolted from my bunk by a tremendous blast, and then a second and a third, and when I reach the wardroom everyone is celebrating and I'm told that our target was an ammunition ship. The captain is permitting the crew to go up to the bridge three at a time to enjoy the spectacle, and upon my turn explosions are still sending flame and debris high into the sky. All who've been bellyaching for days and begrudging each other a civil word are suddenly thick as thieves and best of friends, since with one solitary success all the clouds are dispelled. But soon after that come the sub hunters, and we hang still for twelve hours at one hundred and eighty feet while they thresh around above us like terriers at a rabbit hole. Off-duty crew lie in their bunks trying to read thrillers or magazines. Those working sit right on the deck at their stations to ensure they make as little noise as possible. The chief pores over a technical journal. The captain draws the green curtains round his berth. With the first depth charge a few lights are put out and a roach falls stunned to my chest. The second cracks a glass gauge before me and the welding on a starboard casing. The third knocks me to the floor and the remaining lights go dark and water spritzes from a joint. Pocket torches flash before the emergency lamps come on. More detonations reverberate, farther away and closer, farther away and closer.

The hunters persist until the humidity coalesces into an actual mist and the thinning air plagues everyone with crushing headaches and nausea, and then our hydrophone operators finally report our pursuers moving away.

When we're running on the surface again I find Mills contemplating his photo of the Red Cross nurse, his chin on his filthy mattress. I ask her name and he responds only that one of the last things she requested was that he take the time to consider what she might want, and what she might like, but that instead he gave her the sailor's lament, that he'd soon be shipping out and that they'd perhaps never see one another again, and so she allowed him the kiss and some of the other liberties he'd been desiring. Before his train departed she told him through the carriage window that he was the sort of man who was always at the last second catching his ride in triumph or missing it and not caring. "I think she meant I was selfish," he finally adds, and then turns to me to discover I have nothing to contribute. "What do you think of selfishness, eh, Fisher?" he asks, and some of the torpedomen laugh. "So here we are," he concludes. "Sweating and grease-covered and alone and miserable and sorry for ourselves." And a memory I banished from my time with Margery surfaces: We stood on her front step after our kisses, and she waited for me to respond to what she had confided about the stillness we made together. While she waited she explained that she was trying to ascertain where she could place her trust, and where more supervision would be needed. And when she received no response to that either, she said that if I wanted to swan around the world pretending I didn't understand things, that was my affair, but that I should know that it did cause other people pain.

Another long stretch of empty ocean, which the captain announces as an opportunity for resuming the paper war, and everywhere those of us off duty get busy with pencils writing our patrol reports or toting up stores expended and remaining. Our boat continues to break down. Each day something or other gets jiggered up and someone puts it right. The chief initiates a tournament of Sea Battle, a game he plays on graph paper in which each contestant arranges his hidden fleet, consisting of a battleship, two cruisers, three destroyers, and four submarines and occupying respectively four, three, two, and one square each, while his opponent attempts to destroy them by guesswork, each correct guess on the grid counting as a hit. I'm drawn to the competitions but decline to participate. "That's the way he is on leave, as well," Mills tells everyone. "The Monk likes to watch."

Off Little Andaman Island we pass a jungle of chattering monkeys that cascades right down to the shore. For safety we stay close to the coast in the darkness, and the oily-looking water is filled with sea snakes and jellyfish so that when we surface at nightfall horrid things get stuck in our conning tower gratings and crunch and slide underfoot. The captain takes a bearing on the black hills in the starlight and those of us on watch can hear nothing but the water lapping against our hull and the fans quietly expelling the battery gases. Every so often a rock becomes visible. A little vacant jetty. In the morning we dive in rain like sheets flapping in the wind.

The mattresses grew so foul the captain had them rolled and hauled up through the conning tower and thrown over the side. The coarse pads left on our bunks rub open blisters and sores and our medical officer recommends cornmeal and baking soda to dry the mess. Our new torpedoman had the fingernails and top joints of his first three fingers crushed in a bulkhead door in a crash dive. I helped the medical officer with the bandaging and afterward was surprised at his annoyance. "You could have answered a few of the boy's questions," he complained. "He's new on the ship and looking for a friend."

Mills has begun agitating quietly with other members of the crew to petition the captain to head home, wherever "home" now remains, before it's too late. He explains that his philosophy is to be neither reckless nor overly gun-shy, but to evaluate the situation in light of whether we have any chance at all to make a successful attack and survive to report it. He claims that while the miracle of encountering a lone ammunition ship is all well and good, it's only a matter of time before we confront an entire convoy. He asks for my help to rally support for his position and I agree, and he says we can start with the torpedo officer since his shifts and mine align for the next few days. Each night when I return from duty Mills asks if I've talked to the TO yet and I tell him I haven't.

The next night the watch reports a debris field and the captain goes up to have a look. When he descends to the wardroom the wireless operator says, "It seems that we've finally given them a dose of what they've been giving us, eh, sir?" and the captain answers that it's British wreckage we're sailing through.

At breakfast there are complaints about the mutton, and to provide perspective Mills's cousin tells of having eaten in a mess so rancid they'd had to inspect each mouthful on the fork to ensure there was nothing crawling in it.

Twelve bleary hours later I'm seven minutes late for the dawn watch. The captain is on the conning tower, too, and the enraged mate I'm relieving shoulders past me and heads below. The fresh air smells of seaweed and shellfish. In the heat the sea is so calm it looks like metal. Mist moves across our bow in the early sun. I apologize and the captain remarks that as a midshipman he was flogged for "wasting three minutes of a thousand men's time" by piping a battle cruiser's crew tardy to its first shift. I tell him that when I'm sleepless for long periods I sometimes don't properly attend to things, and after a silence he answers that he had a great uncle who always claimed about himself that he didn't attend to things, and that this great uncle went off to the Crimean War, where as Lord Raglan's aide-de-camp he was more or less responsible for the Charge of the Light Brigade.

He stays on the bridge with me, evidently enjoying the air. "Did you know that *Telemachus* in Greek means 'far from battle'?" he asks. I tell him I didn't.

In the face of the blank sky and still water I return to the problem of how to respond to my cousin's letter. I imagine describing for her all these dawns I've collected on watch: gold over the Norway Deep, scarlet off Singapore, silvery pink in the China Sea. I imagine recounting the morning the sun was behind us and a spray from the bow was arching across the deck so that we carried with us our own rainbow. In my last attempt I wrote that there wasn't much I could say about my position, but that things were presently quiet and I was in excellent health and she shouldn't worry, and then I stopped, since every other man in the crew had the same fatuous and unfinished letter in his locker, as well. I imagine telling her how vividly I could see her face as we left Harwich, the dockyard walls slipping past us like sliding doors, opening up vistas of the harbor, our stem coming round as docile as an old horse. I imagine telling her how some part of me anticipated the Pacific as if a way to discover my father's fate. The sadness of my final glimpse of our escort vessel as it signaled its goodbye and dropped back to its station on our port beam.

Later that day a commotion pulls me from my bunk. The watch spotted something far off in the haze and the captain has taken us to periscope depth. When I get to the wardroom he's climbing into his berth and telling the chief that he'll resume observation in ten minutes and that it's going to be a long approach. In the meantime the chief is to redirect our course to a firing bearing, instruct the torpedo room to stand by, and order the ship's safe opened and the confidential materials packed into a canvas bag and the bag weighed down with wrenches.

The torpedomen are excited, since most believe that Thursdays and Saturdays are our lucky days. Mills is not hiding his dismay. He suggests to the TO that the captain use the wireless to inquire if the Admiralty thinks this action worth the risk, but the TO reminds him that such communications would reveal our position. Mills informs the TO that much of the crew shares his unease and the TO looks around at each of us until finally Mills tells me that if I'm not on duty I'm in the way. As I turn to go he asks when I stuck the photograph over my bunk but doesn't ask who it is.

Back in the wardroom the captain is out of his berth and at the periscope. When the sweat dripping over his eyebrows steams the lens, he wipes it clear with tissue paper the chief hands him. He finally murmurs that the convoy looks to be five miles out and that he estimates it will pass about a quarter mile in front of us. He reports that we've chanced across an escort carrier. He reports that the convoy's rear is lost to the distance, but in its vanguard alone he can make out two destroyers and three sub hunters.

"In this calm and in this channel, once they see our torpedoes' wakes there will be nowhere for us to hide," the chief tells him, as though reciting the solution to an arithmetic problem, and the captain keeps his face to the eyepiece. "Perhaps the wise course is to live to fight another day, sir?" our navigator asks. No one answers him. In the silence it's as if my stomach and legs are urging me on to something.

The chief questions whether we should put on a little speed to close the gap still further, and the captain replies that in this calm any telltale swirl or turbulence would give us away even at this range, and that instead we'll just settle in and get our trim perfect and let them come to us.

We can hear our own breathing. The captain orders the forward torpedo tubes flooded and their doors opened. Our hydrophone operator indicates multiple HEs bearing Green 175 and advancing rapidly. "Are we really going to do this?" our navigator asks again, barely audible. The captain senses the oddity of my presence and glances over before returning his attention to the eyepiece. "Our shipboard wraith," he jokes quietly, and the chief smiles, and I feel a child's pride at the separateness that I've always cultivated.

Then the captain clears his throat and re-grips the handles and calls out a final bearing, and issues the command to fire numbers one through six, and the entire ship jolts with each release. Mills reports in a strangled voice that all tubes have fired electrically, and soon thereafter our hydrophone operator reports that all torpedoes are running hot and straight.

And the image of what I wish I could have put into a letter for my cousin at once appears to me, from the only other time I was allowed at the periscope, along with the rest of the crew, when on a rough day near a reef in a breaking sea we found the spectacle of porpoises on our track above us, leaping through the avalanches of foam and froth six or seven at a time, maneuvering within our field of vision and then surging clean out of the water and reentering smoothly with trailing plumes of white bubbles, all of them flowing together, each a celebration of what the others could be, until finally it seemed as if hundreds had passed us, and in their kinship and coordination had then vanished into the impenetrable green beyond our reach.

CURTIS SITTENFELD

Gender Studies

FROM *The New Yorker*

NELL AND HENRY always said that they would wait until marriage was legal for everyone in America, and now this is the case —it's August 2015—but earlier in the week Henry eloped with his graduate student Bridget. Bridget is twenty-three, moderately but not dramatically attractive (one of the few non-stereotypical aspects of the situation, Nell thinks, is Bridget's lack of dramatic attractiveness), and Henry and Bridget had been dating for six months. They began having an affair last winter, when Henry and Nell were still together, then in April Henry moved out of the house that he and Nell own and directly into Bridget's apartment. Nell and Henry had been a couple for eleven years.

In the shuttle between the Kansas City airport and the hotel where Nell's weekend meetings will occur—the shuttle is a van, and she is its only passenger—a radio host and a guest are discussing the presidential candidacy of Donald Trump. The driver catches Nell's eye in the rearview mirror and says, "He's not afraid to speak his mind, huh? You gotta give him that."

Nell makes a nonverbal sound to acknowledge that, in the most literal sense, she heard the comment.

The driver says, "I never voted before, but, he makes it all the way, maybe I will. A tough businessman like that could go kick some butts in Washington."

There was a time, up to and including the recent past, when Nell would have said something calm but repudiating in response, something professorial, or at least intended as such. Perhaps: *What is it about Trump's business record that you find most persuasive?* But now she thinks, You're a moron. All she says is "Interesting" and looks out the window, at the humidly overcast sky and the prairies of grass behind ranch-style wooden fencing. Though she lives in Wisconsin, not so many states away, she has never been to Kansas City, or even to Missouri.

"I'm not a Republican," the driver says. "But I'm not a Democrat, either, that's for sure. You wouldn't *never* catch me voting for Shrillary." He shudders, or mock-shudders. "If I was Bill, I'd cheat on her, too."

The driver appears to be in his early twenties, fifteen or so years younger than Nell, with narrow shoulders on a tall frame over which he wears a shiny orange polo shirt; the van is also orange, and an orange ballpoint pen is set behind his right ear. He has nearly black hair that is combed back and looks wet, and the skin on his face is pale white and pockmarked. In the rearview mirror, he and Nell make eye contact again, and he says, "I'm not sexist."

Nell says nothing.

"You married?" he asks.

"No," she says.

"Boyfriend?"

"No," she says again, then immediately regrets it—he gave her two chances, and she failed to take either.

"Me, I'm divorced," he says. "Never getting wrapped up in that again. But I've got a four-year-old, Lisette. Total daddy's girl. You have kids?"

"No." This she has no desire to lie about.

Will he scold her? He doesn't. Instead, he asks, "You a lawyer?"

She actually smiles. "You mean like Hillary? No. I'm a professor."

"A professor of what?"

"English." Now she *is* lying. She is a professor of gender and women's studies, but outside academia it's often easier not to get into it.

She pulls her phone from the jacket she's wearing because of how cold the air-conditioning is and says, in a brisk tone, "I need to send an email." Instead, she checks to see how much longer it will take to get to the hotel—twenty-two minutes, apparently. The interruption works, and he doesn't try to talk to her again until they're downtown, off the highway. In the meantime, via Facebook, she accidentally discovers that Henry and Bridget, who got married two days ago in New Orleans (why New Orleans? Nell has no idea), had a late breakfast of beignets this morning and, as of an hour ago, were strolling around the French Quarter.

"How long you in KC?" the driver asks as he stops the van beneath the hotel's porte-cochère. The driveway is busy with other cars coming and going and valets and bellhops sweating in maroon uniforms near automatic glass doors.

"Until Sunday," Nell says.

"Business or pleasure?"

It's the midyear planning meeting for the governing board of the national association of which Nell is the most recent past president, all of which sounds so boring that she is perversely tempted to describe it to him. Instead, she simply says, "Business."

"You have free time, you should check out our barbecue," the guy says. "Best ribs in town are at Winslow's. You're not a vegetarian, are you?"

She and Henry were both vegetarians when they met, which was in graduate school; he was getting a PhD in political science. Then, about five years ago, by coincidence, Henry went to a restaurant where Nell was having lunch with a friend. Nell was eating a BLT. Neither she nor Henry said anything until that night at home, when she asked, "Did you notice what was on my plate today?"

"Actually," Henry said, "I've been eating meat, too."

Nell was stunned. Not upset but truly shocked. She said, "Since when?"

"A year?" Henry looked sheepish as he added, "It's just so satisfying."

They laughed, and they started making steak for dinner, or sausage, although, because of the kind of people they were (insufferable people, Nell thinks now), it had to be grass-fed or free-range or organic. And not too frequent.

All of which is to say that many times since she learned of Henry's affair she has wondered not only if she should have known but even if she is at fault for not cheating on him. Was there an unspoken pact that she failed to discern? And, either way, hadn't she been warned? An admiring twenty-three-year-old graduate student was, presumably, just so satisfying! Plus, Bridget and Henry had become involved at a time when Nell and Henry could go months without sex. They still got along well enough, but if they had ever felt passion or excitement—and truly, in retrospect, she can't remember if they did—they didn't anymore. Actually, what she remembers from their courtship is dinners at a not very good Mexican restaurant near campus, during which she could tell that he was trying to seem smart to her in exactly the way that she was trying to seem smart to him. Maybe for them that *was* passion? Simultaneously, she is furious at him—she feels the standard humiliation and betrayal—and she also feels an unexpected sympathy, which she has been careful not to express to him or to her friends. Their deliberately childless life, their cat, Converse (named not for the shoe but for the political scientist), their free-range beef and nights and weekends of reading and grading and high-quality television series—it was fine and a little horrible. She gets it.

To the driver, she says, "I'm not a vegetarian."

He turns off the van's engine. Although she paid online, in advance, for the ride, an engraved plastic sign above the rearview mirror reads, TIPS NOT REQUIRED BUT APPRECIATED. As he climbs out of the front seat to retrieve her suitcase from the rear of the van, she sees that all she has in her wallet is twenties. If it weren't for his political commentary, she would give him one—her general stance is that if she can pay $300 for a pair of shoes, or $11.99 a pound for Thai broccoli salad from the co-op, she can overtip hourly wage workers—but now she hesitates. She'll ask for ten back, she decides.

She joins the driver behind the van, just as a town car goes by. When she passes him a twenty, she observes him registering the denomination and possibly developing some parting fondness for her. Which means that she can't bring herself to ask for ten back, so instead she says, "There's no way Donald Trump will be the Republican nominee for president."

She wonders if he'll say something like "Fuck you, lady," but he gives no such gratification. He says, seeming concerned, "Hey, I didn't mean offense." From a pocket in his pants he takes a white business card with an orange stripe and the shuttle logo on the front. He adds, "I'm not driving Sunday, but, you need anything while you're here, just call me." Then he kneels, takes the ballpoint pen from behind his ear, and, using her black, wheeled suitcase that's upright on the ground between them as a desk, writes *LUKE* in capital letters and a ten-digit number underneath. (Years ago, Henry had tied a checked red-and-white ribbon, from a Christmas gift his mother had sent them, to the suitcase's handle.) The driver holds the business card up to her.

For what earthly reason would she call him? But the unsettling part is that, with him kneeling, it happens that his face is weirdly close to the zipper of her pants—he didn't do this on purpose, she doesn't think, but his face is maybe three inches away—so how could the idea of him performing oral sex on her *not* flit across her mind? In a clipped voice, she says, "Thanks for the ride."

With CNN on in the background, Nell hangs her shirts and pants in the hotel-room closet and carries her Dopp kit into the bathroom. The members of the governing board will meet in the lobby at six and take taxis to a restaurant a mile away. Nell is moving the things she won't need at dinner out of her purse and setting them on top of the bureau—a water bottle, a manila folder containing the notes for a paper she's in the revise-and-resubmit stage with —when she notices that her driver's license isn't in the front slot of her wallet, behind the clear plastic window. Did she not put it back after going through security in the Madison airport? She isn't particularly worried until she has searched her entire purse twice, and then she is worried. She also doesn't find the license in the pockets of her pants or her jacket, and it wouldn't be in her suitcase. She pictures her license sitting by itself in one of those small, round, gray containers at the end of the X-ray belt—the headshot from 2010, taken soon after she got reddish highlights, the numbers specifying her date of birth and height and weight and address. But she didn't set it in any such container. She probably dropped it on the carpet while walking to her gate, or it fell out of her bag or her pocket on the plane.

Can you board a plane in the United States, in 2015, without an ID? If you're a white woman, no doubt your chances are higher than anyone else's. According to the Internet, she should arrive at the airport early and plan to show other forms of ID, some of which she has (a work badge, a gym ID, a business card) and some of which she doesn't (a utility bill, a check, a marriage license). She also calls the airline, which feels like a futile kind of due dili-

gence. The last call she makes is to the van driver—thank goodness for the twenty-dollar tip—who answers the phone by saying,
in a professional tone, "This is Luke."

"This is the person who was your passenger to the Garden Center Hotel," Nell says. "You dropped me off about forty-five minutes ago."

"Hey there." Immediately, Luke sounds warmer.

Trying to match his warmth, she says, "I might have dropped
my driver's license in your van. Can you check for me? My name
is Eleanor Davies."

"I'm driving now, but I'll look after this drop-off, no problem."

Impulsively, Nell says, "If you find it, I'll pay you." Should she
specify an amount? Another twenty? Fifty?

"Well, it's here or it's not," Luke says. "I'll call you back."

"I was sitting in the first row of the back seat," Nell says, and,
when he speaks again, Luke seems amused.

He says, "Yeah, I remember."

He hasn't called by the time she has to go to dinner. She calls him
again before leaving her room, but the call goes to voicemail. The
dinner, attended by nine people including Nell, is more fun than
she expected—they spend a good chunk of it discussing a gender-
studies department in California that's imploding, plus they drink
six bottles of wine—and the group decides to walk back to the hotel. In her room, Nell realizes that, forty-two minutes ago, she received a call from Luke, and then a text. *Hey call me,* the text reads.

"You at the hotel now?" he says when she calls, and when she
confirms that she is he says, "My shift just ended, so I can be there
in fifteen."

"Wow, thank you so much," Nell says. "I really appreciate this."
He will text when he arrives, they agree, and she'll go outside.

Except that, when she reaches the lobby, he's standing inside it,
near the glass doors. He's not wearing the shiny orange polo shirt;
he has on dark-gray jeans and a black, hooded, sleeveless shirt. His
biceps are stringily well-defined; also, the shirt makes her cringe.
She has decided to give him forty dollars, which she's folded in
half and is holding out even before they speak. He waves away the
money and says, "Buy me a drink and we'll call it even."

"Buy you a drink?" she repeats. If she were sober, she'd definitely make an excuse.

With his chin, Luke gestures across the lobby toward the hotel bar, from which come boisterous conversations and the notes of a live saxophone player. "One Jack and Coke," he says. "You ask me, you're getting a bargain."

Having a drink in the hotel bar with Luke the Shuttle Driver is almost enjoyable, because it's like an anthropological experience. Beyond her wish to get her license back, she feels no fondness for the person sitting across the table, but the structure of his life, the path that brought him from birth to this moment, is interesting in the way that anyone's is. He's twenty-seven, older than she guessed, born in Wichita, the second of two brothers. His parents split up before his second birthday; he's met his father a handful of times and doesn't like him. He'll never disappear from his daughter's life the way that his father disappeared from his. He and his mom and his brother moved to Kansas City when he was in fifth grade —her parents are from here—and he played baseball in junior high and high school and hoped for a scholarship to Truman State (a scout even came to one of his games), but senior year he tore his UCL. After that, he did a semester at UMKC, but the classes were boring and not worth the money. ("No offense," he says, as if Nell, by virtue of being a professor, had a hand in running them.) He met his ex-wife, Shelley, in high school, but the funny thing is that he didn't like her that much then, so he should have known. He thinks she just wanted a kid. They were married for two years, and now she's dating someone else from their high school class, and Luke thinks better that guy than him. Luke and his buddy Tim want to start their own shuttle service, definitely in the next eighteen months; the manager of the one he's working for now is a dick.

Eliciting this information isn't difficult. The one question he asks her is how many years she had to go to school to become a professor. She says, "How many after high school or how many total?"

"After high school," he says, and she says, "Nine."

Without consulting her, he orders them a second round, and after finishing it Nell is the drunkest she's been since she was a bridesmaid in her friend Anna's wedding, in 2003: she's wall shiftingly drunk. She says, "Okay, give me my license now."

Luke grins. "How 'bout I walk you to your room? Be a gentleman and all."

"That's subtle," she says. Does he know what *subtle* means? (It's not that she's unaware that she's an elitist asshole. She's aware! She's just powerless not to be one. Also, seriously, does he know what *subtle* means?) She says, "Is hitting on passengers a thing with you or should I feel special?"

"What makes you think I'm hitting on you?" But he's still grinning, and it's the first thing he's said that a man she'd want to go out with would say. (How will she ever, in real life, meet a man she wants to go out with who wants to go out with her? Should she join Match? Tinder? Will her students find her there?) Then Luke says, "Just kidding, I'm totally hitting on you," and it's double the exact right thing to say—he has a sense of humor *and* he's complimenting her.

She says, "If you give me my license, you can walk me to my room."

"Let me walk you to your room, and I'll give you your license."

Is this how the heroines of romance novels feel? They have, in air quotes, no choice but to submit; they are absolved of responsibility by extenuating circumstances. (Semi-relatedly, Nell was once the first author on a paper titled "Booty Call: Norms of Restricted and Unrestricted Sociosexuality in Hookup Culture," a paper that, when she last checked Google Scholar, which was yesterday, had been cited thirty-one times.)

Nell charges the drinks to her room, and in the elevator up to the seventh floor he is standing behind her, and presses his face between her neck and shoulder and it feels really good; when they are configured like this, it's difficult to remember that she's not attracted to him. Inside her room—the pretense that he is merely walking her to the door has apparently dissolved—they make out for a while by the bathroom. (It's weird, but not bad-weird, to be kissing a man other than Henry. She has not done so for eleven years.) Then they're horizontal on the king-size bed, on top of the white down comforter. They roll over a few times, but mostly she's under him. Eventually, he unbuttons and removes her blouse, then her bra, then pulls off his ridiculous hooded shirt. (Probably, if she were less drunk, she'd turn out the light on the nightstand.) He's taller and thinner than Henry, and he uses his hands in a less habitually proficient but perhaps more natively adept way. He smells like some very fake, very male kind of body wash or deodorant. Intermittently, she thinks of how amused her friend Lisa, who's an economics professor, will be when she texts her to say that she had a one-night stand with the shuttle driver. Though, for it to count as a one-night stand, is penetration required? *Will* penetration occur? Maybe, if he has a condom.

He's assiduously licking her left nipple, then her right one, then kissing down her sternum, though he stops above her navel and starts to come back up. She says, "Keep going," and when he raises his head to look at her she says, "You're allowed to go down on me." This is not a thing she ever said to Henry. Although he did it—not often but occasionally, in years past—neither of them treated it like a privilege she was bestowing.

Luke pulls down her pants and her underwear at the same time. He has to stand to get them over her ankles. From above her, he says, "Wow, you haven't shaved lately, huh? Not a fan of the Brazilian?"

Which might stop her cold if he were a person whose opinion she cared about, a person she'd ever see again. She knows from her students that being mostly or completely hairless is the norm now, unremarkable even among those who consider themselves ardent feminists, and it occurs to her that she may well be the oldest woman Luke has ever hooked up with.

The funny, awful part is that she *did* shave recently—she shaved her so-called bikini line this morning in the shower, because she had seen online that the hotel has a pool and had packed her bathing suit, which in fact is not a bikini. Lightly, she says to Luke, "You're very chivalrous."

Their eyes meet—she's perhaps three percent less hammered than she was down in the lobby, though still hammered enough not to worry about her drunkenness wearing off anytime soon —and at first he says nothing. Then, so seriously that his words almost incite in her a genuine emotion, he says, "You're pretty."

With her cooperation, he tugs her body toward the foot of the bed, so that her legs are dangling off it, then he kneels on the floor and begins his ministrations. (Being eaten out by the shuttle driver! While naked! With the lights on! In Kansas City! Lisa is going to find this hilarious.) Pretty soon, Nell stops thinking of Lisa. Eventually, wondrously, there is the surge, then the cascade. Though she doesn't do it, it crosses her mind to say "I love you" to Luke. That is, in such a situation she can understand why a person would.

He is next to her on the bed again—he's naked, too, though

she doesn't recall when he removed the rest of his clothes—and she closes her eyes as she reaches for his erection and starts moving her hand. In spite of the impulse to declare her love, she's still not crazy about the sight of him. She says, "I'll give you a blow job, but I want my license first. For real."

He doesn't respond, and she stops moving her hand. She says, "Just get it and put it on the bedside table. Then we can quit discussing this."

In a small voice, he says, "I don't have it."

Her eyes flap open. "Seriously?"

"I checked the van, but it wasn't there."

"Are you kidding me?" She sits up. "Then what the fuck are you doing here?"

He says nothing, and she says, "You lied to me."

He shrugs. "I wish I had it."

"Are you planning to, like, sell it?" Who do people sell licenses to? she wonders. Underage kids? Identity thieves?

"I told you, I don't have it."

"Well, it's not like you have any credibility at this point."

After a beat, he says, "Or maybe you didn't really lose it."

"What's that supposed to mean?"

She will reflect on this moment later, will reflect on it extensively, and one of the conclusions she'll come to is that, with more self-possession, he could have recalibrated the mood. He could have done a variation on the thing he did in the bar, when he teased her for assuming he was hitting on her and then admitted he was hitting on her. If he had been more confident, that is, or presumptuous, even—if he'd jokingly pointed out her glaring and abundant complicity. But her life has probably given her far more practice at presumption than his has given him. And, in reality, he looks scared of her. His looking scared makes her feel like a scary woman, and the feeling is both repugnant and pleasurable.

Quietly, he says, "I swear I don't have it."

"You should leave," she says, then adds, "Now."

Again when they look at each other, she is close to puncturing the theatrics of her own anger—certainly she is not oblivious of the non-equitability of their encounter ending at this moment —but she hasn't yet selected the words that she'll use to cause the puncture. As drunk as she is, the words are hard to find.

"I thought we were having fun." His tone is a little pathetic and also a little accusing. "*You* had fun." It's his stating what she has already acknowledged to herself, what she was considering acknowledging to him, that definitively tips the scales the wrong way.

"Get out," she says.

In her peripheral vision, as she looks down at her bare legs, she can see him stand and dress. Her heart is beating rapidly. Clothed, he folds his arms. If he'd reached down and touched her shoulder . . . If he'd sat back down next to her . . .

"Eleanor," he says, and this is the first and only time he uses her name, which of course is her real name, though not one that anybody who knows her calls her by. "I wasn't trying to trick you. I just wanted to hang out."

She says nothing, and after a minute he walks to the door and leaves.

Her headache lasts until midafternoon on Saturday, through the budget meeting, the meeting about the newly proposed journal, the discussion of where to hold future conferences after the ones that are scheduled for 2016 and 2017. She suspects that some of her colleagues are hungover, too, and she'd likely be hungover, anyway, without the additional drinks she had with Luke, so it's almost as if the Luke interlude didn't occur—as if it were a brief and intensely enjoyable dream that took a horrible turn. And yet, after she wakes from a pre-dinner nap, the meetings are a blur and the time with Luke is painfully vivid.

Nell rises from bed and splashes cold water on her face. She wants days and weeks to have passed, so that she can revert to being her boring self, her wronged-by-her-partner, high-road self; she wants to build up the capital, if only in her own mind, of not being cruel. She no longer thinks that she'll tell Lisa anything.

Which means that when, while dressing to meet her colleagues for dinner, she finds her driver's license in the left pocket of her jacket the discovery only amplifies her distress. The lining of the jacket's left pocket is ripped, which she knew about, because a dime had been slipping around inside it since last spring. But she hadn't realized that the hole was large enough for a license to pass through.

When she was a sophomore in high school, the father of a kind and popular classmate died of cancer. Nell didn't know the boy well, and she wasn't sure if it was appropriate to write him a condolence note. He came back to school after a week, at which point she hadn't written one. It seemed like perhaps it was too late. But, a few days later, she wondered, *had* it been too late? Weeks later, was it too late? Months? She occasionally still recalls this boy, now a man who is, like her, nearly forty, and she wishes she had expressed compassion.

This is how she will feel about Luke. She could have summoned him back on Friday night. She could have called him on Saturday, after finding the license. She could have texted him on Sunday, or after she returned to Madison. However, though she thinks of him regularly—she thinks of him especially during the Republican debates, then during the primaries, the caucuses, the convention, and the election (the election!)—she never initiates contact. She does join Match, she goes to a salon and gets fully waxed, she starts dating an architect whom she didn't meet on Match, who is eight years older than her, pro women's pubic hair, and appalled by how readily a gender-studies professor will capitulate to arbitrary standards of female beauty. Nell finds his view to be a relief personally, but intellectually a facile and unendearing failure of imagination.

Sometimes, when she's half asleep, she remembers Luke saying, *You're pretty,* how serious and sincere his voice was. She remembers when his face was between her legs, and she feels shame and desire. But by daylight it's hard not to mock her own overblown emotions. He didn't have anything to do with her losing the license, no, but it's his fault that she thought he did. Besides, he was a Trump supporter.

Famous Actor

FROM *Tin House*

I LOOKED AROUND the party: forty or so people clustered in threes and fours, pretending not to look at the Famous Actor (even here in Bend, we know not to go goony around celebrities), but no one went more than four or five seconds without stealing a glance at him. Nobody but me seemed to notice what his right elbow was up to.

After a few minutes, he stopped elbow-fucking me and turned so that we were face-to-face. It was weird staring into those pale blues, eyes I'd known for years, eyes I'd seen in, what, fifteen or sixteen movies, in a couple of seasons of TV, staring out from magazine covers. He muttered something I couldn't quite hear.

I leaned in. "I'm sorry—what?"

"I *said* . . ." he bent in closer, so that his mouth was inches from my left ear ". . . the universe is an endless span of darkness occasionally broken by moments of unspeakable celestial violence."

I was pretty sure that wasn't what he'd said.

He laughed as if he recognized what an insane thing that was for someone to say. "You ever think shit like that at parties?"

I tend to think about crying at parties, or if someone might be trying to kill me. But I didn't say that. I don't very often say what I think.

"Hey," he said, "this is going to sound like a line, but . . . do you maybe want to get out of here?"

He was right. It did sound like a line.

And I did want to get out of there.

"Okay," I said.

I disliked him from the moment I decided to sleep with him.

In one of his first movies, *Fire in the Hole,* he plays a scared young soldier. I can't even remember which war but it's not Vietnam. It's maybe one of the gulf wars, or Afghanistan, or something. It's a truly awful movie, but somehow too earnest to *really* hate. Still, you know you've made a bad war movie when they don't even show it on TNT. At the time he was cast, the Famous Actor was still known as the kid from the Disney Channel. I think the role in that war movie was supposed to launch him as an adult actor. But you got the sense that people watched the movie thinking, *Wait, what's the kid from* The Terrific Todd Chronicles! *doing carrying a rifle, for Christ's sake.* Still, I guess it did turn him into a real adult actor because he started doing more movies after that.

We made our way through the party. He didn't ask how it was that I didn't need to tell anyone that I was leaving. I was glad I didn't have to explain that I wasn't actually invited to the party.

There were a few people I knew outside and I wondered what they would say about him leaving with me. The Famous Actor climbed in the passenger seat of my Subaru. He sat on my makeup bag, held it up, then tossed it into the back seat. He had a small hiker's backpack with him, which he sat at his feet. "Must be weird to go to a party in Bend, Oregon, and end up leaving with me," he said.

I shrugged. "There's always a party at that house. Everybody knows about it."

"No, I didn't mean the party. I just meant this probably wasn't how you figured your Friday night would go."

"This is my Wednesday," I said. I explained that I had Mondays and Tuesdays off from the coffee shop, so I always thought of Fridays as my Wednesdays. He looked at me as if he couldn't tell if I was crazy or if I was fucking with him. It's hard to explain, but I can make myself distant, make my face as blank as possible.

"Huh, funny," he said. He stared out the window as I drove. He hadn't buckled his seat belt and my car bonged at him.

"You know that thing I said at the party—about the universe being an endless span of darkness? It was really a comment on how it gets old, everyone looking at you like you're going to say something profound. Sometimes I play off that expectation by saying something totally crazy." He laughed at himself. "You know?" My car bonged at him again.

When he dies in *Fire in the Hole,* you can tell it's meant to be the emotional peak of the movie. The soldiers are walking through this destroyed city and a sniper's bullet zips into the spot where his neck meets his chest, just above his body armor. He slaps at the wound like he's been stung by a wasp, and only then does he seem to realize what's happening to him. That he's dying. It should be a profound moment. Those tuna-blue eyes get all wide and he frantically reaches around his back to feel whether the bullet has gone all the way through. His line is something like, *Sarge! Did it go through? Did . . . it . . . go through?* And then he just falls over. It's hard to say what's wrong with it, but it became one of those unintentional laugh lines. Like: *Sure, war is hell, but it's nothing compared to Terrific Todd's acting.*

He pulled a cigarette pack from his pocket. "You mind?" Natural Spirits. Naturally. I can't remember the last time I dated a guy who didn't smoke Natural Spirits. Every guy in Bend smokes them. He blew the smoke to the roof of the car, which answered by bonging at him again about his seat belt.

The Famous Actor explained that he'd been making a movie nearby — I knew this, of course; everyone knew they were filming a postapocalyptic movie called *The Beats* in the high desert, and we all knew the cast. Someone had told the Famous Actor that Bend was known for its rock-climbing, so he'd called a climbing guide and they'd gone bouldering that day. Then the guide invited him to the party.

I knew the dick-guide he'd called. Wayne Bolls. Wayne's website is covered with pictures of celebrities he's climbed with, like he's some old New York dry cleaner. *Starfucker Tours,* we call it in Bend. *We put the climber in climbing.*

"It's so great to get away from the bullshit," he said. I guess the bullshit was Hollywood, and wealth and fame — pretty much everything that everyone else in the world completely craves. He took a long drag of that cigarette. "But hey, Bend's a cool town, huh?"

I nodded. That's the worst thing about Bend. Its coolness. That and its size, how everyone thinks they know you.

He picked a piece of tobacco off his tongue. "For me it's just a treat to be around normal people."

I made a noise that must've sounded like a laugh.

"What's so funny?" He took another drag of his cigarette. "I'm serious." He seemed genuinely hurt. "I don't see why people have so much trouble believing that famous people just want to be normal."

In his last movie, *New Year's Love Song*, he is one of like a hundred celebrities paired off in parallel love stories. He was cast as the manager of a rock band that is doing a concert on New Year's Day in New York. The band is supposed to be a modern-day Fleetwood Mac, I guess—two young guys and two young girls—but without the hard drugs or anything else that made Fleetwood Mac interesting. The cute singer is married to the drummer and, as the band's tongue-tied manager, the Famous Actor needs to keep the press from finding out that they're divorcing until after the concert—although they never really make it clear why that would matter. The singer is played by the girl from that Nickelodeon show *You Can't Fool Tara!*—it was billed as a kind of Disney meets Nickelodeon thing; this was right after her whole sex-tape scandal, so the movie was meant to redeem her image or something. The movie ends with the Famous Actor's band manager character stumbling out onstage in Rockefeller Plaza and telling the singer that he's always loved her in front of, like, a jillion people. But here's what I don't get: Why do we find that romantic? Are men such liars that it's a turn-on to have so many witnesses? It's one of those movies that make you sad to be female, that make you want to stab yourself in the ovaries. It's truly a hateful movie, but I was still teary at the end, in a completely involuntary way, the way crying babies are supposed to make women lactate. "I want to start every year from now on with you in my arms," the Famous Actor says to the singer on the stage, in front of everyone in the world. There should be a German word for wanting to gouge out your own teary eyes.

"I like your apartment," the Famous Actor said. He walked around like someone sizing up a hotel room. He ran his hand along the spines of the books on my shelf and crouched in front of my albums. "Vinyl," he said. "Cool." When he got to a band he approved of, he would say the name. "Love this old Beck. Ooh, Talking Heads. Nice. The New Pornographers. Yes."

I put my keys on the kitchen table and looked through my mail. There was a late notice for a credit card bill, a late notice for a water bill, a solicitation for a fake college, and a postcard from my ex.

The postcard showed some old 1960s tourist trap in Idaho called the Snake Pit. On the back he'd written, *Expected to see you here.* It's this thing my ex and I have: we send each other old postcards with slights on them. I sent him one from Crater Lake on which I wrote: *The second biggest a-hole in Oregon.* We never really broke up; he just moved to Portland with his band. Not that we had this great relationship. He always said I needed help. I always said he was a pig who fucked any girl who would have him. But I'll say this for him: he was *not* a liar. He told me all about it every time he strayed. He'd get back from some gig in Ashland or Eureka and say, "Dude, I got something to tell you." After a while I'd get anxious even seeing his name on my phone because I thought he was going to tell me about some new girl he'd junked. But I couldn't seem to break up with him. When he finally left for Portland I wasn't sad, just more deadened, the way I get. Sometimes I think our real problem wasn't his infidelity; it was his honesty.

I think we sent old postcards to say—*Hey. Still here.* I wondered if he'd be jealous if he saw who was in my apartment.

The Famous Actor plopped down on my couch. "It's so great to just be in, like, a fucking *apartment!* Right? You know? A *real place?* With just, like . . . walls . . . and furniture and books and a TV and real posters and . . ." I wondered if he was going to name everything in my apartment, room by room: dresser, nightstand, alarm clock . . . toothbrush, antibacterial soap, Tampax . . .

I opened my fridge. "You want a drink?"

"I'm in recovery," he said. "But you go ahead." He held up his pack of Natural Spirits again. "This okay?" When I said it was, he lit up, took a deep pull of smoke, and let it go in the air. "No, this is really nice," he said again. "Just what I needed." He pulled a piece of tobacco off his tongue again. Or, actually, I suspect that he pretended to pull a piece of tobacco off his tongue. He leaned his head back onto the couch. "I just get so fucking tired of . . ."

But he couldn't seem to think of what it was that made him so fucking tired.

In *Amsterdam Deadly* he plays a UN investigator who goes to The Hague to testify in the trial of a vicious African warlord. As soon as you see the cast you know he's going to fall in love with the beautiful blond South African lawyer defending the warlord. The actress is that girl from *My One True,* and because she's as American as Velveeta she got knocked pretty bad for her South African accent, which sounded like an Irish girl crossed with a Jamaican auctioneer. Still, she and the Famous Actor really do have chemistry. Watching that movie is like watching the two best-looking single people at a wedding reception; not a lot of drama about who's going to fuck whom later. But if the romance in that movie is okay, the politics make no sense. The dialogue is like someone reading stories out of the *New York Times*. The Famous Actor has a speech near the end where he yells, "If the Security Council won't pass this joint resolution then *I* will get these refugees across the border to the safe zone!" Not exactly *Henry V.* I think sometimes movies, like people, just try too hard.

We had straight missionary paint-by-numbers sex: some foreplay, exactly enough oral to get us both going, then he pulled a condom out of that backpack he carried and rolled it over his dick. It was ribbed, which I could see he believed was thoughtful of him. There was nothing weird or obsessive or porny about the sex. Or particularly memorable. First sex is always kind of awkward, though; you don't yet know what the other person likes. Everything's basically in the right place, but it doesn't feel right, or it takes a minute to find.

First sex is like being in a stranger's kitchen, trying all the drawers, looking for a spoon. There was one point where he was over me, his eyes closed, head back, weight on his arms like he was doing a pushup, and it was kind of weird—like, *Oh, hey, look, Terrific Todd is boning someone. Oh wait, it's me.* But I shouldn't make it sound like the sex was bad. It was fine. Really, the only disappointing thing was how much stomach fat the Famous Actor had—I mean, really, when you have that much money, how hard is it to do a few sit-ups? Of course that might have been intentional, too, part of his normalcy campaign.

Afterward, we were lying on my bed naked and he was smoking another Natural Spirit. He smoked so many I wanted to buy stock in it. "That was great," he said. "And thanks for not taking a selfie or anything weird like that."

I must've made a face like, *Christ, are you kidding me?*

He sat up. "Oh, you'd be surprised how often that happens. I know actors who have, like, a contract they have women sign before they'll have sex." He named two actors of his generation, both of whom had been in movies with him. "I mean, can you imagine?" he asked. "Making a woman sign a contract before you fuck?"

He offered me his cigarette. I took a small drag. Those organic cigarettes tasted a little like dog shit.

"That's the part I really don't think people get." He picked another fake tobacco bit off his tongue. "You know? About fame? How dispiriting it is, how dehumanizing? It's like you're this . . . product. Right? I mean: I'm not some product. I'm a fuckin' person." He slapped his little intentional belly fat. "Right? Why can't people understand I'm just a regular guy?"

"I think people understand that," I said.

In *Big Bro,* he plays a guy in a fraternity whose older brother is a Wall Street trader who shows up after his divorce to act out some *Animal House* fantasies, only to find that frats now are full of serious students. The actor who plays the Wall Street brother had recently left *Saturday Night Live* and you can really tell the difference between someone used to making live audiences laugh and someone who falls into a giant birthday cake and reads lines like, "Oh boy! Here we go again!" to a Disney laugh track. Still, *Big Bro* was the Famous Actor's breakout. It must've made $200 million and it's watchable in part because the Famous Actor seems so easygoing and likeable in it (in other words, exactly like *no* fraternity guy *ever,* in the history of the world). People saw him differently after that. I think when an actor exudes such charm we assume the character must be close to his real self. But there's no reason to think that: he could just as easily be the selfish loser who raids his senile dad's retirement account in *Forty Reasons for Dying,* for instance. We really want to like people, even famous people.

It's not really possible to sleep next to someone the first time you've had sex together. That's something I'd like to take up with Hollywood if I ever get the chance: how they always cut from the kissing couple to them lying peacefully in bed postsex, snoozing with smiles on their faces. I'd like to grab some screenwriter by his ears: "Hey, *you* fuck a stranger and then try sleeping afterward!"

We were lying there on our backs, staring at the ceiling. He was smoking another cigarette. Our legs were touching.

"If you want me to go, I can call for a ride," he said.

"Only if you want to," I said.

"Cool," he said. "Yeah, cool. I'll stay. I like it here. It's chill."
I didn't say anything.

He sniffed. "I think people would be surprised at how hard it is
for someone like me to find a place where I can just . . . you know
—*be?* Where there's not some PA constantly buzzing around asking
if I want a Sprite."

"You want a Sprite?"

He laughed a little, took a pull of smoke, and when he started
to reach for his mouth, I watched him closely. He looked like he
was picking something off the end of his tongue again, but I'll be
damned if I saw any tobacco bits there. He looked right at me with
those Pepsi-blue eyes.

"Sometimes I daydream about hiding out someplace like this.
Just saying 'Fuck you' to the fake industry stuff and just dropping
the fuck out. Not tell anyone either, just chill in Bend, Oregon,
for a month, go out to breakfast, rock-climb, maybe get a bike,
read poetry in the park, go to parties like last night, hang out with
someone cool like you? Know what I mean?"

"Yes," I said. I didn't say the rest of what I was thinking, which
was: Who *doesn't* daydream of that, of not having a job or any worries, playing around all day, riding a bike and reading poetry and
having sex? The difference is that most of us would fucking starve
to death in a week.

I started to imagine the Famous Actor hanging around my
apartment for the next month like some unwanted houseguest.
A month becoming two, and three, him smoking forty cartons of
organic cigarettes and never finishing that book of poetry he was
supposedly reading, me coming home every day to Terrific Todd
marveling still at all the normal shit in my normal apartment—
dish soap, spatula, salt pig, can opener!—that band of fat around
his middle getting bigger and realer all the time.

He leaned over, got his tennis shoe off the ground, put his cigarette out on its sole, and put the butt in the pocket of his jeans.
Then he propped himself up on one elbow—the one that I had
gotten to know so well earlier. "Hey, can I ask you a personal question?"

Look, I don't mean to go all double-standard feminist—I mean,
I wasn't some victim; *I'd* fucked *him,* too—but that seemed like
such a guy thing to say right then. *Hey, remember a few minutes ago my
dick was inside you? Well, now I was wondering if we could talk.*

"Sure," I said.

"It's just . . . I can't get a read on you."

I didn't say anything.

I get that a lot from guys.

Also, it wasn't technically a question.

"I just keep feeling like . . . I don't know . . . like you think I'm . . . kind of a douchebag or something."

Also not a question.

Toward the end of *Big Bro,* after this huge party where Snoop Dogg inexplicably shows up with a bunch of hookers, the rest of the frat pulls the Famous Actor's character aside and tells him that his big brother has to go. He's nearly gotten them all expelled and they're all flunking classes and in danger of losing their fraternity charter. It's probably the most moving scene in the movie, the Famous Actor telling his brother he's got to leave. "Hey, Charlie, *these* are my brothers now," the Famous Actor says, "but they'll never be . . . *my brother.*" Chastened for his boorish behavior, the older brother slinks away sadly. Of course, he doesn't really go away, but shows up three minutes later with Mark Cuban and Donald Trump to save the day at his brother's oral presentation in his business class.

"I don't think you're a douchebag," I said to the Famous Actor.

"No, I think you do." He sat up higher.

"It's not that," I said. "It's just . . ." What are you supposed to say—after years of therapy to untangle your difficulty in forming relationships, your self-destructive behavior, the depressive periods and suicidal thoughts? And some narcissist expects you to pillow-talk it out?

"Seriously," he said, "I need you to tell me what you think of me."

What I thought of *him?* That his insecurity was infinite? Instead, after a minute, I said, "You'll always be my brother."

You have to wonder how a movie like *Big Bro 2* even gets made. In it, the younger brother has graduated from college and been hired by the older brother's company, which has somehow morphed from a Wall Street firm in the first movie to a tech company in the second. They're about to unveil this new kind of biocomputer, but an evil tech company called Gorgle wants to take over the brothers' company, so the old *SNL* comedian has to gather all the old frat guys together to use their special skills to defeat—Ugh, you know, it actually hurts my head to even think of the plot of that movie. It's like having to recount all the sexual positions your parents might have used in conceiving you. The best thing I can say about the second *Big Bro* is that the Famous Actor is barely in it, and only because he's clearly fulfilling some line in a contract that required his presence in a sequel. The *SNL* guy's career had stalled, and most of those frat guys would've starred in animal porn just to work again, but the Famous Actor had gone on to become the Famous Actor by then. He seems truly apologetic in the six or seven scenes he's in—like, I'm sorry America. I really am sorry.

He had that same sorry look on his face as he sat on the edge of the bed and looked back over his shoulder at me. "You know, I think you're not being very generous."

"Sorry," I said.

"I mean, maybe *you're* the asshole. Did that ever occur to you?"

"Yes," I said.

He turned away. "You can't know how weird this fame shit is. It's like you're see-through. Everyone assumes they know everything about you, but you know what? Nobody knows a fucking thing about me!" He stood and rubbed his forehead. "Always trying to be what people want—after a while, it's like you don't even know how to trust yourself anymore. You're always second-guessing, like, *Wait, how do I talk again? Is this how I react to things or how I want people to see me react?* And when no one's watching, you feel totally fucked—like, *Am I even here?* You don't know how hard that is—to not know yourself!"

He really seemed to think famous people were the only ones who didn't know themselves.

"Then I meet someone like you, someone I might genuinely like, someone I don't want to think that I'm a celebrity dick-head . . . and what do I do?" He laughed. "Act like a dickhead."

He walked across my tiny bedroom to my dresser. Behind a pile of clothes there was a picture of me with my sister, the last picture of us before she disappeared. He picked up the picture and stared at it. In the picture I'm eleven and Megan's thirteen and we're standing in front of the hammer ride at the county fair. We both have huge grins on our face and Megan's giving the thumbs-up because we're so proud of riding that scary ride together. Three months later she would run away from home. We never found out

what happened to her, if her body is somewhere or if she's working as a hooker in Alaska or whatever. She could be in the Taliban,
or she could be in the circus, or she could be rotting in a field in
Utah. That was the hardest thing for my parents—just never knowing. Our house was a tomb after that; my parents never the same.
The Famous Actor stared at the picture a moment and then put it
down. He turned and faced me.

"So if I've been a little self-absorbed, I apologize."

"It's fine," I said.

"No," he said. "It's not fine." He was getting worked up again.
"You can't just say, *It's fuckin' fine* and then keep acting like some
zombie! You can't fuckin' do that! You have to give something
back! You can't just sit there in judgment thinking that I'm an asshole and not give me the chance to show you I'm not! I mean, am
I asking too much? For a little human interaction!"

"What's my name?" I said.

He stared at me for a few seconds. "Aw fuck," he said.

If I was trapped on an island or something and I could only have
one movie to watch, but it had to be one of *his* movies, I'd choose
Been There, Done That. It's telling that my favorite of his movies is
one where he's just a supporting actor. I think it's hard for even
good actors to carry a whole movie. He's great as the gay brother
of the heroine, who has come back to her family's home in 1980s
Louisiana with her black boyfriend. He has several opportunities
to go too broad with the gay brother, or go all AIDS-victim-TV-
movie-of-the-week or something, but he's really restrained. And
when the gay brother ends up being the most racist person in the
family, the Famous Actor turns in a really nuanced and smart per-
formance. It's even a little bit brave. I suspect it's what happens
when you work with a great director. But I also think there's something deeper that he managed to find in himself in that movie.

He snapped his fingers and pointed at me. "Katherine!"

I shook my head.

"But it's something with a *K* sound, though, right? Caroline or
Cassidy or . . ."

"Sorry."

He had his eyes closed, concentrating. "You work at a bar."

"Coffee shop."

"Well *fuck me*," he said. "Fuck me fuck me fuck me." He opened his eyes, as if suddenly finding out someone he'd known for years was not who he thought they were.

"You had a lot on your mind," I said. "And your elbow."

He shook his head—like, *Can you believe me?*

"Don't worry about it," I said. "I suspect it's harder to not be a douchebag than people think."

He gave a little laugh, but I think, of all the things I said, that might've hurt the most. The condescension and truth of it. I felt okay then, in control of things.

"Well, thanks for understanding, Katherine," he said, "or whatever your name is."

I just smiled.

He reached into his backpack for his phone. "I should probably —" He turned on his phone and it buzzed and buzzed. He began reading messages. "Oh shit."

"Girlfriend?"

"What?" He scowled. "No. No. I have an earlier call tomorrow than I thought. I'm gonna have someone come get me."

"Sure."

He pressed a number and put his iPhone to his ear. "Hey. It's me. I'm at this girl's house. Yeah, in Bend. I know. I know. Hey, is there any way . . ." He didn't have to finish the sentence. I guessed there were a lot of sentences he didn't have to finish. "Yeah. Cool. Just a sec." He looked up at me. "Hey, what's the address here?"

In *Been There, Done That,* he has a great scene where he has a beer with the black boyfriend, who, it turns out, is super religious and has a problem with gay people. It ends with the two of them laughing together, two otherwise decent men confronting their old biases. As Hollywood pat as it sounds, the scene comes off as entirely genuine.

I have to say, right before he left, it felt that way in my apartment, too. Genuine. Like we'd come through something. He took a quick shower, and came out dressed in the same jeans and gray T-shirt.

He bowed. "Well, nameless queen of Bend, it was a pleasure to meet you tonight. Thank you."

I'd put a T-shirt on.

"Can I kiss you goodbye?"

I said he could.

It would be hard being with an actor. Figuring out what's real. That goodbye kiss he gave me—honestly, I don't know if I've ever been kissed like that: one hand behind my neck, the other on my waist. It was a great, generous kiss and I felt myself opening up to him, more than I had in bed. In fact, the kiss was so good I started to think about that laughter in *Been There, Done That*. I mean, clearly, they weren't *really* laughing like that, but in a way they sort of *were*. I guess in acting, you become the very thing you're portraying. In sex scenes, if you act turned on, you get turned on. Act like something is hilarious, it becomes hilarious. And that's how that kiss was—

My God, if that kiss wasn't real, I don't even care. I'll take fake over real any day. I've seen real.

Maybe it's that way with our lives, too. Normal people. I mean, we're all acting all of the time anyway, putting on our not-crazy faces for people, acting like making someone a cappuccino is the greatest thrill in the world, pretending to care about things you don't, pretending *not* to care about things you do care about, pretending your name isn't Katherine when it is, acting like you have your shit together when, the truth is, well—

I didn't want to look out the window as he left—it seemed like such a stupid movie-cliché thing to do—but I couldn't help myself. I looked out. He gave a small glance over his shoulder to my window, but I think the light was wrong and he couldn't see my face. Then he flicked at his hair and jumped into the passenger seat of a blue Audi, which zipped away. I imagined his Big Bro driving the car. I imagined the Famous Actor lighting up a Natural Spirit while the car bonged at him to put on his seat belt. He hated seat belts. It was three in the morning. I wasn't tired.

I looked around my apartment.

The Famous Actor was in a serial killer movie, too. It's called *Over Tumbled Graves* and he plays this young cop, the love interest of the girl detective hunting a serial killer. It might be the only movie of his that I've never seen—because of Megan, I guess. If you suffer night terrors and insomnia you sort of learn to avoid serial killer movies. Not that I begrudge him being in it. We all make choices. And he generally makes good ones. I just read that he is getting a franchise superhero in one of those reboots. And that he's engaged to the girl who is going to play Blue Aura in the same movie.

I'm really glad for him. He's been through a lot the last year. It wasn't even two weeks after the postapocalyptic movie finished production in Bend that I read that the Famous Actor was going back into rehab. Of course, I might have been the least surprised person in the world.

The morning he left, I rubbed lotion on my arms so that I wouldn't start scratching. I cried for a while, then I cried for crying. I went back to bed but I couldn't fall back to sleep. I had to be at the coffee shop at six. I repeated the steps: Get out of bed. Keep moving. Take care of yourself. I got up to take a shower. That's when I noticed my medicine cabinet door was slightly ajar. I opened it all the way. He had cleaned it out. The Zoloft I take for depression. The Ativan I take for anxiety. The Ambien I sometimes have to take to sleep. But not just that. He took the Benadryl and the Advil and the Gas-X. He even took the Lysteda I sometimes take when I get these ungodly heavy periods. I can't imagine what he thought he was going to do with that one. Two days later I got a visit from a nice young woman from the production company. I signed the nondisclosure documents without negotiating. She gave me a check for $6,000. All I had to do was promise never to mention his name. But what's a name anyway?

That morning, as I stood there, staring at that empty medicine cabinet, I felt the strangest sense of pride in him. Warmth. Love, even. Well, look at you, I thought, you are normal—as normal as the most fucked-up barista in Bend, Oregon. Relax, Terrific Todd, wherever you are, you're one of us.

Contributors' Notes

Other Distinguished Stories of 2016

American and Canadian Magazines Publishing Short Stories

Contributors' Notes

CHAD B. ANDERSON is a writer and editor living in Washington, DC. Born and raised in Virginia's Shenandoah Valley, he earned his BA from University of Virginia and his MFA in creative writing from Indiana University where he served as fiction editor for *Indiana Review*. He has been a resident at the Ledig House International Writers' Colony, and his fiction was published in *Salamander, Black Warrior Review,* and *Nimrod International Journal.* He has also published nonfiction with *The Hairsplitter* and several articles and reports on higher education.

• "Maidencane" started as a feverish and spontaneous writing exercise one morning in fall 2015 when I wasn't writing fiction as much as I wanted. I began with a kind of synecdoche for rambunctious, rural childhood: the scraping of sneakers on soil, the snatching of hands, cloudbursts of red dirt. I drew the camera backward, answering a series of questions: Who do the feet and hands belong to? What are they snatching? Where are they? By the end of that morning, I had these characters, somewhere in the South, but it wasn't a fully formed story and I didn't know it was a character's memory. It was just a kid's perfect day, and of course, I decided to destroy it: the brother gone, the neighbor girl dead, and the protagonist's childhood in the distant past. Gradually, over several months and several drafts, the story expanded from there.

At the time, the only writing I was doing was nonfiction in my personal journal, and I had fallen into this habit of writing in second person, speaking to myself, but also, in some ways, distancing myself from my own experiences, actions, and feelings, for better or for worse. The second person just slipped into "Maidencane" by accident, and I always intended to change it. But at some point, I realized the second person fit because this was an introspective but distant character who wasn't fully attached to anything: emotion, family, lovers, work. The protagonist only seems attached to this memory of a person who would otherwise be a footnote in anyone else's history. At the same time, "Maidencane" is a very introspective story, mostly (re)played in the protagonist's head, the way we all replay and repackage experiences internally, creating our own narratives of who we and others are, which may or may not be the truth.

I have a memory of hurting an adult cousin's feelings with an unintentionally offhanded comment when I was seven years old. Although it was a minor incident occurring decades ago, the memory sticks with me and it stings. It shaped the way I interact with others into adulthood. And yet, there are bigger family events I barely remember. Why—like the protagonist with that memory of the girl on the dock—do I cling to this memory? Around the time that I was writing "Maidencane," my family and I experienced a series of challenging events, including the death of my grandfather. During those difficult times, through our many and sometimes profound differences, we clung to what we hoped were shared memories, seeking connection to him, to each other, and to ourselves. In some ways, we succeeded, and in others, we failed. "Maidencane," in part, is an attempt to capture that experience, one that I suspect all families grapple with in some form or another.

T. C. BOYLE is the author of twenty-eight books of fiction, including *The Terranauts* (2016) and *The Relive Box and Other Stories,* due out this fall. He published his collected stories in two volumes, *T. C. Boyle Stories* (1998) and *T. C. Boyle Stories II* (2013), and was awarded the PEN/Malamud Award for his short fiction in 1999 and the Rea Award for the Short Story in 2014. He is a member of the American Academy of Arts and Letters.

• In my long career and even longer life on this earth, I have come to one conclusion: things always get worse. The deniers and revisionists have seized control of Washington, the hundred-year storms are coming once a week, the seas are rising and the polar bears paddling toward a distant horizon that will suck them down into the void of extinction any day now. In the absence of God, we look to science for hope. But science has now given us perhaps the most frightening agent of change yet, CRISPR-Cas9 gene-editing technology. Reports of it are all but inescapable, and, just as in "Are We Not Men?," we are now barraged with ads for DIY kits to enable us to toy with evolution over the kitchen sink. Is this a good idea? Well, again, as in the story, science croons to us in the most reasonable of voices, telling us of the great boon such technology promises humanity by way of permanently editing inherited disorders out of the germline, but once the dogcat is out of the bag . . . So. I am a satirist, I am a wise guy, I am a nudger and winker. In the face of the horror, what else is left to us but to laugh?

Along these lines, I should say that the suite of transgenic creatures mentioned so casually toward the end of the story includes but two of my own invention—the aforementioned dogcat and the crowparrot. The other five are already among us. And tell me, what parent, eager for his/her offspring to have a little head start in life, won't renounce the old dirty way of mixing genes between the sheets, when science offers us a shining new way to personhood? Or no, not simply personhood, but super-person-hood? What do I say? *Good luck.*

KEVIN CANTY's eighth book, a novel called *The Underworld,* was published by W. W. Norton in March 2017. He is also the author of three previous collections of short stories (*Where the Money Went, Honeymoon,* and *A Stranger in This World*) and four novels (*Nine Below Zero, Into the Great Wide Open, Winslow in Love,* and *Everything*). His short stories have appeared in *The New Yorker, Granta, Esquire, Tin House, GQ, Glimmer Train, Story, New England Review, The Best American Short Stories 2015,* and elsewhere; essays and articles in *Vogue, Details, Playboy,* the *New York Times,* and the *Oxford American,* among others. He lives and writes in Missoula, Montana.

• The literal roots of this story are neither surprising nor interesting: I was working at my dining table, right by my open door, on a sunny, warm summer day. The table sits in front of a big window with a view of the mountain half a block away; I have an office and a desk but I often prefer to sit here for the view. When the proselytizers came to the door, though, I was in plain sight. I couldn't pretend that I wasn't home.

It was a woman and a boy and the boy never spoke. The woman was kindly, measured, and very sincere. Did I take the pamphlet? I can't remember. I often do, meaning to be kind, though I discard them unread. The encounter was over quickly and uneventfully.

When they were gone, though, I found myself thinking of a passage I had read by Annie Dillard, about looking down at the singers in the street, bearing witness with their songs, and how much more interesting it would be to be inside the circle looking out, rather than outside looking in. I have no idea if I am remembering this accurately; it's been years since I read the essay, and I didn't go back to try to find it. But this was the version I remembered in the moment, and this set the story in motion. What was that boy's life about? What did it feel like?

And then, inevitably, my own Catholic boyhood came into play—that moment in particular when the saintly eleven-year-old was turning into a twelve-year-old pervert. So I made the boy a little older than he had been in real life and gave him strong unresolvable feelings: real faith, real desire. You can't be both at once. And yet he is. The tables are tipped a bit by the fact that he loves an abstract God but an actual breathing girl. But the tension of these two elements is where I found the story.

JAI CHAKRABARTI was born in Kolkata, India, and grew up between India and half a dozen American states. He was a 2015 Emerging Writer Fellow with *A Public Space* and received his MFA from Brooklyn College. His work has appeared in *A Public Space, Barrow Street, Hayden's Ferry Review,* and other publications. He lives with his family in Brooklyn, New York.

• When I walk through my grandparents' house in Kolkata, a sprawling colonial built at the turn of the last century, I can sense the stories that these old walls must have seen. On the bottom floor lived the maids, the cleaners, the cooks, as well as their children, and on the floors above, an extended family whose ghosts now roam from the kitchen to the parlor. With its crumbling verandahs and empty rooms, the house of Nikhil echoes my family's grand home gone to disrepair. When I climb the steps to the rooftop and see how closely the buildings lean on each other, a clothesline running from one family's roof to the next, I imagine Nikhil's perilous journey, up those same steps and into the humid air that feels at once constricting and full of possibility.

EMMA CLINE is the author of *The Girls,* which was a finalist for the National Book Critic Circle's John Leonard Prize. Her stories have appeared in *The New Yorker, Granta, Tin House,* and *Paris Review.* In 2014, she was the winner of the Plimpton Prize.

• This story really began with the setting: a certain kind of farm that is very familiar to me from growing up in Northern California, the kind of place where there always seems to be blue tarps everywhere. At the same time that the landscape of these places is so idyllic, the isolation and separation breeds the possibility of great violence. I liked exploring that idea of beauty or innocence, and its latent darkness—Heddy is still childish, in so many ways, with her lists and college classes, but her relationship with Otto, and their history together on the farm, is unsettling, bordering on perverse. Those are the parts of Heddy that ensure she will forever remain unknowable to Peter, and that is maybe the biggest loss in the story —the people we love will always, in some fundamental way, be beyond our reach.

LEOPOLDINE CORE was born and raised in New York's East Village and graduated from Hunter College. She is the author of the poetry collection *Veronica Bench* and the short story collection *When Watched,* which was a finalist for the PEN/Hemingway Award. Her fiction and poetry have appeared in *Joyland, Open City, PEN America,* and *Apology Magazine,* among others. She is the recipient of a 2015 Whiting Award for fiction, as well as fellowships from the Center for Fiction and the Fine Arts Work Center. She lives in New York.

• I had been writing dialogue between two women for months—just talking, no descriptions of any kind. I must have written a hundred pages of their banter. And they revealed themselves to me—Kit and Lucy did. It seemed at first to be a moral story, but then I realized that it was actually about the construction of morality—how fixed states of virtue and evil are falsely projected onto people, much the way gender is. I wanted to portray a deep bond between women in what might be considered the most unlikely of circumstances—the sex industry—and watch them come to understand how rare friendship is—much rarer than lust, in my opinion. This is a story about the early life of the writer—that moment of becoming obsesses me—maybe because in some way it never ends. And a young writer, especially if they are a marginalized individual, is not encouraged —they have to write in spite of being routinely demoralized. And somehow they do—many do. I wanted to track some of the ways misogyny is internalized by women—and watch Kit and Lucy deconstruct the experience out loud. I wanted to show how fluid identity really is—how the self in each case consists of many, often conflicting parts. No one is all good or all bad. Everyone has the capacity to violate others—and be violated. We are all so fragile, really.

PATRICIA ENGEL is the author of *Vida,* a finalist for the PEN/Hemingway Award and a *New York Times* Notable Book, *It's Not Love, It's Just Paris,* winner of the International Latino Book Award, and most recently, *The Veins of the Ocean,* named a *San Francisco Chronicle* Best Book of the Year. Her books have been widely translated and her short fiction has appeared in *The Atlantic, A Public Space, Boston Review,* and *ZYZZYVA,* among other journals, and anthologies including *The Best American Mystery Stories 2014.* She lives in Miami.

• Over a period of three years, I traveled to Cuba about a dozen times to do research for a novel. During that time, I learned about the Campoamor theater, so abandoned that somehow the entire city had forgotten where it was. A Cuban friend and I searched every map and asked around yet nobody could tell us exactly where it was. After about a week, we mentioned it to another friend's mother, well into her seventies, who told us to look just behind the Capitolio building, where the Campoamor ruins were hidden in plain sight. I wanted to write a story that reflected the ambiguous loyalties I observed in so many young people in Cuba, the ways that patriotism and survival are often in direct conflict, the negotiation of public and private life, and respective hidden desires. A lot of this story comes from things I saw, people I knew, and gossip I heard. I wrote it to remind myself of that particular time at the end of 2014, when there was a blend of cautious hope and skepticism that change might come to the island after decades of suffocating stillness. I'm Colombian-American, not

Cuban, and knew I was approaching this as an outsider, so to displace my
sensibility even further, I decided to try it from a male perspective, which
was also something new for me.

DANIELLE EVANS is the author of the story collection *Before You Suffocate
Your Own Fool Self.* Her stories have appeared in magazines and anthologies
including *Paris Review, A Public Space, American Short Fiction, Callaloo, New
Stories from the South,* and *The Best American Short Stories 2008* and *2010.* She
teaches creative writing at the University of Wisconsin–Madison.

  ▪ The first thread of this story came from hearing a sermon on Noah's
Ark. It's rare for me to be in a church as an adult, and it had been years
since I thought about Noah. Even set in a joyful sermon, the story seemed
to me profoundly tragic. When I was very small, one of my favorite books
to be read at bedtime was an illustrated retelling of the Noah's Ark story.
I do not know whether it was the story itself, or the idea of a boat full of
animals, or the theatrics with which my parents would oblige me when I
demanded they read, again and again, my favorite page, which read in
its entirety "Hmm, said Noah." How, I wondered, had this story been so
comforting to me as a child? How had I missed the weight of all that loss?
  "Richard of York Gave Battle in Vain" started there for me, with the
idea of putting a character in a similar state of discomfort. I meant to write
the first few pages and see where they got me, but I was in the middle of a
cross-country move and a family emergency and a novel, and the story hovered at idea for months. Eventually I stumbled into a good writing space
and had one of those magical writing days when things just work; I drafted
the first half of the story and thought I'd finish the rest of the draft over
the semester break. The semester break came; I lost the keys to the writing
space, and my sense of the story, and some other things that made writing
feel like a distant priority. I'd nudge the story every few months, but if it
moved at all it moved slowly and aimlessly. Dori became more and more
interesting to me, but to what end I couldn't say. I began to superstitiously
believe that the story had vanished with my access to the place where I'd
started writing it.
  When the story finally cracked open for me, more than a year after
I'd started it, it was because I got that it had never been about a wedding
or how anyone felt about the groom. The real loneliness of the story had
been underneath the opening bit all along, in what it means to understand
that every triumphant story of the things we survive is also the story of the
losses haunting it.

MARY GORDON is the author of eight novels, two collections of novellas, two collections of short stories, two memoirs, two collections of essays,
a writer's interpretation of the Gospels, and a biography of Joan of Arc.

She has been awarded the Story Prize, a Guggenheim Fellowship, and an Academy Award for Literature from the American Academy of Arts and Letters. She lives in New York City. Her latest novel, *There Your Heart Lies*, was published in May by Pantheon.

• I attended a lecture by my colleague at Barnard on the idea of Ugliness in the Renaissance. I thought: "what a terrible word *ugly* is." Soon afterward, I bought something beautiful in a store full of beautiful things, owned by a woman who I could not but think of as "ugly." The juxtaposition was the source of the story.

LAUREN GROFF is the author of four books: *The Monsters of Templeton, Delicate Edible Birds, Arcadia,* and *Fates and Furies,* which was a finalist for the National Book Award, the National Book Critics Circle Award, and the Kirkus Prize, and which won the American Booksellers Association Indies Choice Book Award. This is her fifth story in *The Best American Short Stories* anthology. She lives in Gainesville, Florida, with her husband and two sons.

• This story came from two places. The first was my friend's sighting of a Florida panther far to the north of where panthers supposedly roam, at his camp way out in the scrub where my husband and all of his friends often take their children camping. The panther haunted me for months, but the story didn't come together until spring break at the beach last year, when my husband had to go back to work in Gainesville, leaving me stranded without a car and with our two small boys. We weren't far from humanity: I could hear the neighbors grilling out, and could see the pickups driving up the beach (on a sea turtle nesting habitat! Humans are egregious). But when the boys went to bed, I started spinning out about the worst possible thing that could happen now that I was alone with the boys. I worked myself into sleeplessness, and the first draft came before dawn.

AMY HEMPEL'S *The Collected Stories* won the Ambassador Book Award for Best Fiction of the Year, and was one of the *New York Times* Ten Best Books of the Year in 2006. She has won the PEN/Malamud Award and the Rea Award, and received the Harold D. Vursell Memorial Award from the American Academy of Arts and Letters. She was awarded fellowships from the Guggenheim Foundation and the United States Artists, and is a founding board member of the Deja Foundation, a nonprofit rescue organization for dogs (www.dejafoundation.org).

• Being haunted is the way many of my stories begin. And nothing has haunted me more than the object at the center of "The Chicane," the tape in a vault in another country. I learned about it before I had begun writing. I began the story that is powered by it more than thirty years ago. I have been thinking about it for that long. I knew it needed to be framed, but I had only one incident, not the two required. No story has taken this long for me to write. Because a part of it is true, and because of the person who inspired it, I felt a particular weight of responsibility to get it right.

NOY HOLLAND'S *I Was Trying to Describe What It Feels Like: New and Selected Stories* was published by Counterpoint in January 2017. Her debut novel, *Bird* (Counterpoint), appeared in 2015, to great critical acclaim. Holland's collections of short fiction and novellas include *Swim for the Little One First* (FC2), *What Begins with Bird* (FC2), and *The Spectacle of the Body* (Knopf). She has published work in *Kenyon Review, Antioch Review, Conjunctions, The Quarterly, Glimmer Train, Electric Literature, Publishers Weekly, The Believer, Noon,* and *New York Tyrant,* among others. She was a recipient of a Massachusetts Cultural Council award for artistic merit and a National Endowment for the Arts Fellowship. She has taught for many years in the MFA Program for Poets and Writers at the University of Massachusetts. www.noyholland.com

• I wrote all but the first sentence of "Tally" during a residency at the MacDowell Colony last September. I'd been carrying the first sentence, and the notion behind it—that we are sometimes driven into the mouth of what we most fear—since my days tending bar in Montana. Cowboy bar, hoarfrost, not much on the jukebox. I had a bird dog and a tiny cheap apartment.

SONYA LARSON'S fiction and essays have appeared in *American Literary Review, American Short Fiction, Poets & Writers,* the *Writer's Chronicle,* Audible. com, *West Branch, Salamander, Red Mountain Review, Del Sol Review,* and others. She has received fellowships and awards from the Bread Loaf Writers' Conference, the Vermont Studio Center, the University of Wisconsin–Madison, and the St. Botolph Club Foundation, and more. She is studying fiction in the MFA Program for Writers at Warren Wilson College, and is writing a novel about Chinese immigrants living in the swamps of 1930s Mississippi. Sonya lives in Cambridge, Massachusetts, and works at Grub-Street, an independent creative writing center in Boston.

• A few years ago, I found myself suddenly single, and feeling like a fuckup in most areas of my life.

I tried to date again. But I started hearing more comments than usual—in bars, in texts, in bed—about my race. "I can't wait to meet you," said one guy. "Half-Asians are the holy grail." Said another, who was white, "I like you, but if we had kids, they'd totally be watered down." I felt confused and a little enraged, watching people use my race to evaluate our potential.

I complained to my friends, who laughed and commiserated. "This is why I only date people of color," a Bengali friend said over breakfast. "So that I don't have to explain." "Me too," another nodded. "But I'd rather not date another Korean. I already bring that to the table." I blinked into my eggs, feeling weird all over again. Their predilections made sense, but unsettled me too.

It occurred to me that the dating world may be one of the last remaining realms in which people openly and regularly express racial preference. Sites like OkCupid and Match invite this, and have revealed disturbing trends (most racial groups, as of this writing, pursue white men and Asian women; few pursue Asian men and black women).

We tend to think of attraction as a deeply personal force—something mysterious, "biological," and otherwise out of our control. But even this raw sensation can be shaped by external forces we don't realize. Forces of history, of stereotyping, and even public policy.

Of course, we don't exactly contemplate this stuff as we're sipping beer at a bar and catching someone's gaze. *Does he intrigue me?* we ask ourselves. *Do I think about her when she's gone?* Following our gut here seems obvious and unavoidable. But what if our gut contains some racial bias?

So I tried to write a story that houses these ideas, and lets them resonate like a bell tower around a bell. And I tried to embrace my fuckuppery, in both context and form. It may seem like a simple dating story, but for me its consequences are much larger. What's at stake for Chuntao —and for all of us—is nothing less than who we make available to ourselves to love.

FIONA MAAZEL is the author of three novels: *Last Last Chance* (2008); *Woke Up Lonely* (2013); and *A Little More Human* (2017). Her stories have appeared in *Conjunctions, Harper's Magazine, Ploughshares, Tin House,* and elsewhere. She lives in Brooklyn, New York.

  • Parents spend a lot of time talking about the detrimental influence of social media on their kids. But one thing I noticed when I became a parent was how alarmingly addictive and questionably helpful social media became for me. Suddenly I was a part of a community whose only shared interest was parenting, but whose hold on me was powerful. I'd post questions about my daughter's well-being—*she's* snoring, *is that okay??*—and wait, with a mixture of anxiety and delight, for all the reassurance to pour in. Not just that snoring was *okay,* but that *I* was okay. And not just okay, but great. Because one thing social media is skilled at is tearing you down or building you up.

Even so, I was incredibly uncomfortable with all this. And then uncomfortable with being uncomfortable. Is camaraderie necessarily fake simply because you don't know the people with whom you're exchanging intimacies? Does publicizing personal details about your life signal the end of real friendship, this being premised on the idea that friendship is about a communing of private selves? What does this mean for people who routinely share and consume each other's secrets? And who gets hurt as a result?

Enter "Let's Go to the Videotape." I wanted to find a framework for thinking through how all this stuff might play out in the life of someone who is hobbled by grief and unsure of how to work through it for the benefit of his son. I wanted to develop a good man who's faced with too many options, who is desperate for help and community, and who basically exploits his son to get it. Though of course he doesn't know as much. He's just muddling along as best he can. Just like the rest of us, I figure.

KYLE MCCARTHY's work has appeared in *Southwest Review, American Short Fiction, Harvard Review,* and *Los Angeles Review of Books.* A graduate of the Iowa Writers' Workshop, she lives in Brooklyn, New York.

• I work as a private tutor in Manhattan, where the displays of wealth and naked ambition continually astonish me. Once after listening to a particularly outrageous tale, my father jokingly suggested I write a *Nanny Diaries* for the tutoring world. For a few weeks I played with this idea, imagining a beleaguered narrator beset by coddled children.

At about the same time I had the great pleasure of reading Geoff Dyer's *Out of Sheer Rage: Wrestling with D. H. Lawrence.* One early March evening, walking home from the park, I heard my narrator unspooling a Dyeresque rant, saying things like *something was in fact wrong with today's females.* Probably I was sort of twitching and talking to myself, but I didn't care: I just wanted to follow that voice.

So I began to imagine the person witnessing all this wealth as a *particular* someone. I began to see her girlhood, and her relationship to sex, beauty, and ambition, as something odd, as culturally determined as the milieu in which she found herself.

It's strange. Like my students, I'm a millennial—though just barely. Sometimes the young women I teach seem like a new species, and sometimes their desire to be perfect, brilliant, and beautiful feels achingly familiar. And sometimes, simply, their inner lives are mysteries. So I suppose "Ancient Rome" came from a place of wondering, too.

ERIC PUCHNER is the author of the novel *Model Home,* a finalist for the PEN/Faulkner Award, and two collections of stories, *Music Through the Floor* and *Last Day on Earth.* His work has appeared in many magazines and anthologies, including *GQ, Granta, Tin House, Zoetrope, The Best American Nonrequired Reading, Pushcart Prize: Best of the Small Presses,* and *The Best American Short Stories 2012.* He has received an NEA fellowship, a California Book Award, and an Award in Literature from the American Academy of Arts and Letters. A professor at Johns Hopkins University, he lives in Baltimore with his wife, the novelist Katharine Noel, and their two children.

• Most of my short stories aren't particularly autobiographical, at least in the conventional sense, but this one is based on something that really happened: my father, chasing some kind of California dream, moved us out to suburban LA when I was twelve and ended up losing all of his money in the savings and loan crisis in the eighties. (More than all of his money, actually—he went $2 million into debt.) Soon afterward, he moved out of the house and got involved with a much younger woman. Among the casualties of his disappearance from our life were his two hunting dogs, whom he left cooped up in a pen in our backyard. My mother, whose only experience with hunting was cleaning and cooking the smelly birds my dad used to bring home, asked him many times to come get the dogs, two German shorthaired pointers she didn't know how to care for. But he never did. Finally, after months of pleading, she loaded the dogs into her car and took them to the pound to get put down. I only found out about this years afterward, when my mother told me the truth about where the pointers had gone. She said that it was the hardest thing she'd ever had to do. Later, I began to imagine what it might be like for a boy, one who tragically idolizes his father, to accompany his mother on such a trip. Despite having some obvious similarities, the parents in "Last Day on Earth" aren't my real parents, and like everything else in the plot—the trip to the beach, the maligned girlfriend, the father's dumpy apartment—they're largely made up. For a long time I wrote stories wishing that my mother wouldn't read them, but this is a story I wish with all my heart she could read. In any case, I wrote it for her.

MARIA REVA was born in Ukraine and grew up in Vancouver, British Columbia. Her stories have appeared in *The Atlantic, Tin House* Flash Fridays, the *New Quarterly*, and *Malahat Review*. Her musical collaborations include an opera libretto for Erato Ensemble, texts for Vancouver International Song Institute's Art Song Lab, and a script for City Opera Vancouver. She is currently pursuing an MFA at the Michener Center for Writers (University of Texas–Austin). "Novostroïka" is part of a linked story collection in progress.

• "Without papers, you're a bug," wrote the Soviet poet and lyricist Vasily Lebedev-Kumach in "Bureaucrat's Song." The words morphed into an expression still used in the former Eastern Bloc: "Without papers, you're a turd." Without an internal passport, *propiska* (residence permit), and the myriad other documents required of a Soviet citizen, your very personhood was held in question.

"Novostroïka" came out of a conversation with my parents. They recounted how our panel building in Brovary, Ukraine, hadn't made it into the city's registry. None of the municipal services recognized the address. If an entire building is "without papers," what happens to the people living inside it? If you are repeatedly told that something does not exist, when do you start believing it?

JIM SHEPARD has written seven novels, including *The Book of Aron,* which won the Sophie Brody Medal for Excellence in Jewish Literature, the Harold U. Ribalow Prize for Jewish Literature, the PEN/New England Award for Fiction, and the Clark Fiction Prize, and five story collections, including *Like You'd Understand, Anyway,* a finalist for the National Book Award and a Story Prize winner, and most recently *The World to Come.* He's also won the Library of Congress / Massachusetts Book Award for Fiction, the Alex Award from the American Library Association, and a Guggenheim Fellowship. He teaches at Williams College.

• From my earliest childhood I've been continually stirred and appalled by the combination of intrepidness and lunacy that you'll find reliably on display over the course of British military history. I probably first wrote about it in graduate school, with a short story about young contemporary newlyweds who inexplicably find themselves in the middle of the Charge of the Light Brigade. I've also always found the combination of helplessness and terror and claustrophobia in the submarine service during the world wars to be equally compelling, and in my nerdy reading around in the subject came across two details that stuck with me. The first was that the Admiralty during World War II had refused to equip its submarines with snorkels—periscopic breathing tubes—that would allow a refreshed air supply without surfacing, arguing that there was no tactical requirement for such a fitting. The second was that in those dark days in 1942 in the Pacific following the fall of Singapore and the Dutch East Indies and the sinking of the *Prince of Wales* and the *Repulse,* the British found themselves with *two or three combat ships in total* standing between the entire Japanese Navy and the rest of the Indian Ocean. That sort of juxtaposition—one tiny schlumpy unit against a stupefyingly large menace—always snags my imagination. And then my wife, Karen, and I were talking about the kind of guy who likes to blunder through the world pretending that he doesn't know things and who needs to be reminded every so often that his ignorance *is* causing other people pain, and suddenly I had my protagonist.

CURTIS SITTENFELD is the best-selling author of five novels: *Prep, The Man of My Dreams, American Wife, Sisterland,* and *Eligible.* Her first story collection, *You Think It, I'll Say It,* will be published in 2018 and will include "Gender Studies." Her books have been selected by the *New York Times, Time, Entertainment Weekly,* and *People* for their Ten Best Books of the Year lists, optioned for television and film, and translated into twenty-five languages. Her short stories have appeared in *The New Yorker,* the *Washington Post,* and *Esquire,* and her nonfiction has appeared in the *New York Times,*

Time, Vanity Fair, The Atlantic, Slate, and on *This American Life.* She lives with her family in St. Louis.

• Like many fiction writers, I wrote short stories before I wrote novels, and I loved reading and writing the form. But after my first novel was published in 2005, I mostly stopped writing stories, even though I continued to read them. (The exceptions were a few times when magazines invited me to write fiction about topics of their choosing.) In May 2016, after the publication of my fifth novel, I was feeling a bit of what-do-I-do-with-myself-now? agitation, and the best way I know to address agitation is by writing. During the years I'd been writing novels, I'd stored up ideas, including one about a woman who loses her driver's license while on a work trip, which is how I conceived of this story; I didn't see it as a political allegory, though I understand that to some extent it is. Also, of course, I wrote it at a time when I and most Americans believed Hillary Clinton would win the 2016 election, and—full disclosure—I've added four words to accommodate the way its meaning changed after she didn't. Anyway, all of this is to say that "Gender Studies" just might be the first story I wrote as a bona fide adult, about a topic I'd chosen. The only other thing I have to add is that I first read a *Best American Short Stories* anthology in the summer of 1992, between my junior and senior years of high school, and I was enthralled and delighted by it. It's such an honor to now contribute to the series.

A former National Book Award finalist, JESS WALTER is the author of eight books, most recently the novel *Beautiful Ruins* and the story collection *We Live in Water.* His stories were also selected for *The Best American Short Stories 2012* and *2015.* He lives in Spokane, Washington, with his family.

• I got to know a famous actor once. We were working on a script together for a movie that would never get made, and we spent some time drinking, hanging out, and talking about our lives. We'd send each other texts and emails, exchange music and book recommendations, and I was surprised how open he seemed. In fact, we got so close that after our film's funding fell apart, I sent him a text: *This doesn't mean you and I can't stay in touch.*

He texted back, *Who is this?*

I'd made the classic Hollywood blunder: I forgot that actor friendships are basically summer camp friendships. No matter how deep it goes, as soon as camp (or your movie) ends, the friendship ends, too. I had gotten to know a few other famous people, so I should've seen this coming, but it was surprising how vulnerable I felt, how close this felt to romantic rejection.

I had been fame-ghosted.

That feeling of vulnerability made me want to write a story about a romantic encounter with a famous actor. I wrote the title "Famous Actor" in my journal, and for weeks that's all I had. I began inventing a very different famous actor than the one I had known. I happened to be in Bend, Oregon, for a reading and when I walked by a house party, I pictured this young Famous Actor bounding up the steps and grabbing a beer. Generally, I can tell if a story is going to work if I'm having fun writing it. It was so fun creating his filmography and imagining the Disney Channel TV show — *The Terrific Todd Chronicles!*—that launches his career.

As usual, the story went somewhere I never expected when the woman he met at the party turned out to be so interesting. It's her story in the end, this acerbic, complex, haunted woman who manages to find some humanity in the Famous Actor, while revealing herself as the greatest barista/film critic of all time.

Other Distinguished Stories of 2016

American and Canadian Magazines Publishing Short Stories

Able Muse Review
African American Review
AGNI
Alaska Quarterly Review
Alligator Juniper
American Fiction
American Short Fiction
Antioch Review
Appalachian Heritage
Arcadia
Arkansas Review
Ascent
The Atlantic
Baltimore Review
Bellevue Literary Review
Black Warrior Review
Bomb
Booth
Bosque
Boston Review
Boulevard
Brain, Child: The Magazine for Thinking Mothers
Briar Cliff Review
BuzzFeed
Callaloo
Carolina Quarterly
Carve Magazine
Catamaran Literary Reader
Catapult
Chattahoochee Review

Chautauqua
Cherry Tree
Chicago Quarterly Review
Chicago Tribune, Printers Row
Cicada
Cimarron Review
Cincinnati Review
Colorado Review
Commentary
Confrontation
Conjunctions
Consequence
Copper Nickel
Cossack Review
Crazyhorse
Cream City Review
CutBank
December
Denver Quarterly
Descant
Dogwood
East
Ecotone
805 Lit + Art
Electric Literature
Eleven Eleven
Emrys Journal
Epiphany
Epoch
Esquire
Event

Fantasy and Science Fiction
Faultline
Fence
Fiction
Fiction International
The Fiddlehead
Fifth Wednesday
Five Points
Florida Review
The Forge
Fourteen Hills
Freeman's
F(r)iction
Georgia Review
Gettysburg Review
Glimmer Train
Grain
Granta
Green Mountains Review
Grist
Grub Street
Guernica
Gulf Coast
Hanging Loose
Harper's Magazine
Harvard Review
Hayden's Ferry Review
Heart and Mind Zine
High Desert Journal
Hopkins Review
Hotel Amerika
Hudson Review
Hunger Mountain
Idaho Review
Image
Indiana Review
Iowa Review
Iron Horse Literary Review
Isthmus
Jabberwock Review
Joyland
Kenyon Review
Kweli Journal
Lady Churchill's Rosebud Wristlet
Lake Effect
Lalitamba
Lightspeed

Literary Review
Little Patuxent Review
Los Angeles Review of Books
Louisiana Literature
Make
Mary
Massachusetts Review
Masters Review
McSweeney's Quarterly
Memorious
Meridian
Michigan Quarterly Review
Mid-American Review
Midwestern Gothic
Minnesota Review
Minola Review
Mississippi Review
Missouri Review
Moon City Review
Mount Hope
n + 1
Narrative Magazine
Natural Bridge
New England Review
New Genre
New Guard
New Haven Review
New Letters
New Madrid
New Ohio Review
New South
New York Review of Books
The New Yorker
Nimrod International Journal
Ninth Letter
Noon
The Normal School
North American Review
North Carolina Literary Review
North Dakota Quarterly
Northern New England Review
Notre Dame Review
Ocean State Review
The Offing
One Story
One Throne Magazine
Opossum

Orion
Oxford American
Pakn Treger
PANK
Paper Darts
Paris Review
Pembroke Magazine
The Pinch
Pleiades
Ploughshares
PoemMemoirStory
Portland Review
Post Road
Potomac Review
Prairie Fire
Prairie Schooner
Prism International
Profane
Provincetown Arts
Provo Canyon Review
A Public Space
Pulp Literature
Raritan
Redivider
River Styx
Room Magazine
Ruminate
Salamander
Salmagundi
Santa Monica Review
Saturday Evening Post
Sewanee Review
Sierra Nevada Review
Sixfold
Slice
Solstice
Southampton Review
South Dakota Review
Southeast Review
Southern Humanities Review
Southern Indiana Review

Southern Review
Southwest Review
Sou'wester
StoryQuarterly
StringTown
Subtropics
Summerset Review
The Sun
Sycamore Review
Tablet
Tahoma Literary Review
Tampa Review
Terraform
Territory
Third Coast
This Land
Threepenny Review
Timber Creek Review
Tin House
TriQuarterly
upstreet
Vermont Literary Review
Virginia Quarterly Review
War, Literature, and the Arts
Washington Square Review
Waxwing Magazine
Weber Studies
West Branch
Western Humanities Review
Whitefish Review
Willow Springs
Wired
Witness
World Literature Today
Yale Review
Yellow Medicine Review
Your Impossible Voice
Zoetrope: All-Story
Zone 3
ZYZZYVA

THE BEST AMERICAN SERIES®

FIRST, BEST, AND BEST-SELLING

The Best American Comics

The Best American Essays

The Best American Mystery Stories

The Best American Nonrequired Reading

The Best American Science and Nature Writing

The Best American Science Fiction and Fantasy

The Best American Short Stories

The Best American Sports Writing

The Best American Travel Writing

Available in print and e-book wherever books are sold.

Visit our website: *www.hmhco.com/bestamerican*